IMAGE COMICS
PRESENTS

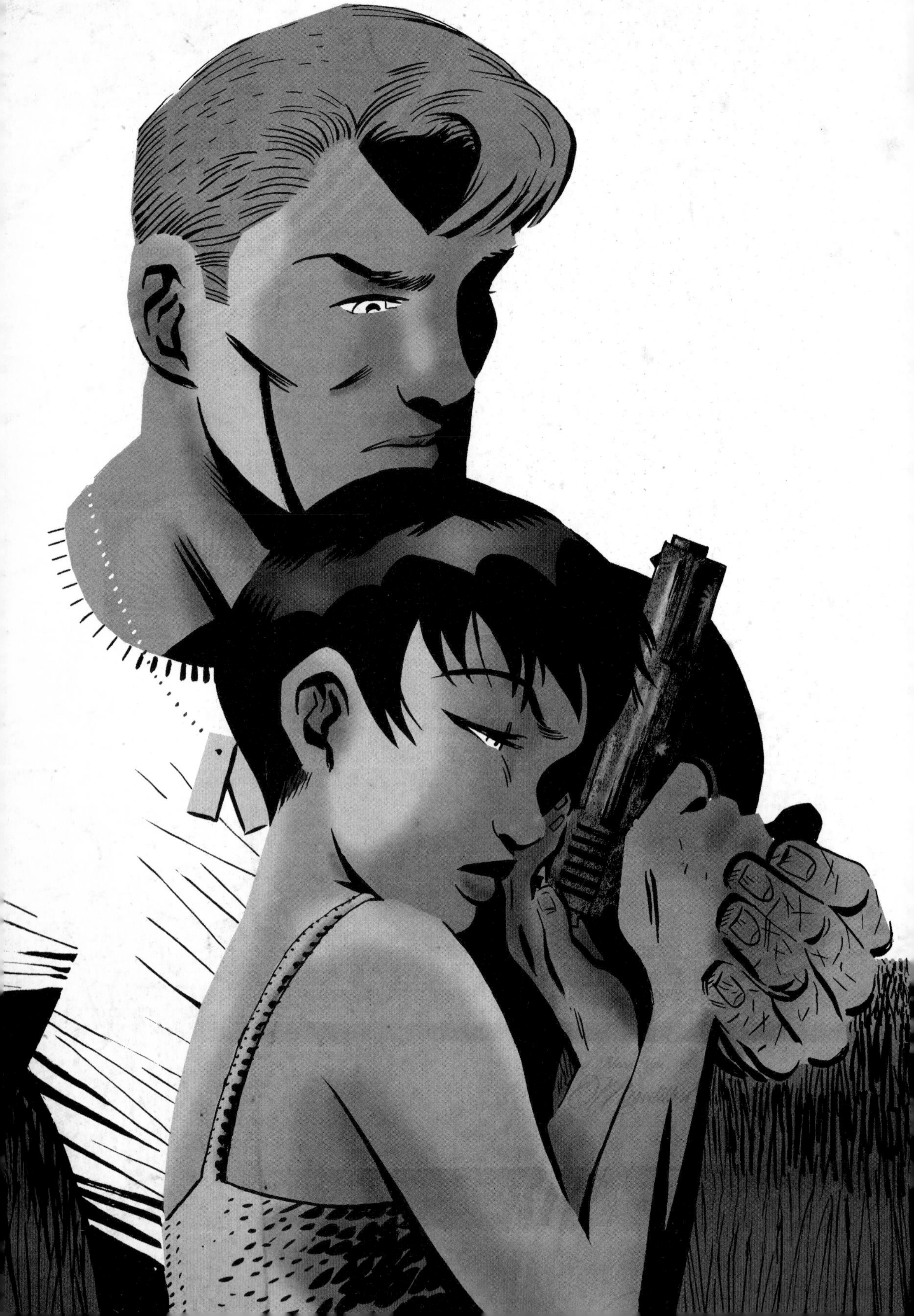

VIOLENT LOVE

VIOLENT LOVE
VOLUME ONE
"STAY DANGEROUS"

WRITTEN BY **FRANK J. BARBIERE**   ART BY **VICTOR SANTOS**
DESIGN BY **DYLAN TODD**

image

FRANK
TO ALL THE HEARTBREAKERS.

VICTOR
TO FRANK, DYLAN AND
ALL THE VIOLENT BUNCH
FROM IMAGE

TO ALL THE KICK-ASS 70s
ACTRESSES LIKE ISABELLE ADJANI,
ALI MacGRAW AND FAYE DUNAWAY

TO GENE COLAN, DOUG MOENCH,
SAM PECKINPAH, DENYS COWAN,
JIM STERANKO AND JOHN BOORMAN
FOR THE INSPIRATION

TO SILVIA, MY DAISY JANE.
THANK YOU FOR YOUR
ENDLESS SUPPORT

VIOLENT LOVE, VOLUME 1: STAY DANGEROUS First printing. May 2017. Published by Image Comics, Inc. Office of publication: 2701 NW Vaughn St., Suite 780, Portland, OR 97210. Copyright © 2017 Frank J. Barbiere & Victor Santos. All rights reserved. Contains material originally published in single magazine form as VIOLENT LOVE #1-5. "Violent Love," its logos, and the likenesses of all characters herein are trademarks of Frank J. Barbiere & Victor Santos, unless otherwise noted. "Image" and the Image Comics logos are registered trademarks of Image Comics, Inc. No part of this publication may be reproduced or transmitted, in any form or by any means (except for short excerpts for journalurial or review purposes), without the express written permission of Frank J. Barbiere, Victor Santos, or Image Comics, Inc. All names, characters, events, and locales in this publication are entirely fictional. Any resemblance to actual persons (living or dead), events, or places, without satiric intent, is coincidental. Printed in the USA. For information regarding the CPSIA on this printed material call: 203-595-3636 and provide reference #RICH–736906. For international rights, contact: foreignlicensing@imagecomics.com. ISBN: 978-1-5343-0044-6.

PUBLISHED BY **IMAGE COMICS, INC**

ROBERT KIRKMAN CHIEF OPERATING OFFICER ERIK LARSEN CHIEF FINANCIAL OFFICER TODD McFARLANE PRESIDENT MARC SILVESTRI CHIEF EXECUTIVE OFFICER
JIM VALENTINO VICE-PRESIDENT ERIC STEPHENSON PUBLISHER COREY MURPHY DIRECTOR OF SALES JEFF BOISON DIRECTOR OF PUBLISHING PLANNING & BOOK TRADE SALES
CHRIS ROSS DIRECTOR OF DIGITAL SALES JEFF STANG DIRECTOR OF SPECIALTY SALES KAT SALAZAR DIRECTOR OF PR & MARKETING BRANWYN BIGGLESTONE CONTROLLER
SUE KORPELA ACCOUNTS MANAGER DREW GILL ART DIRECTOR BRETT WARNOCK PRODUCTION MANAGER MEREDITH WALLACE PRINT MANAGER
TRICIA RAMOS TRAFFIC MANAGER BRIAH SKELLY PUBLICIST ALY HOFFMAN EVENTS & CONVENTIONS COORDINATOR SASHA HEAD SALES & MARKETING PRODUCTION DESIGNER
DAVID BROTHERS BRANDING MANAGER MELISSA GIFFORD CONTENT MANAGER DREW FITZGERALD PUBLICITY ASSISTANT VINCENT KUKUA PRODUCTION ARTIST
ERIKA SCHNATZ PRODUCTION ARTIST RYAN BREWER PRODUCTION ARTIST SHANNA MATUSZAK PRODUCTION ARTIST CAREY HALL PRODUCTION ARTIST
ESTHER KIM DIRECT MARKET SALES REPRESENTATIVE EMILIO BAUTISTA DIGITAL SALES REPRESENTATIVE LEANNA CAUNTER ACCOUNTING ASSISTANT
CHLOE RAMOS-PETERSON LIBRARY MARKET SALES REPRESENTATIVE MARLA EIZIK ADMINISTRATIVE ASSISTANT

IMAGECOMICS.COM

"Our heads are blurry
Our hearts are sharp things
I bet on you
To make me nervous
To stay dangerous
Good love is not safe."

BEACH SLANG

CHAPTER ONE

"THE BALLAD OF DAISY JANE"

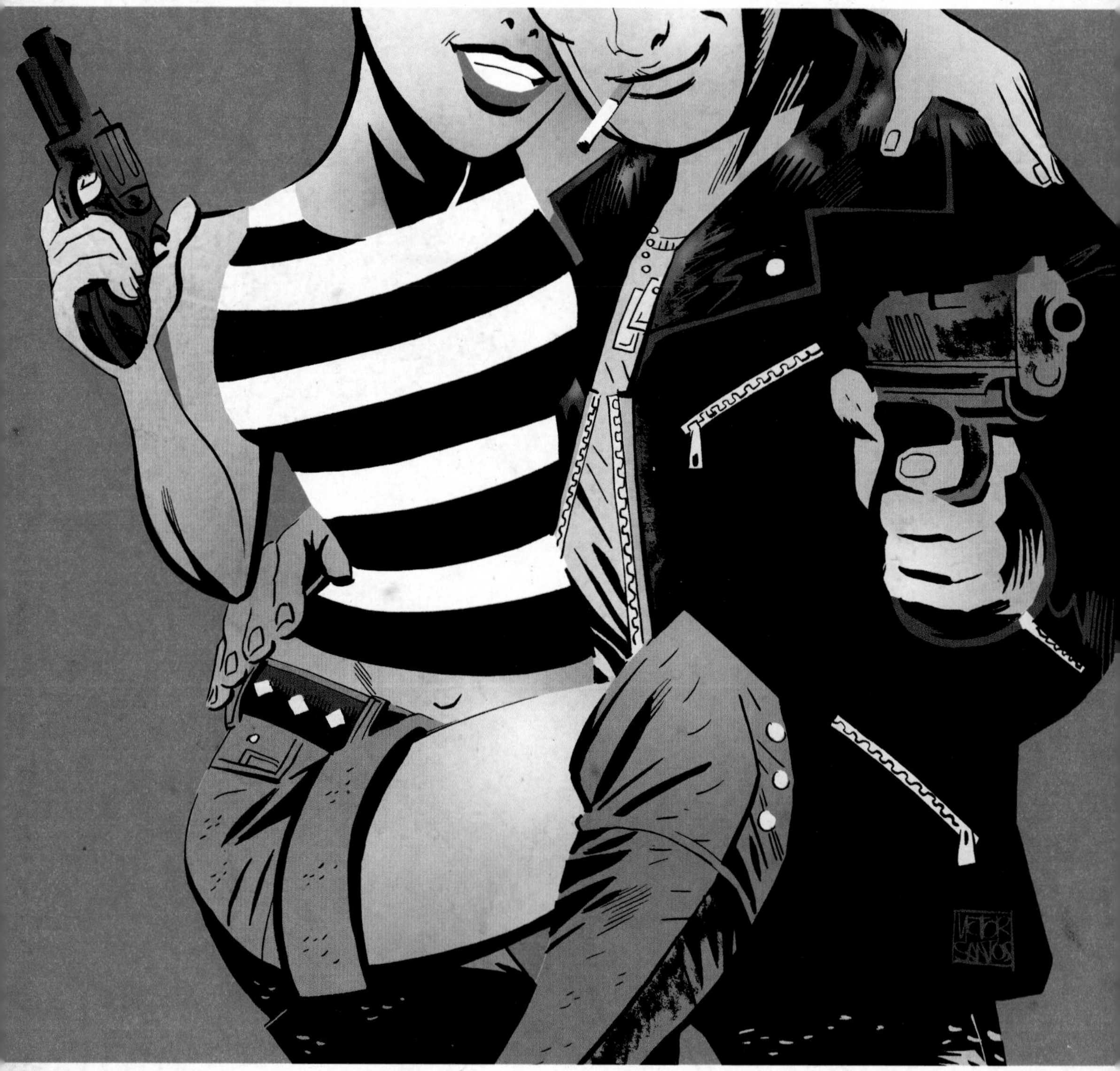

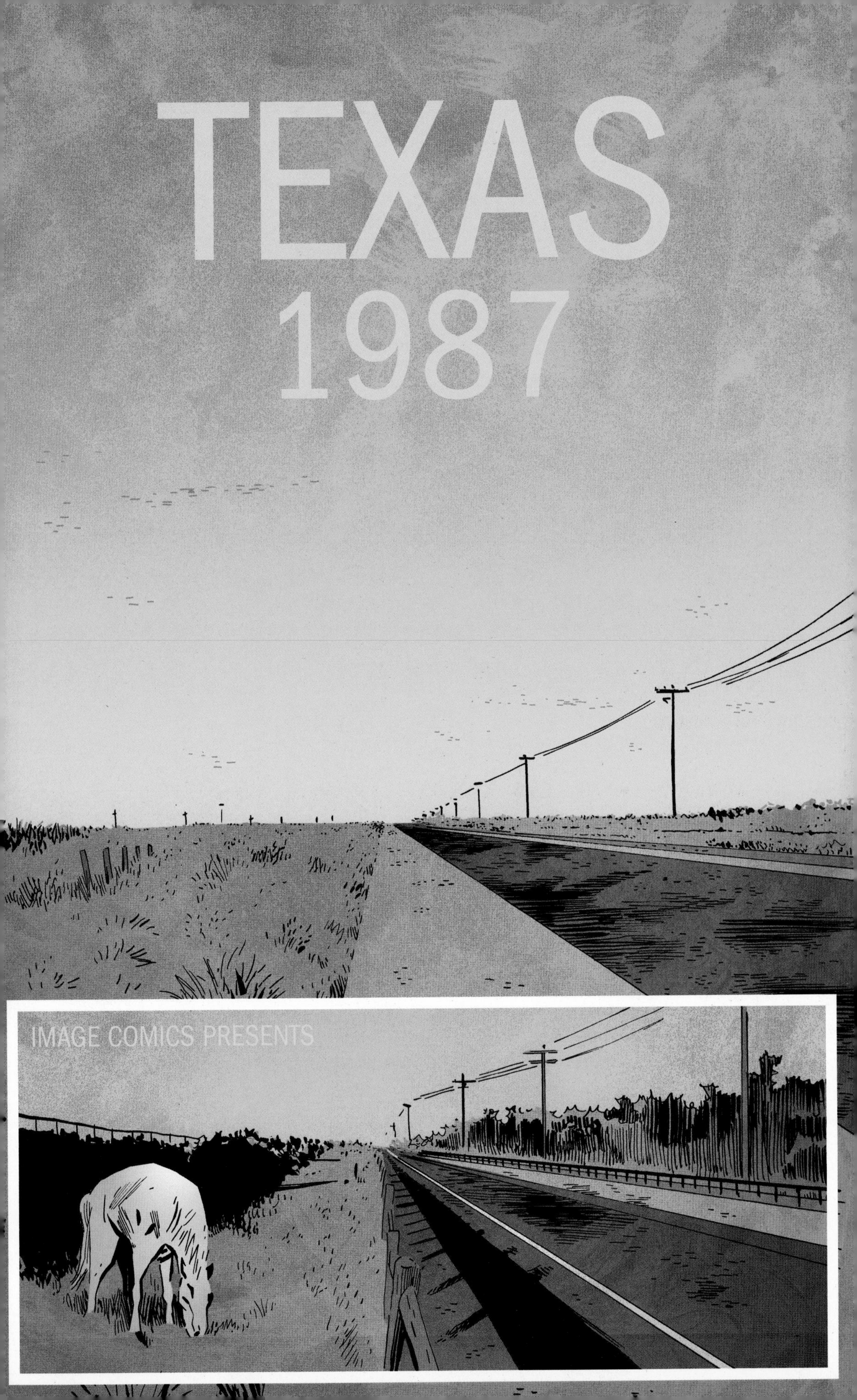
TEXAS
1987
IMAGE COMICS PRESENTS

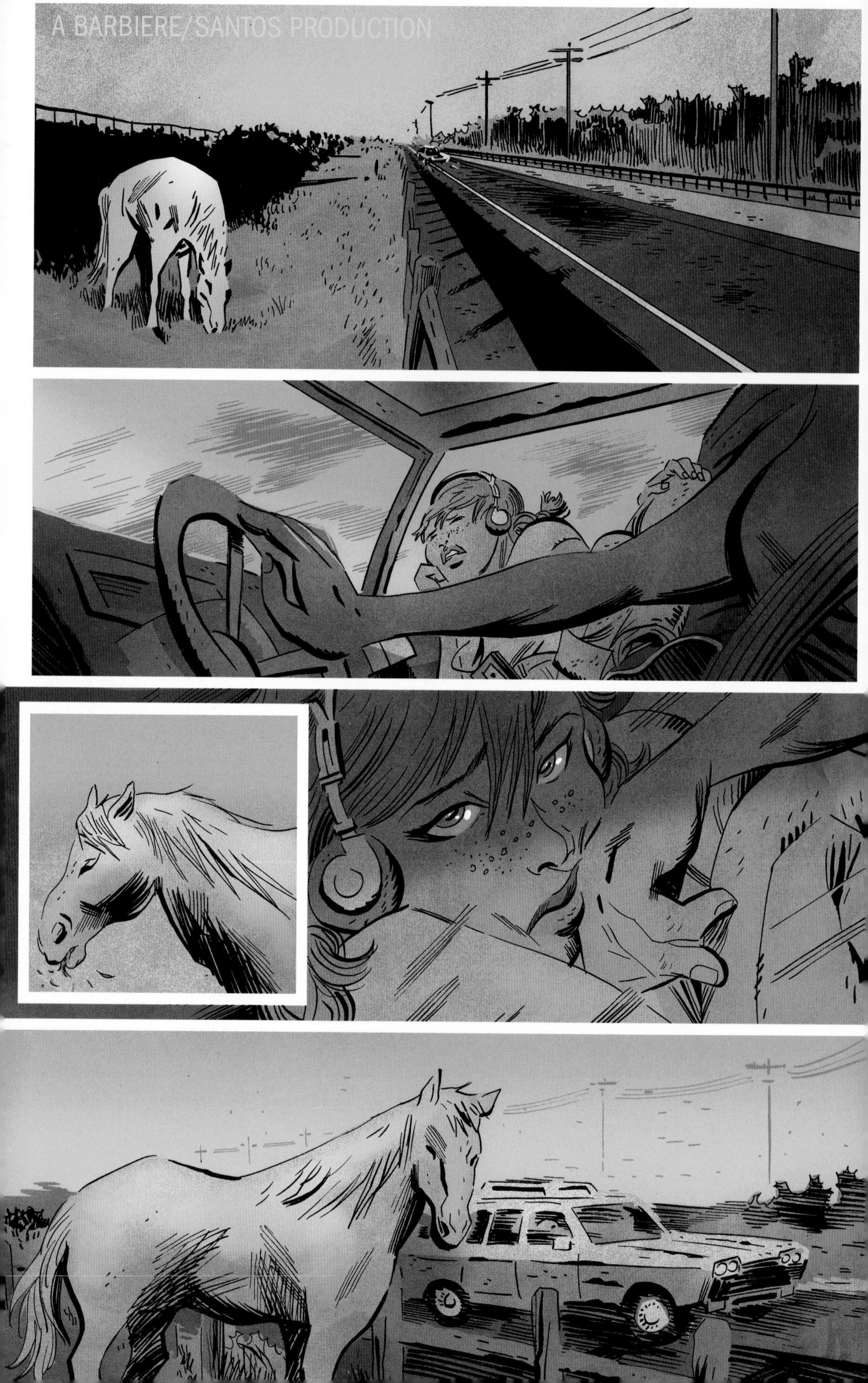
A BARBIERE/SANTOS PRODUCTION

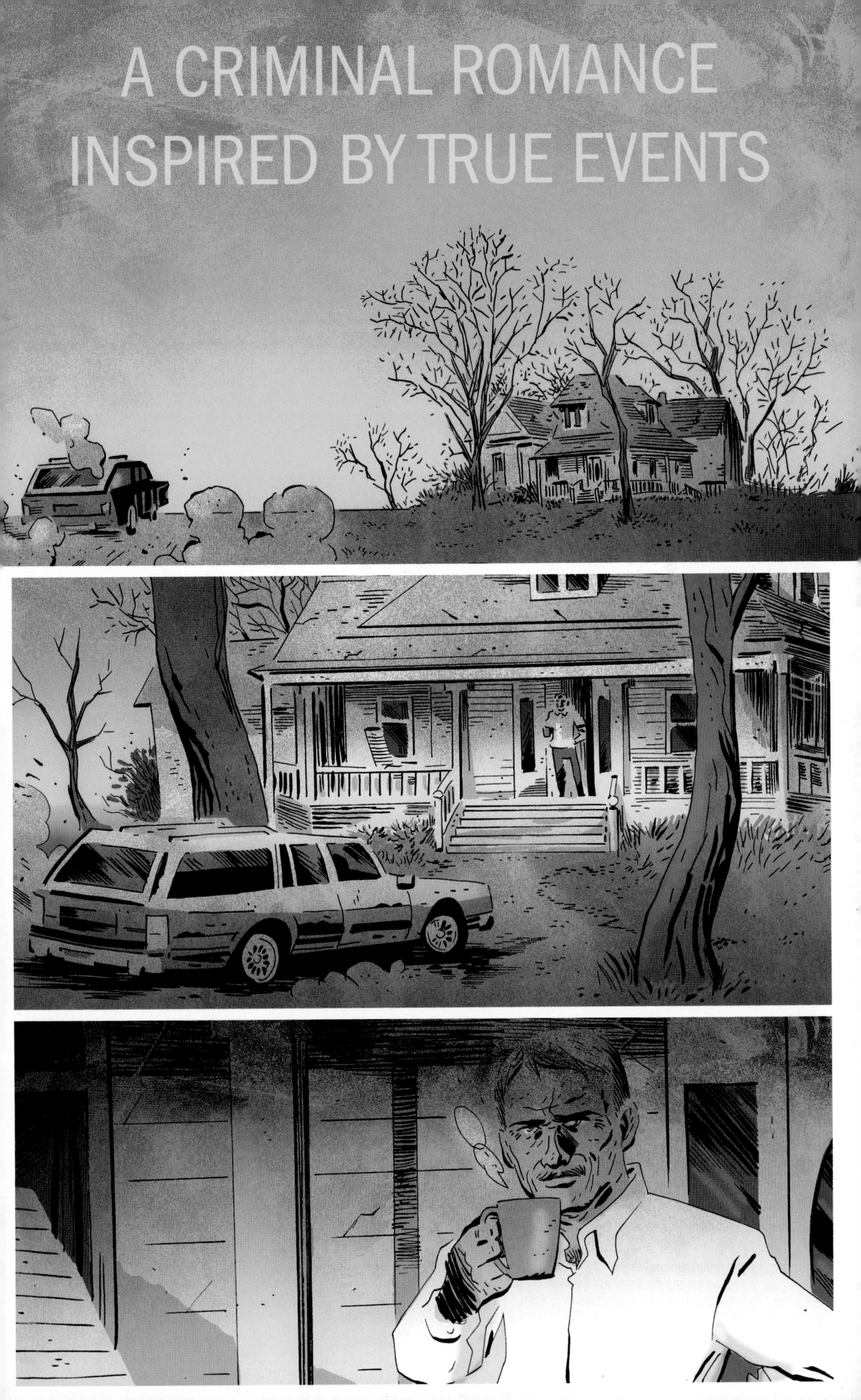
A CRIMINAL ROMANCE
INSPIRED BY TRUE EVENTS

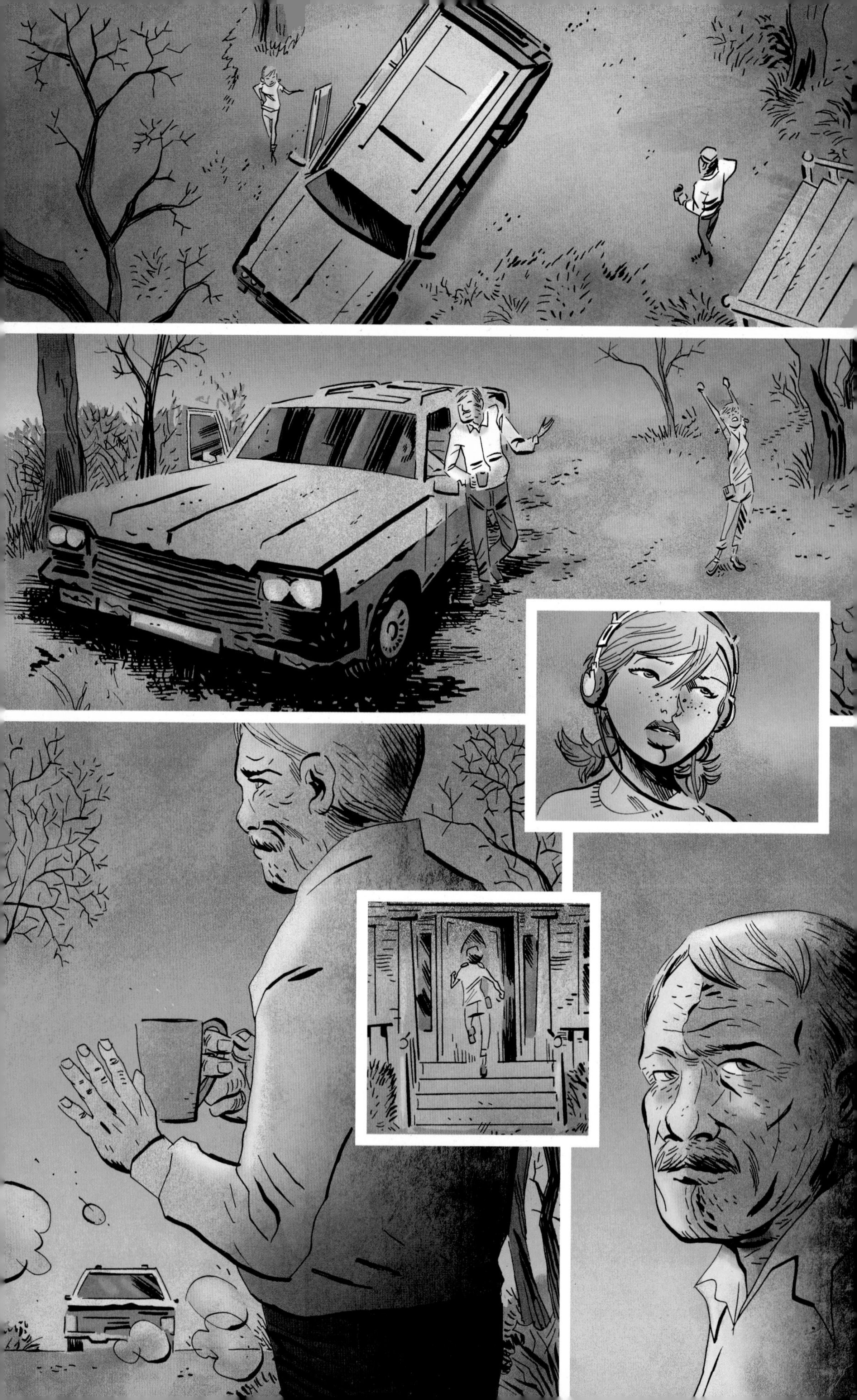

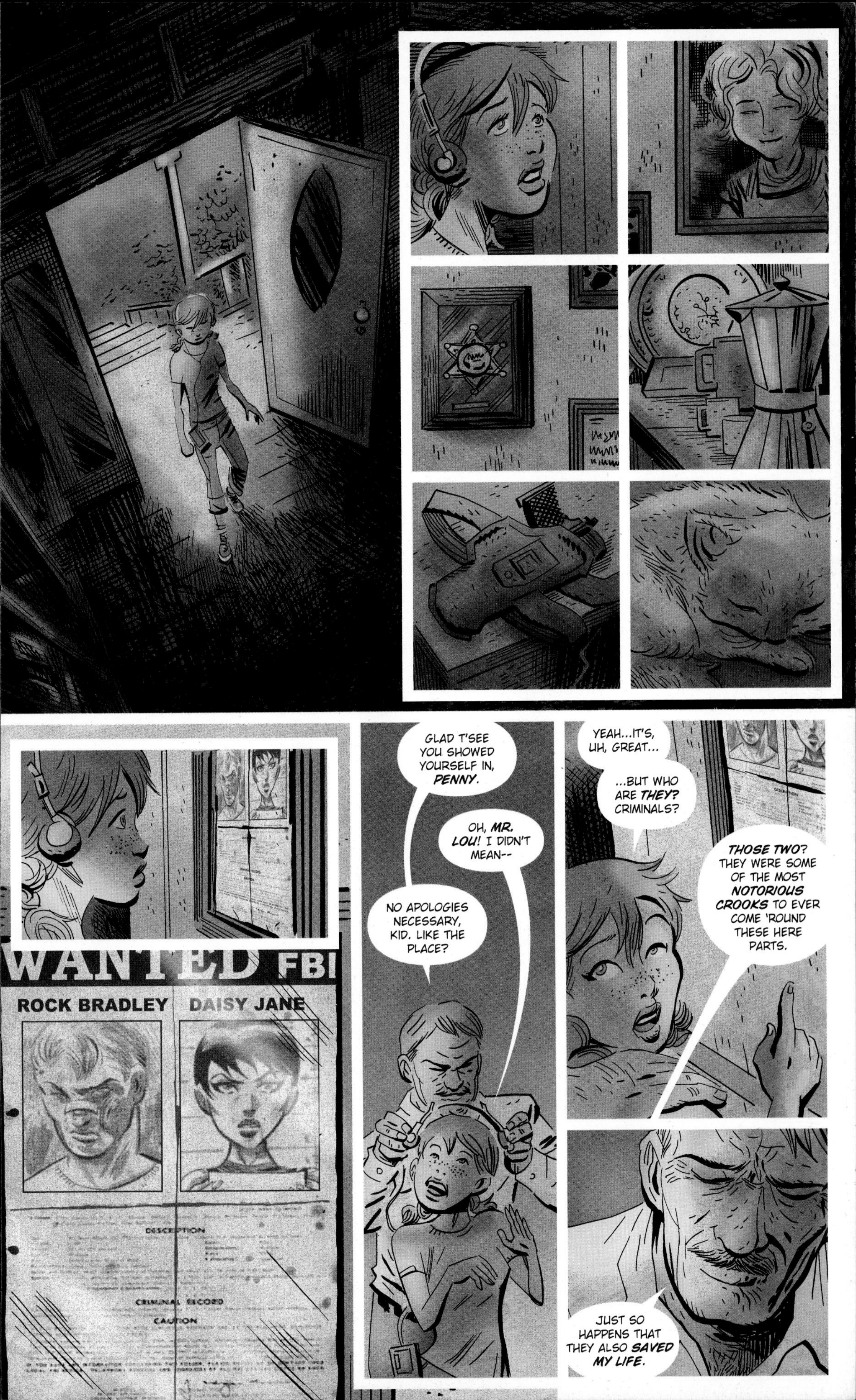
WANTED FBI
ROCK BRADLEY
DAISY JANE
DESCRIPTION
CRIMINAL RECORD
CAUTION
GLAD T'SEE YOU SHOWED YOURSELF IN, PENNY.
OH, MR. LOU! I DIDN'T MEAN--
NO APOLOGIES NECESSARY, KID. LIKE THE PLACE?
YEAH...IT'S, UH, GREAT...
...BUT WHO ARE THEY? CRIMINALS?
THOSE TWO? THEY WERE SOME OF THE MOST NOTORIOUS CROOKS TO EVER COME 'ROUND THESE HERE PARTS.
JUST SO HAPPENS THAT THEY ALSO SAVED MY LIFE.

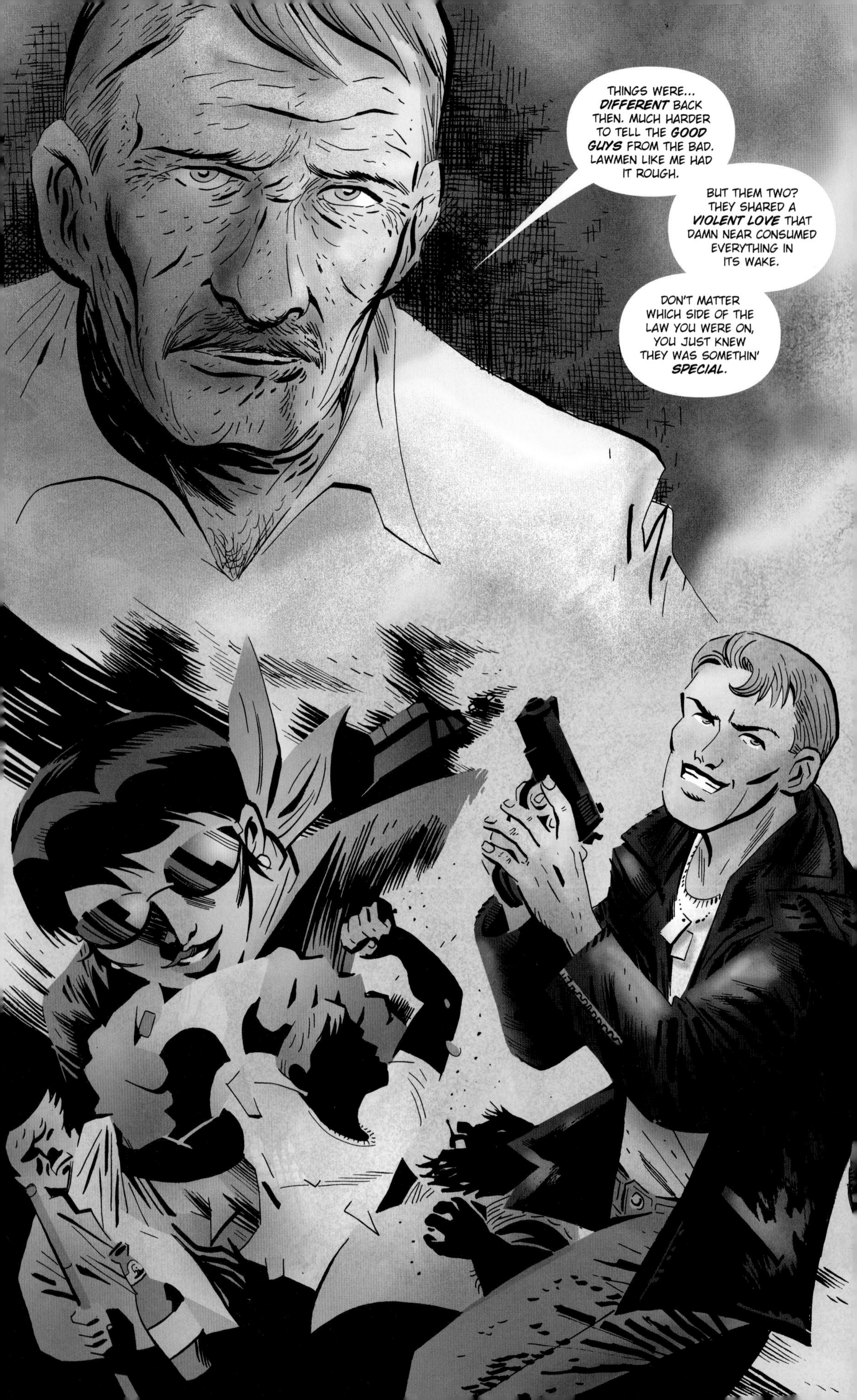
THINGS WERE... DIFFERENT BACK THEN. MUCH HARDER TO TELL THE GOOD GUYS FROM THE BAD. LAWMEN LIKE ME HAD IT ROUGH.
BUT THEM TWO? THEY SHARED A VIOLENT LOVE THAT DAMN NEAR CONSUMED EVERYTHING IN ITS WAKE.
DON'T MATTER WHICH SIDE OF THE LAW YOU WERE ON, YOU JUST KNEW THEY WAS SOMETHIN' SPECIAL.

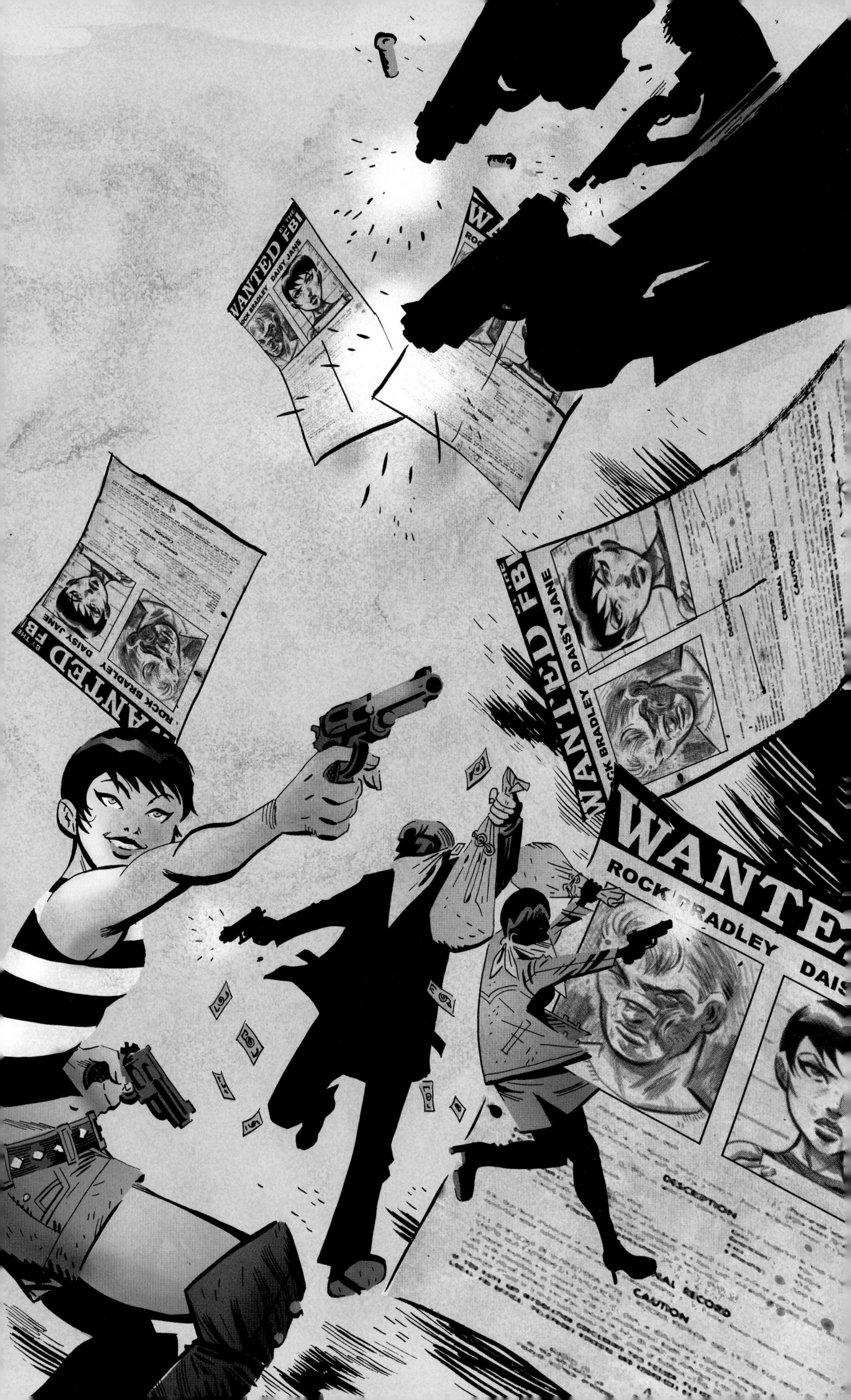

WANTED BY THE FBI
DAISY JANE
WANTED BY THE FBI
ROCK BRADLEY
DAISY JANE
CRIMINAL RECORD
CAUTION
WANTED BY THE FBI
DAISY JANE
DESCRIPTION
CRIMINAL RECORD
CAUTION
ROCK BRADLEY
DESCRIPTION
CAUTION

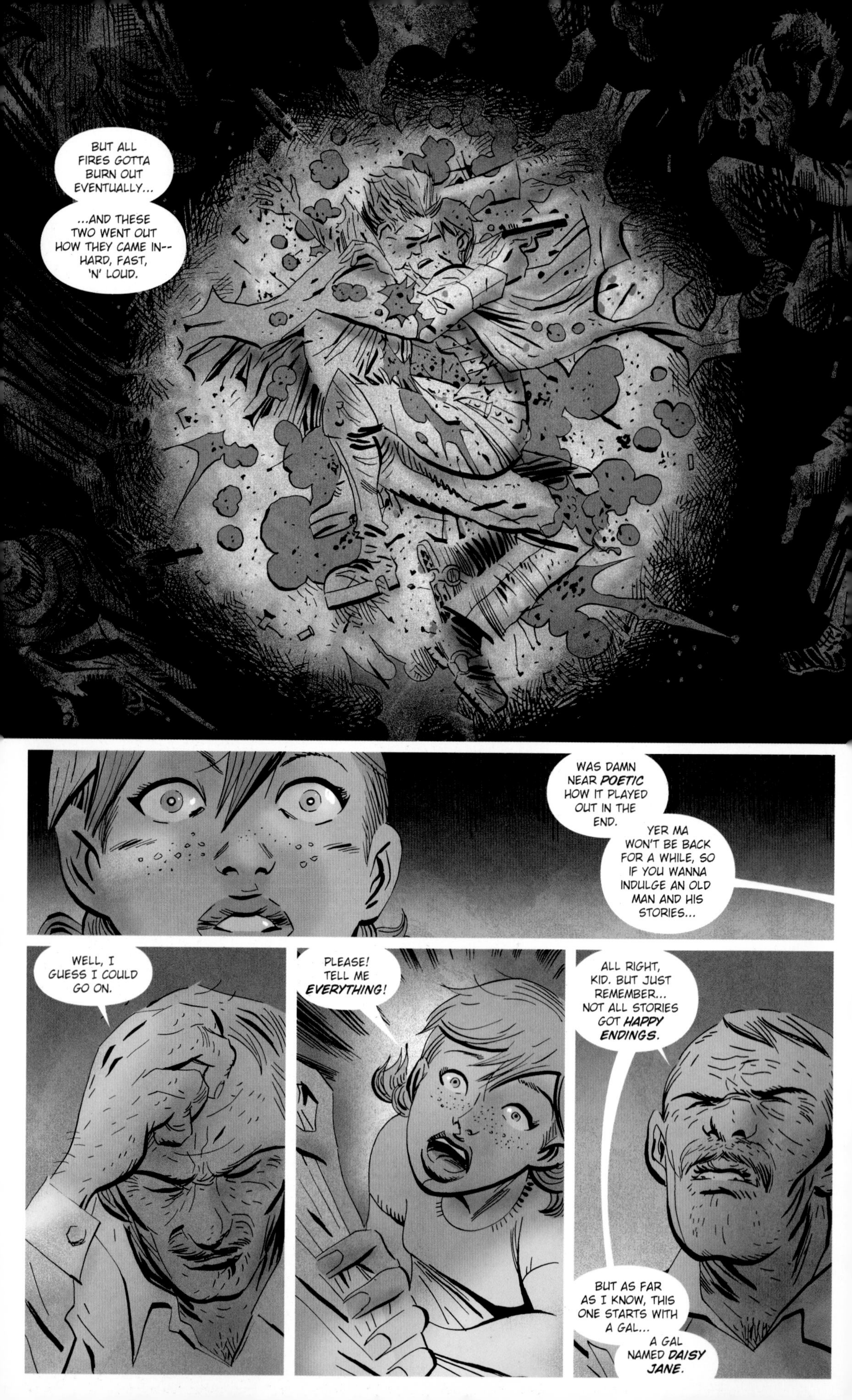
BUT ALL FIRES GOTTA BURN OUT EVENTUALLY...
...AND THESE TWO WENT OUT HOW THEY CAME IN-- HARD, FAST, 'N' LOUD.
WAS DAMN NEAR POETIC HOW IT PLAYED OUT IN THE END.
YER MA WON'T BE BACK FOR A WHILE, SO IF YOU WANNA INDULGE AN OLD MAN AND HIS STORIES...
WELL, I GUESS I COULD GO ON.
PLEASE! TELL ME EVERYTHING!
ALL RIGHT, KID. BUT JUST REMEMBER... NOT ALL STORIES GOT HAPPY ENDINGS.
BUT AS FAR AS I KNOW, THIS ONE STARTS WITH A GAL...
A GAL NAMED DAISY JANE.

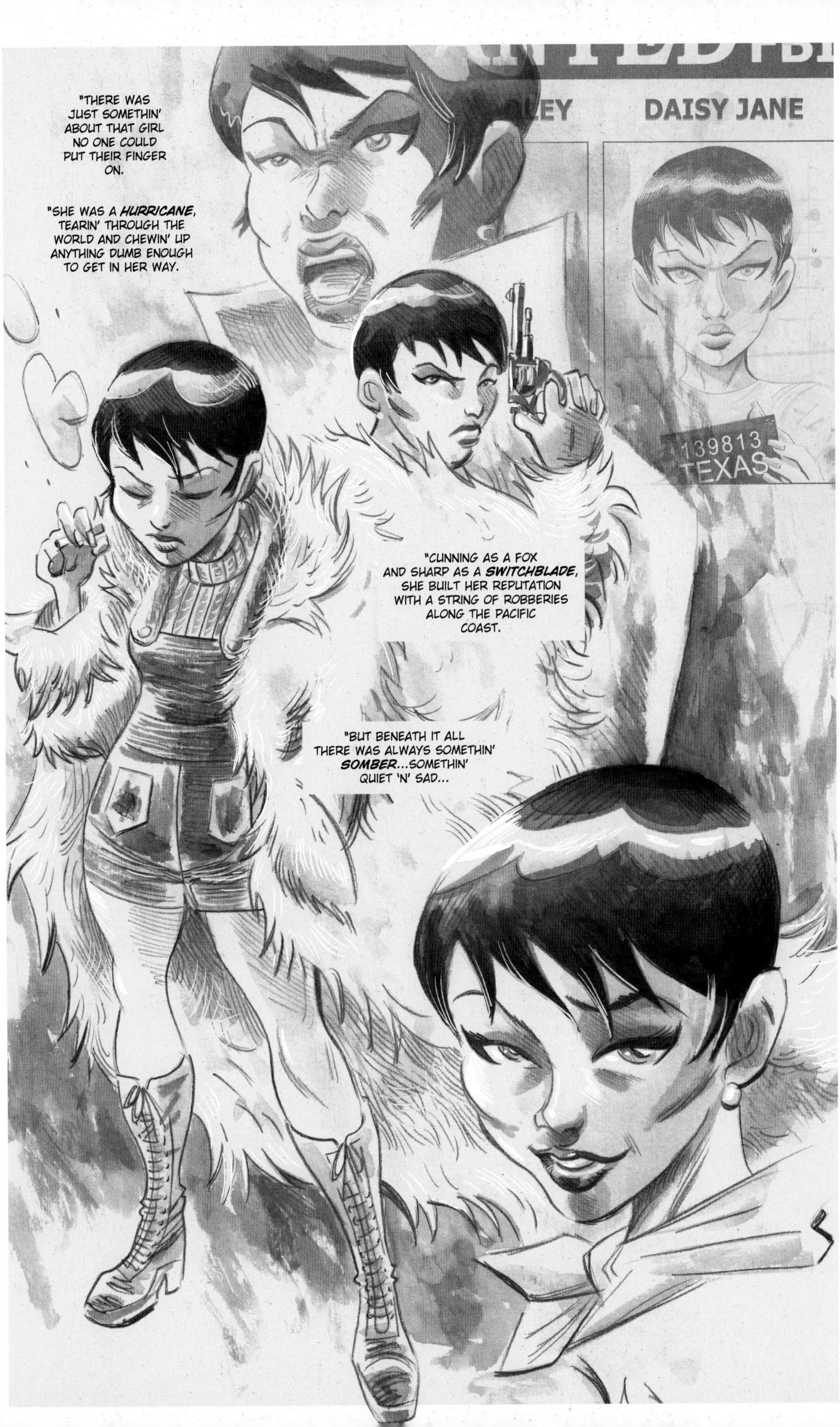
"THERE WAS JUST SOMETHIN' ABOUT THAT GIRL NO ONE COULD PUT THEIR FINGER ON.
"SHE WAS A HURRICANE, TEARIN' THROUGH THE WORLD AND CHEWIN' UP ANYTHING DUMB ENOUGH TO GET IN HER WAY.
DAISY JANE
139813
TEXAS
"CUNNING AS A FOX AND SHARP AS A SWITCHBLADE, SHE BUILT HER REPUTATION WITH A STRING OF ROBBERIES ALONG THE PACIFIC COAST.
"BUT BENEATH IT ALL THERE WAS ALWAYS SOMETHIN' SOMBER...SOMETHIN' QUIET 'N' SAD...

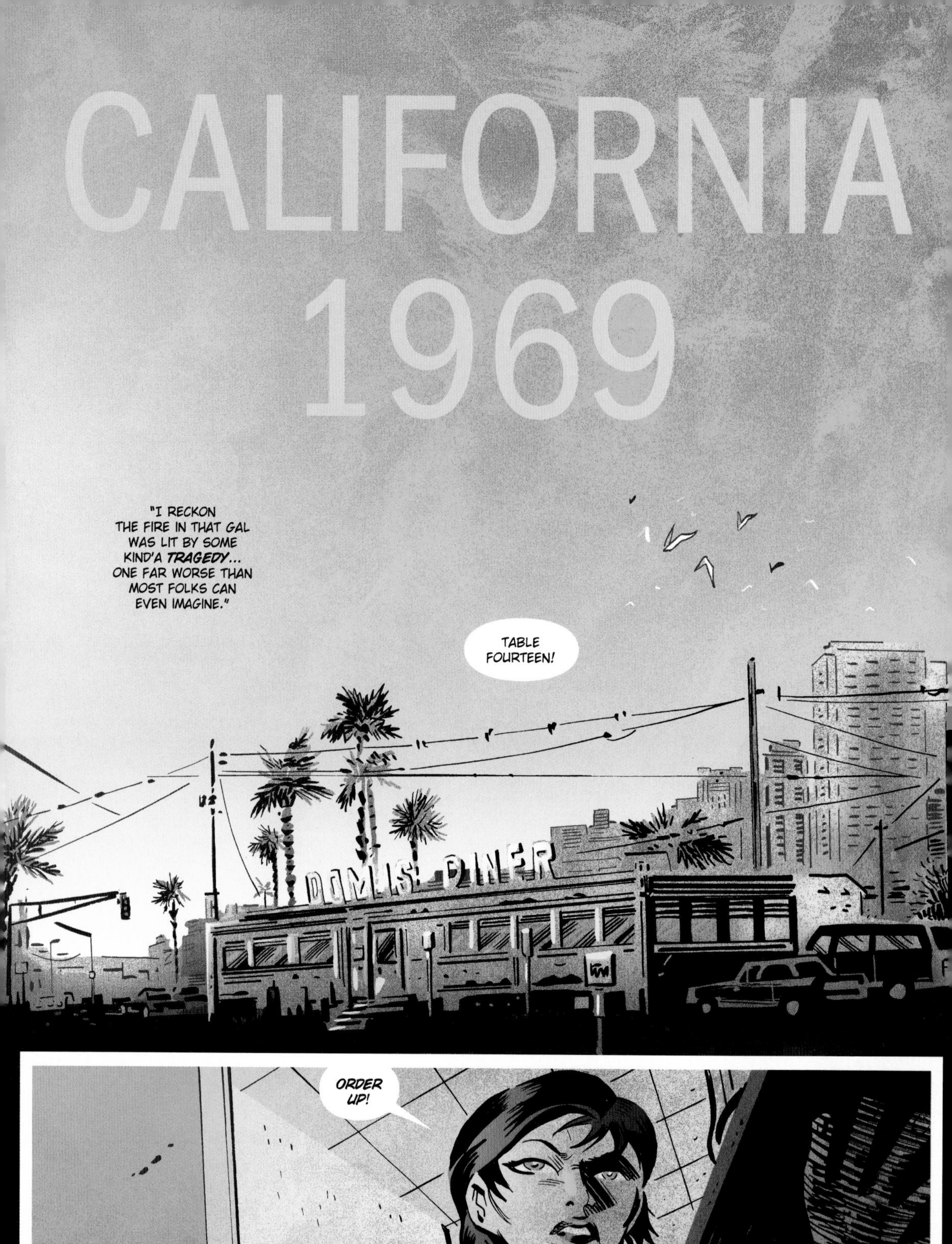
CALIFORNIA
1969
"I RECKON THE FIRE IN THAT GAL WAS LIT BY SOME KIND'A ***TRAGEDY***... ONE FAR WORSE THAN MOST FOLKS CAN EVEN IMAGINE."
TABLE FOURTEEN!
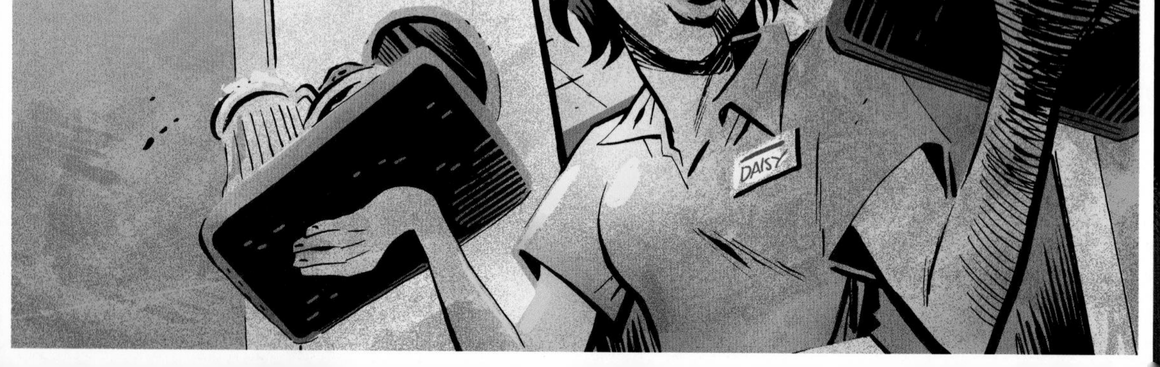
ORDER UP!
DAISY

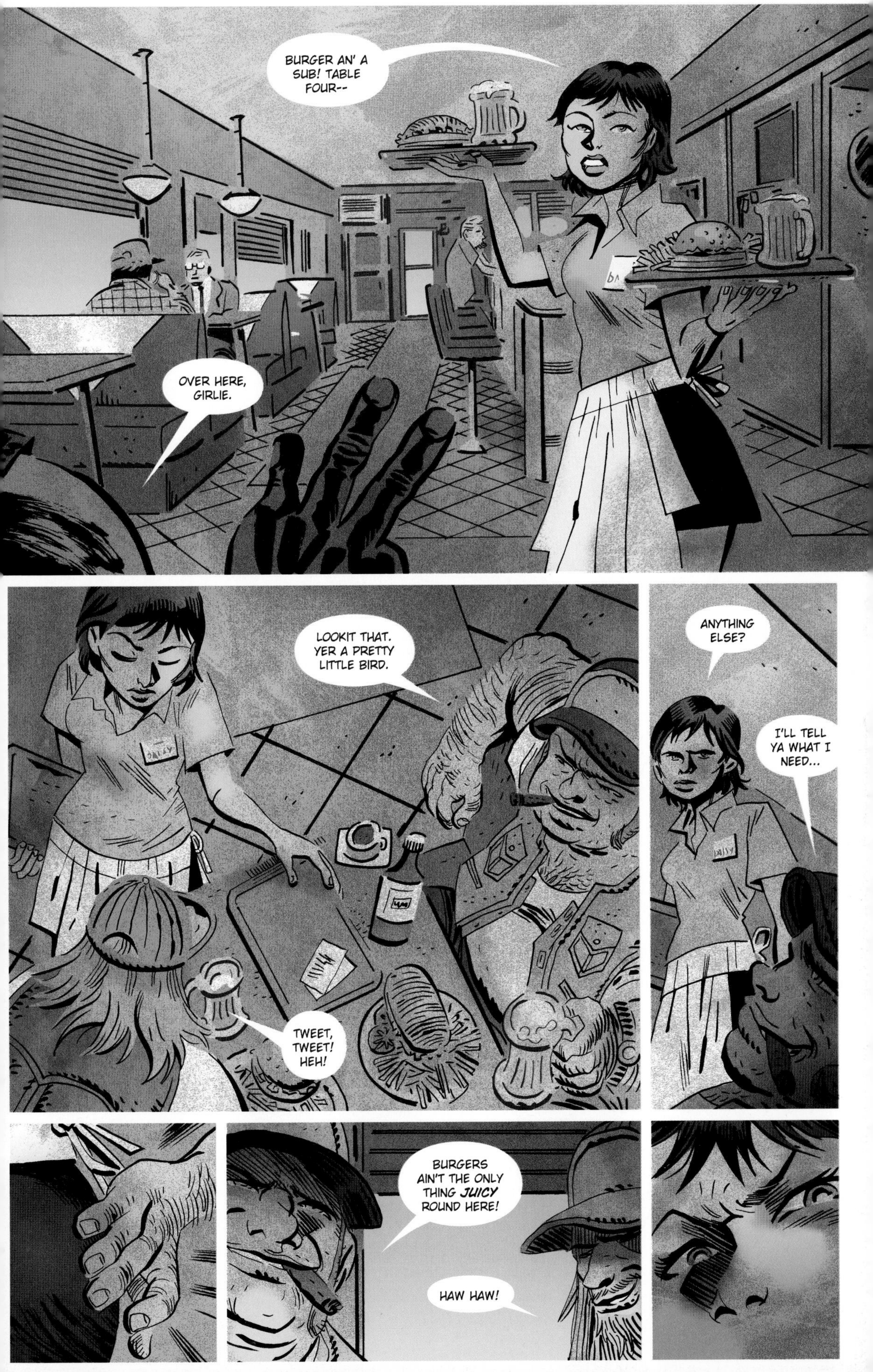
BURGER AN' A SUB! TABLE FOUR--
OVER HERE, GIRLIE.
LOOKIT THAT. YER A PRETTY LITTLE BIRD.
TWEET, TWEET! HEH!
ANYTHING ELSE?
I'LL TELL YA WHAT I NEED...
BURGERS AIN'T THE ONLY THING JUICY ROUND HERE!
HAW HAW!

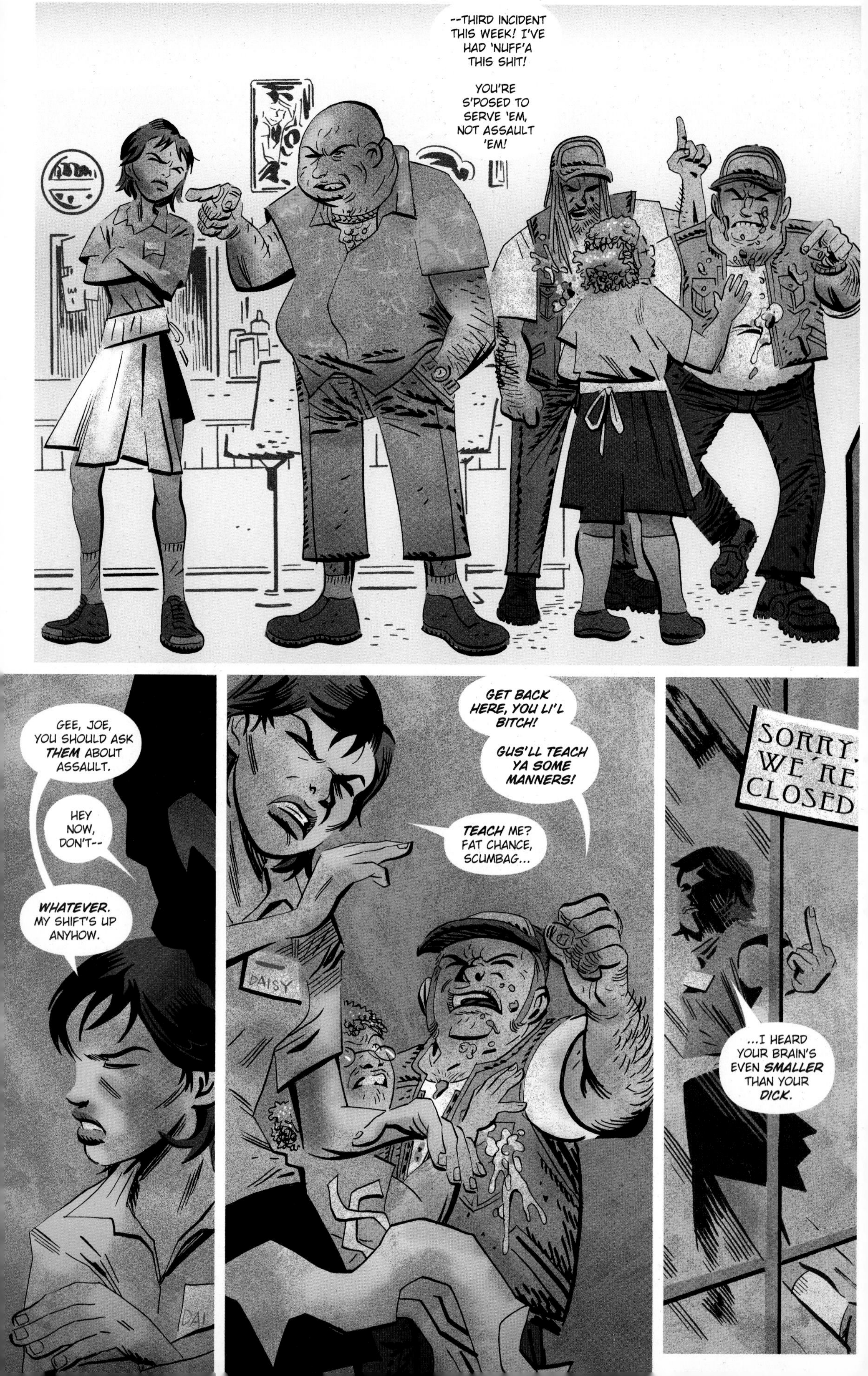
--THIRD INCIDENT THIS WEEK! I'VE HAD 'NUFF'A THIS SHIT!
YOU'RE S'POSED TO SERVE 'EM, NOT ASSAULT 'EM!
GEE, JOE, YOU SHOULD ASK THEM ABOUT ASSAULT.
HEY NOW, DON'T--
WHATEVER. MY SHIFT'S UP ANYHOW.
GET BACK HERE, YOU LI'L BITCH!
GUS'LL TEACH YA SOME MANNERS!
TEACH ME? FAT CHANCE, SCUMBAG...
DAISY
SORRY, WE'RE CLOSED
...I HEARD YOUR BRAIN'S EVEN SMALLER THAN YOUR DICK.

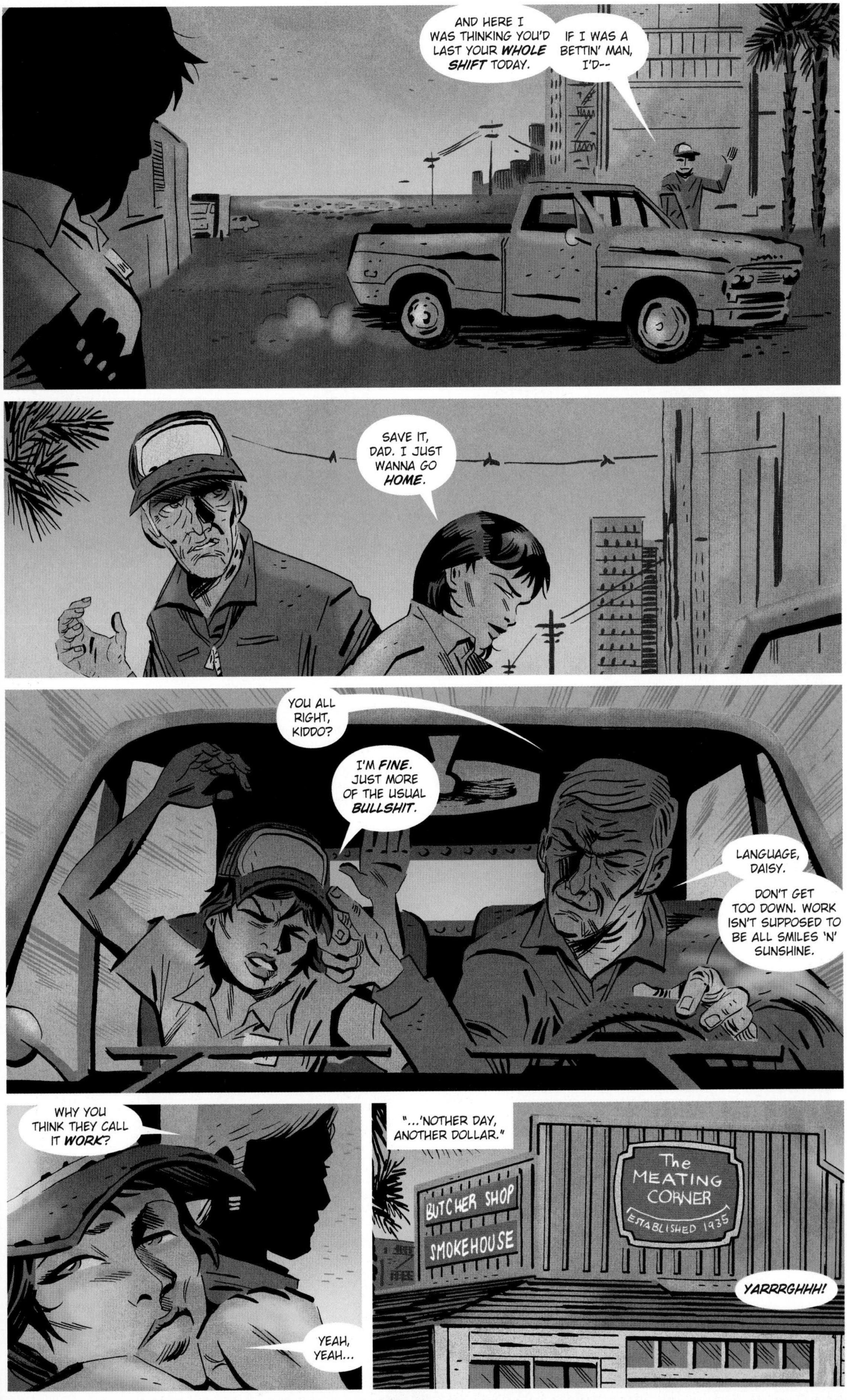
AND HERE I WAS THINKING YOU'D LAST YOUR WHOLE SHIFT TODAY.
IF I WAS A BETTIN' MAN, I'D--
SAVE IT, DAD. I JUST WANNA GO HOME.
YOU ALL RIGHT, KIDDO?
I'M FINE. JUST MORE OF THE USUAL BULLSHIT.
LANGUAGE, DAISY.
DON'T GET TOO DOWN. WORK ISN'T SUPPOSED TO BE ALL SMILES 'N' SUNSHINE.
WHY YOU THINK THEY CALL IT WORK?
YEAH, YEAH...
"...'NOTHER DAY, ANOTHER DOLLAR."
The MEATING CORNER
ESTABLISHED 1935
BUTCHER SHOP
SMOKEHOUSE
YARRRGHHH!

P-PLEASE... NO...MORE...

MR. WILLIS, YOU REALLY OUGHTA *KEEP IT DOWN.*

WHAT'S THAT, FRIENDO?

YAAARGHHH!

I'LL...I'LL DO WHATEVER YOU SAY...JUST PLEASE DON'T...DON'T--

THAT'S VERY GENEROUS OF YOU, GUY-- BUT UNFORTUNATELY THE TIME FOR *FORGIVENESS* HAS PASSED.

THIS? THIS IS MEANT TO BE A...*TEACHABLE MOMENT.*

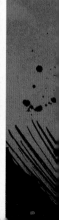

IT'S ABOUT *RESPECT.*

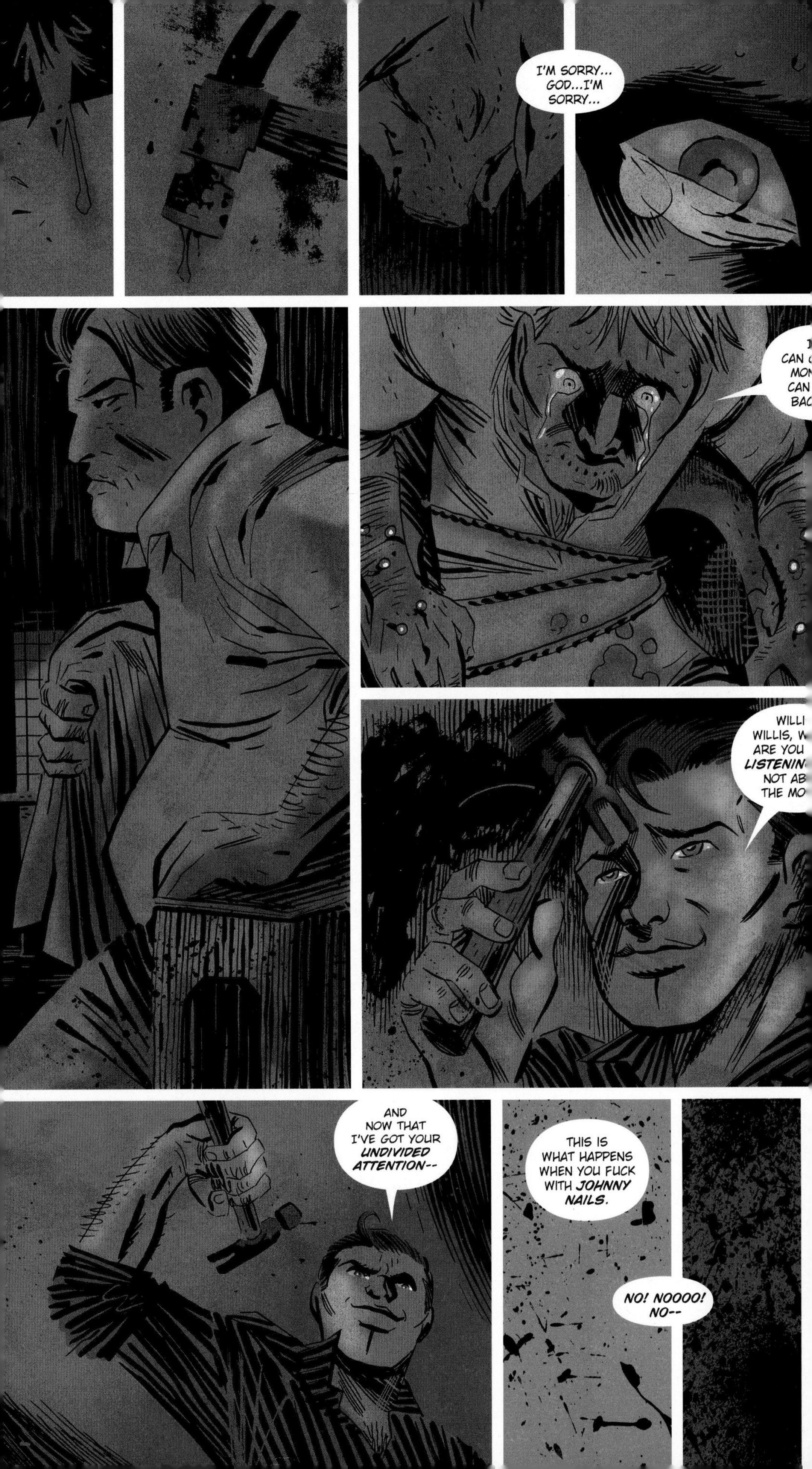
I'M SORRY... GOD...I'M SORRY...
AND NOW THAT I'VE GOT YOUR *UNDIVIDED ATTENTION--*
THIS IS WHAT HAPPENS WHEN YOU FUCK WITH *JOHNNY NAILS*.
NO! NOOOO! NO--

I KNOW THIS ISN'T THE LIFE YOU ASKED FOR, DAISY...

BUT NOTHING IN THIS WORLD'S HANDED TO YOU.

YOU GOTTA *WORK* FOR IT.

AND SOMETIMES THAT MEANS DOING THINGS THAT FEEL...*BENEATH YOU.*

"I MEAN...ME? I *LIKE* FIXING CARS. I'M GOOD AT IT.

"PEOPLE ARE GOOD AT *ALL KINDS OF THINGS.*

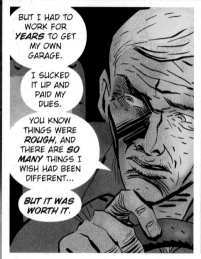

BUT I HAD TO WORK FOR *YEARS* TO GET MY OWN GARAGE.

I SUCKED IT UP AND PAID MY DUES.

YOU KNOW THINGS WERE *ROUGH,* AND THERE ARE *SO MANY* THINGS I WISH HAD BEEN DIFFERENT...

BUT IT WAS WORTH IT.

YOU... YOU JUST GOTTA FIND THAT *ONE THING.* THE ONE YOU LOVE MORE THAN ANYTHING ELSE.

AND THEN YOU FIGHT FOR IT.

MAYBE I'M JUST A RAMBLING OLD MAN...

"...BUT YOU GOT A FIRE IN YOU, DAISY. YOU'RE STILL YOUNG-- ONLY *NINETEEN*-- I KNOW, IF YOU WORK FOR IT, YOU GOT SOMETHING *BIG* COMING YOUR WAY.

"YOU'RE ON A CRASH COURSE WITH DESTINY. SOONER THAN LATER IT'S GONNA BE YOUR TIME."

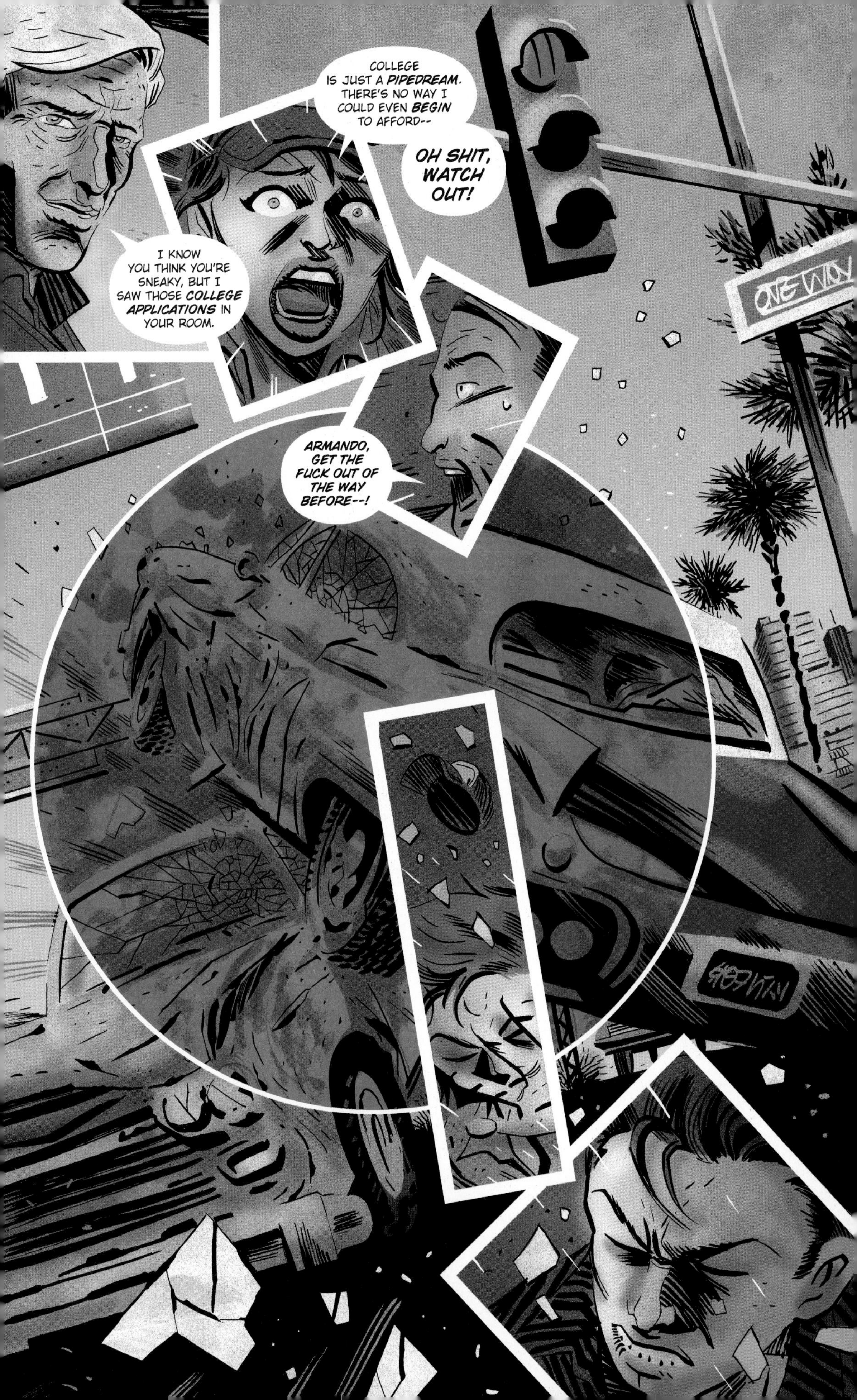
I KNOW YOU THINK YOU'RE SNEAKY, BUT I SAW THOSE COLLEGE APPLICATIONS IN YOUR ROOM.
COLLEGE IS JUST A PIPEDREAM. THERE'S NO WAY I COULD EVEN BEGIN TO AFFORD--
OH SHIT, WATCH OUT!
ARMANDO, GET THE FUCK OUT OF THE WAY BEFORE--!

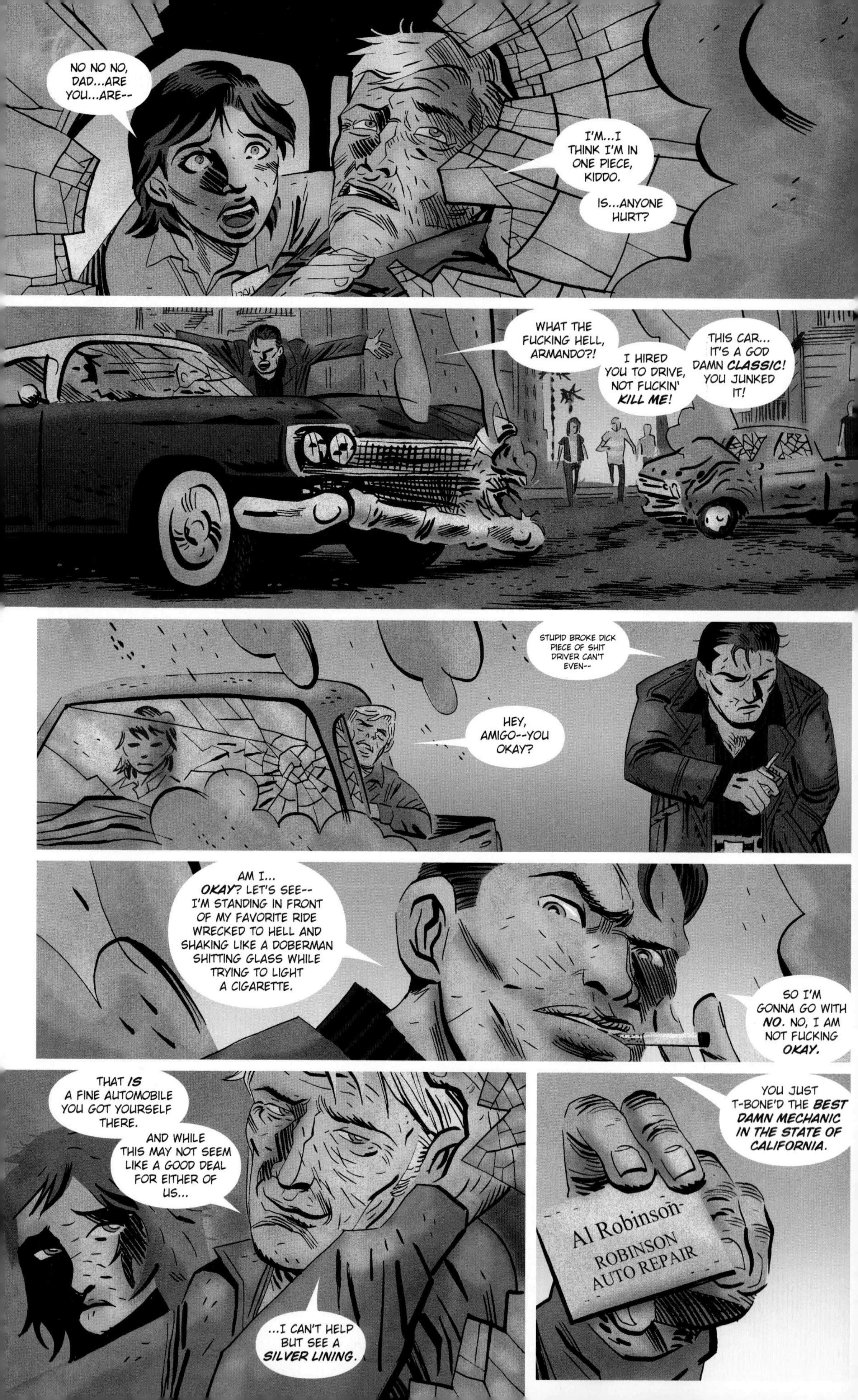
NO NO NO, DAD...ARE YOU...ARE--
I'M...I THINK I'M IN ONE PIECE, KIDDO.
IS...ANYONE HURT?
WHAT THE FUCKING HELL, ARMANDO?!
I HIRED YOU TO DRIVE, NOT FUCKIN' KILL ME!
THIS CAR... IT'S A GOD DAMN CLASSIC! YOU JUNKED IT!
STUPID BROKE DICK PIECE OF SHIT DRIVER CAN'T EVEN--
HEY, AMIGO--YOU OKAY?
AM I... OKAY? LET'S SEE-- I'M STANDING IN FRONT OF MY FAVORITE RIDE WRECKED TO HELL AND SHAKING LIKE A DOBERMAN SHITTING GLASS WHILE TRYING TO LIGHT A CIGARETTE.
SO I'M GONNA GO WITH NO. NO, I AM NOT FUCKING OKAY.
THAT IS A FINE AUTOMOBILE YOU GOT YOURSELF THERE.
AND WHILE THIS MAY NOT SEEM LIKE A GOOD DEAL FOR EITHER OF US...
...I CAN'T HELP BUT SEE A SILVER LINING.
YOU JUST T-BONE'D THE BEST DAMN MECHANIC IN THE STATE OF CALIFORNIA.
Al Robinson
ROBINSON AUTO REPAIR

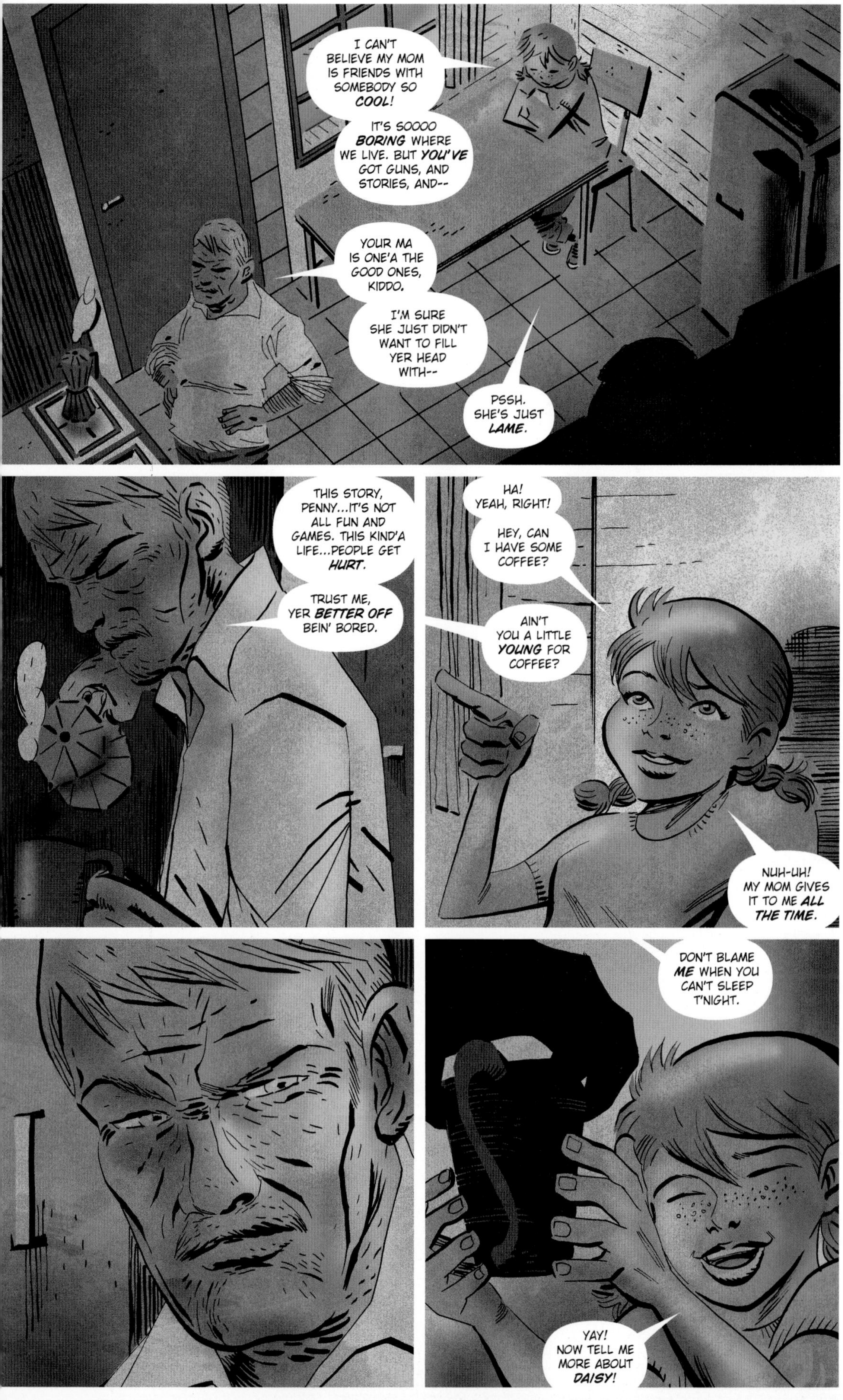
I CAN'T BELIEVE MY MOM IS FRIENDS WITH SOMEBODY SO COOL!
IT'S SOOOO BORING WHERE WE LIVE. BUT YOU'VE GOT GUNS, AND STORIES, AND--
YOUR MA IS ONE'A THE GOOD ONES, KIDDO.
I'M SURE SHE JUST DIDN'T WANT TO FILL YER HEAD WITH--
PSSH. SHE'S JUST LAME.
THIS STORY, PENNY...IT'S NOT ALL FUN AND GAMES. THIS KIND'A LIFE...PEOPLE GET HURT.
TRUST ME, YER BETTER OFF BEIN' BORED.
HA! YEAH, RIGHT!
HEY, CAN I HAVE SOME COFFEE?
AIN'T YOU A LITTLE YOUNG FOR COFFEE?
NUH-UH! MY MOM GIVES IT TO ME ALL THE TIME.
DON'T BLAME ME WHEN YOU CAN'T SLEEP T'NIGHT.
YAY! NOW TELL ME MORE ABOUT DAISY!

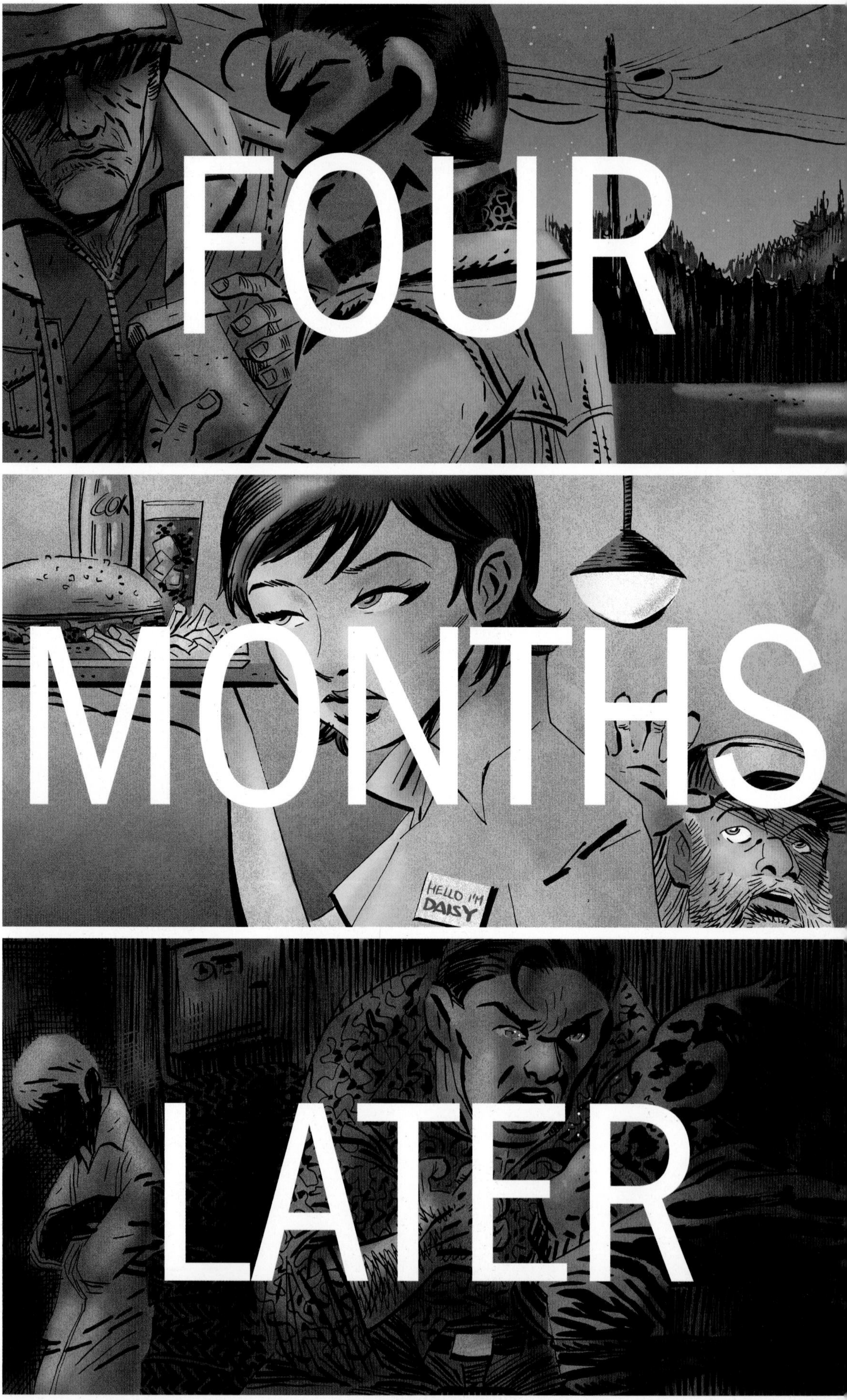
FOUR
MONTHS
LATER
HELLO I'M
DAISY

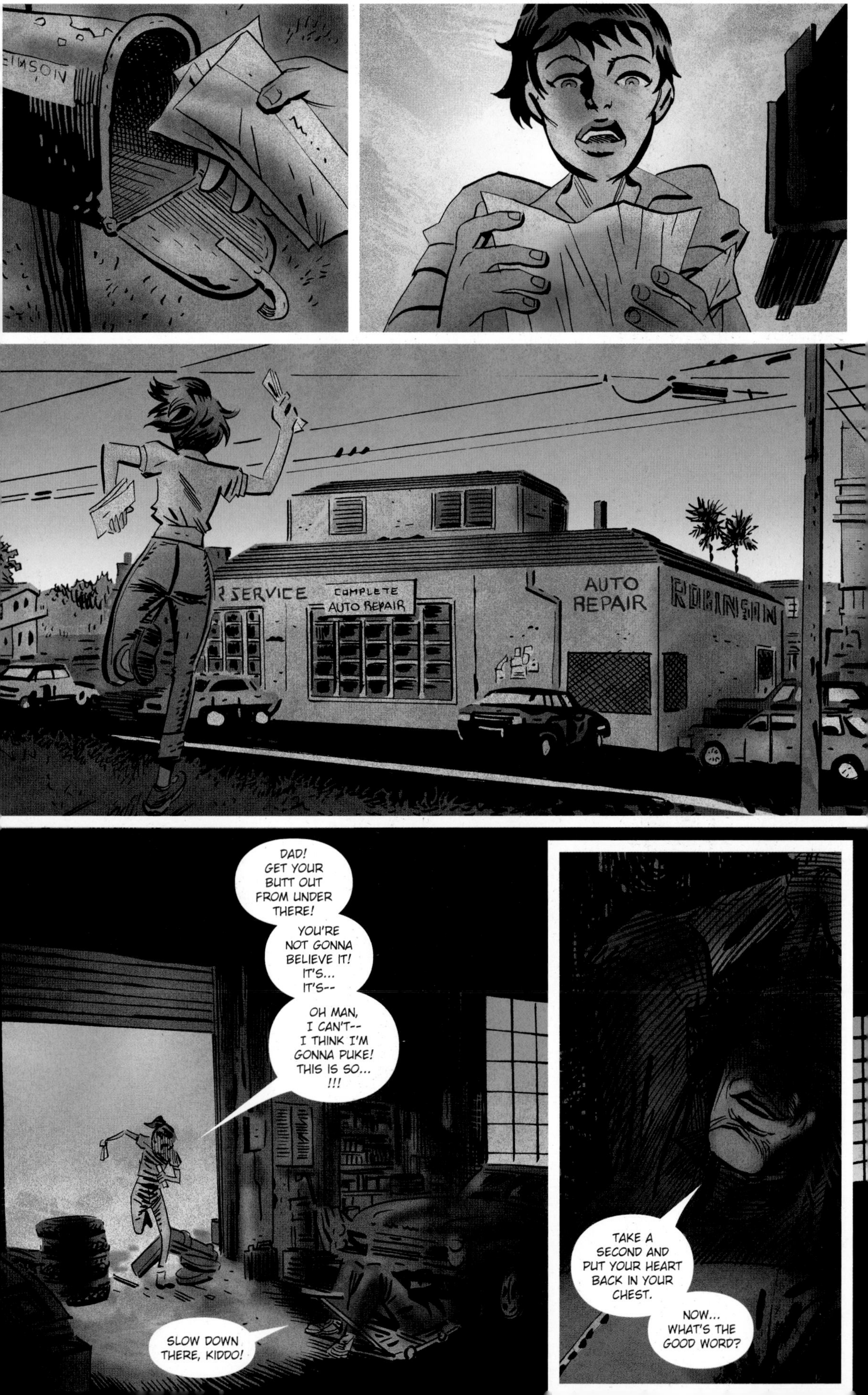

IMSON
R SERVICE
COMPLETE AUTO REPAIR
AUTO REPAIR
ROBINSON
DAD! GET YOUR BUTT OUT FROM UNDER THERE!
YOU'RE NOT GONNA BELIEVE IT! IT'S... IT'S--
OH MAN, I CAN'T-- I THINK I'M GONNA PUKE! THIS IS SO... !!!
SLOW DOWN THERE, KIDDO!
TAKE A SECOND AND PUT YOUR HEART BACK IN YOUR CHEST.
NOW... WHAT'S THE GOOD WORD?

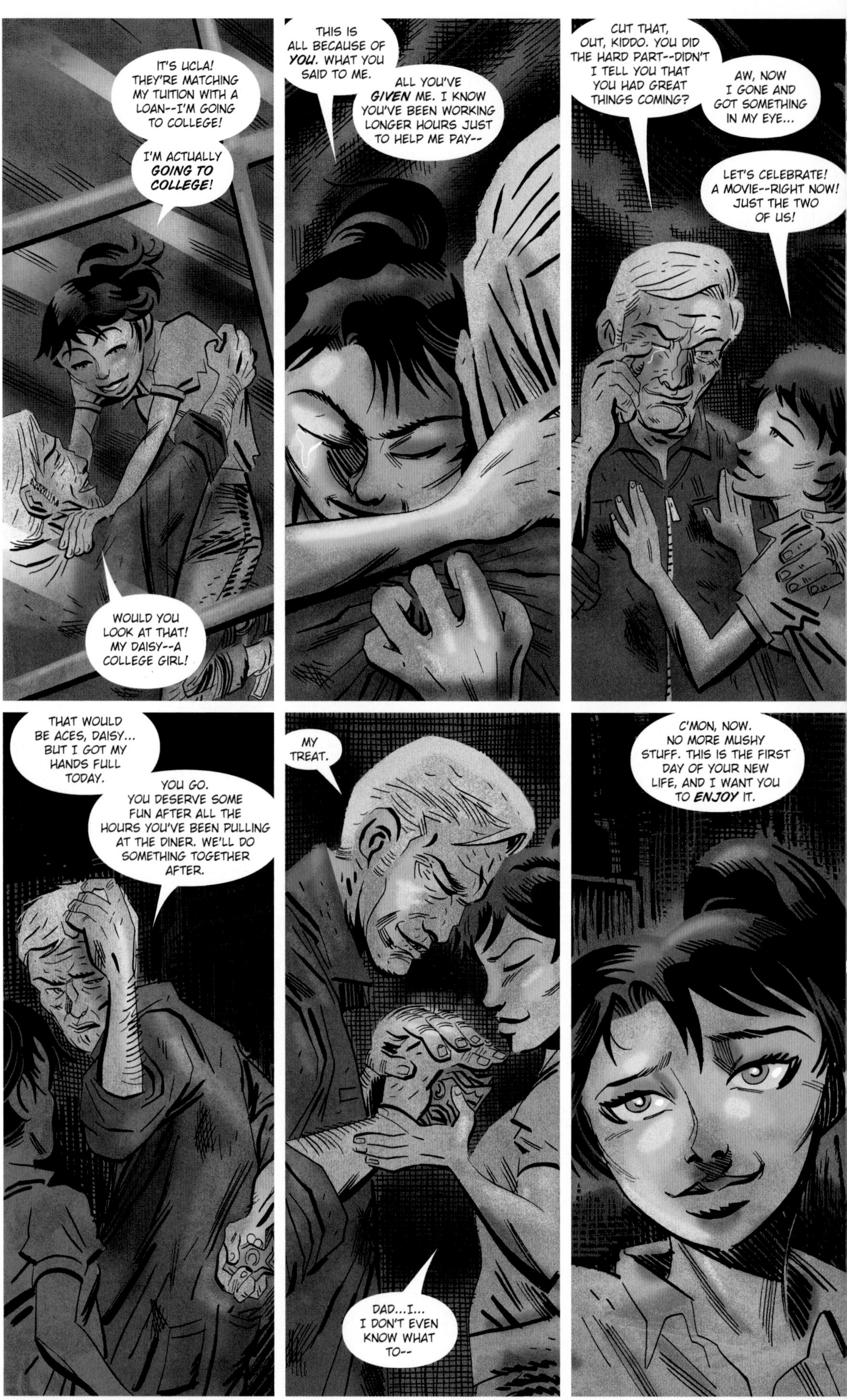
IT'S UCLA! THEY'RE MATCHING MY TUITION WITH A LOAN--I'M GOING TO COLLEGE!
I'M ACTUALLY GOING TO COLLEGE!
WOULD YOU LOOK AT THAT! MY DAISY--A COLLEGE GIRL!
THIS IS ALL BECAUSE OF YOU. WHAT YOU SAID TO ME.
ALL YOU'VE GIVEN ME. I KNOW YOU'VE BEEN WORKING LONGER HOURS JUST TO HELP ME PAY--
CUT THAT, OUT, KIDDO. YOU DID THE HARD PART--DIDN'T I TELL YOU THAT YOU HAD GREAT THINGS COMING?
AW, NOW I GONE AND GOT SOMETHING IN MY EYE...
LET'S CELEBRATE! A MOVIE--RIGHT NOW! JUST THE TWO OF US!
THAT WOULD BE ACES, DAISY... BUT I GOT MY HANDS FULL TODAY.
YOU GO. YOU DESERVE SOME FUN AFTER ALL THE HOURS YOU'VE BEEN PULLING AT THE DINER. WE'LL DO SOMETHING TOGETHER AFTER.
MY TREAT.
DAD...I... I DON'T EVEN KNOW WHAT TO--
C'MON, NOW. NO MORE MUSHY STUFF. THIS IS THE FIRST DAY OF YOUR NEW LIFE, AND I WANT YOU TO ENJOY IT.

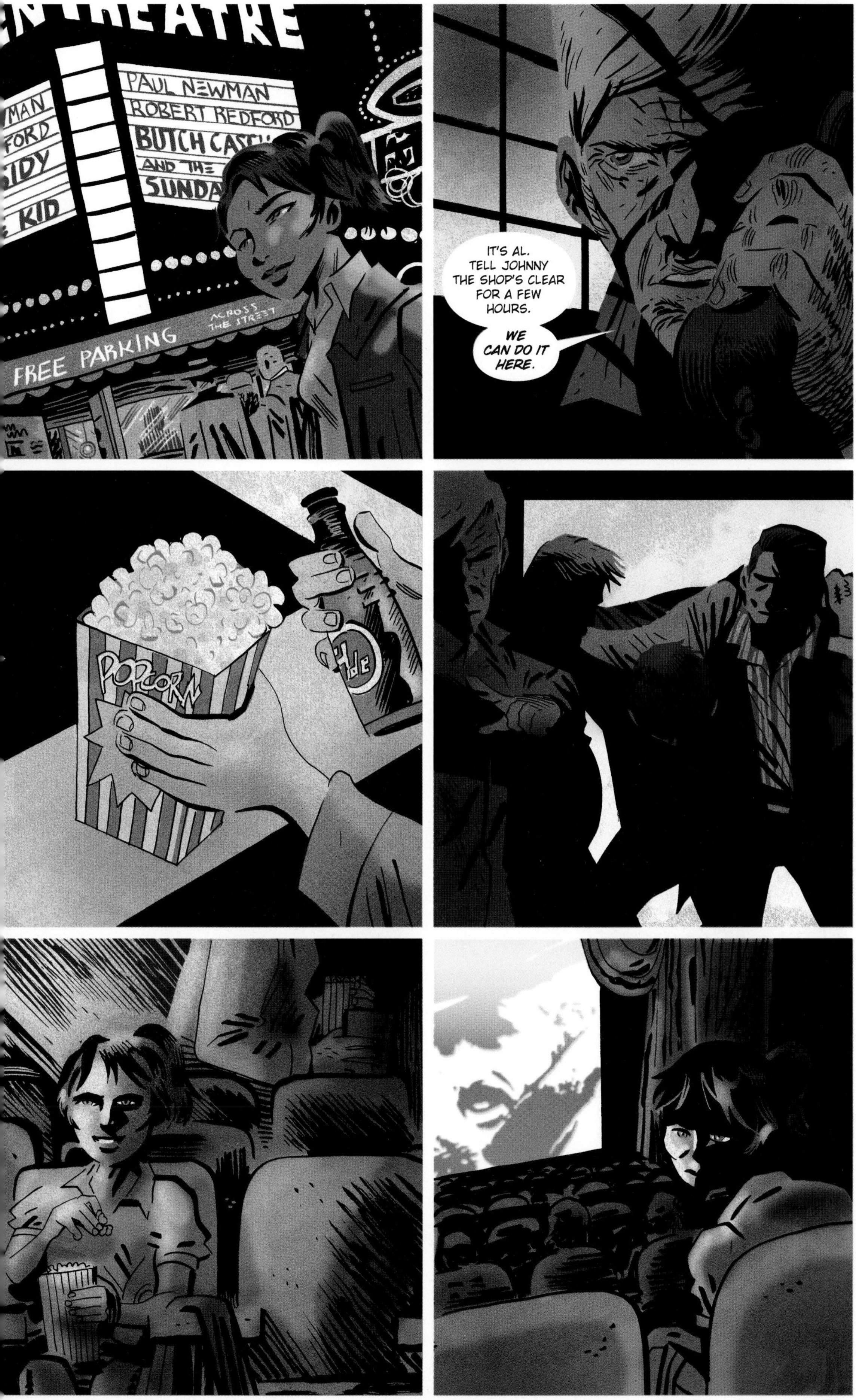
PAUL NEWMAN
ROBERT REDFORD
AND THE
FREE PARKING
ACROSS THE STREET
IT'S AL. TELL JOHNNY THE SHOP'S CLEAR FOR A FEW HOURS.
WE CAN DO IT HERE.
POPCORN

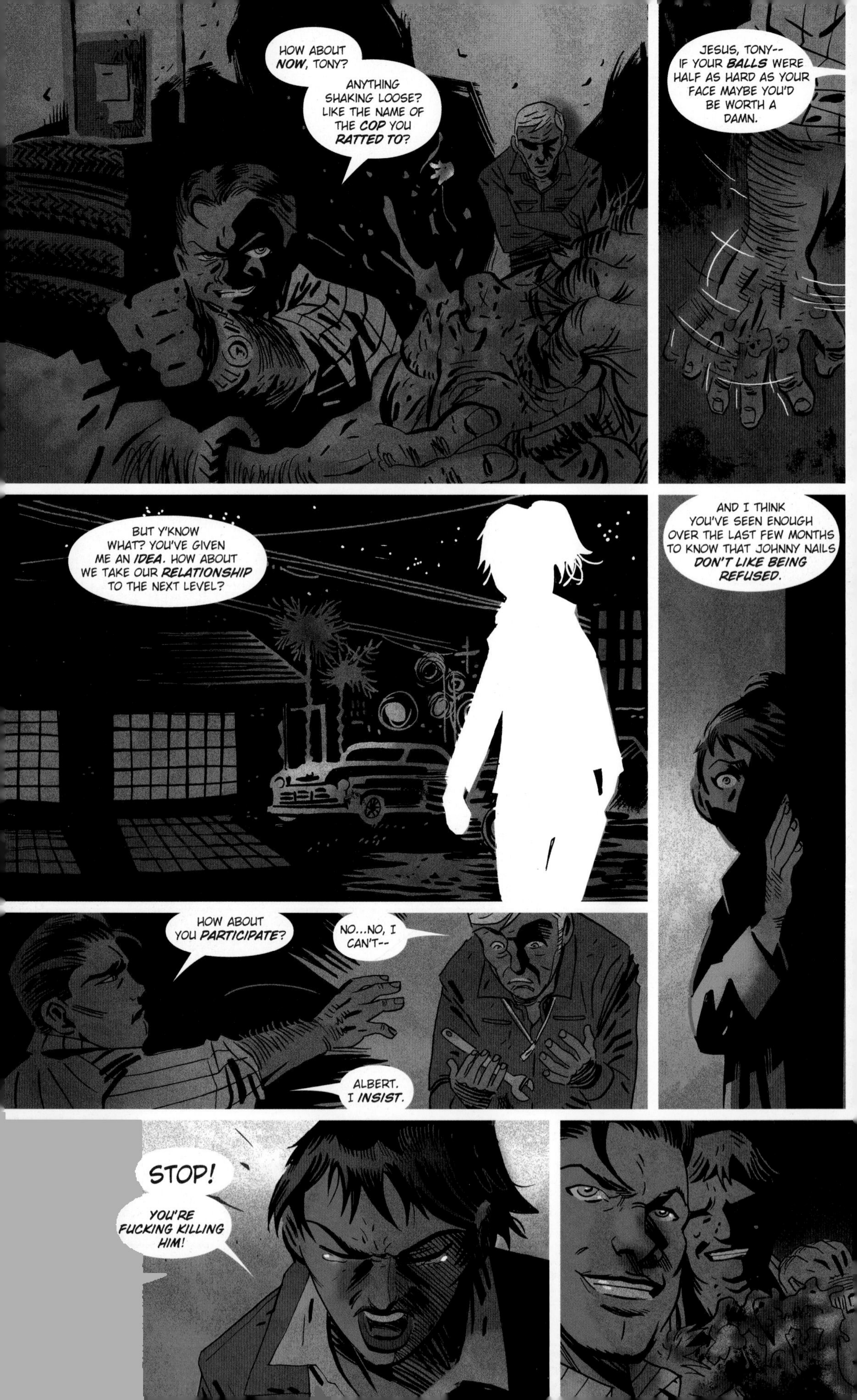
HOW ABOUT NOW, TONY?
ANYTHING SHAKING LOOSE? LIKE THE NAME OF THE COP YOU RATTED TO?
JESUS, TONY-- IF YOUR BALLS WERE HALF AS HARD AS YOUR FACE MAYBE YOU'D BE WORTH A DAMN.
BUT Y'KNOW WHAT? YOU'VE GIVEN ME AN IDEA. HOW ABOUT WE TAKE OUR RELATIONSHIP TO THE NEXT LEVEL?
AND I THINK YOU'VE SEEN ENOUGH OVER THE LAST FEW MONTHS TO KNOW THAT JOHNNY NAILS DON'T LIKE BEING REFUSED.
HOW ABOUT YOU PARTICIPATE?
NO...NO, I CAN'T--
ALBERT. I INSIST.
STOP!
YOU'RE FUCKING KILLING HIM!

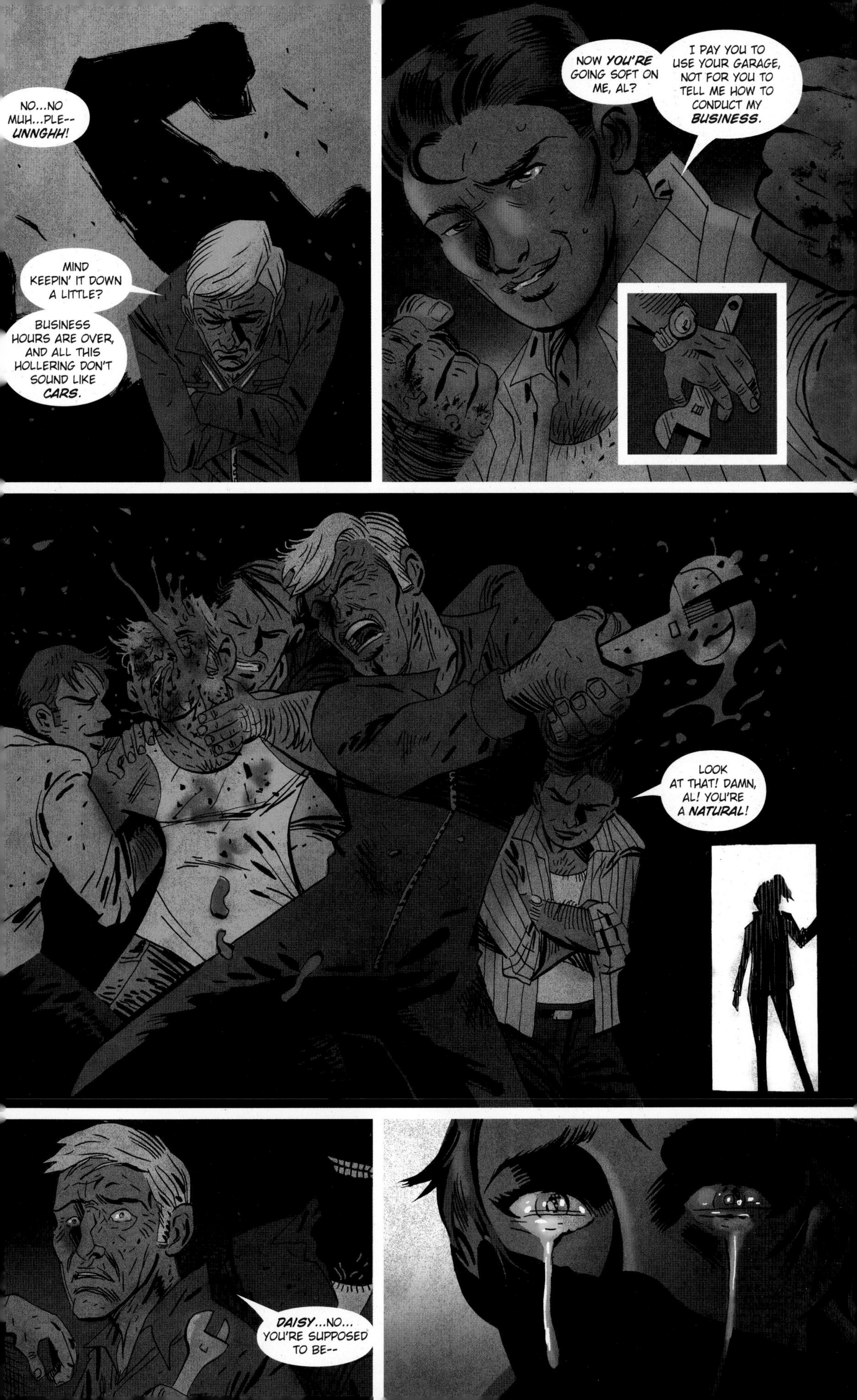
NO...NO MUH...PLE-- UNNGHH!
MIND KEEPIN' IT DOWN A LITTLE?
BUSINESS HOURS ARE OVER, AND ALL THIS HOLLERING DON'T SOUND LIKE CARS.
NOW YOU'RE GOING SOFT ON ME, AL?
I PAY YOU TO USE YOUR GARAGE, NOT FOR YOU TO TELL ME HOW TO CONDUCT MY BUSINESS.
LOOK AT THAT! DAMN, AL! YOU'RE A NATURAL!
DAISY...NO... YOU'RE SUPPOSED TO BE--

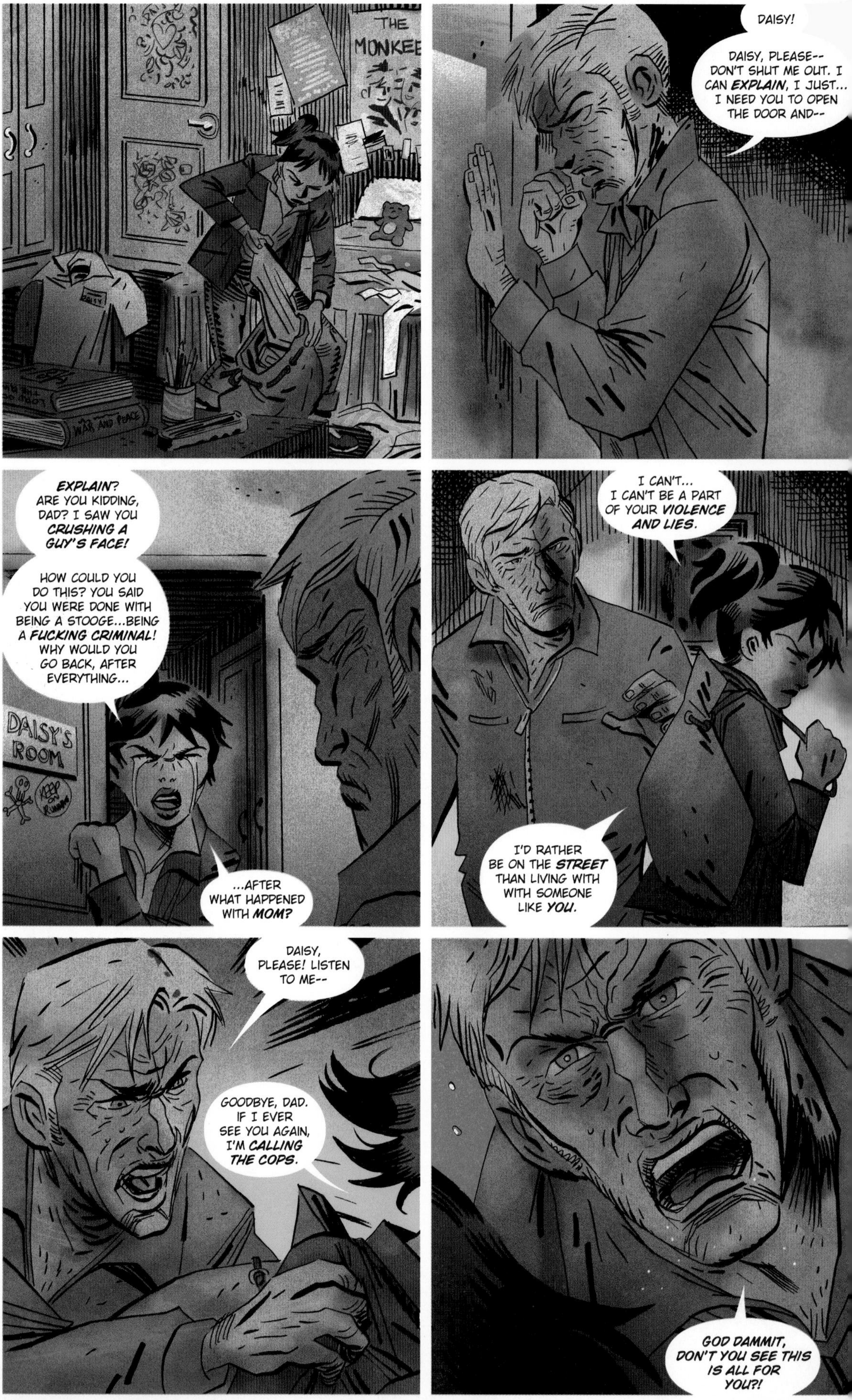
THE MONKEE
WAR AND PEACE
DAISY!
DAISY, PLEASE-- DON'T SHUT ME OUT. I CAN EXPLAIN, I JUST... I NEED YOU TO OPEN THE DOOR AND--
EXPLAIN? ARE YOU KIDDING, DAD? I SAW YOU CRUSHING A GUY'S FACE!
HOW COULD YOU DO THIS? YOU SAID YOU WERE DONE WITH BEING A STOOGE...BEING A FUCKING CRIMINAL! WHY WOULD YOU GO BACK, AFTER EVERYTHING...
DAISY'S ROOM
...AFTER WHAT HAPPENED WITH MOM?
I CAN'T... I CAN'T BE A PART OF YOUR VIOLENCE AND LIES.
I'D RATHER BE ON THE STREET THAN LIVING WITH WITH SOMEONE LIKE YOU.
DAISY, PLEASE! LISTEN TO ME--
GOODBYE, DAD. IF I EVER SEE YOU AGAIN, I'M CALLING THE COPS.
GOD DAMMIT, DON'T YOU SEE THIS IS ALL FOR YOU?!

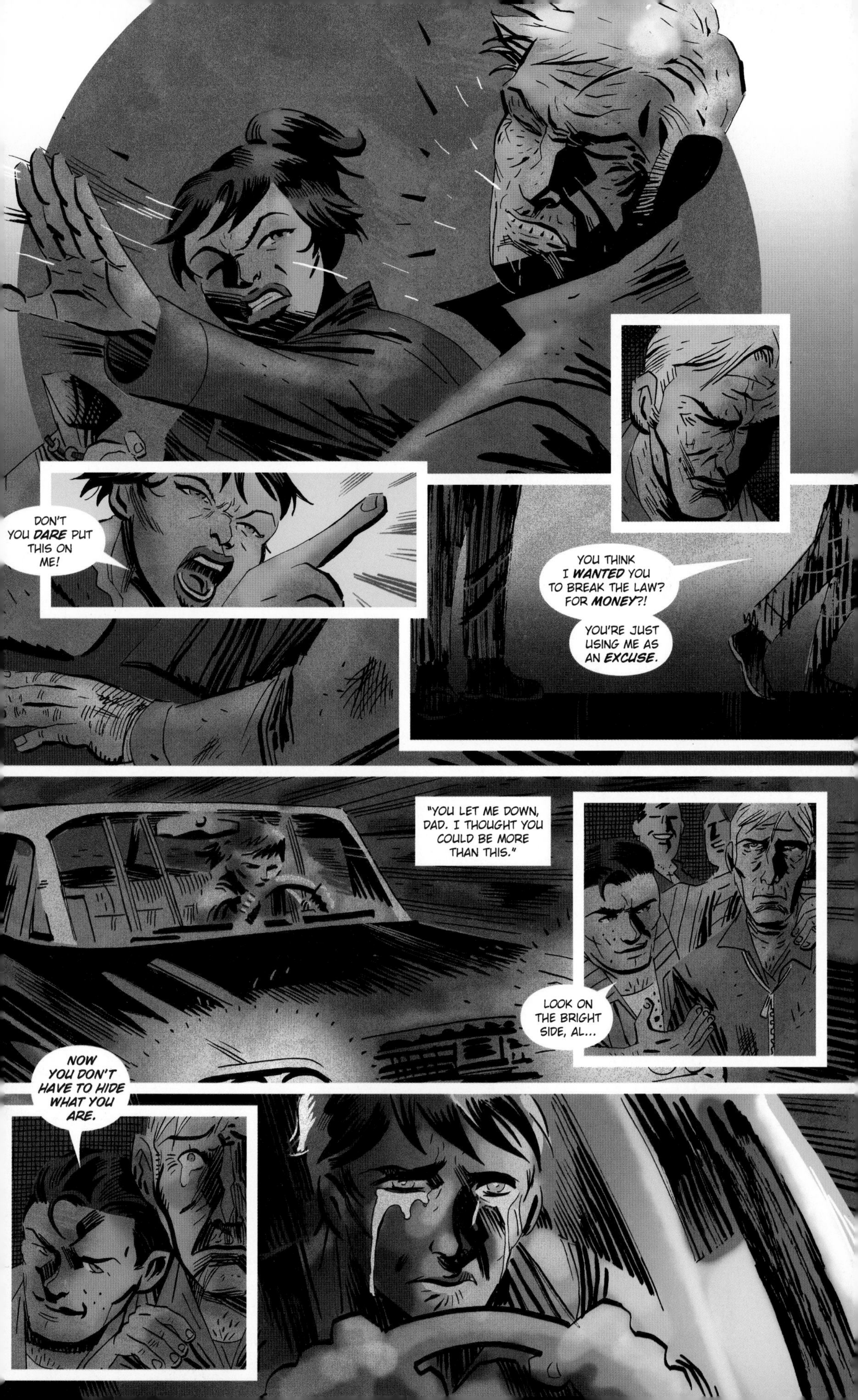
DON'T YOU DARE PUT THIS ON ME!
YOU THINK I WANTED YOU TO BREAK THE LAW? FOR MONEY?!
YOU'RE JUST USING ME AS AN EXCUSE.
"YOU LET ME DOWN, DAD. I THOUGHT YOU COULD BE MORE THAN THIS."
LOOK ON THE BRIGHT SIDE, AL...
NOW YOU DON'T HAVE TO HIDE WHAT YOU ARE.

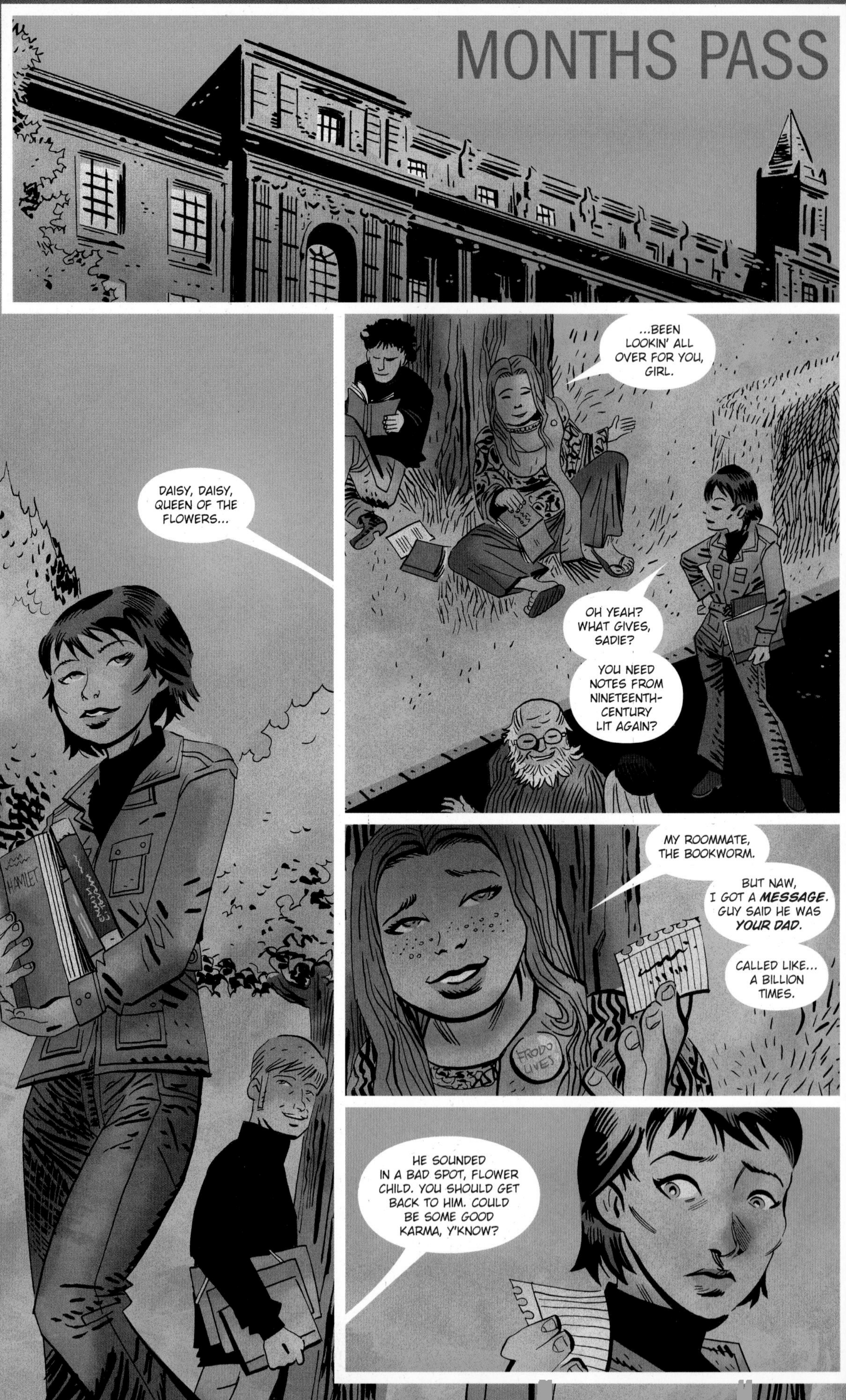
MONTHS PASS
DAISY, DAISY, QUEEN OF THE FLOWERS...
...BEEN LOOKIN' ALL OVER FOR YOU, GIRL.
OH YEAH? WHAT GIVES, SADIE?
YOU NEED NOTES FROM NINETEENTH-CENTURY LIT AGAIN?
MY ROOMMATE, THE BOOKWORM.
BUT NAW, I GOT A **MESSAGE**. GUY SAID HE WAS **YOUR DAD**.
CALLED LIKE... A BILLION TIMES.
FRODO LIVES
HE SOUNDED IN A BAD SPOT, FLOWER CHILD. YOU SHOULD GET BACK TO HIM. COULD BE SOME GOOD KARMA, Y'KNOW?

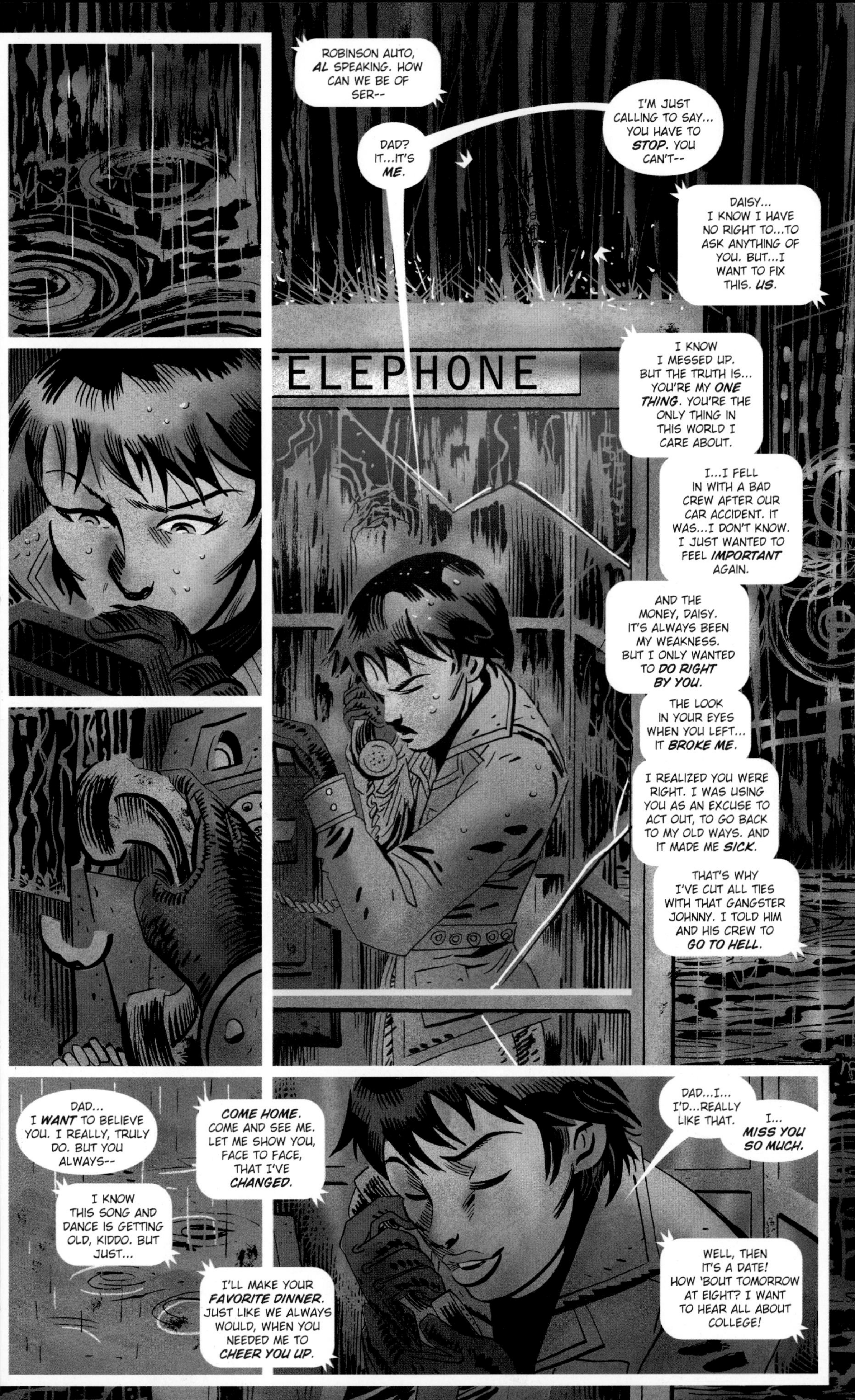
ROBINSON AUTO, AL SPEAKING. HOW CAN WE BE OF SER--
DAD? IT...IT'S ME.
I'M JUST CALLING TO SAY... YOU HAVE TO STOP. YOU CAN'T--
DAISY... I KNOW I HAVE NO RIGHT TO...TO ASK ANYTHING OF YOU. BUT...I WANT TO FIX THIS. US.
TELEPHONE
I KNOW I MESSED UP. BUT THE TRUTH IS... YOU'RE MY ONE THING. YOU'RE THE ONLY THING IN THIS WORLD I CARE ABOUT.
I...I FELL IN WITH A BAD CREW AFTER OUR CAR ACCIDENT. IT WAS...I DON'T KNOW. I JUST WANTED TO FEEL IMPORTANT AGAIN.
AND THE MONEY, DAISY. IT'S ALWAYS BEEN MY WEAKNESS. BUT I ONLY WANTED TO DO RIGHT BY YOU.
THE LOOK IN YOUR EYES WHEN YOU LEFT... IT BROKE ME.
I REALIZED YOU WERE RIGHT. I WAS USING YOU AS AN EXCUSE TO ACT OUT, TO GO BACK TO MY OLD WAYS. AND IT MADE ME SICK.
THAT'S WHY I'VE CUT ALL TIES WITH THAT GANGSTER JOHNNY. I TOLD HIM AND HIS CREW TO GO TO HELL.
DAD... I WANT TO BELIEVE YOU. I REALLY, TRULY DO. BUT YOU ALWAYS--
I KNOW THIS SONG AND DANCE IS GETTING OLD, KIDDO. BUT JUST...
COME HOME. COME AND SEE ME. LET ME SHOW YOU, FACE TO FACE, THAT I'VE CHANGED.
I'LL MAKE YOUR FAVORITE DINNER. JUST LIKE WE ALWAYS WOULD, WHEN YOU NEEDED ME TO CHEER YOU UP.
DAD...I... I'D...REALLY LIKE THAT.
I... MISS YOU SO MUCH.
WELL, THEN IT'S A DATE! HOW 'BOUT TOMORROW AT EIGHT? I WANT TO HEAR ALL ABOUT COLLEGE!

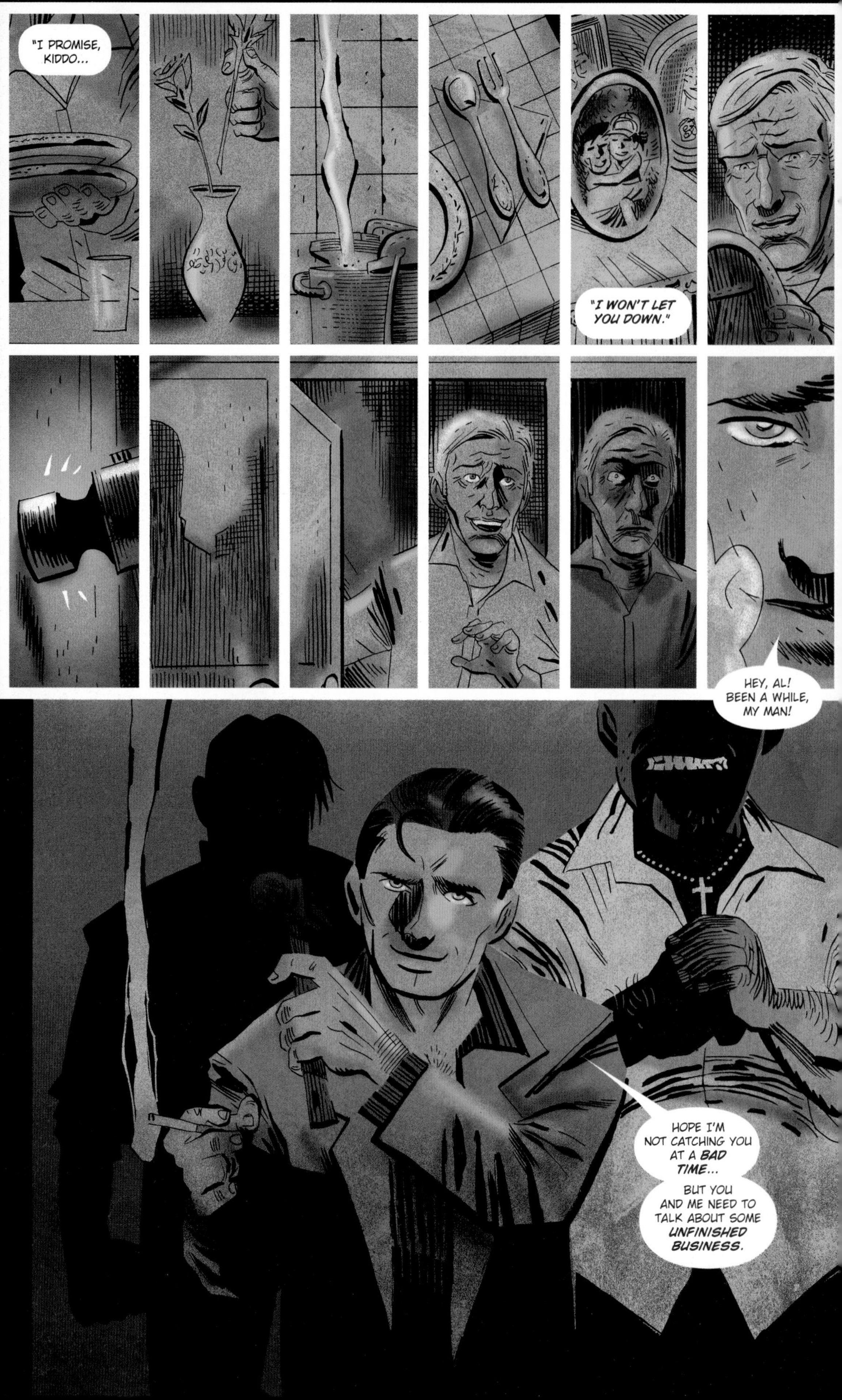
"I PROMISE, KIDDO...
"I WON'T LET YOU DOWN."
HEY, AL! BEEN A WHILE, MY MAN!
HOPE I'M NOT CATCHING YOU AT A BAD TIME...
BUT YOU AND ME NEED TO TALK ABOUT SOME UNFINISHED BUSINESS.

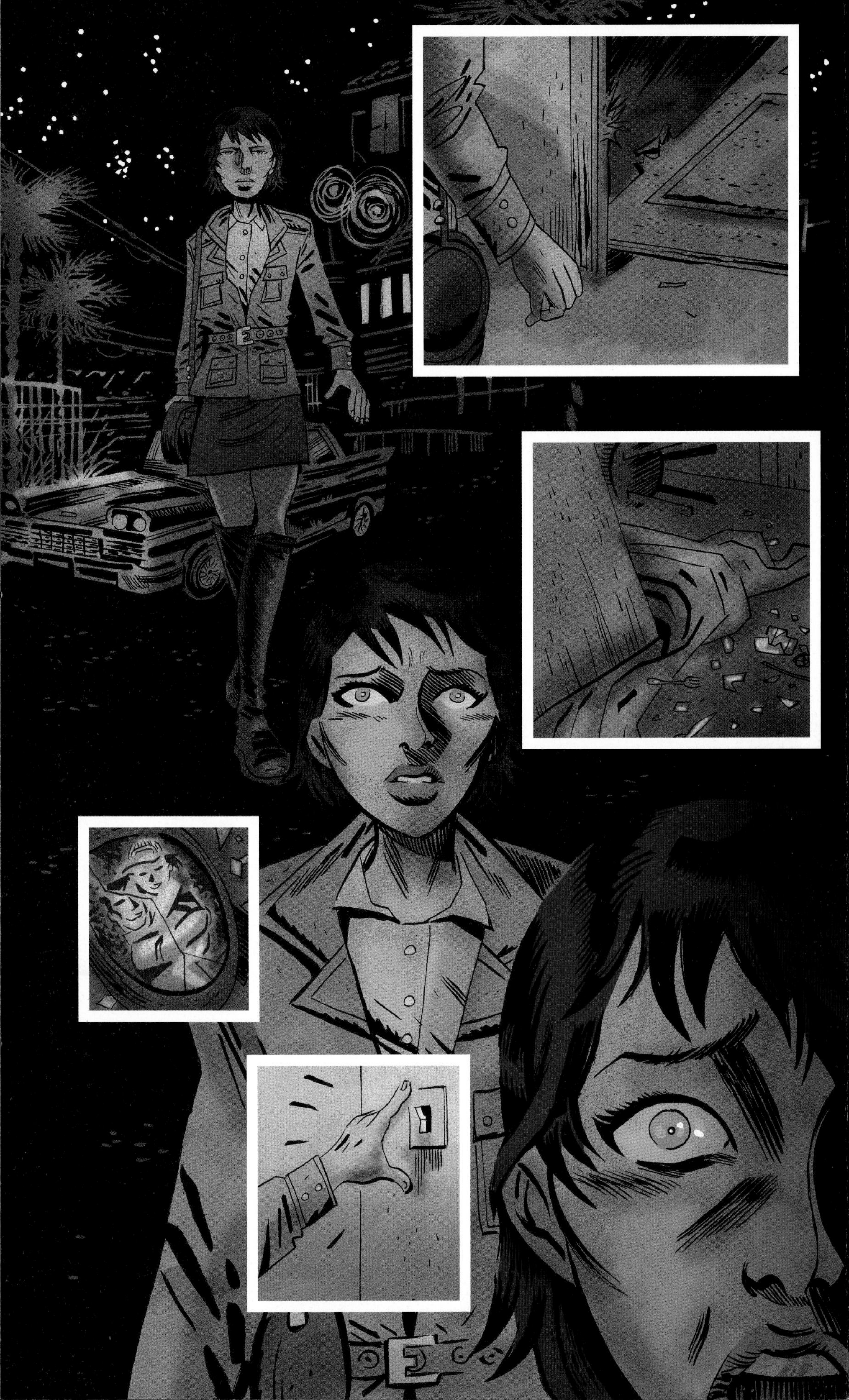

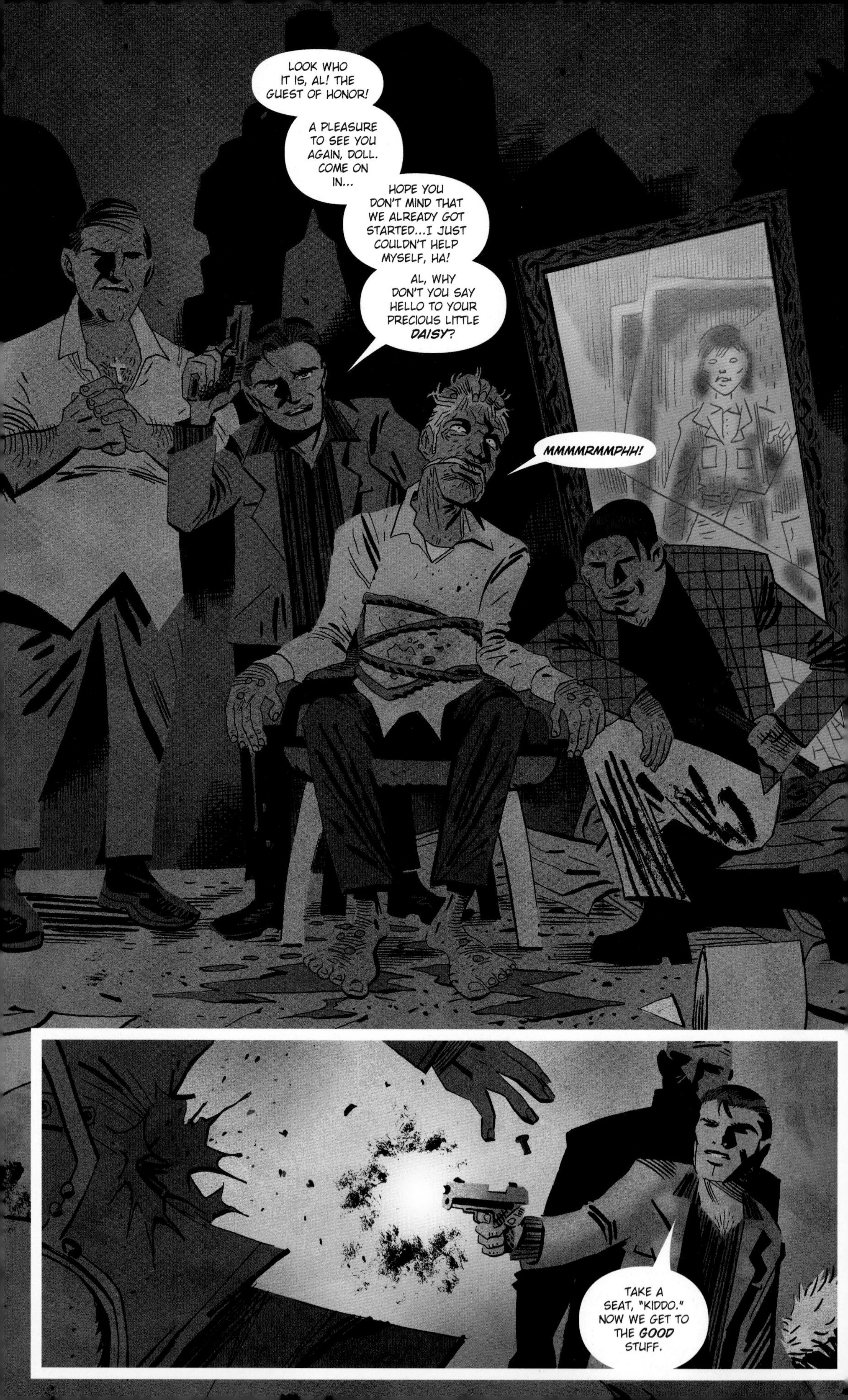
LOOK WHO IT IS, AL! THE GUEST OF HONOR!
A PLEASURE TO SEE YOU AGAIN, DOLL. COME ON IN...
HOPE YOU DON'T MIND THAT WE ALREADY GOT STARTED...I JUST COULDN'T HELP MYSELF, HA!
AL, WHY DON'T YOU SAY HELLO TO YOUR PRECIOUS LITTLE *DAISY*?
MMMMRMMPHH!
TAKE A SEAT, "KIDDO." NOW WE GET TO THE *GOOD* STUFF.

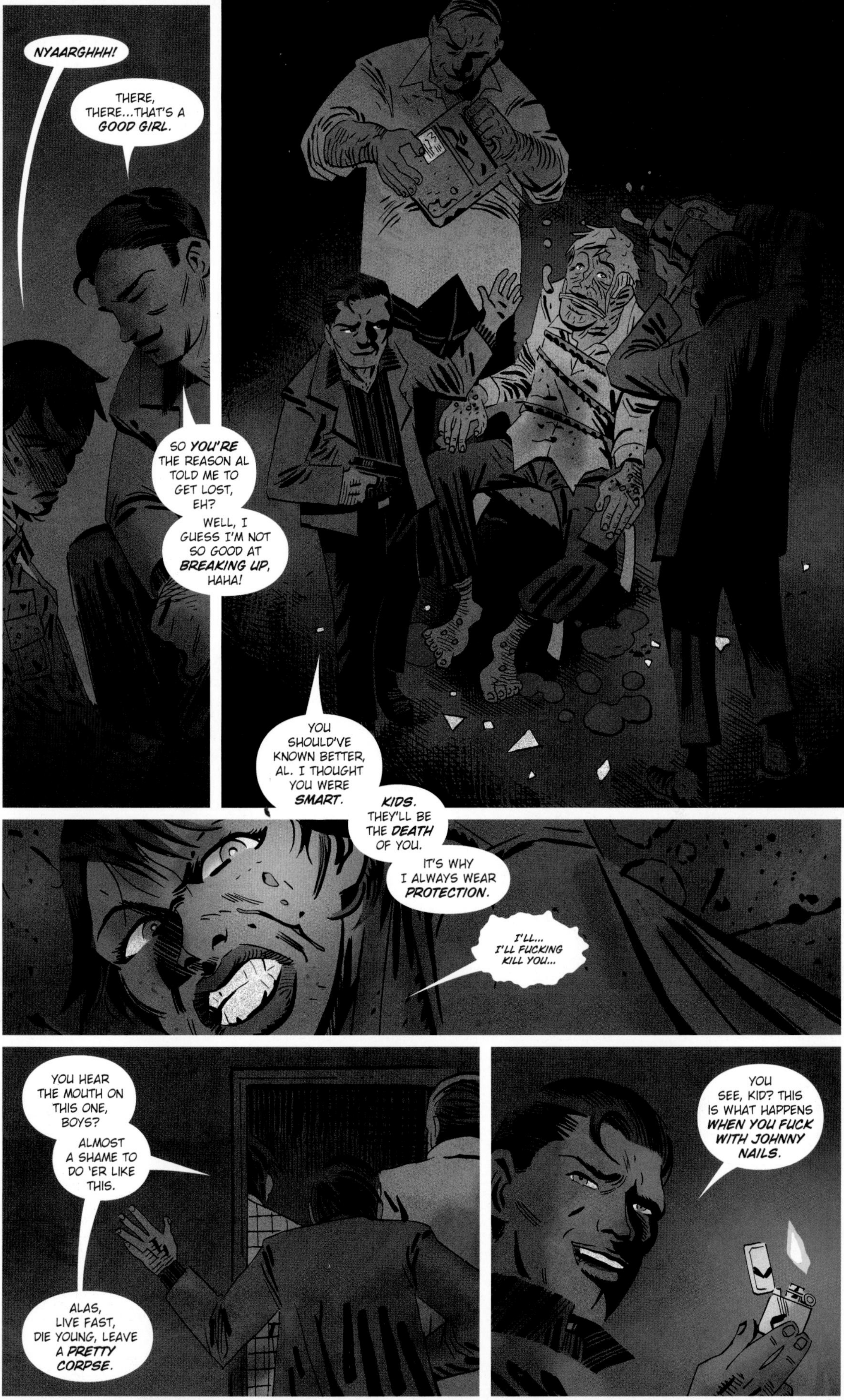
NYAARGHHH!
THERE, THERE...THAT'S A GOOD GIRL.
SO YOU'RE THE REASON AL TOLD ME TO GET LOST, EH?
WELL, I GUESS I'M NOT SO GOOD AT BREAKING UP, HAHA!
YOU SHOULD'VE KNOWN BETTER, AL. I THOUGHT YOU WERE SMART.
KIDS. THEY'LL BE THE DEATH OF YOU.
IT'S WHY I ALWAYS WEAR PROTECTION.
I'LL... I'LL FUCKING KILL YOU...
YOU HEAR THE MOUTH ON THIS ONE, BOYS?
ALMOST A SHAME TO DO 'ER LIKE THIS.
ALAS, LIVE FAST, DIE YOUNG, LEAVE A PRETTY CORPSE.
YOU SEE, KID? THIS IS WHAT HAPPENS WHEN YOU FUCK WITH JOHNNY NAILS.

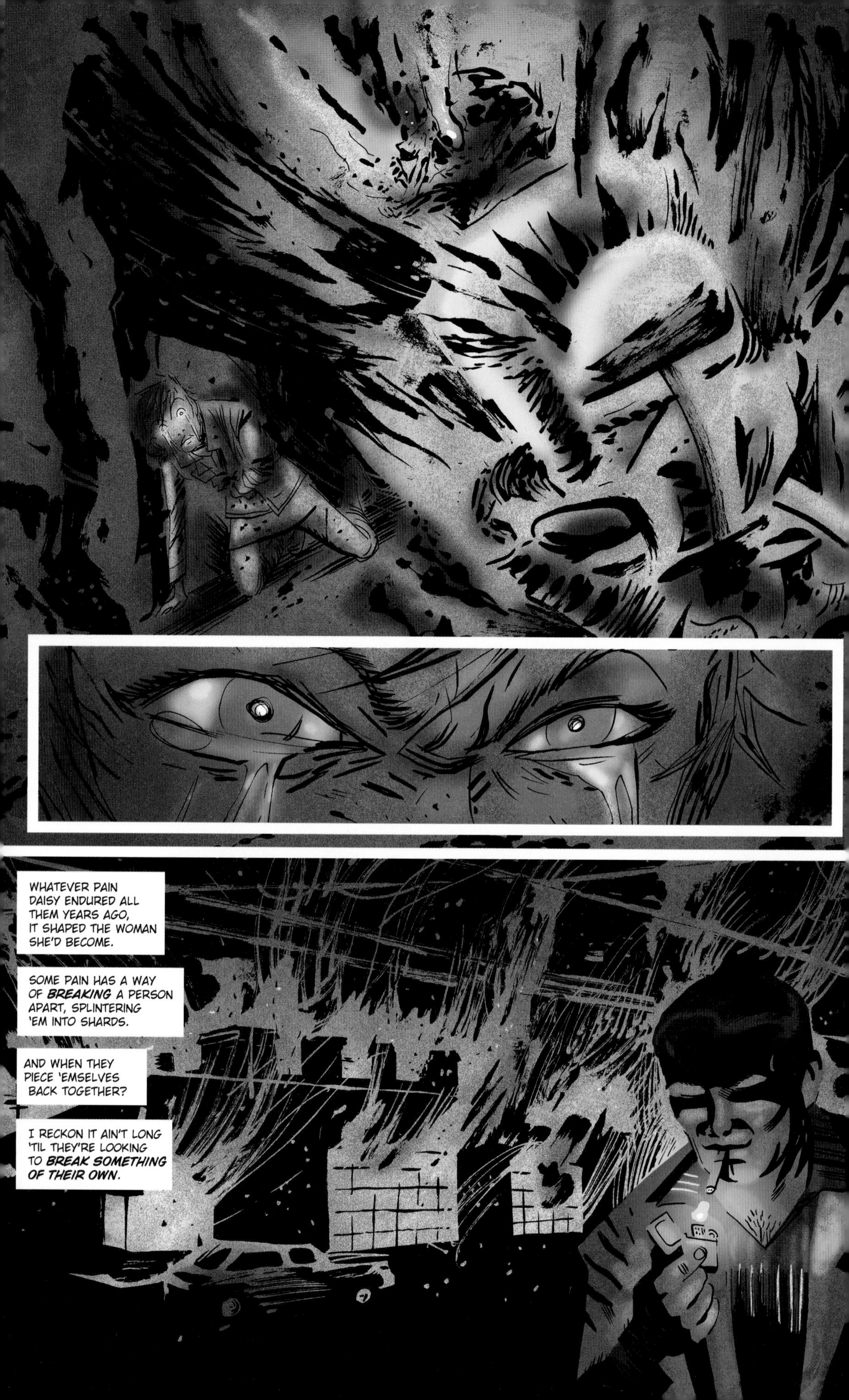
WHATEVER PAIN DAISY ENDURED ALL THEM YEARS AGO, IT SHAPED THE WOMAN SHE'D BECOME.
SOME PAIN HAS A WAY OF **BREAKING** A PERSON APART, SPLINTERING 'EM INTO SHARDS.
AND WHEN THEY PIECE 'EMSELVES BACK TOGETHER?
I RECKON IT AIN'T LONG 'TIL THEY'RE LOOKING TO **BREAK SOMETHING OF THEIR OWN**.

CHAPTER TWO

"SEX & MONEY"

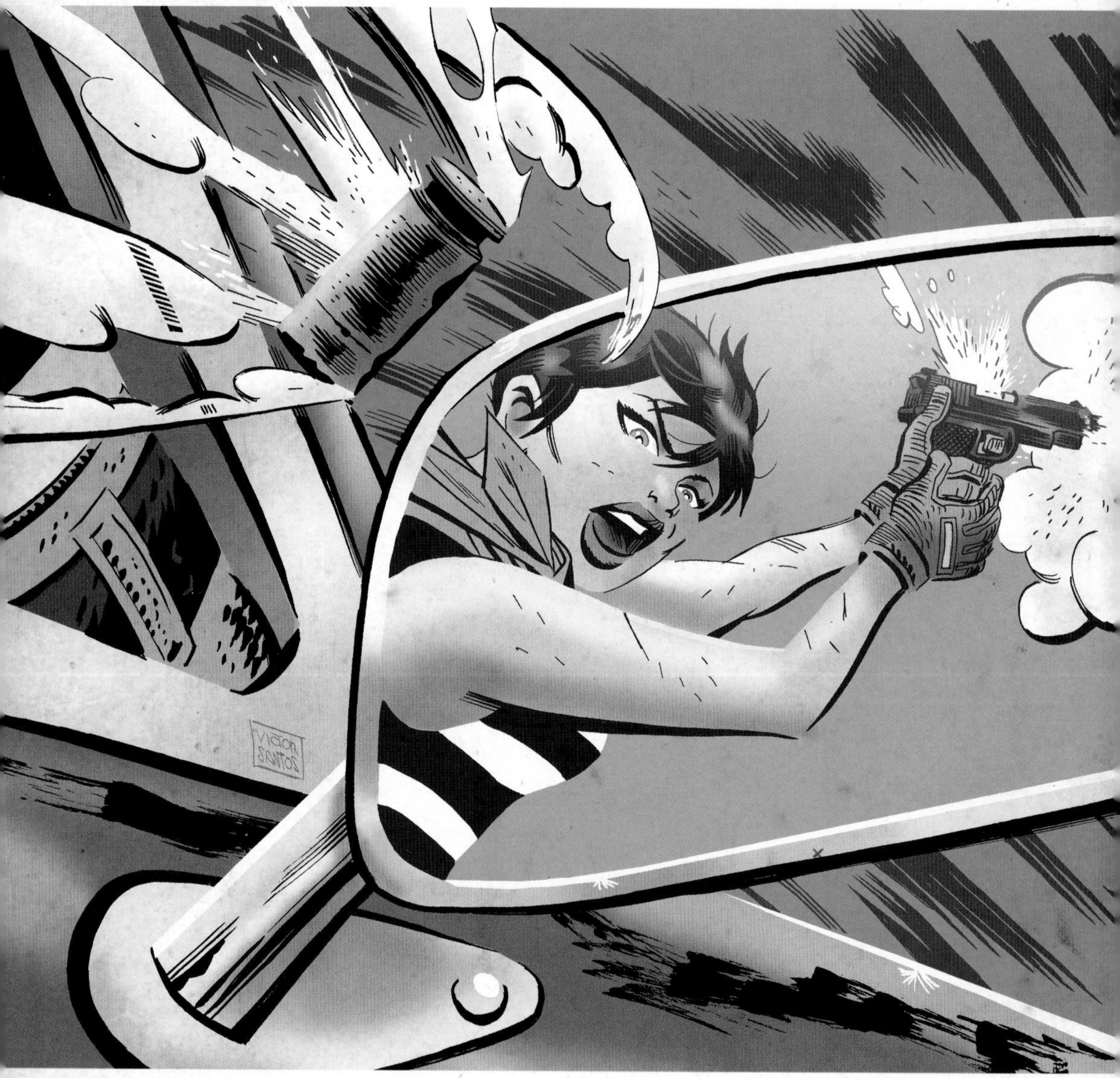
VICTOR SANTOS

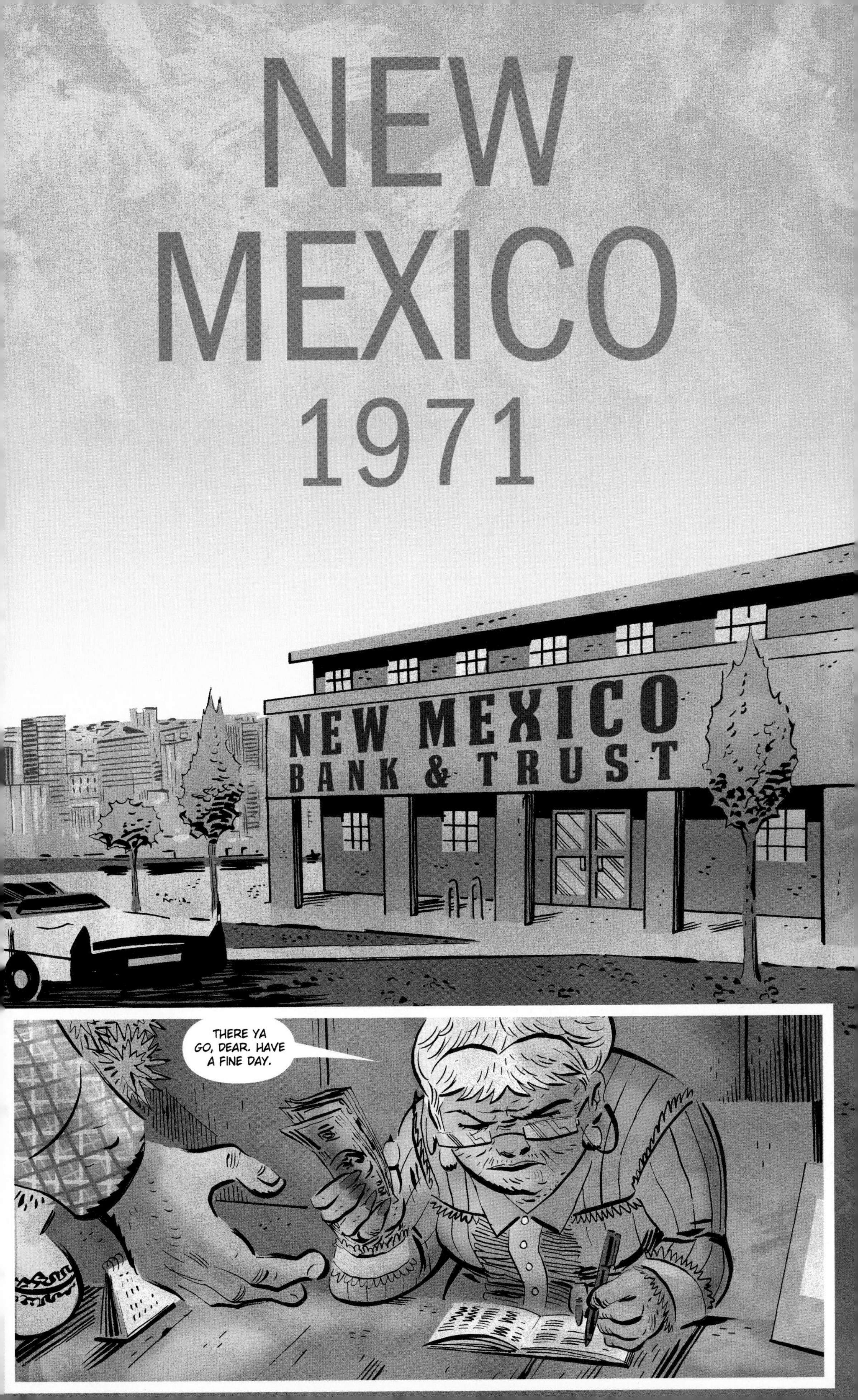
NEW MEXICO 1971
NEW MEXICO BANK & TRUST
THERE YA GO, DEAR. HAVE A FINE DAY.

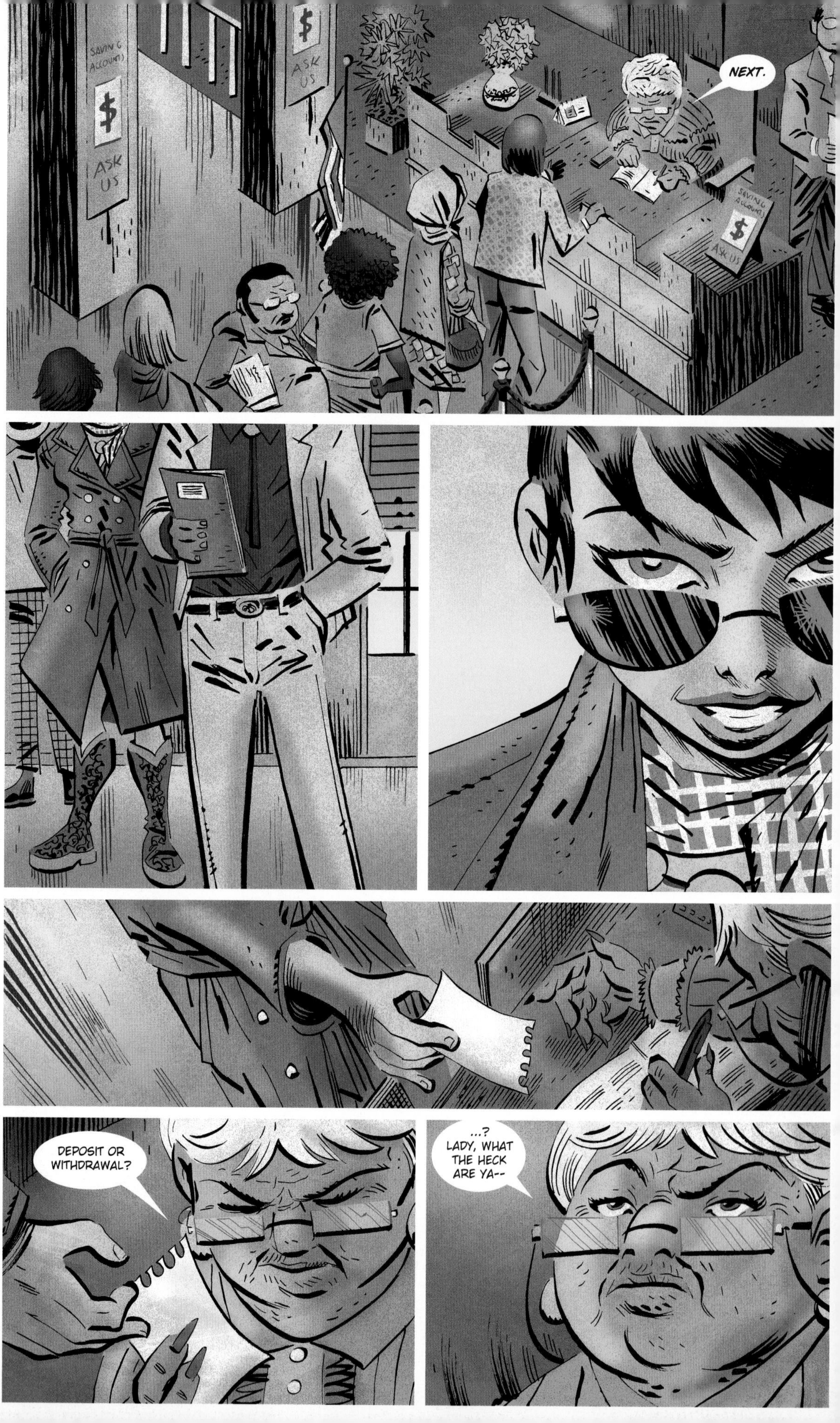
SAVING ACCOUNTS
$
ASK US
$
ASK US
NEXT.
SAVING ACCOUNTS
$
ASK US
DEPOSIT OR WITHDRAWAL?
...? LADY, WHAT THE HECK ARE YA--

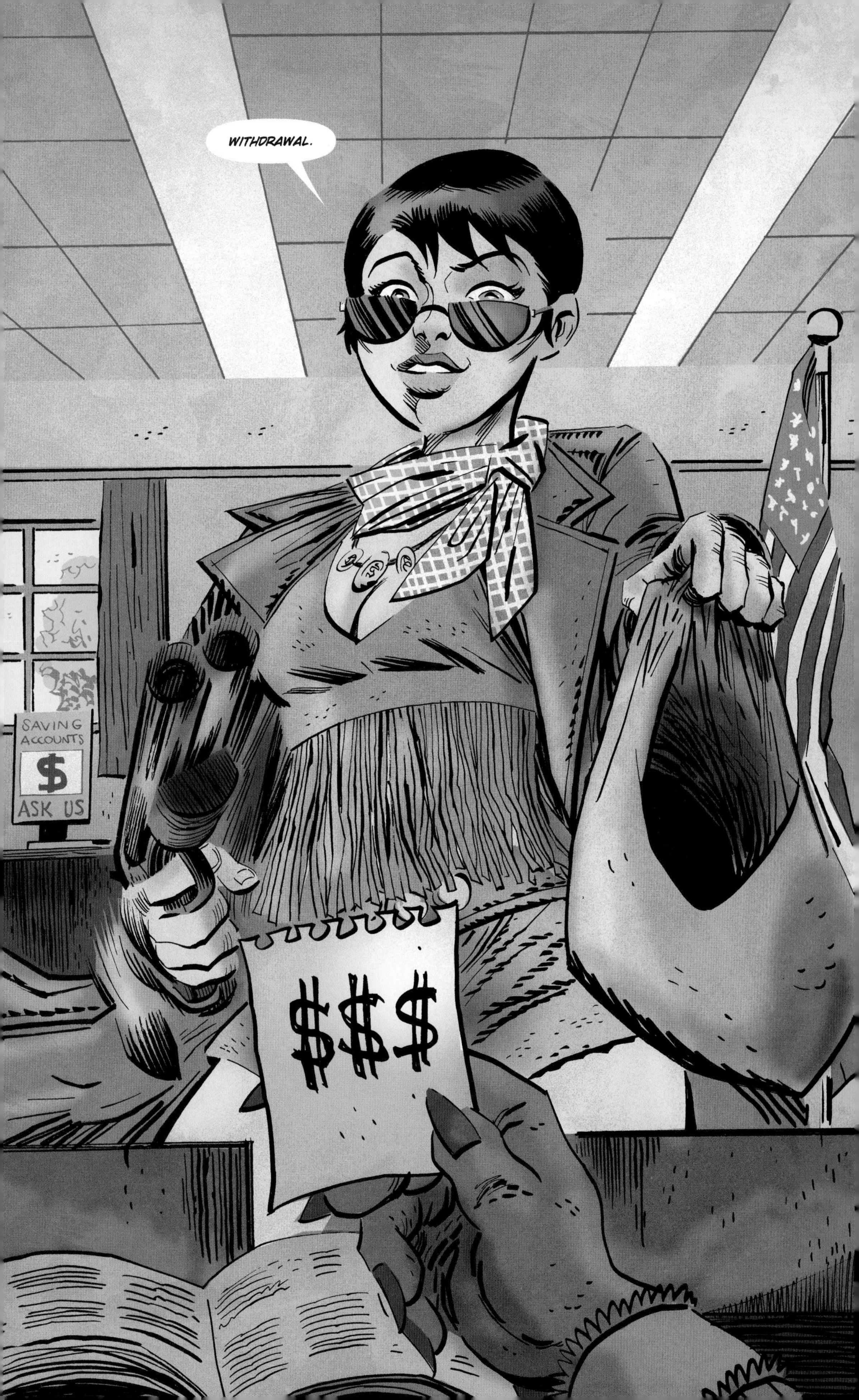
WITHDRAWAL.
SAVING ACCOUNTS
$
ASK US
$$$

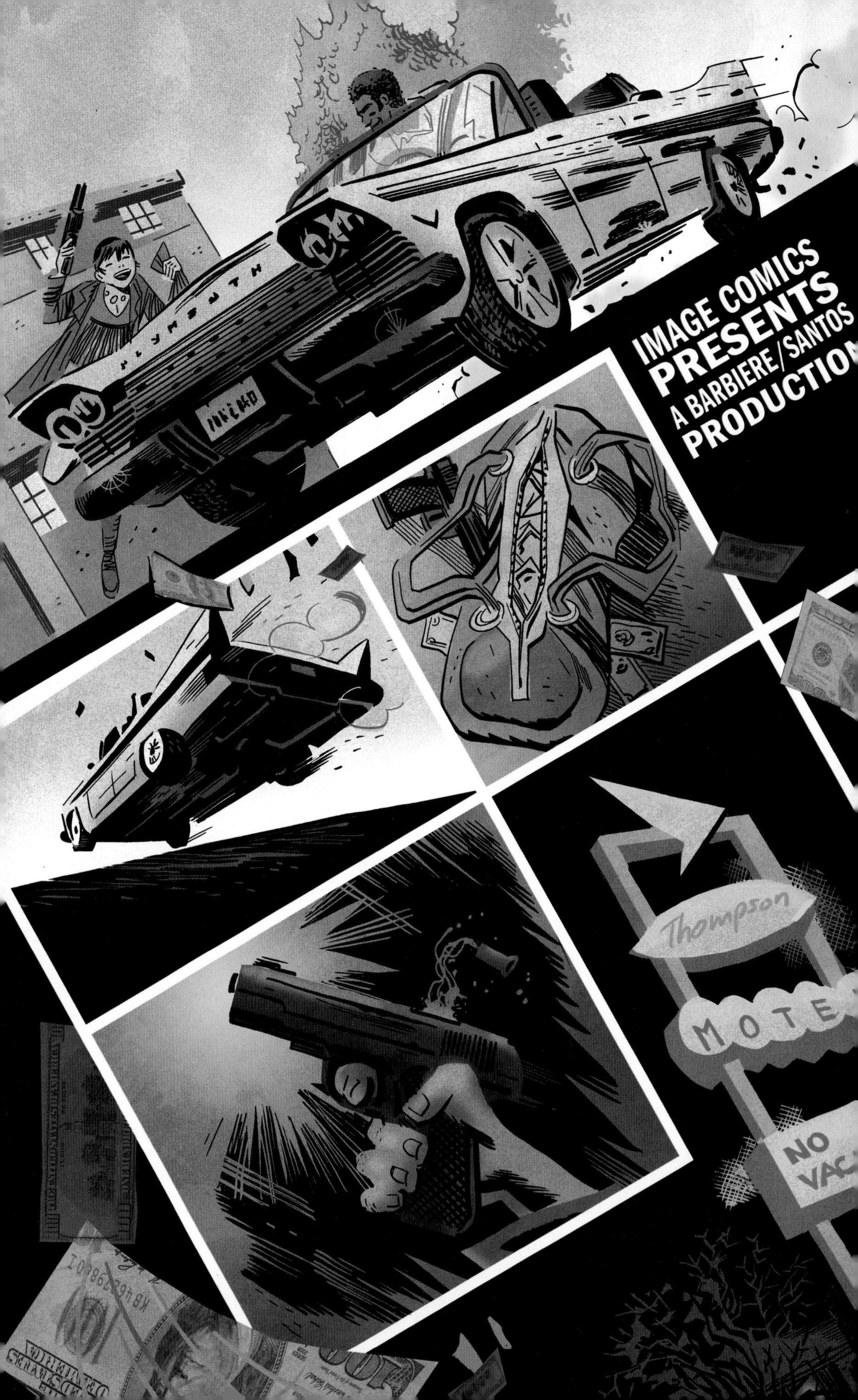
IMAGE COMICS
PRESENTS
A BARBIERE/SANTOS
PRODUCTIO
Thompson
MOTE
NO
VAC

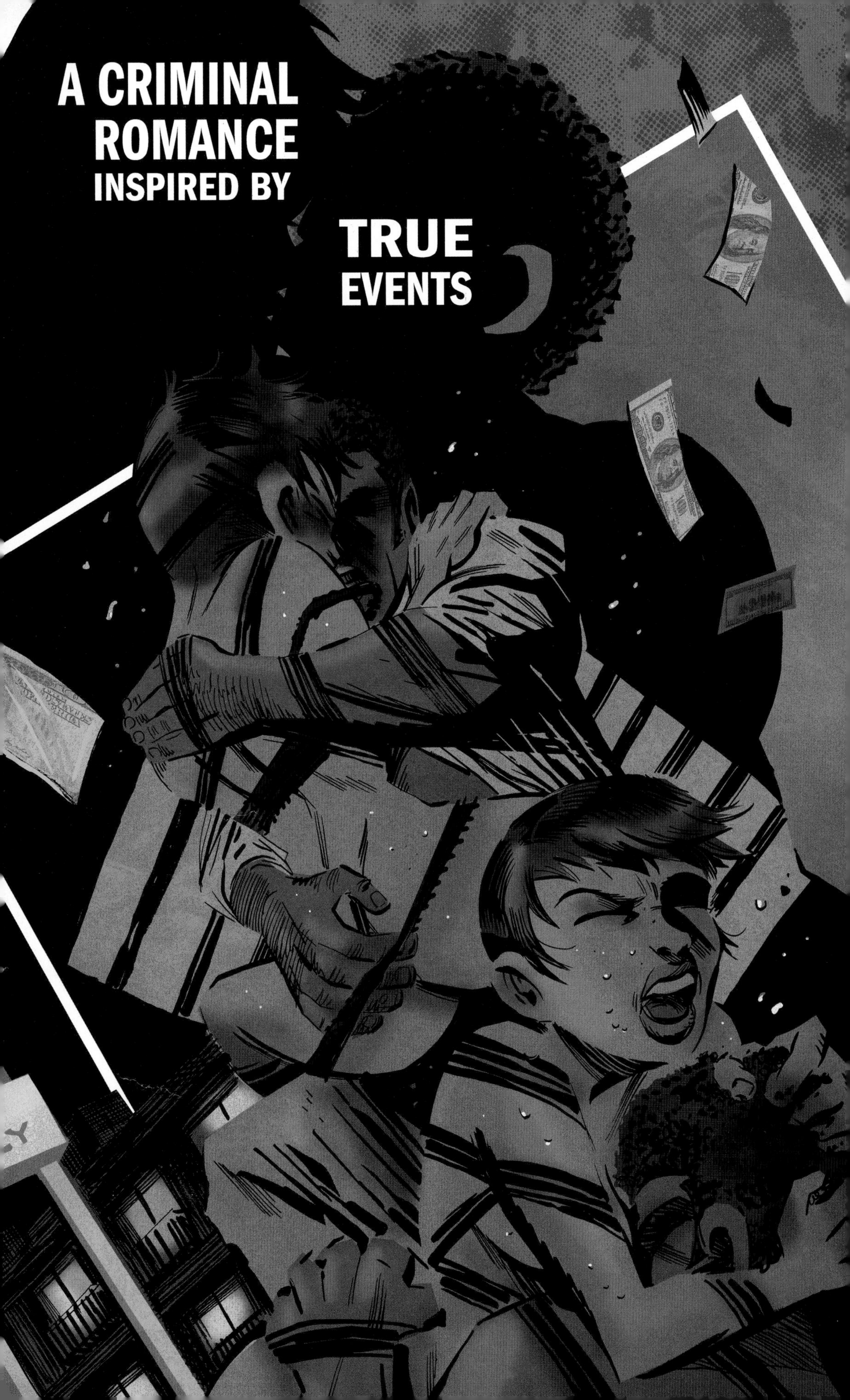
A CRIMINAL
ROMANCE
INSPIRED BY
TRUE
EVENTS

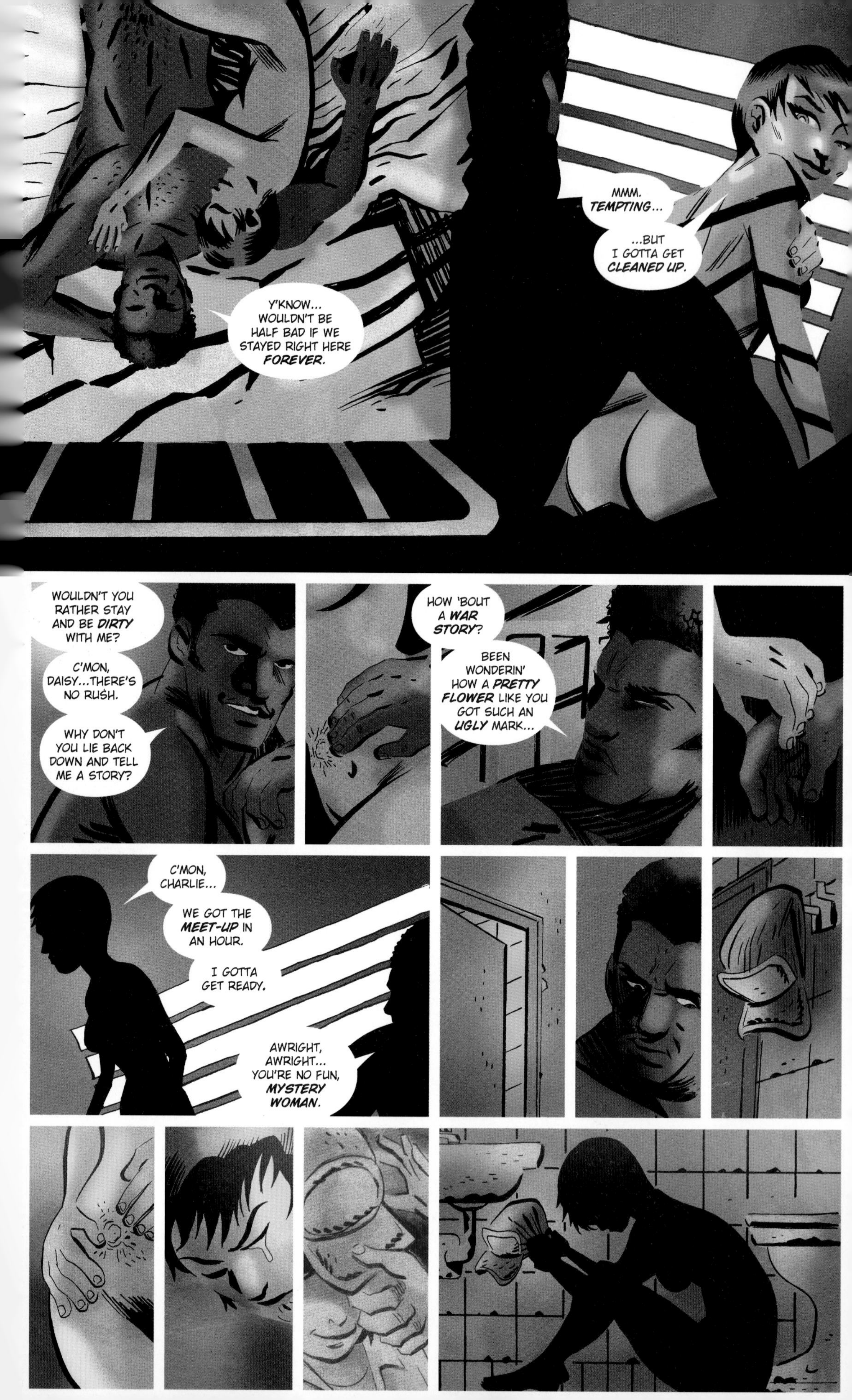
Y'KNOW... WOULDN'T BE HALF BAD IF WE STAYED RIGHT HERE FOREVER.
MMM. TEMPTING...
...BUT I GOTTA GET CLEANED UP.
WOULDN'T YOU RATHER STAY AND BE DIRTY WITH ME?
C'MON, DAISY...THERE'S NO RUSH.
WHY DON'T YOU LIE BACK DOWN AND TELL ME A STORY?
HOW 'BOUT A WAR STORY?
BEEN WONDERIN' HOW A PRETTY FLOWER LIKE YOU GOT SUCH AN UGLY MARK...
C'MON, CHARLIE...
WE GOT THE MEET-UP IN AN HOUR.
I GOTTA GET READY.
AWRIGHT, AWRIGHT... YOU'RE NO FUN, MYSTERY WOMAN.

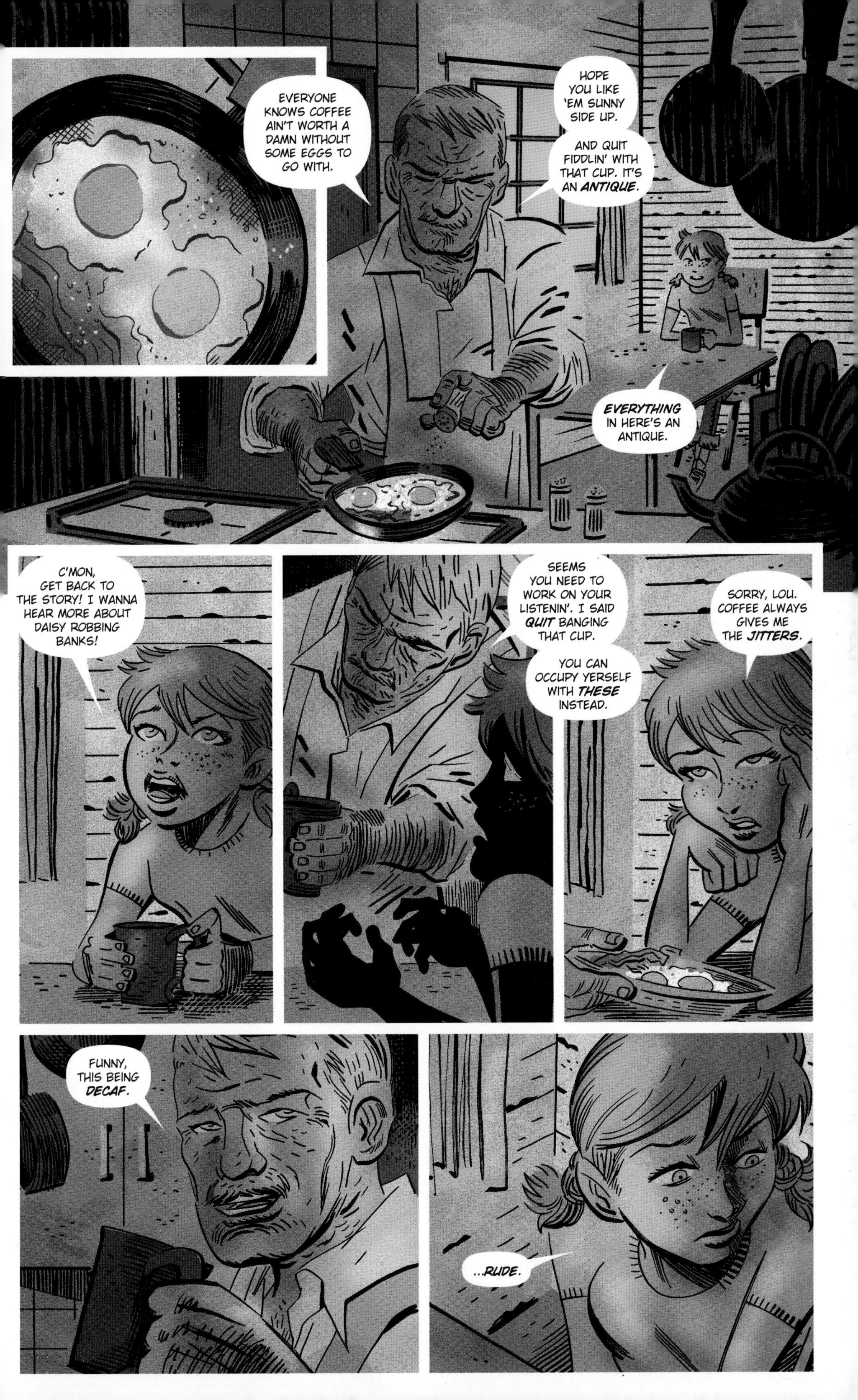
EVERYONE KNOWS COFFEE AIN'T WORTH A DAMN WITHOUT SOME EGGS TO GO WITH.
HOPE YOU LIKE 'EM SUNNY SIDE UP.
AND QUIT FIDDLIN' WITH THAT CUP. IT'S AN ANTIQUE.
EVERYTHING IN HERE'S AN ANTIQUE.
C'MON, GET BACK TO THE STORY! I WANNA HEAR MORE ABOUT DAISY ROBBING BANKS!
SEEMS YOU NEED TO WORK ON YOUR LISTENIN'. I SAID QUIT BANGING THAT CUP.
YOU CAN OCCUPY YERSELF WITH THESE INSTEAD.
SORRY, LOU. COFFEE ALWAYS GIVES ME THE JITTERS.
FUNNY, THIS BEING DECAF.
...RUDE.

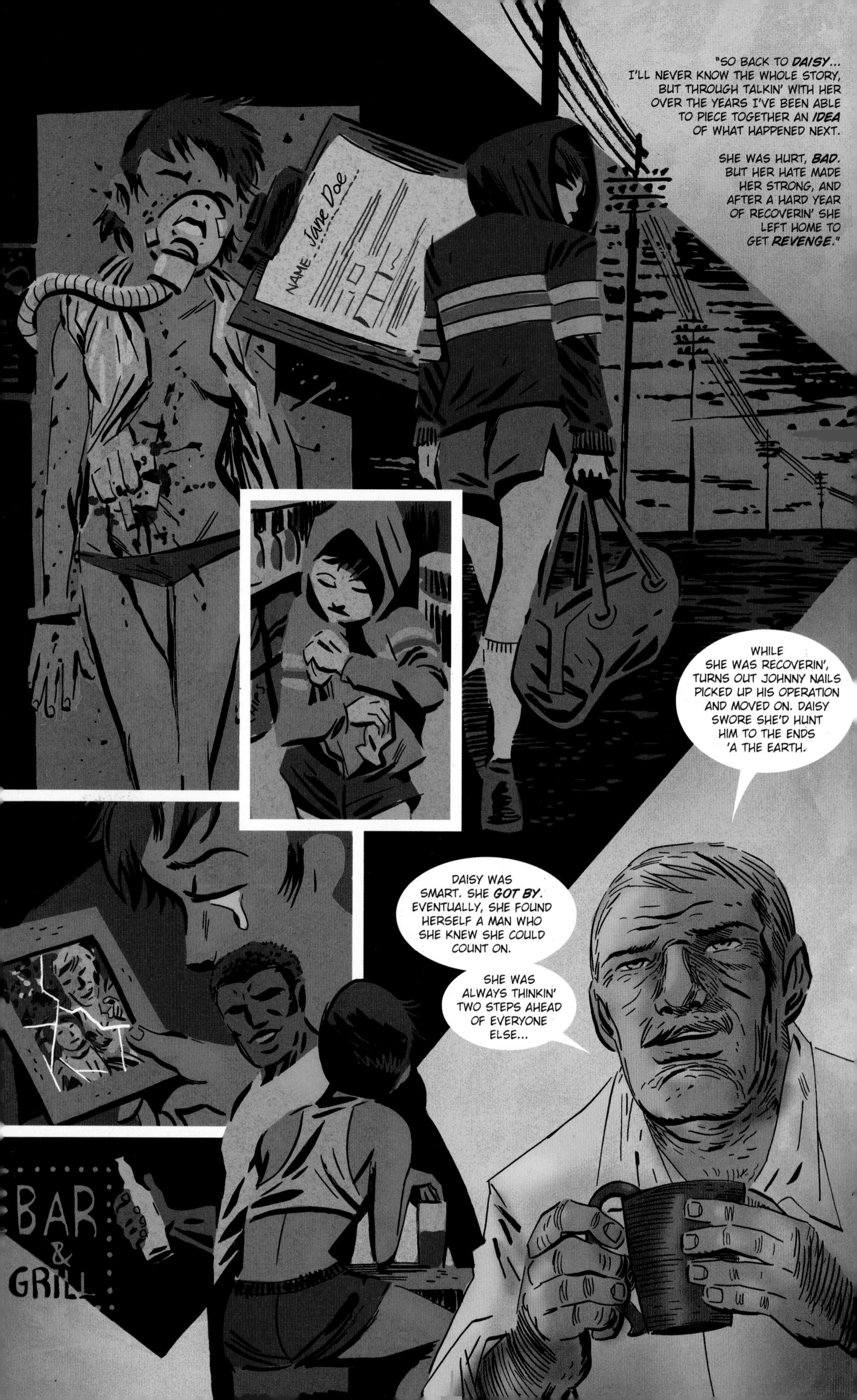
"SO BACK TO DAISY... I'LL NEVER KNOW THE WHOLE STORY, BUT THROUGH TALKIN' WITH HER OVER THE YEARS I'VE BEEN ABLE TO PIECE TOGETHER AN IDEA OF WHAT HAPPENED NEXT.
SHE WAS HURT, BAD. BUT HER HATE MADE HER STRONG, AND AFTER A HARD YEAR OF RECOVERIN' SHE LEFT HOME TO GET REVENGE."
NAME Jane Doe
WHILE SHE WAS RECOVERIN', TURNS OUT JOHNNY NAILS PICKED UP HIS OPERATION AND MOVED ON. DAISY SWORE SHE'D HUNT HIM TO THE ENDS 'A THE EARTH.
DAISY WAS SMART. SHE GOT BY. EVENTUALLY, SHE FOUND HERSELF A MAN WHO SHE KNEW SHE COULD COUNT ON.
SHE WAS ALWAYS THINKIN' TWO STEPS AHEAD OF EVERYONE ELSE...
BAR & GRILL

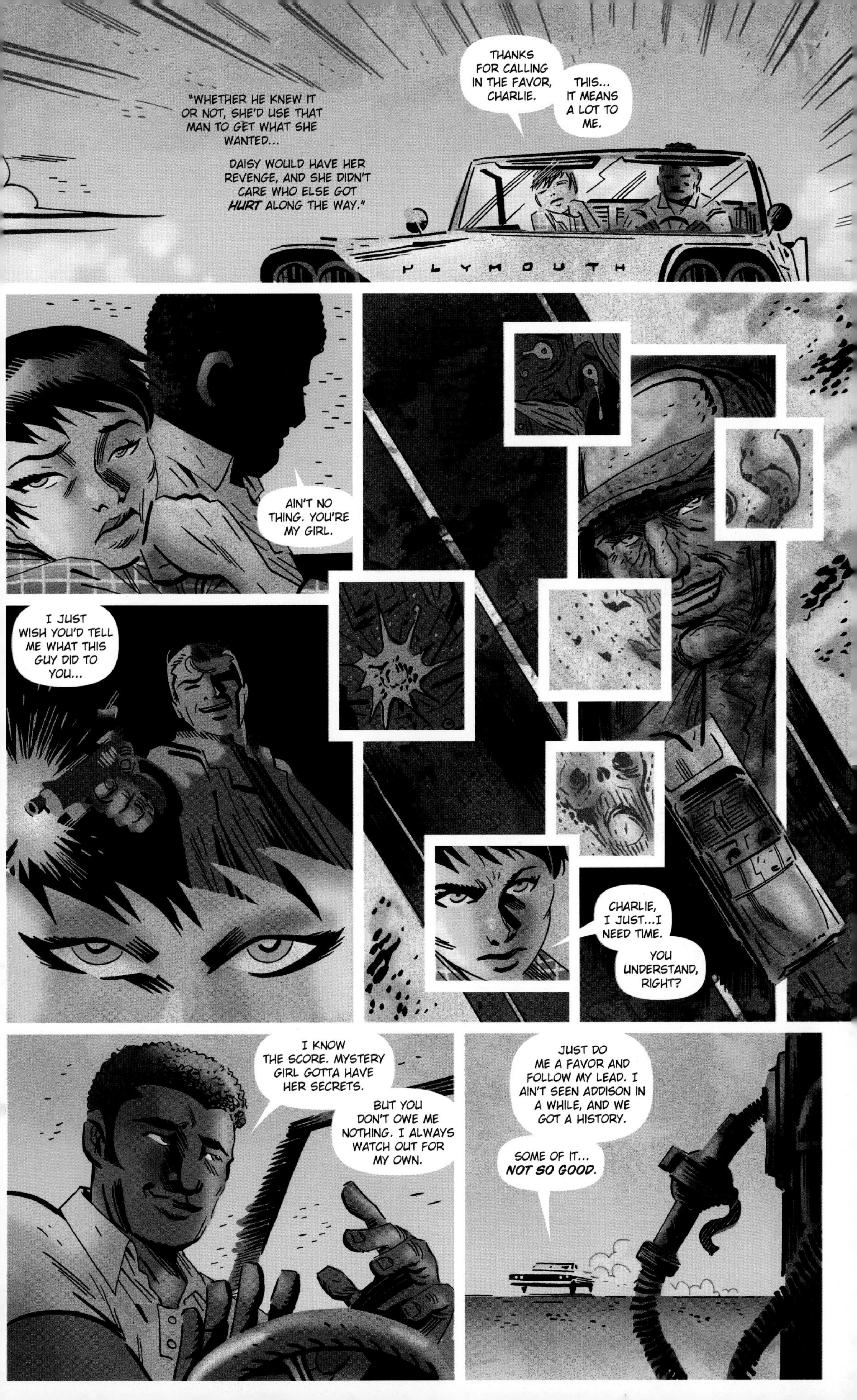

"WHETHER HE KNEW IT OR NOT, SHE'D USE THAT MAN TO GET WHAT SHE WANTED...
DAISY WOULD HAVE HER REVENGE, AND SHE DIDN'T CARE WHO ELSE GOT HURT ALONG THE WAY."
THANKS FOR CALLING IN THE FAVOR, CHARLIE.
THIS... IT MEANS A LOT TO ME.
PLYMOUTH
AIN'T NO THING. YOU'RE MY GIRL.
I JUST WISH YOU'D TELL ME WHAT THIS GUY DID TO YOU...
CHARLIE, I JUST...I NEED TIME.
YOU UNDERSTAND, RIGHT?
I KNOW THE SCORE. MYSTERY GIRL GOTTA HAVE HER SECRETS.
BUT YOU DON'T OWE ME NOTHING. I ALWAYS WATCH OUT FOR MY OWN.
JUST DO ME A FAVOR AND FOLLOW MY LEAD. I AIN'T SEEN ADDISON IN A WHILE, AND WE GOT A HISTORY.
SOME OF IT... NOT SO GOOD.

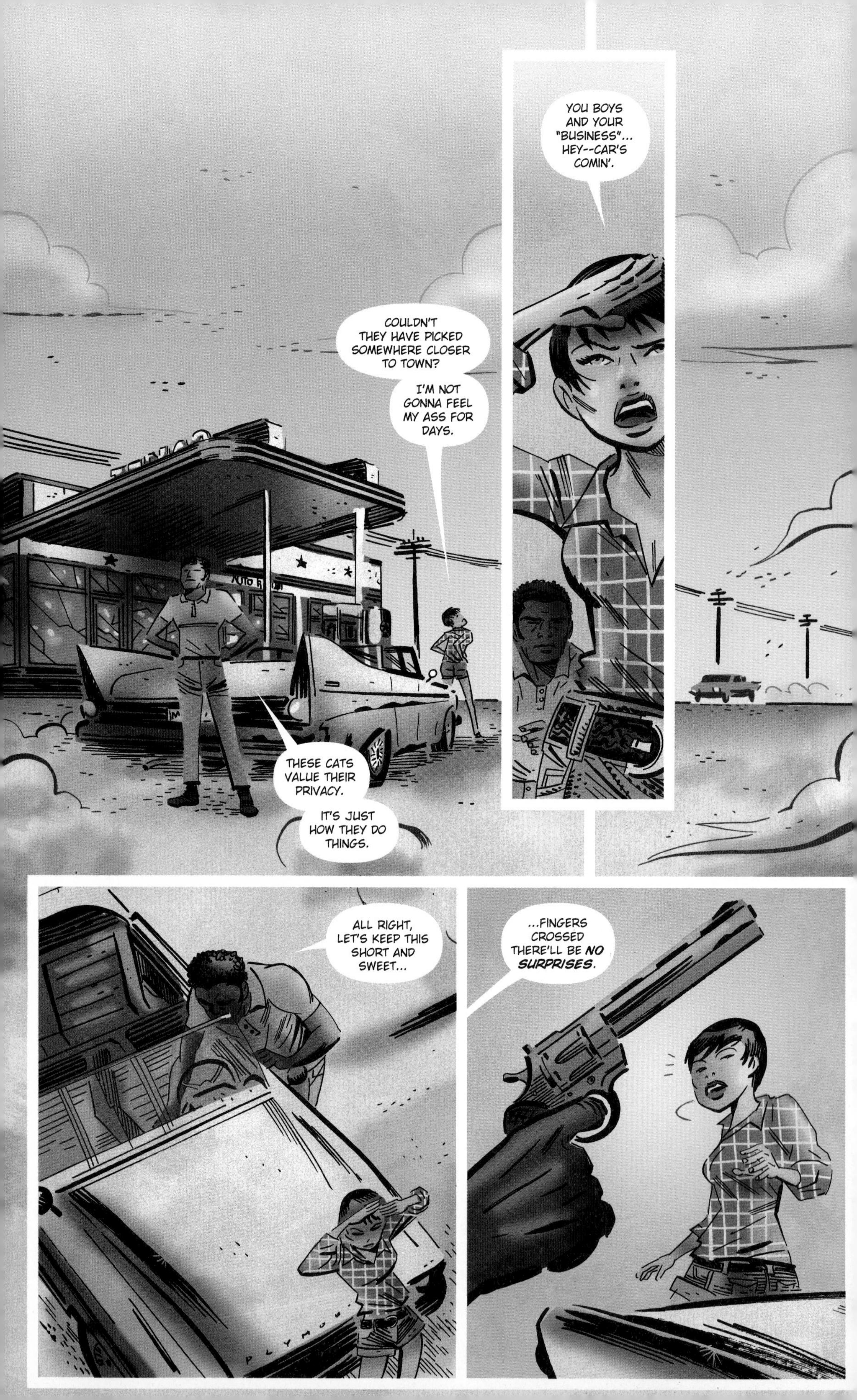
COULDN'T THEY HAVE PICKED SOMEWHERE CLOSER TO TOWN?
I'M NOT GONNA FEEL MY ASS FOR DAYS.
THESE CATS VALUE THEIR PRIVACY.
IT'S JUST HOW THEY DO THINGS.
YOU BOYS AND YOUR "BUSINESS"... HEY--CAR'S COMIN'.
ALL RIGHT, LET'S KEEP THIS SHORT AND SWEET...
...FINGERS CROSSED THERE'LL BE ***NO SURPRISES***.

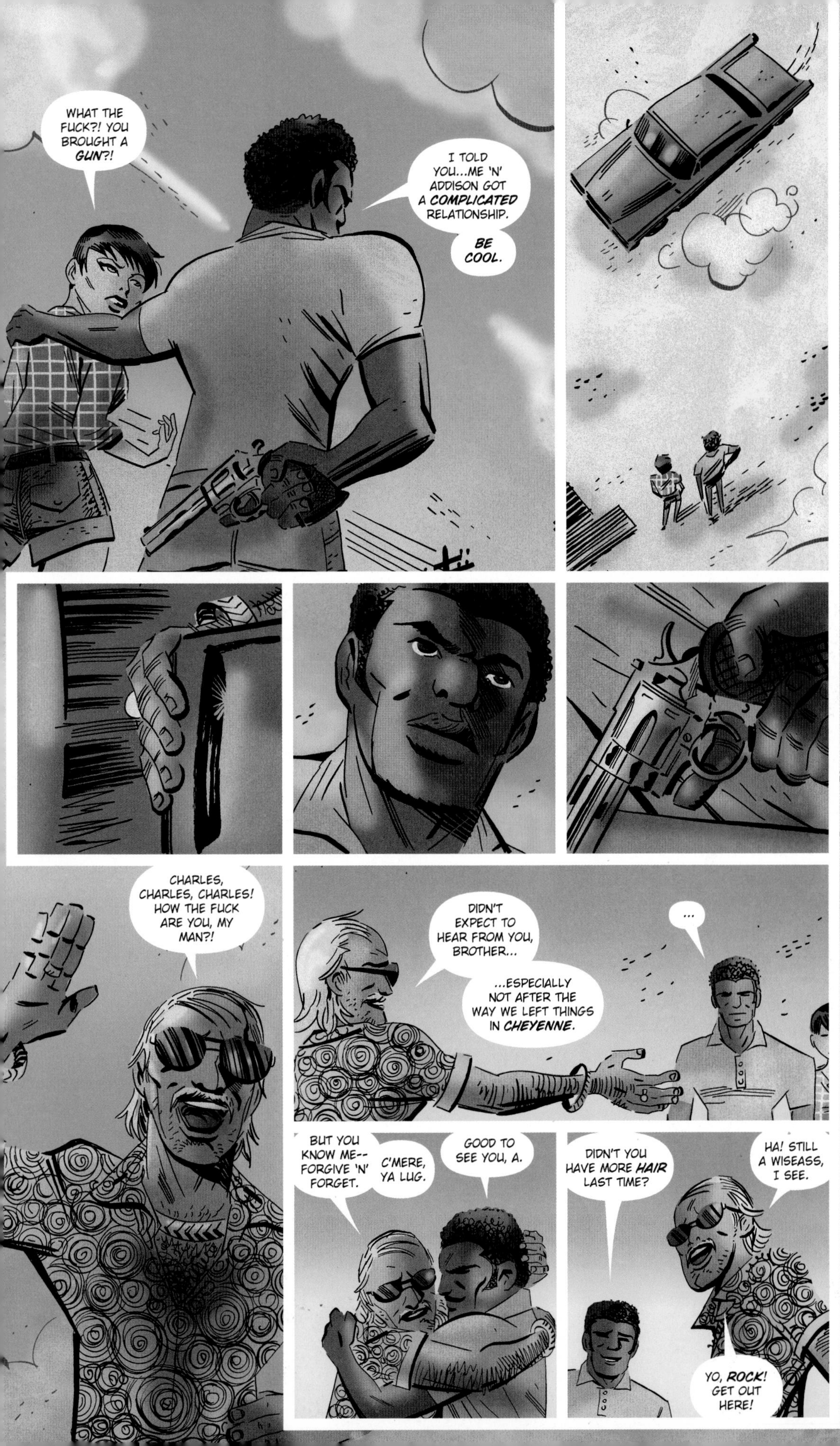
WHAT THE FUCK?! YOU BROUGHT A GUN?!
I TOLD YOU...ME 'N' ADDISON GOT A COMPLICATED RELATIONSHIP.
BE COOL.
CHARLES, CHARLES, CHARLES! HOW THE FUCK ARE YOU, MY MAN?!
DIDN'T EXPECT TO HEAR FROM YOU, BROTHER...
...ESPECIALLY NOT AFTER THE WAY WE LEFT THINGS IN CHEYENNE.
...
BUT YOU KNOW ME-- FORGIVE 'N' FORGET.
C'MERE, YA LUG.
GOOD TO SEE YOU, A.
DIDN'T YOU HAVE MORE HAIR LAST TIME?
HA! STILL A WISEASS, I SEE.
YO, ROCK! GET OUT HERE!

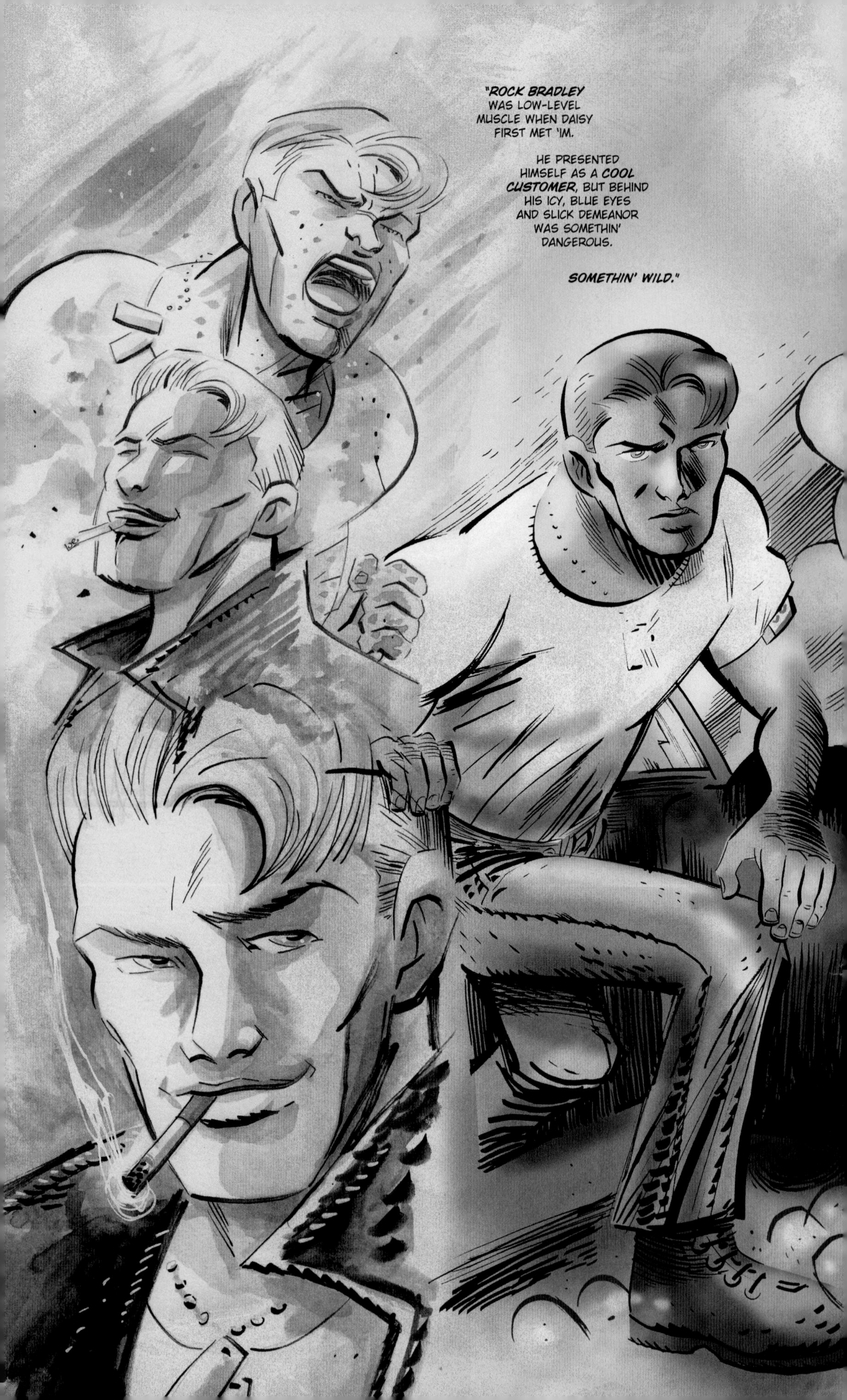
"ROCK BRADLEY WAS LOW-LEVEL MUSCLE WHEN DAISY FIRST MET 'IM.
HE PRESENTED HIMSELF AS A COOL CUSTOMER, BUT BEHIND HIS ICY, BLUE EYES AND SLICK DEMEANOR WAS SOMETHIN' DANGEROUS.
SOMETHIN' WILD."

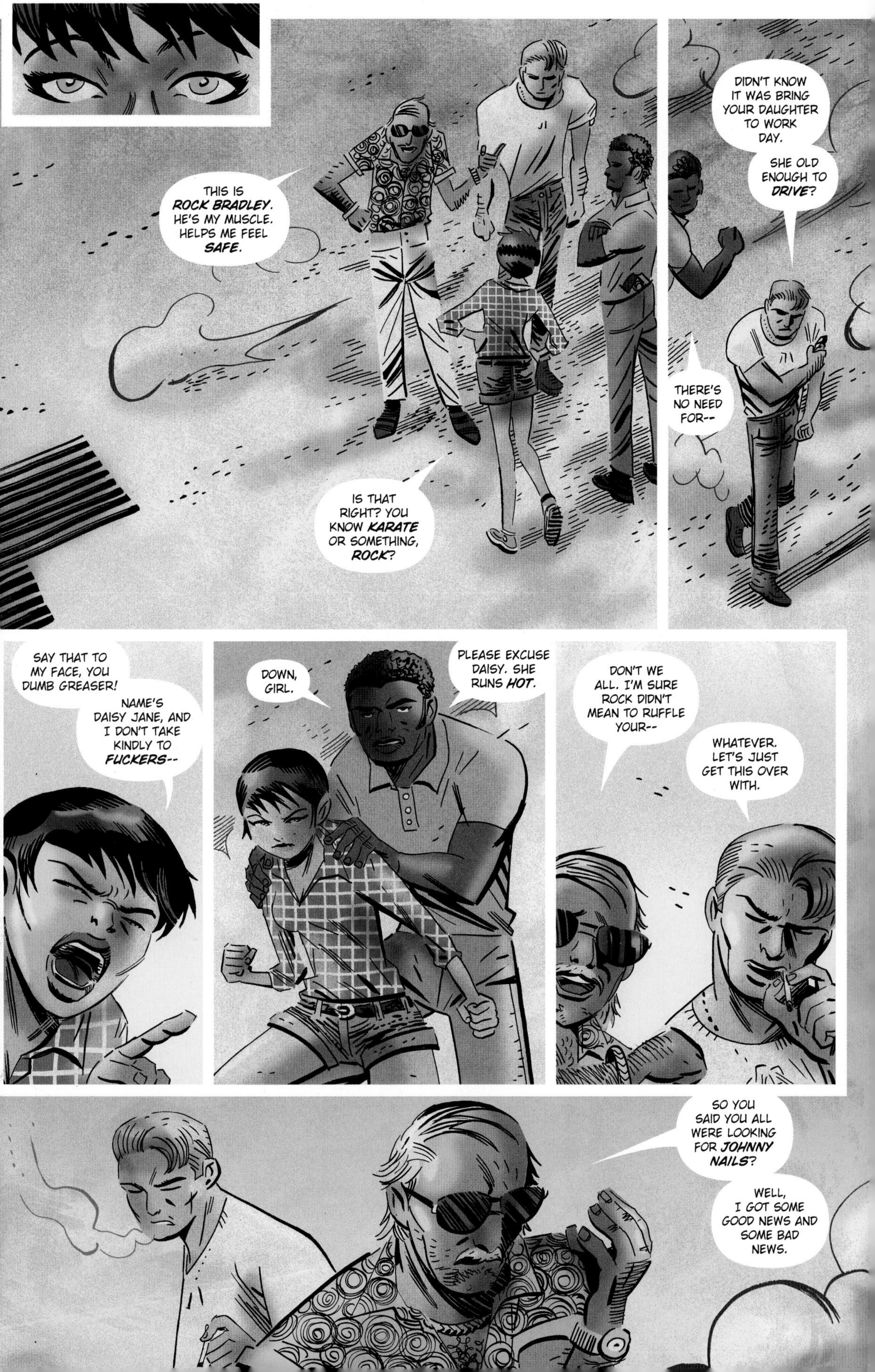
THIS IS ROCK BRADLEY. HE'S MY MUSCLE. HELPS ME FEEL SAFE.
IS THAT RIGHT? YOU KNOW KARATE OR SOMETHING, ROCK?
DIDN'T KNOW IT WAS BRING YOUR DAUGHTER TO WORK DAY.
SHE OLD ENOUGH TO DRIVE?
THERE'S NO NEED FOR--
SAY THAT TO MY FACE, YOU DUMB GREASER!
NAME'S DAISY JANE, AND I DON'T TAKE KINDLY TO FUCKERS--
DOWN, GIRL.
PLEASE EXCUSE DAISY. SHE RUNS HOT.
DON'T WE ALL. I'M SURE ROCK DIDN'T MEAN TO RUFFLE YOUR--
WHATEVER. LET'S JUST GET THIS OVER WITH.
SO YOU SAID YOU ALL WERE LOOKING FOR JOHNNY NAILS?
WELL, I GOT SOME GOOD NEWS AND SOME BAD NEWS.

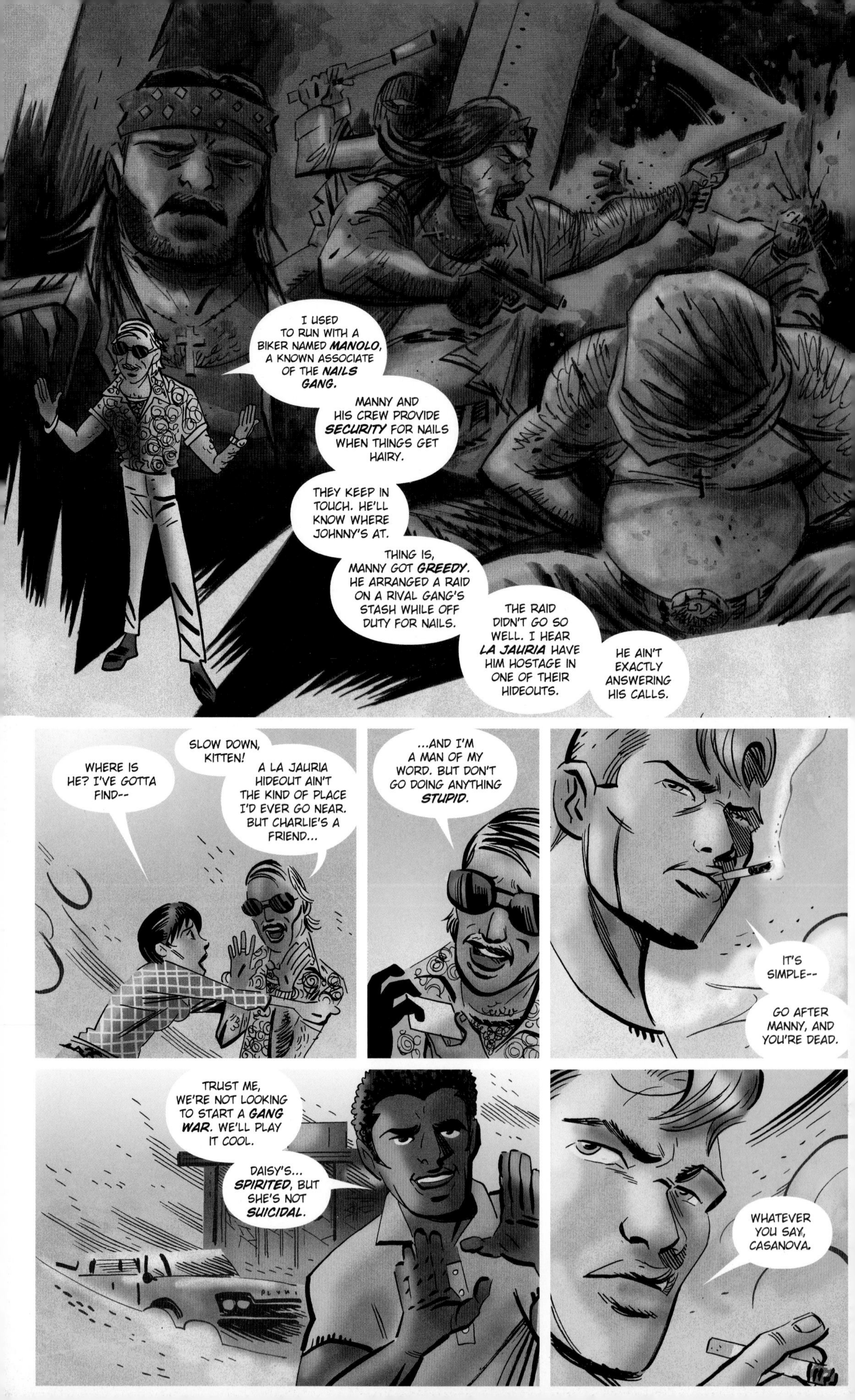
I USED TO RUN WITH A BIKER NAMED MANOLO, A KNOWN ASSOCIATE OF THE NAILS GANG.
MANNY AND HIS CREW PROVIDE SECURITY FOR NAILS WHEN THINGS GET HAIRY.
THEY KEEP IN TOUCH. HE'LL KNOW WHERE JOHNNY'S AT.
THING IS, MANNY GOT GREEDY. HE ARRANGED A RAID ON A RIVAL GANG'S STASH WHILE OFF DUTY FOR NAILS.
THE RAID DIDN'T GO SO WELL. I HEAR LA JAURIA HAVE HIM HOSTAGE IN ONE OF THEIR HIDEOUTS.
HE AIN'T EXACTLY ANSWERING HIS CALLS.
WHERE IS HE? I'VE GOTTA FIND--
SLOW DOWN, KITTEN!
A LA JAURIA HIDEOUT AIN'T THE KIND OF PLACE I'D EVER GO NEAR. BUT CHARLIE'S A FRIEND...
...AND I'M A MAN OF MY WORD. BUT DON'T GO DOING ANYTHING STUPID.
IT'S SIMPLE--
GO AFTER MANNY, AND YOU'RE DEAD.
TRUST ME, WE'RE NOT LOOKING TO START A GANG WAR. WE'LL PLAY IT COOL.
DAISY'S... SPIRITED, BUT SHE'S NOT SUICIDAL.
WHATEVER YOU SAY, CASANOVA.

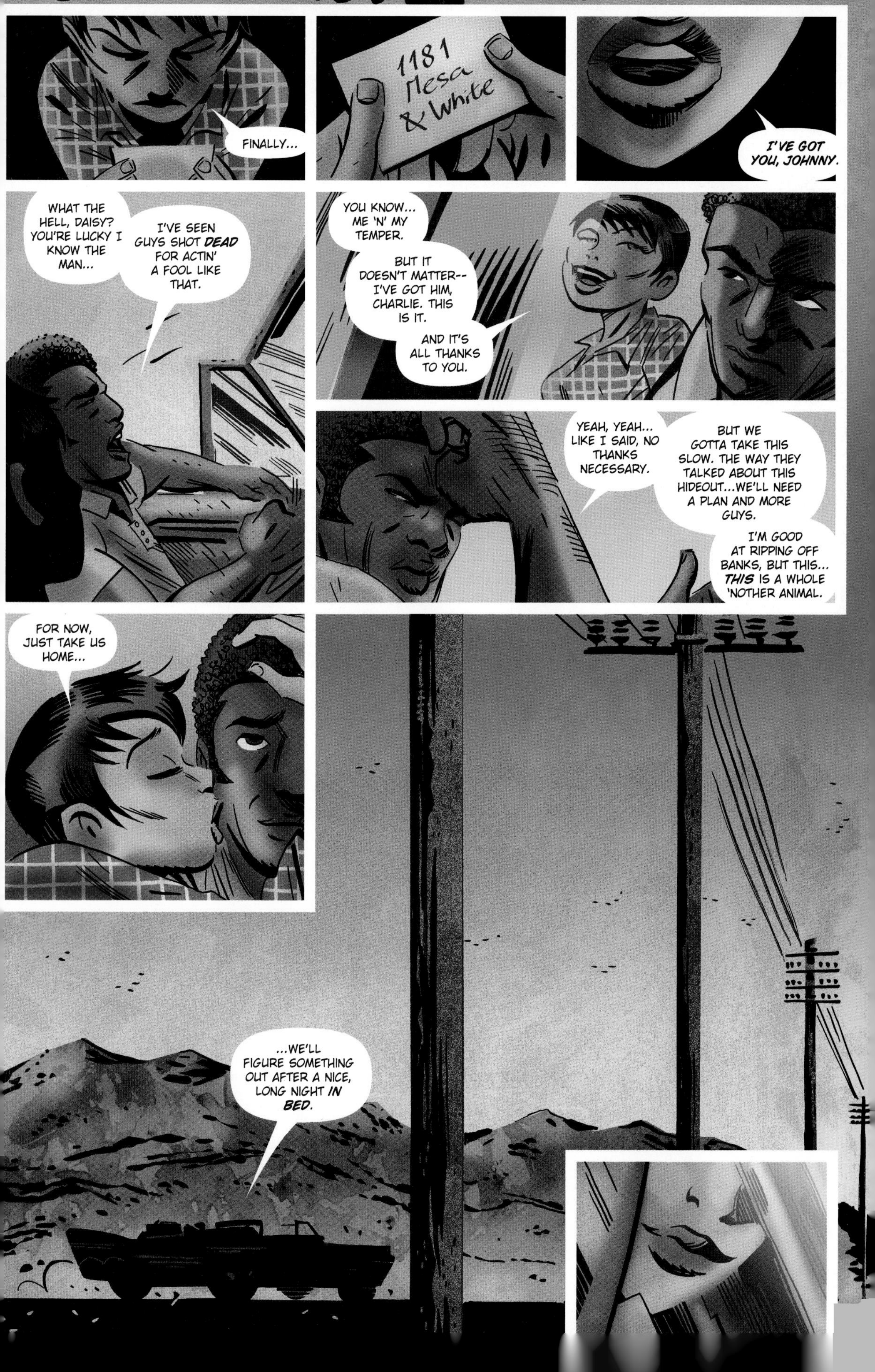
FINALLY...
1181 Mesa & White
I'VE GOT YOU, JOHNNY.
WHAT THE HELL, DAISY? YOU'RE LUCKY I KNOW THE MAN...
I'VE SEEN GUYS SHOT DEAD FOR ACTIN' A FOOL LIKE THAT.
YOU KNOW... ME 'N' MY TEMPER.
BUT IT DOESN'T MATTER-- I'VE GOT HIM, CHARLIE. THIS IS IT.
AND IT'S ALL THANKS TO YOU.
YEAH, YEAH... LIKE I SAID, NO THANKS NECESSARY.
BUT WE GOTTA TAKE THIS SLOW. THE WAY THEY TALKED ABOUT THIS HIDEOUT...WE'LL NEED A PLAN AND MORE GUYS.
I'M GOOD AT RIPPING OFF BANKS, BUT THIS... THIS IS A WHOLE 'NOTHER ANIMAL.
FOR NOW, JUST TAKE US HOME...
...WE'LL FIGURE SOMETHING OUT AFTER A NICE, LONG NIGHT IN BED.

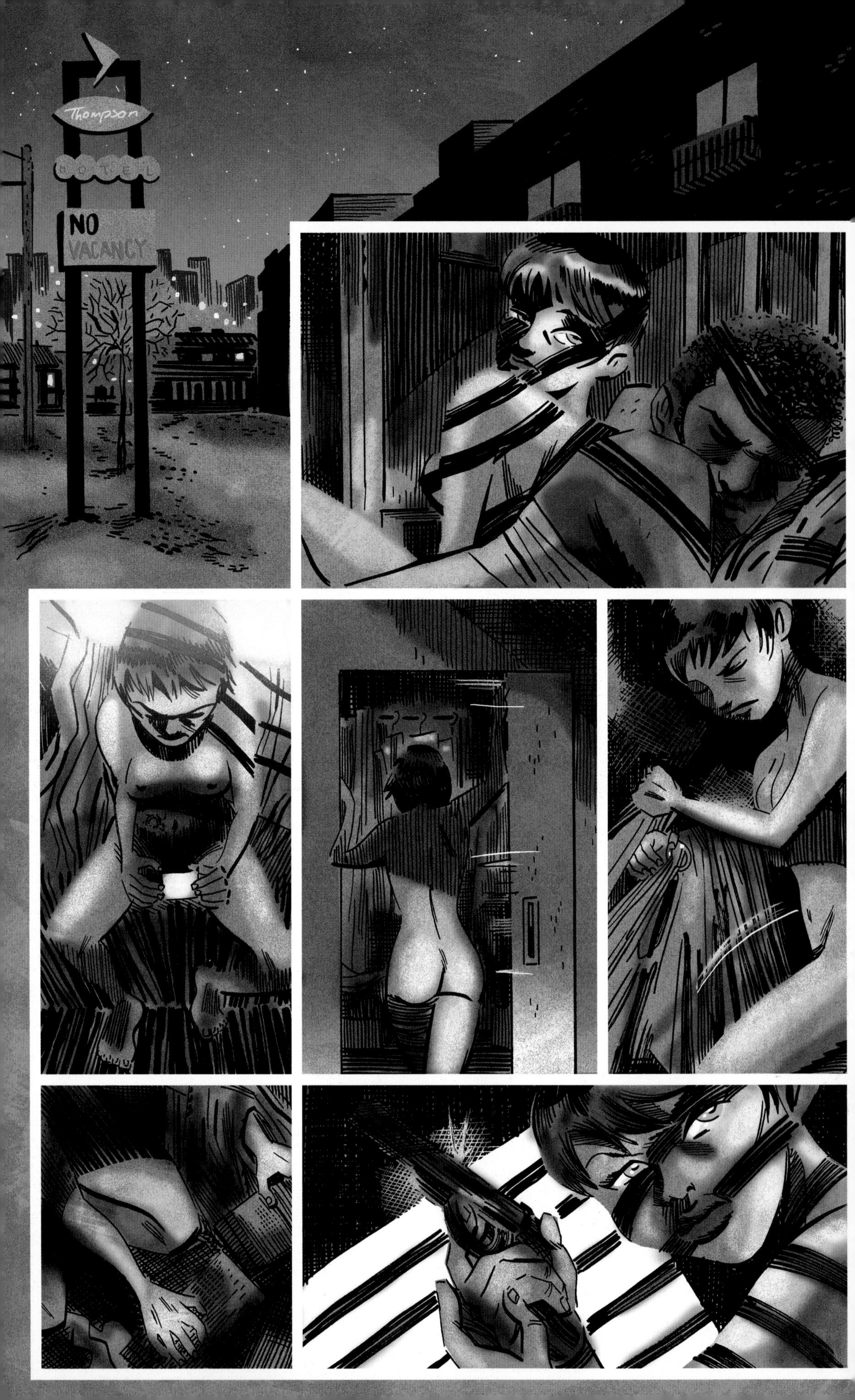
Thompson
NO
VACANCY

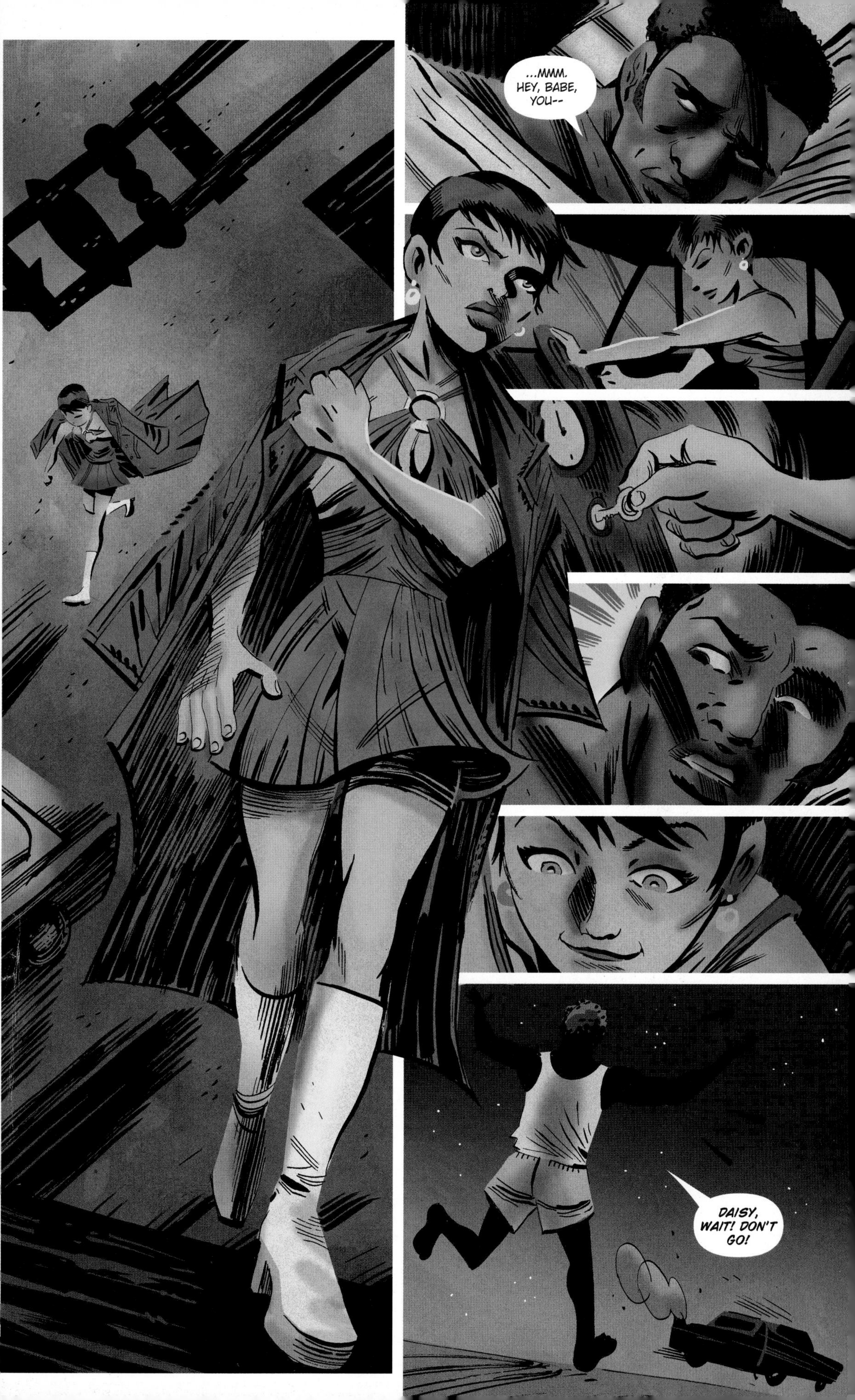
...MMM. HEY, BABE, YOU--
DAISY, WAIT! DON'T GO!

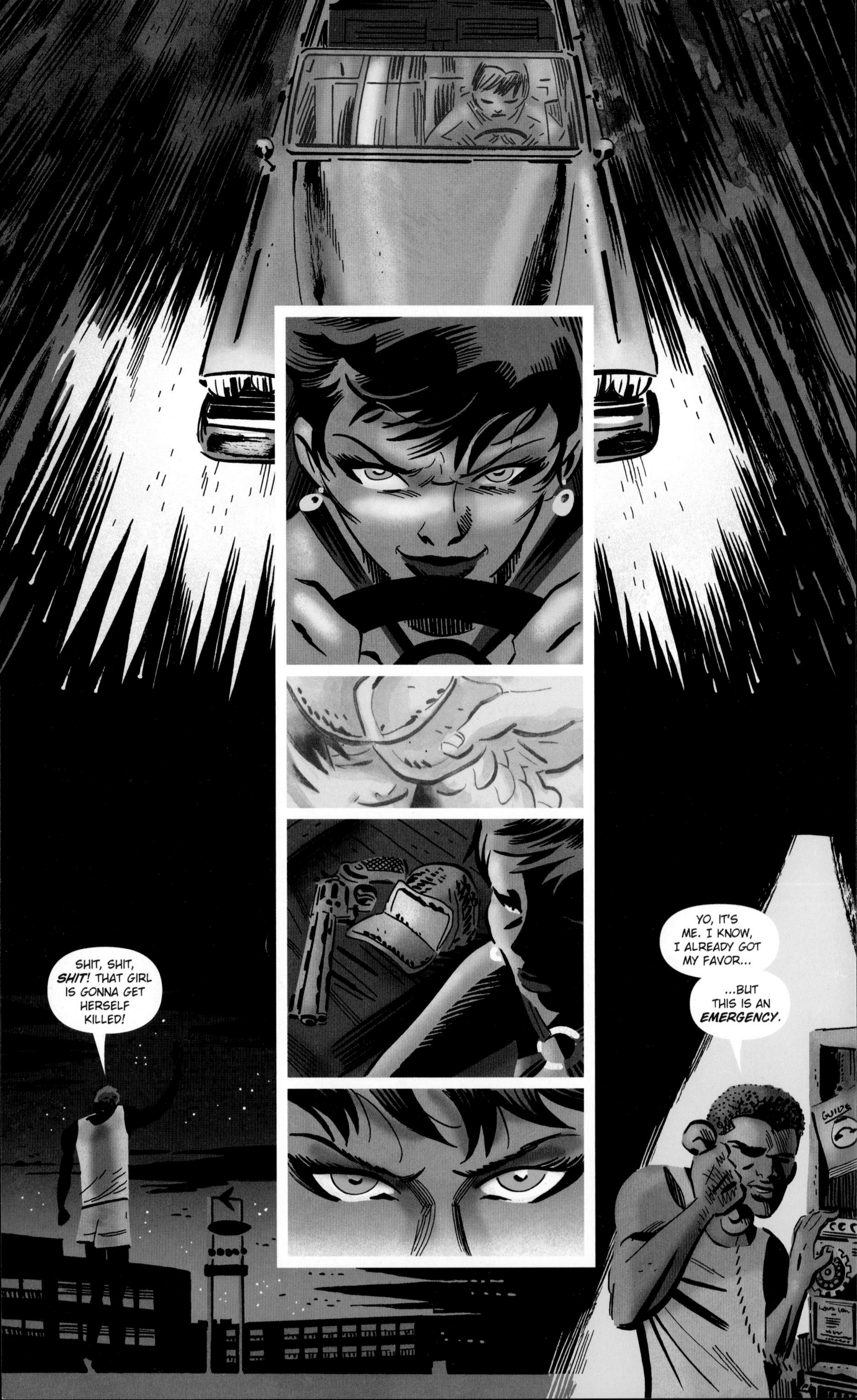
SHIT, SHIT, SHIT! THAT GIRL IS GONNA GET HERSELF KILLED!
YO, IT'S ME. I KNOW, I ALREADY GOT MY FAVOR...
...BUT THIS IS AN EMERGENCY.

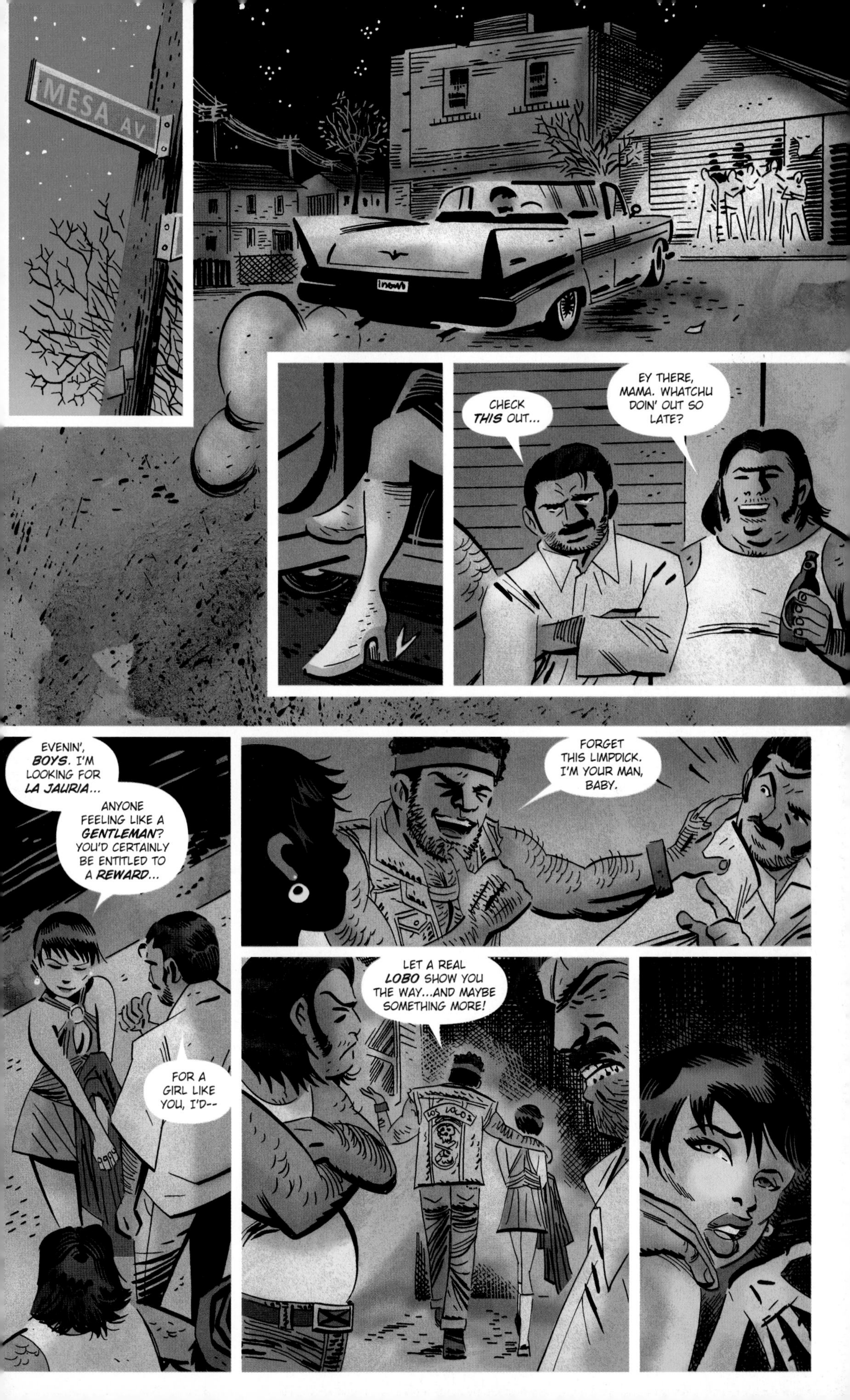
MESA AV
CHECK THIS OUT...
EY THERE, MAMA. WHATCHU DOIN' OUT SO LATE?
EVENIN', BOYS. I'M LOOKING FOR LA JAURIA...
ANYONE FEELING LIKE A GENTLEMAN? YOU'D CERTAINLY BE ENTITLED TO A REWARD...
FOR A GIRL LIKE YOU, I'D--
FORGET THIS LIMPDICK. I'M YOUR MAN, BABY.
LET A REAL LOBO SHOW YOU THE WAY...AND MAYBE SOMETHING MORE!

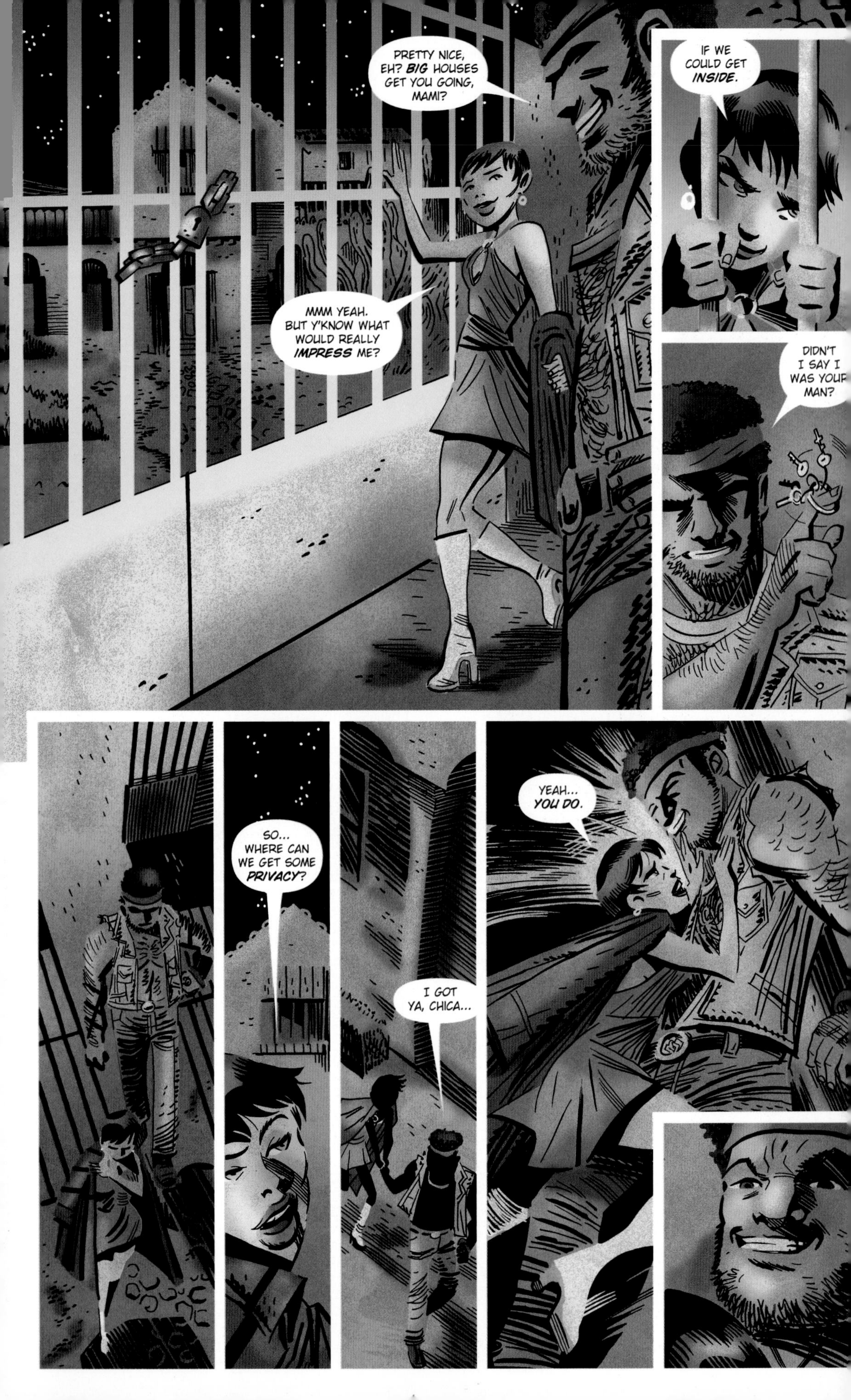
PRETTY NICE, EH? BIG HOUSES GET YOU GOING, MAMI?
MMM YEAH. BUT Y'KNOW WHAT WOULD REALLY IMPRESS ME?
IF WE COULD GET INSIDE.
DIDN'T I SAY I WAS YOUR MAN?
SO... WHERE CAN WE GET SOME PRIVACY?
I GOT YA, CHICA...
YEAH... YOU DO.

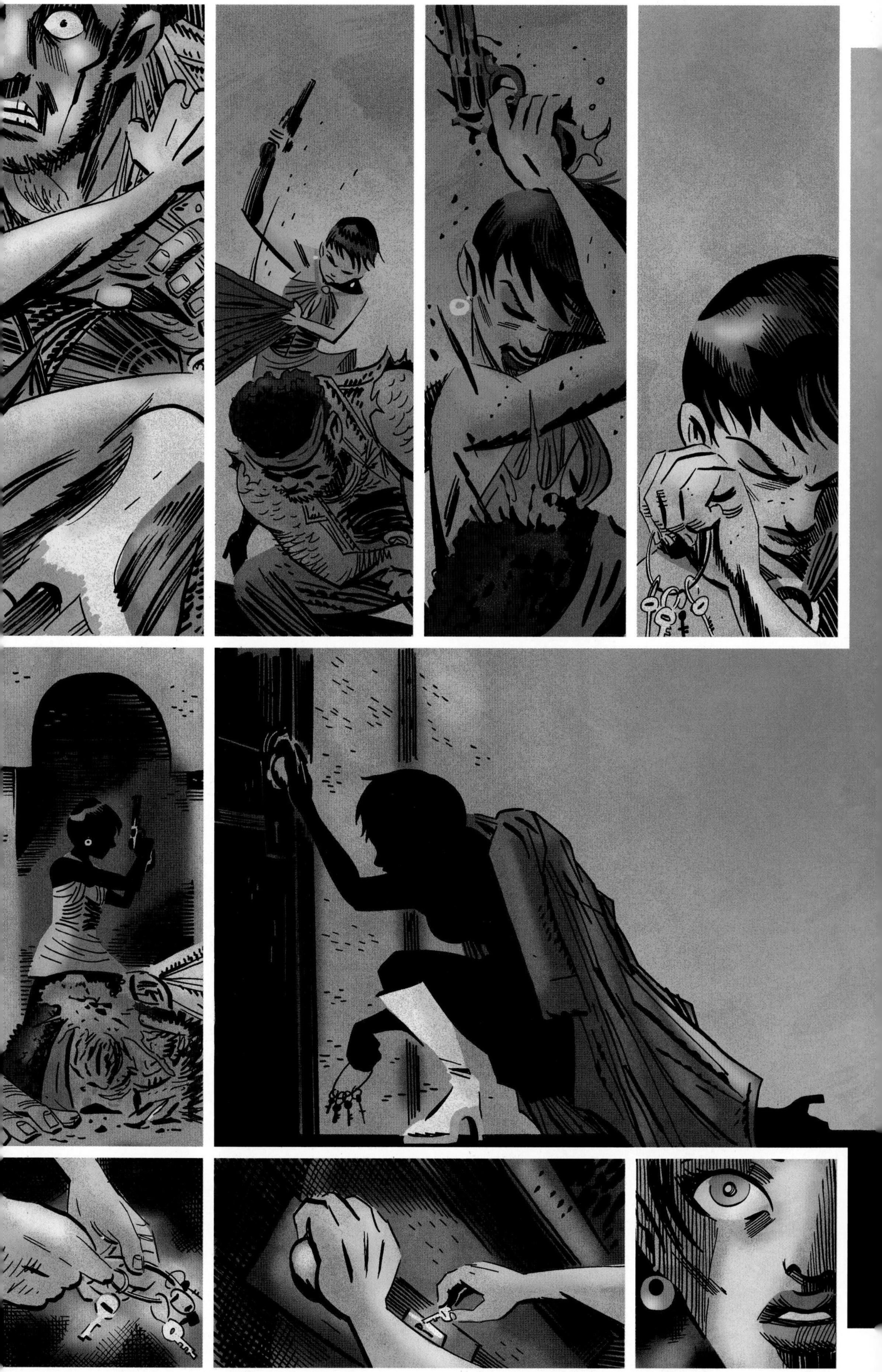

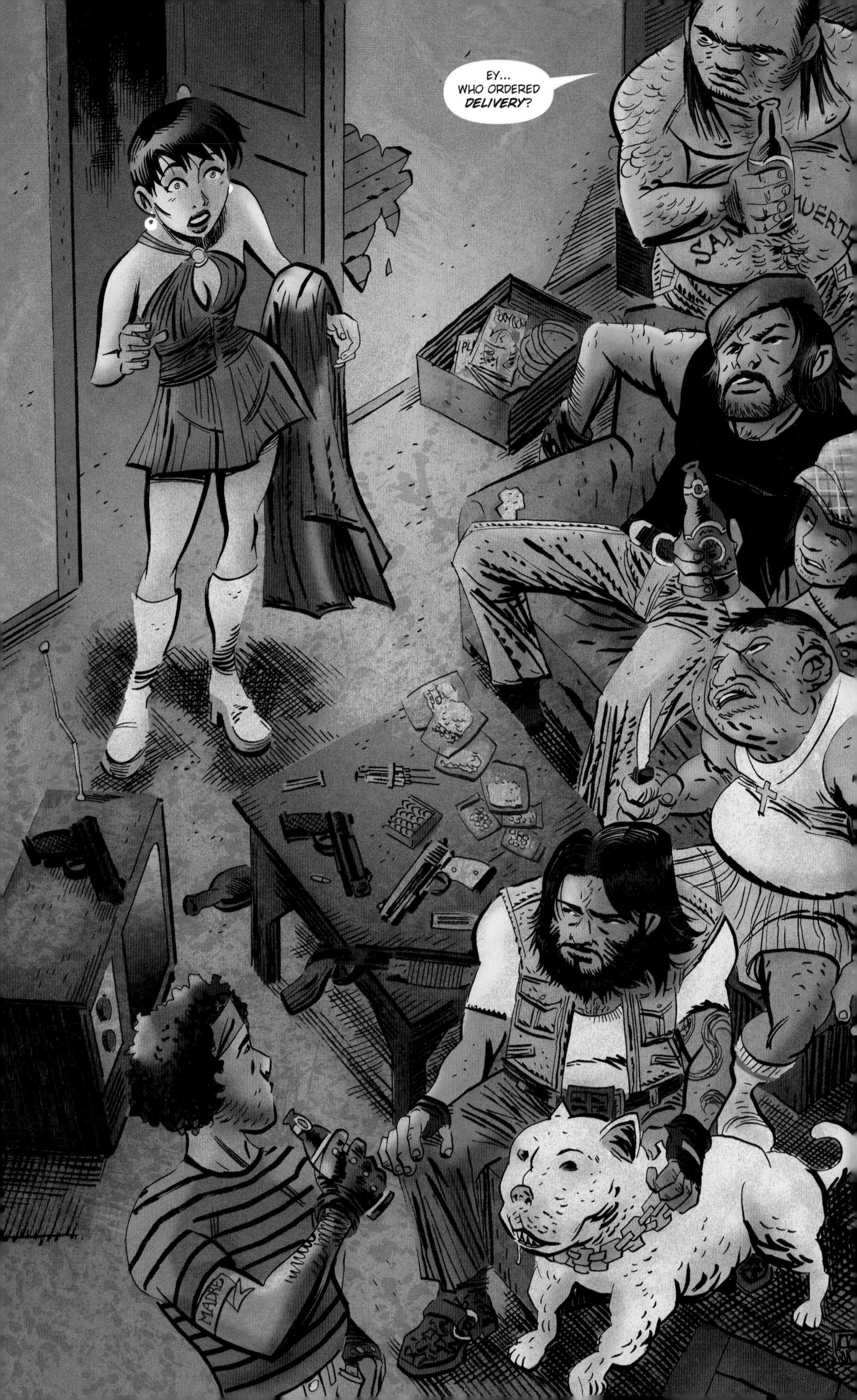
EY... WHO ORDERED DELIVERY?
MADRE

CHAPTER THREE
"VOLATILE MOLOTOV"

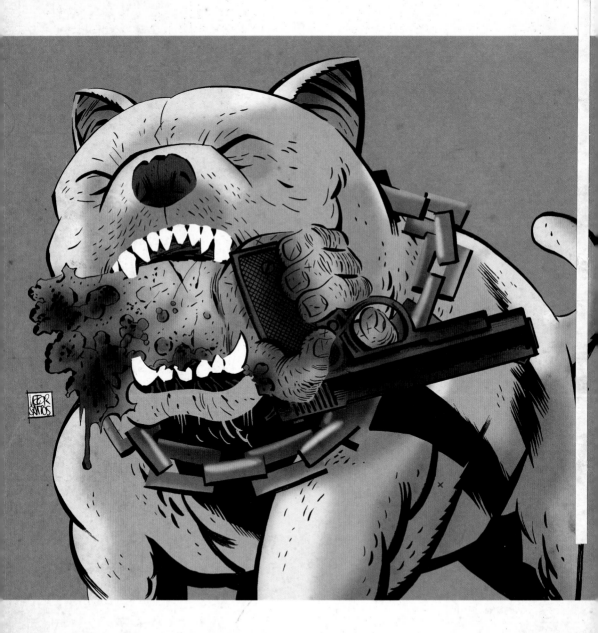

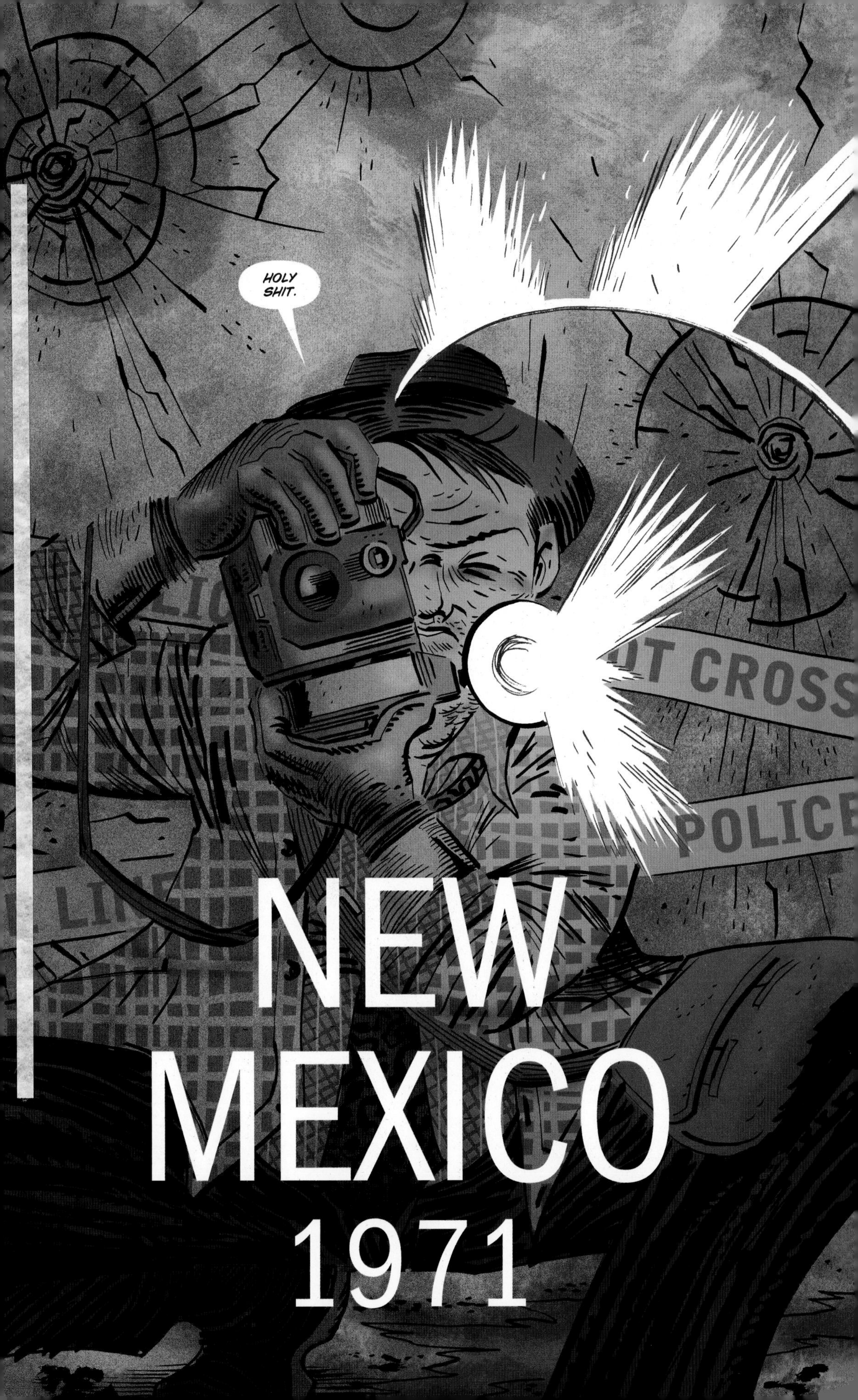
HOLY SHIT.
POLICE
NEW MEXICO
1971

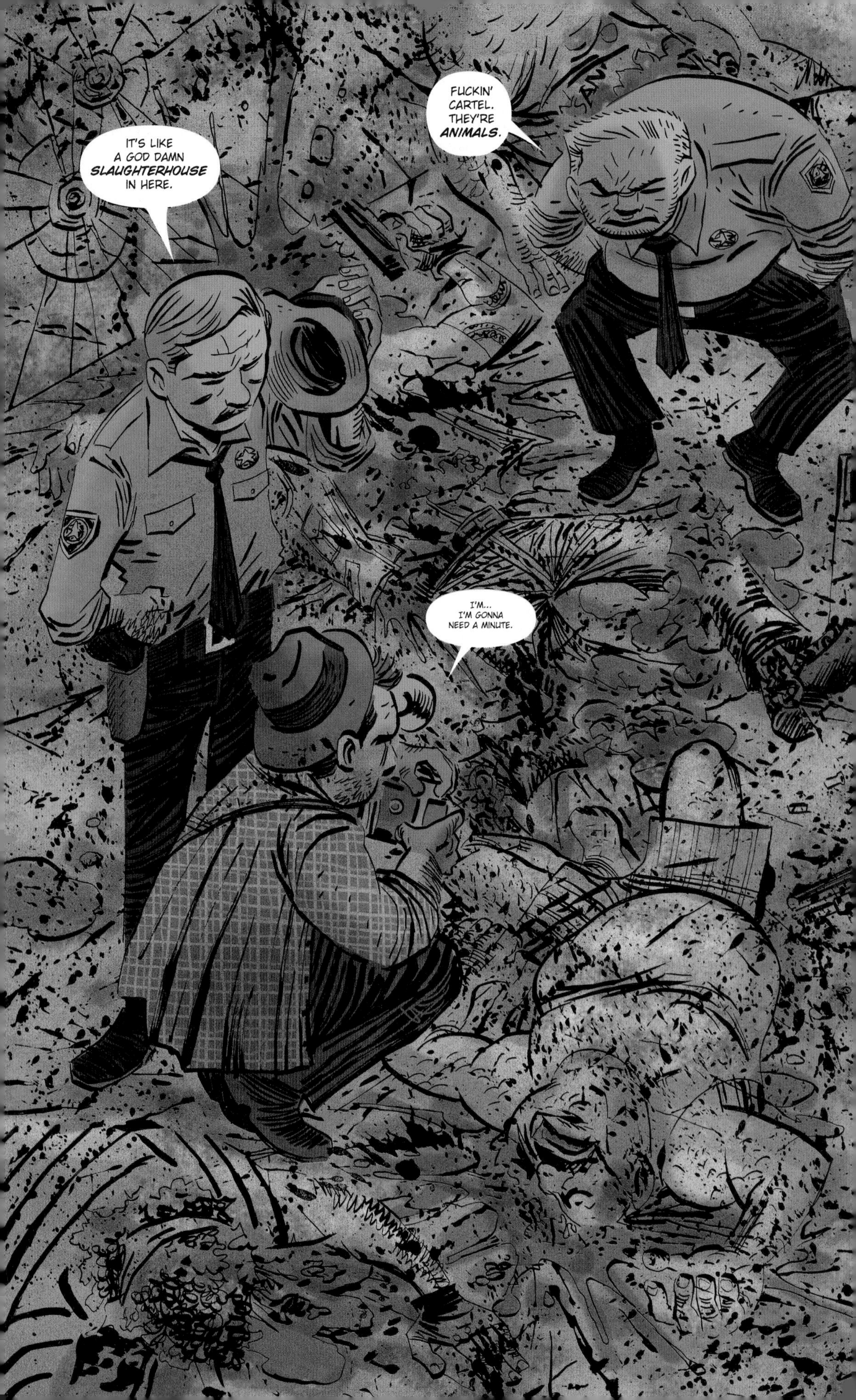
IT'S LIKE A GOD DAMN SLAUGHTERHOUSE IN HERE.
FUCKIN' CARTEL. THEY'RE ANIMALS.
I'M... I'M GONNA NEED A MINUTE.

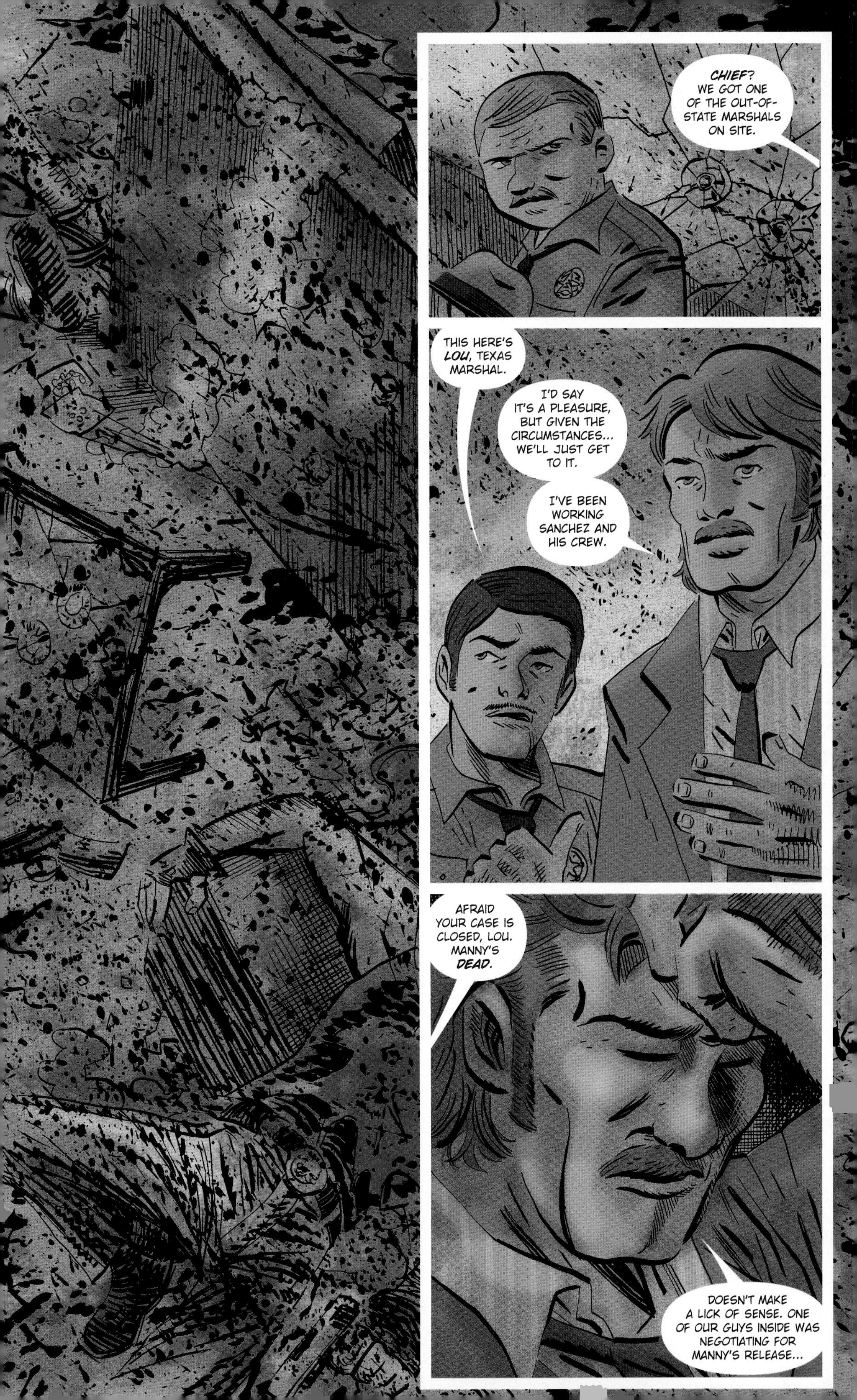
CHIEF? WE GOT ONE OF THE OUT-OF-STATE MARSHALS ON SITE.
THIS HERE'S LOU, TEXAS MARSHAL.
I'D SAY IT'S A PLEASURE, BUT GIVEN THE CIRCUMSTANCES... WE'LL JUST GET TO IT.
I'VE BEEN WORKING SANCHEZ AND HIS CREW.
AFRAID YOUR CASE IS CLOSED, LOU. MANNY'S DEAD.
DOESN'T MAKE A LICK OF SENSE. ONE OF OUR GUYS INSIDE WAS NEGOTIATING FOR MANNY'S RELEASE...

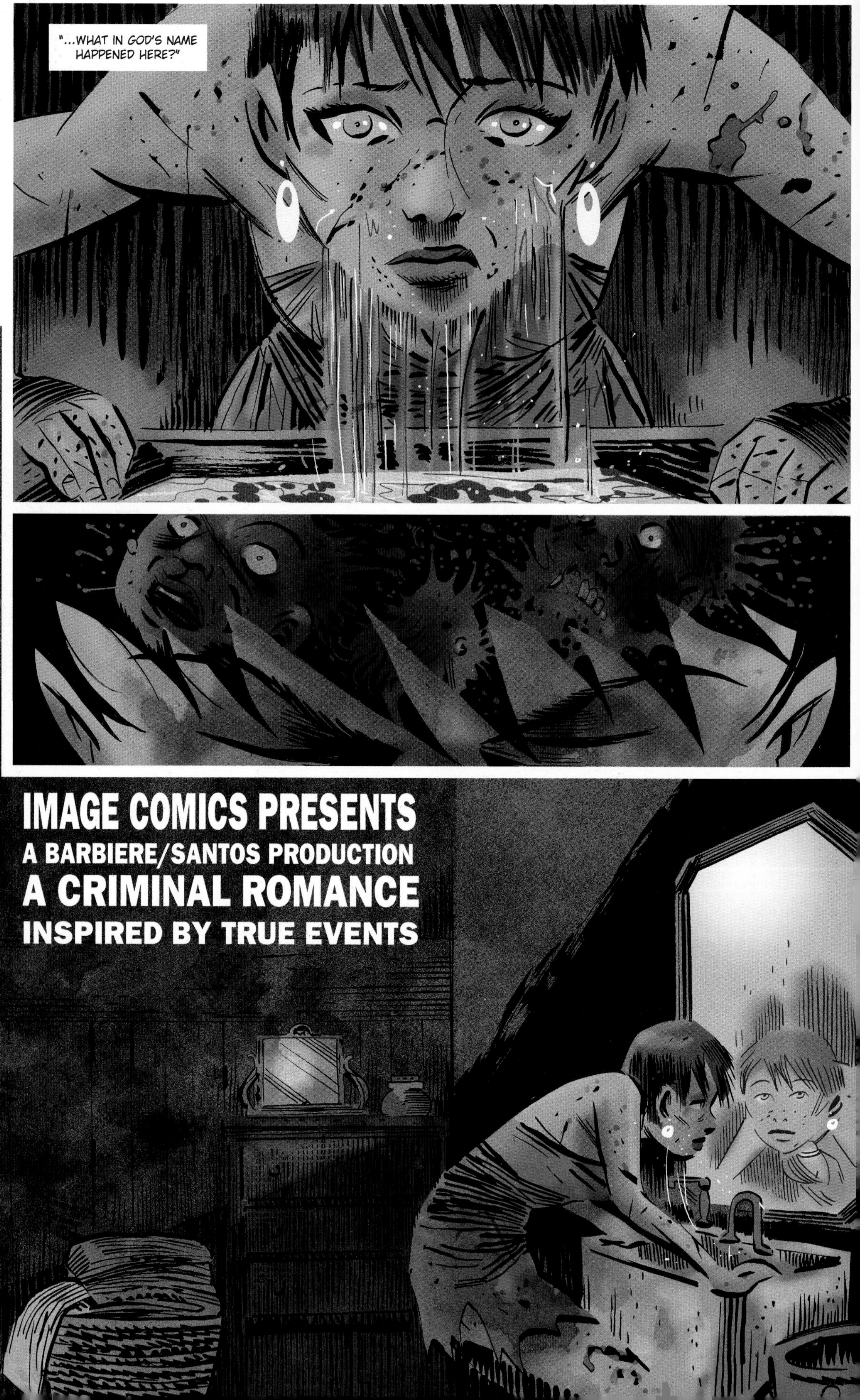
"...WHAT IN GOD'S NAME HAPPENED HERE?"
IMAGE COMICS PRESENTS
A BARBIERE/SANTOS PRODUCTION
A CRIMINAL ROMANCE
INSPIRED BY TRUE EVENTS

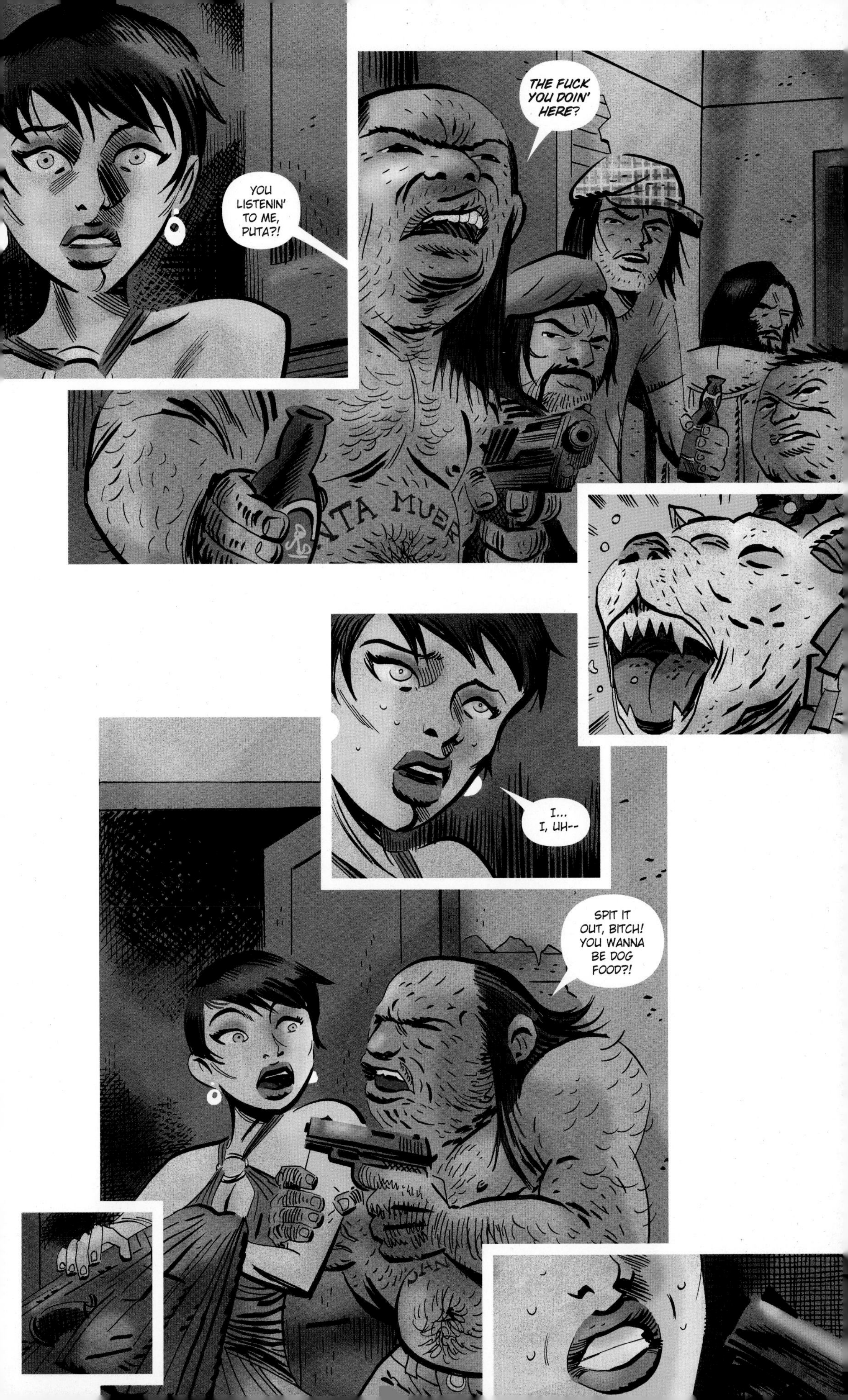
YOU LISTENIN' TO ME, PUTA?!
THE FUCK YOU DOIN' HERE?
I... I, UH--
SPIT IT OUT, BITCH! YOU WANNA BE DOG FOOD?!

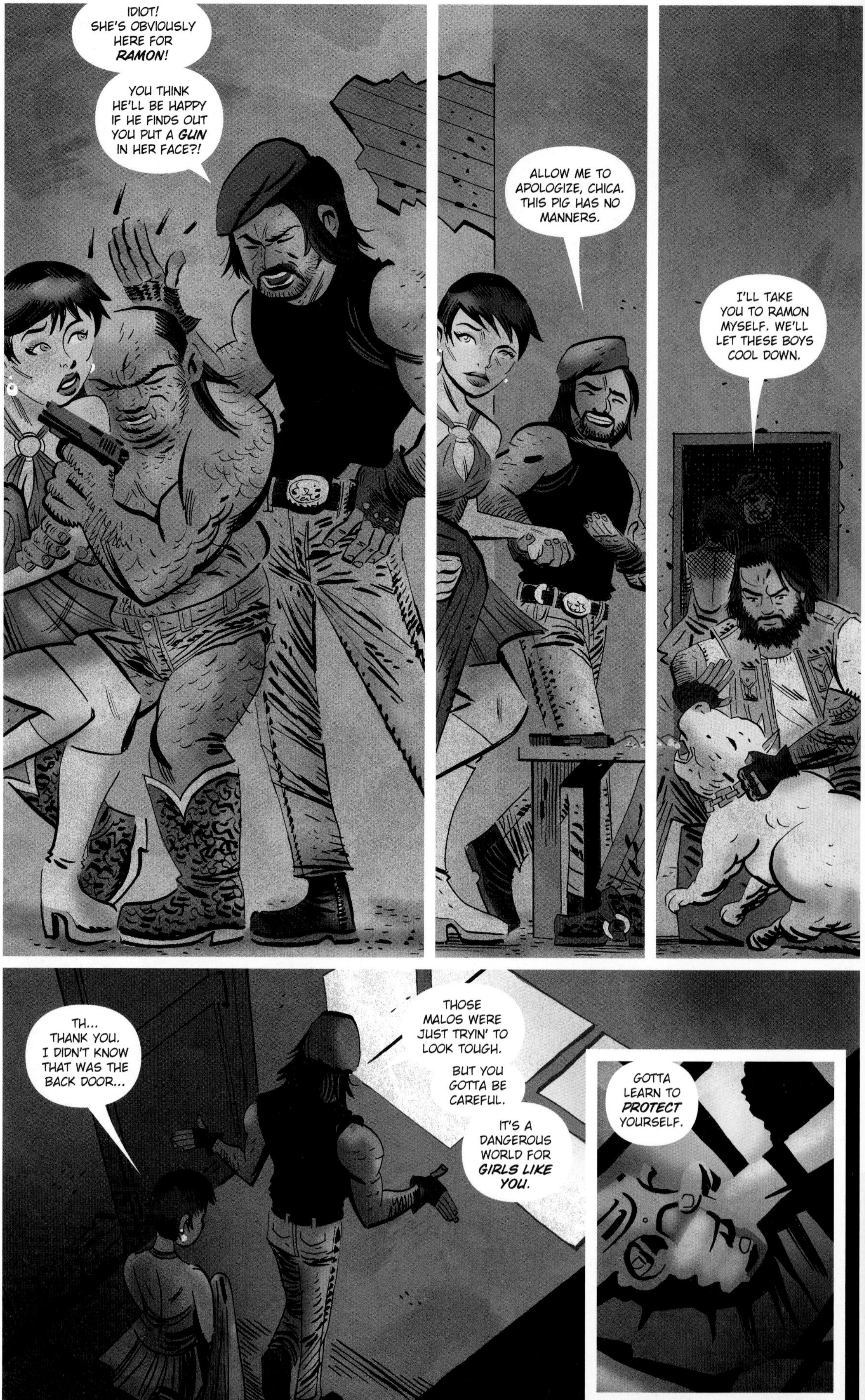
IDIOT! SHE'S OBVIOUSLY HERE FOR RAMON!
YOU THINK HE'LL BE HAPPY IF HE FINDS OUT YOU PUT A GUN IN HER FACE?!
ALLOW ME TO APOLOGIZE, CHICA. THIS PIG HAS NO MANNERS.
I'LL TAKE YOU TO RAMON MYSELF. WE'LL LET THESE BOYS COOL DOWN.
TH... THANK YOU. I DIDN'T KNOW THAT WAS THE BACK DOOR...
THOSE MALOS WERE JUST TRYIN' TO LOOK TOUGH.
BUT YOU GOTTA BE CAREFUL.
IT'S A DANGEROUS WORLD FOR GIRLS LIKE YOU.
GOTTA LEARN TO PROTECT YOURSELF.

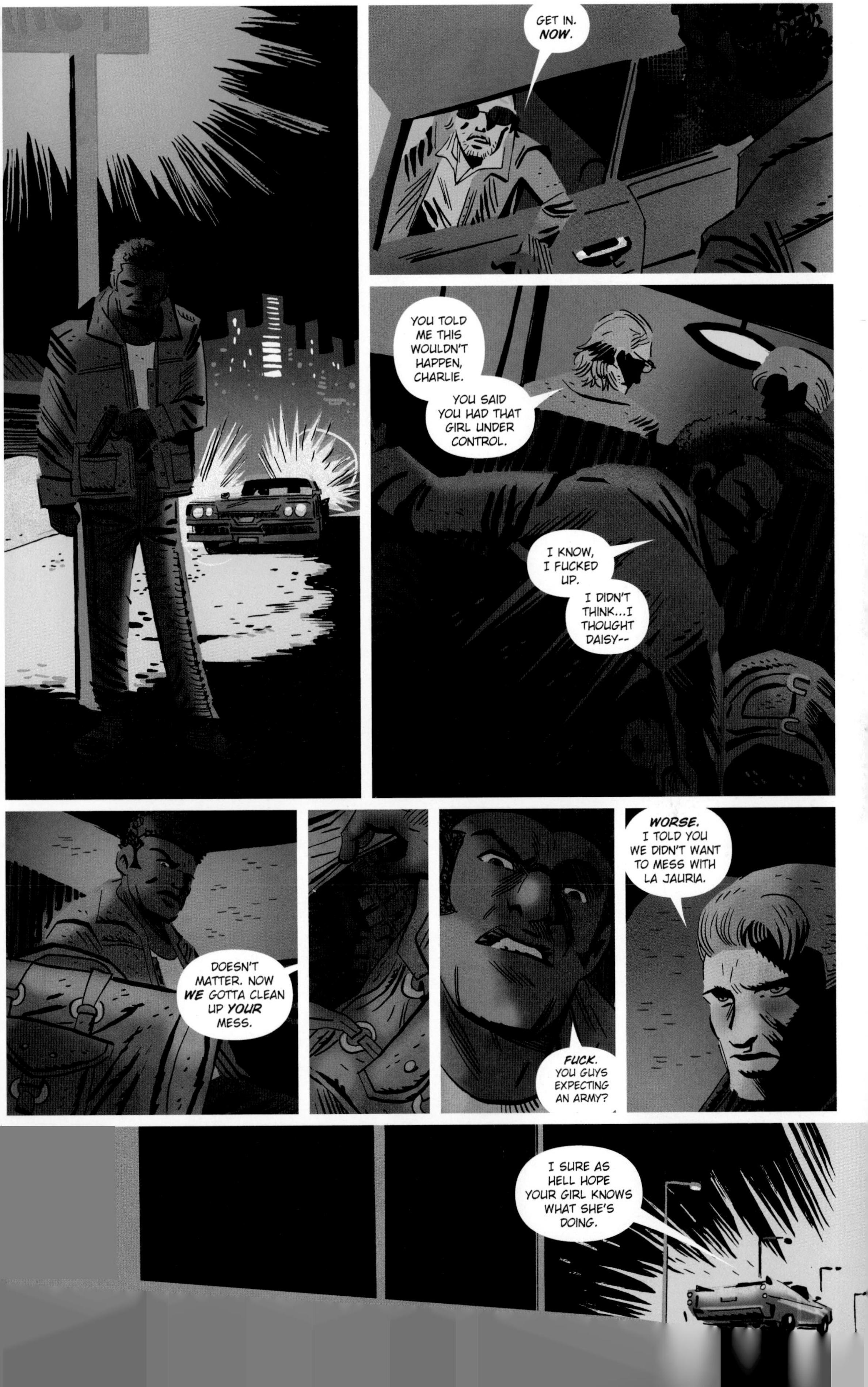
GET IN. NOW.
YOU TOLD ME THIS WOULDN'T HAPPEN, CHARLIE.
YOU SAID YOU HAD THAT GIRL UNDER CONTROL.
I KNOW, I FUCKED UP.
I DIDN'T THINK...I THOUGHT DAISY--
DOESN'T MATTER. NOW WE GOTTA CLEAN UP YOUR MESS.
FUCK. YOU GUYS EXPECTING AN ARMY?
WORSE. I TOLD YOU WE DIDN'T WANT TO MESS WITH LA JAURIA.
I SURE AS HELL HOPE YOUR GIRL KNOWS WHAT SHE'S DOING.

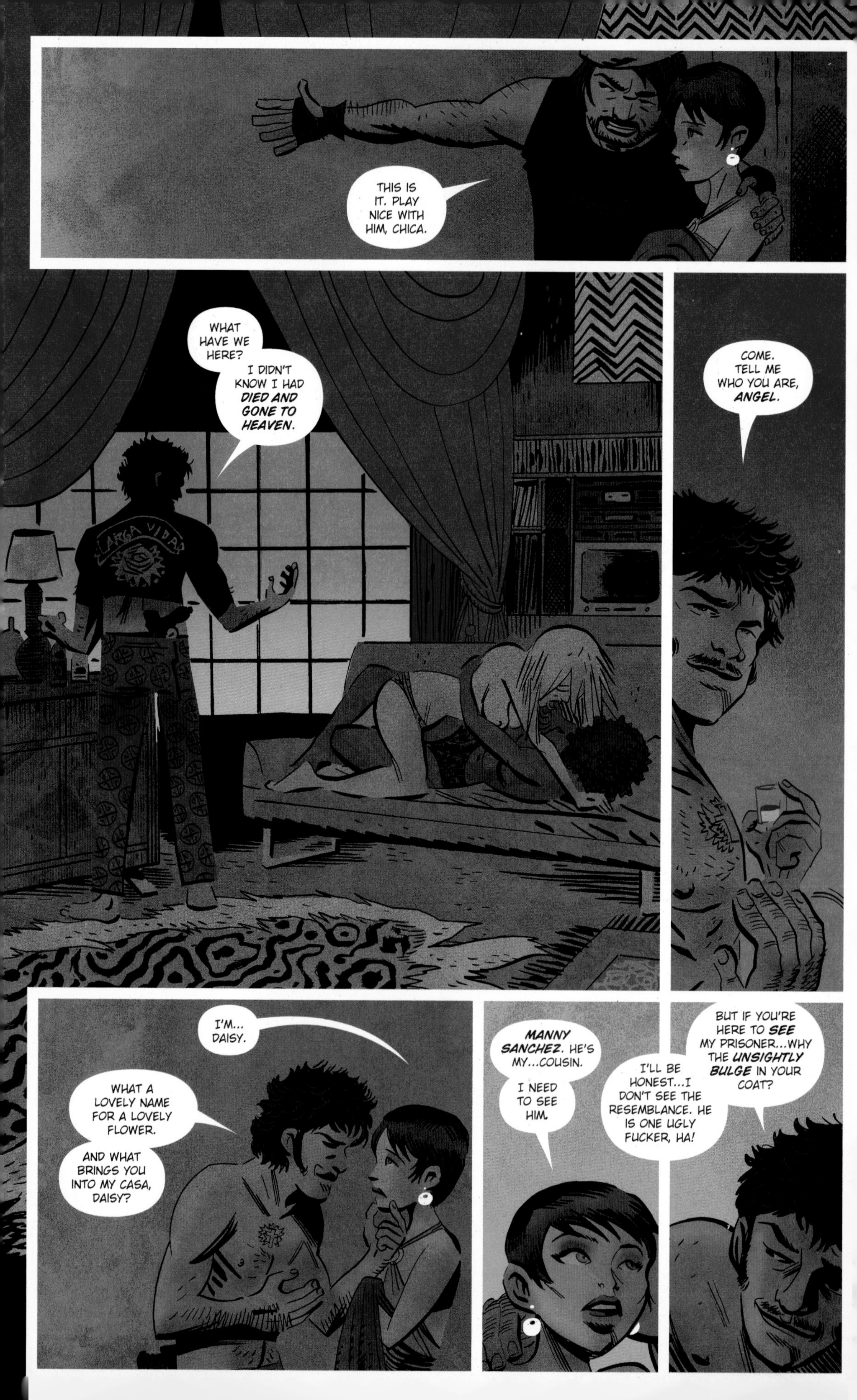
THIS IS IT. PLAY NICE WITH HIM, CHICA.
WHAT HAVE WE HERE?
I DIDN'T KNOW I HAD DIED AND GONE TO HEAVEN.
COME. TELL ME WHO YOU ARE, ANGEL.
I'M... DAISY.
WHAT A LOVELY NAME FOR A LOVELY FLOWER.
AND WHAT BRINGS YOU INTO MY CASA, DAISY?
MANNY SANCHEZ. HE'S MY...COUSIN.
I NEED TO SEE HIM.
I'LL BE HONEST...I DON'T SEE THE RESEMBLANCE. HE IS ONE UGLY FUCKER, HA!
BUT IF YOU'RE HERE TO SEE MY PRISONER...WHY THE UNSIGHTLY BULGE IN YOUR COAT?

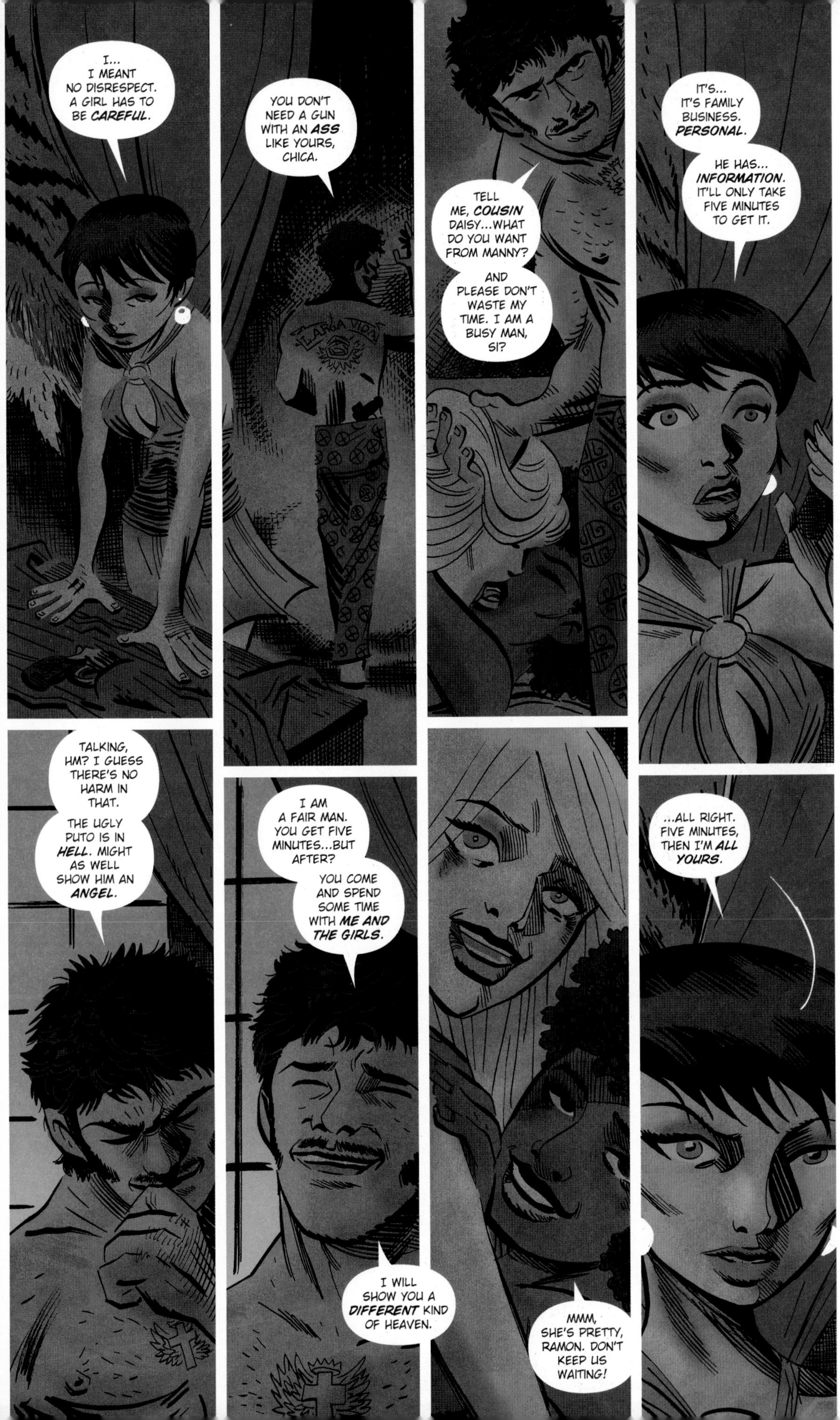
I... I MEANT NO DISRESPECT. A GIRL HAS TO BE CAREFUL.
YOU DON'T NEED A GUN WITH AN ASS LIKE YOURS, CHICA.
LARGA VIDA
TELL ME, COUSIN DAISY...WHAT DO YOU WANT FROM MANNY?
AND PLEASE DON'T WASTE MY TIME. I AM A BUSY MAN, SI?
IT'S... IT'S FAMILY BUSINESS. PERSONAL.
HE HAS... INFORMATION. IT'LL ONLY TAKE FIVE MINUTES TO GET IT.
TALKING, HM? I GUESS THERE'S NO HARM IN THAT.
THE UGLY PUTO IS IN HELL. MIGHT AS WELL SHOW HIM AN ANGEL.
I AM A FAIR MAN. YOU GET FIVE MINUTES...BUT AFTER?
YOU COME AND SPEND SOME TIME WITH ME AND THE GIRLS.
I WILL SHOW YOU A DIFFERENT KIND OF HEAVEN.
MMM, SHE'S PRETTY, RAMON. DON'T KEEP US WAITING!
...ALL RIGHT. FIVE MINUTES, THEN I'M ALL YOURS.

I APOLOGIZE FOR THE SMELL... MANNY IS NOT EXACTLY A *GUEST OF HONOR.*

YOU... YOU'RE MANNY SANCHEZ?

NO. WE'RE JUST GONNA *TALK.* YOU NEED TO TELL ME WHERE I CAN FIND THE *NAILS GANG.*

THERE. CLOCK IS RUNNING, MY LITTLE FLOWER.

AND NO FUCKING AROUND. I NEED THIS PIECE OF SHIT *ALIVE.*

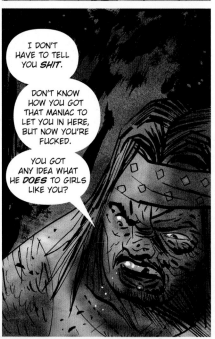

I DON'T HAVE TO TELL YOU *SHIT.*

DON'T KNOW HOW YOU GOT THAT MANIAC TO LET YOU IN HERE, BUT NOW YOU'RE FUCKED.

YOU GOT ANY IDEA WHAT HE *DOES* TO GIRLS LIKE YOU?

I CAN HANDLE HIM JUST FINE. BUT YOU...

YOU'RE GONNA TELL ME WHERE NAILS IS. *NOW.*

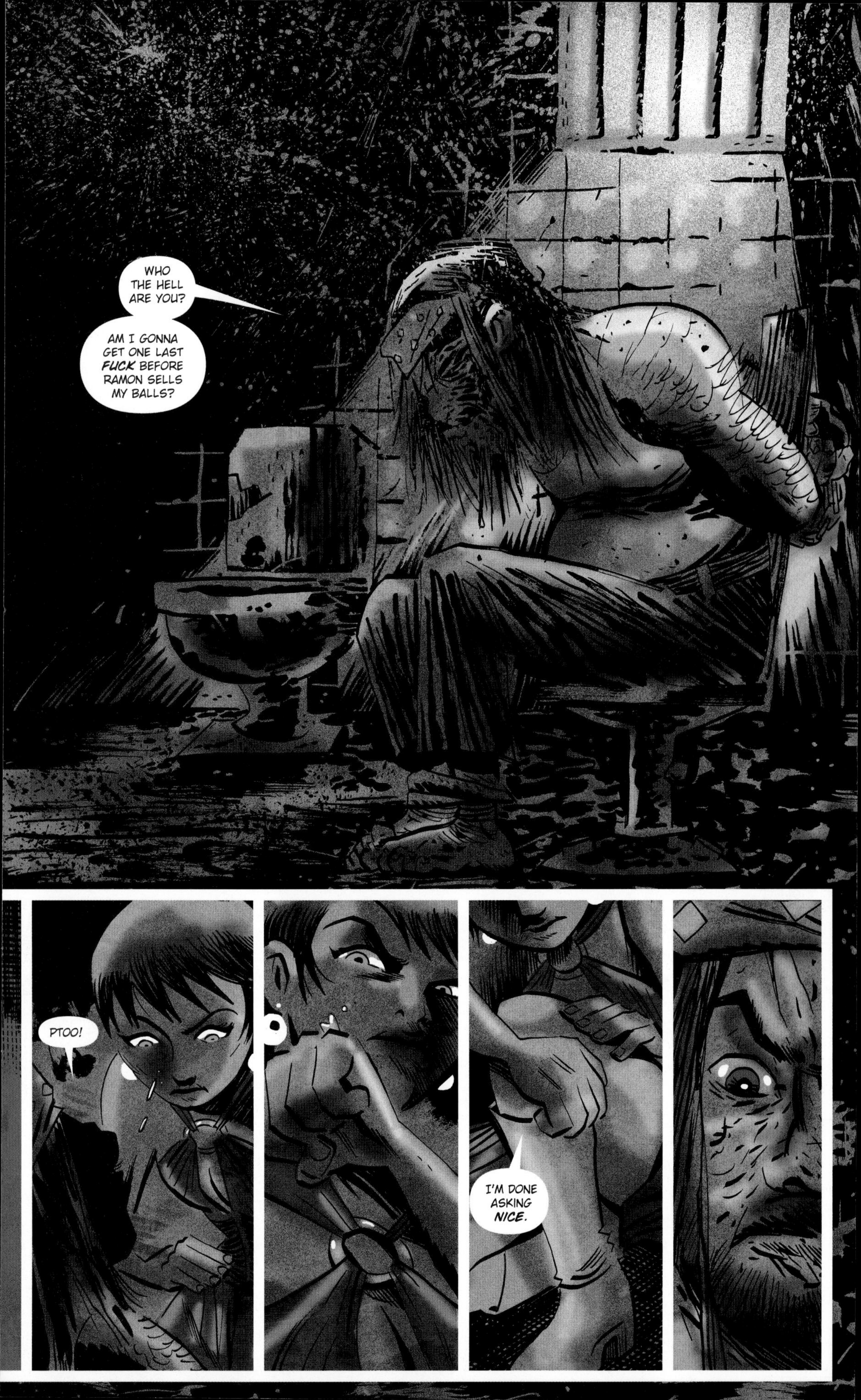
WHO THE HELL ARE YOU?
AM I GONNA GET ONE LAST **FUCK** BEFORE RAMON SELLS MY BALLS?
PTOO!
I'M DONE ASKING **NICE**.

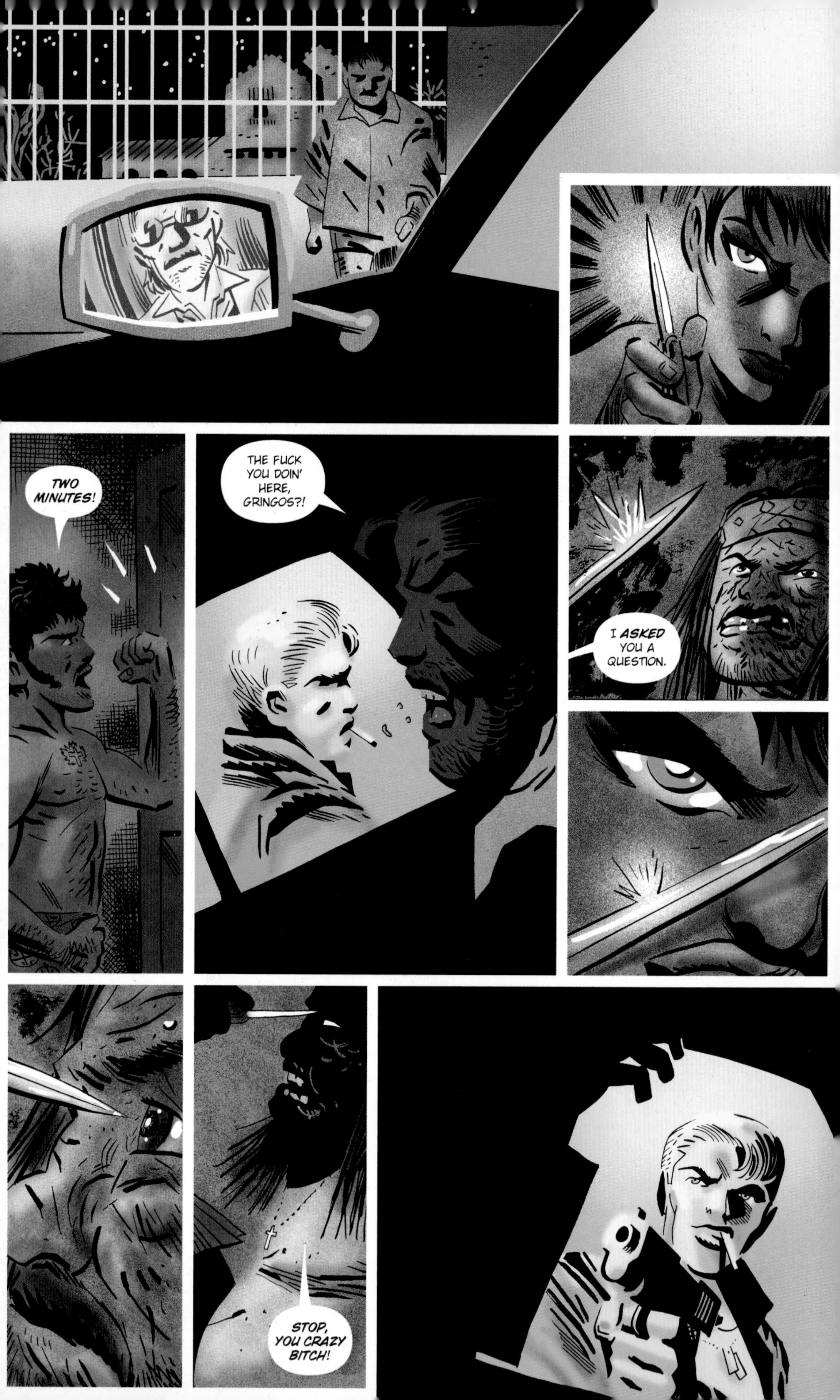
TWO MINUTES!
THE FUCK YOU DOIN' HERE, GRINGOS?!
I ASKED YOU A QUESTION.
STOP, YOU CRAZY BITCH!

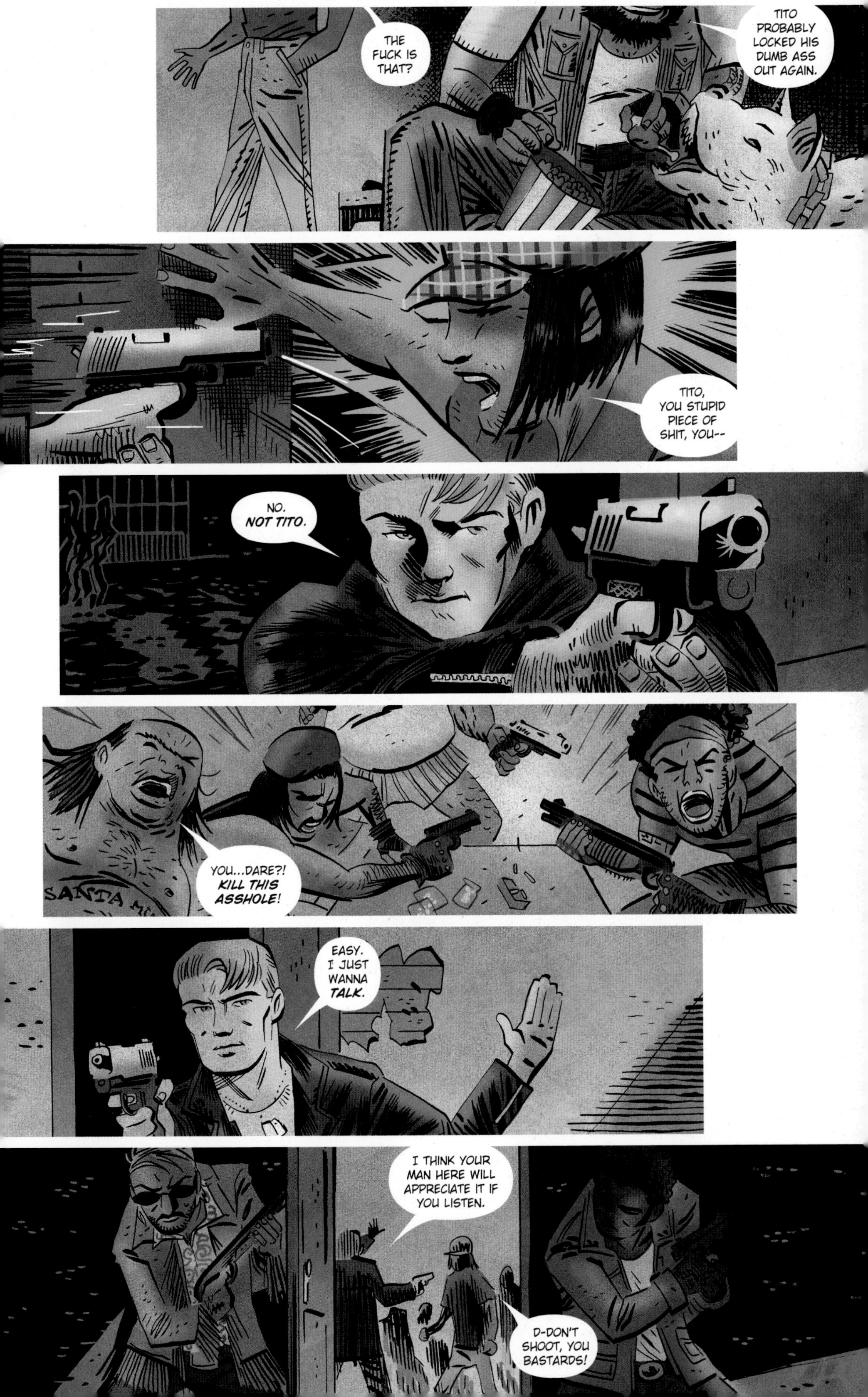
THE FUCK IS THAT?
TITO PROBABLY LOCKED HIS DUMB ASS OUT AGAIN.
TITO, YOU STUPID PIECE OF SHIT, YOU--
NO. NOT TITO.
YOU...DARE?! KILL THIS ASSHOLE!
SANTA M
EASY. I JUST WANNA TALK.
I THINK YOUR MAN HERE WILL APPRECIATE IT IF YOU LISTEN.
D-DON'T SHOOT, YOU BASTARDS!

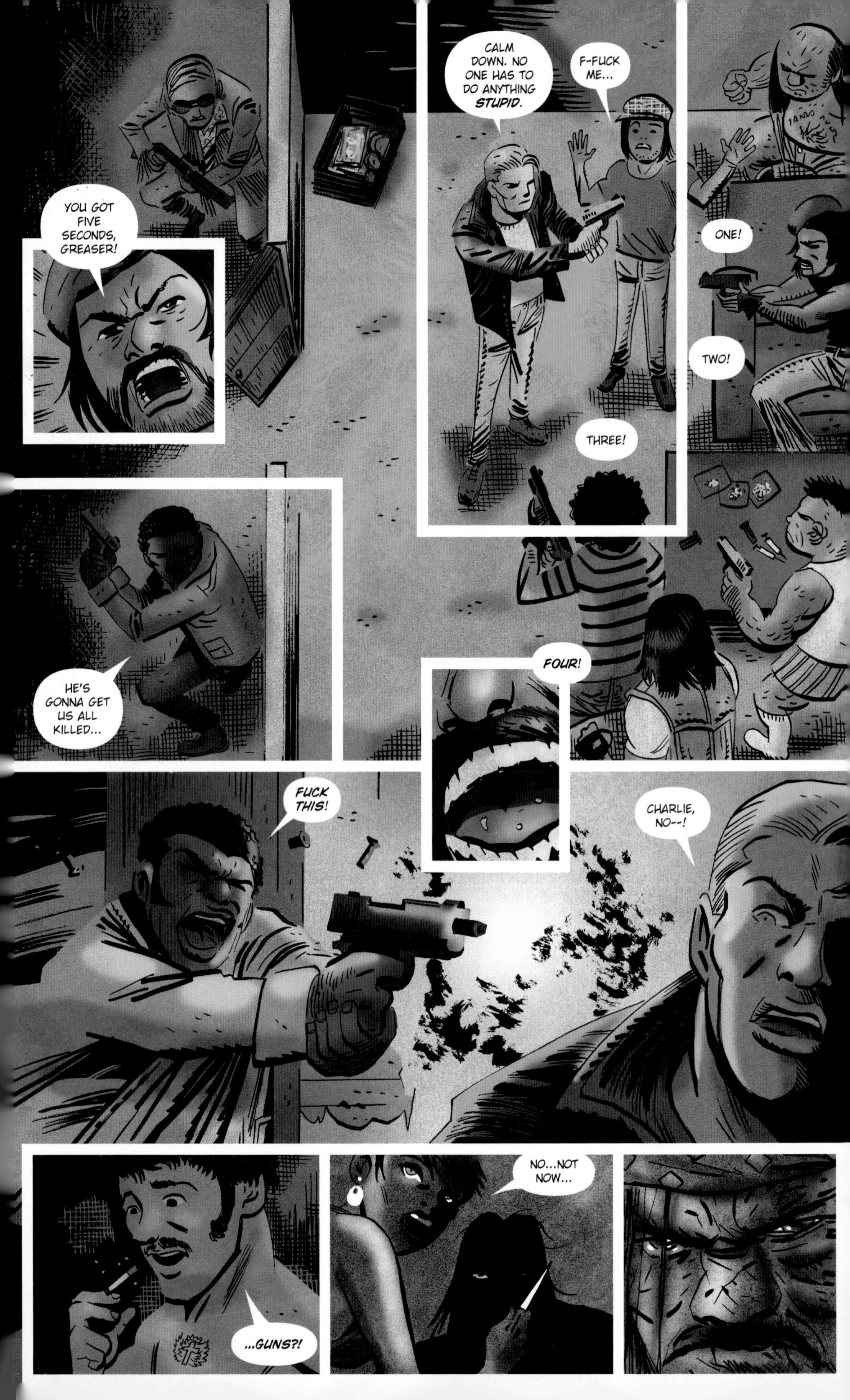
YOU GOT FIVE SECONDS, GREASER!
CALM DOWN. NO ONE HAS TO DO ANYTHING STUPID.
F-FUCK ME...
ONE!
TWO!
THREE!
HE'S GONNA GET US ALL KILLED...
FOUR!
FUCK THIS!
CHARLIE, NO--!
...GUNS?!
NO...NOT NOW...

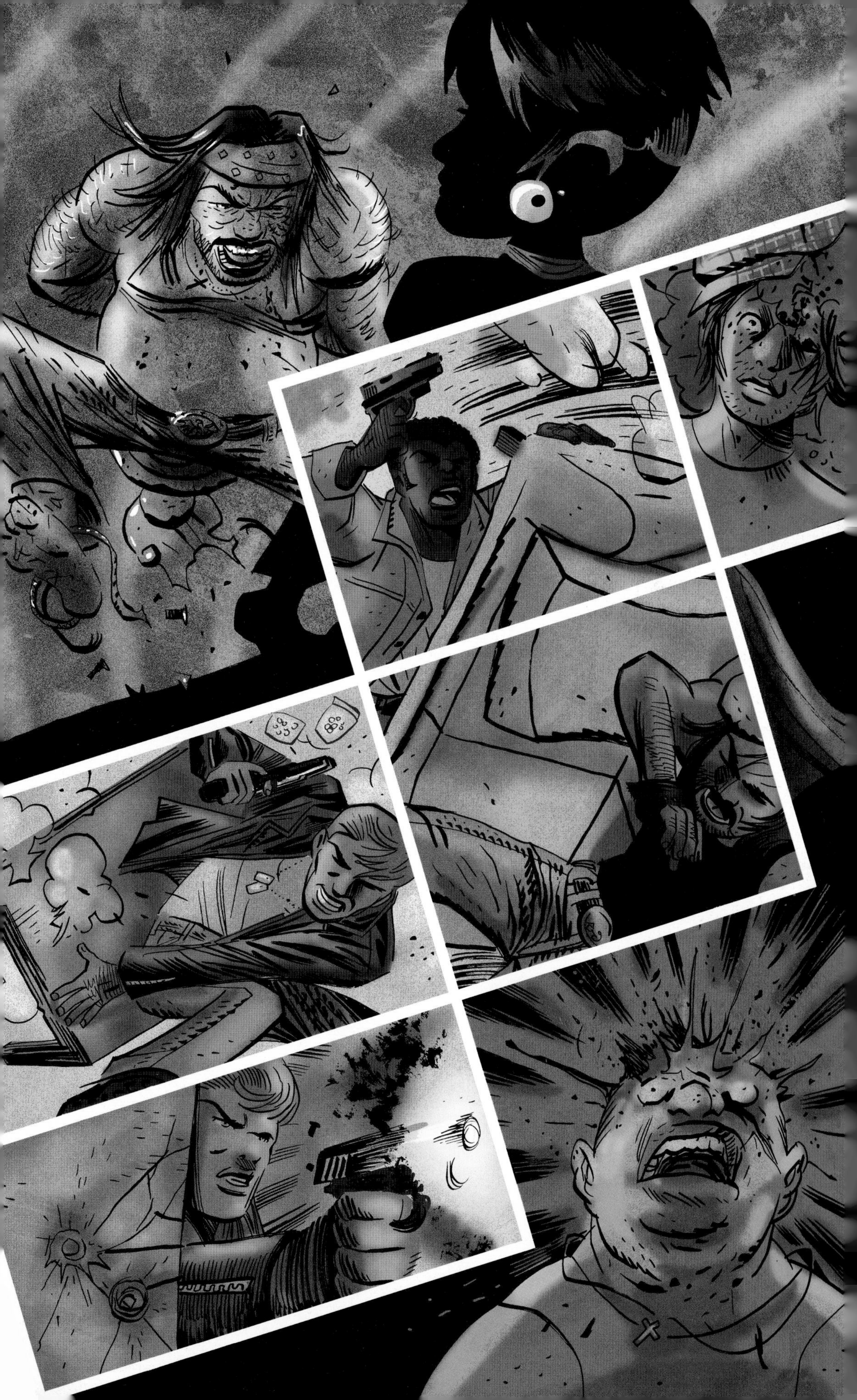

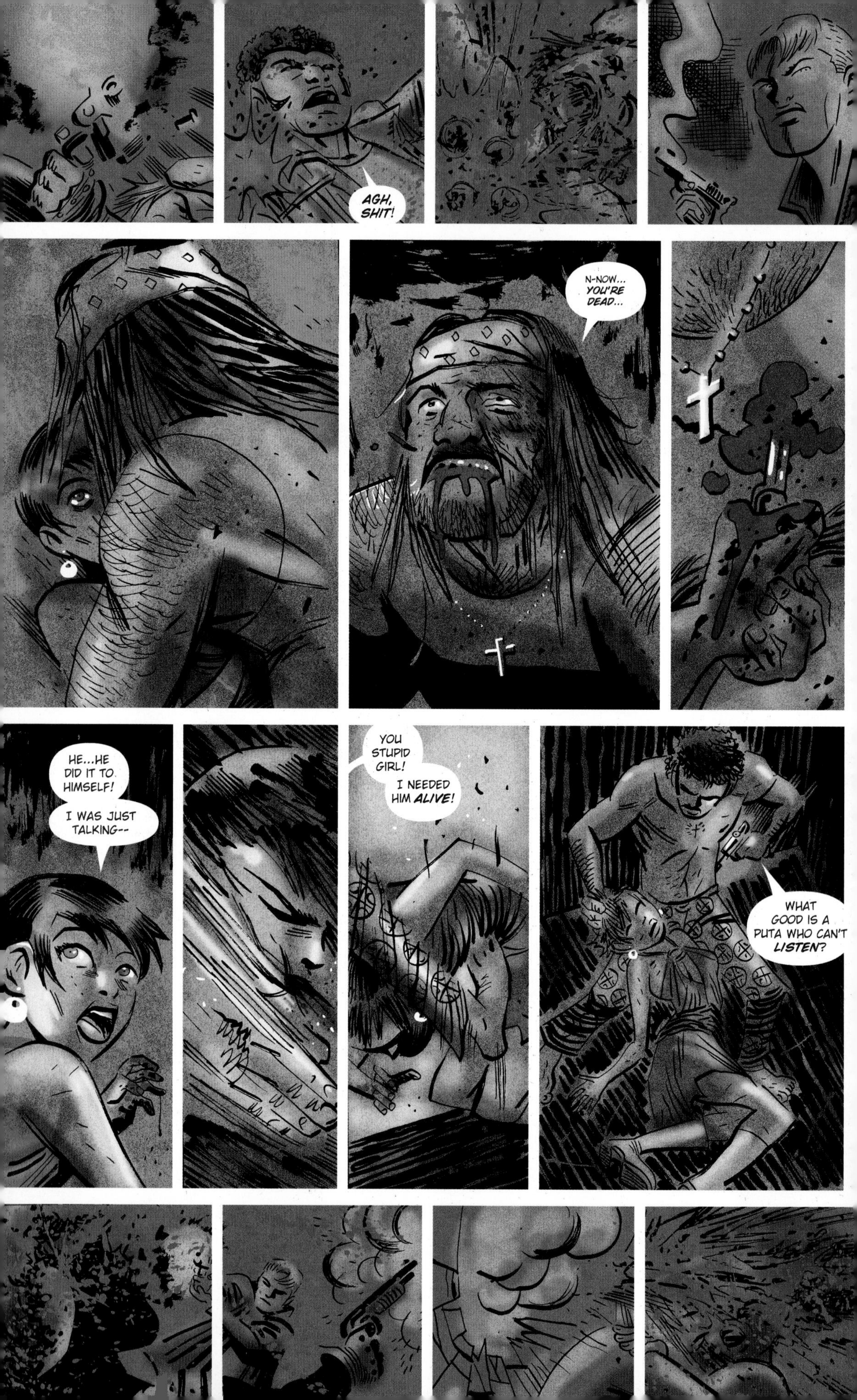
AGH, SHIT!
N-NOW... YOU'RE DEAD...
HE...HE DID IT TO HIMSELF!
I WAS JUST TALKING--
YOU STUPID GIRL!
I NEEDED HIM ALIVE!
WHAT GOOD IS A PUTA WHO CAN'T LISTEN?

MAN DOWN!

ROCK, GO FIND THE GIRL!

...D-DAISY...

NO...

WHAT DID YOU DO?

ANSWER ME, BITCH!

SUCH A WASTE OF A BEAUTIFUL GIRL.

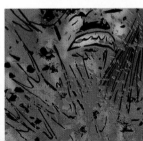

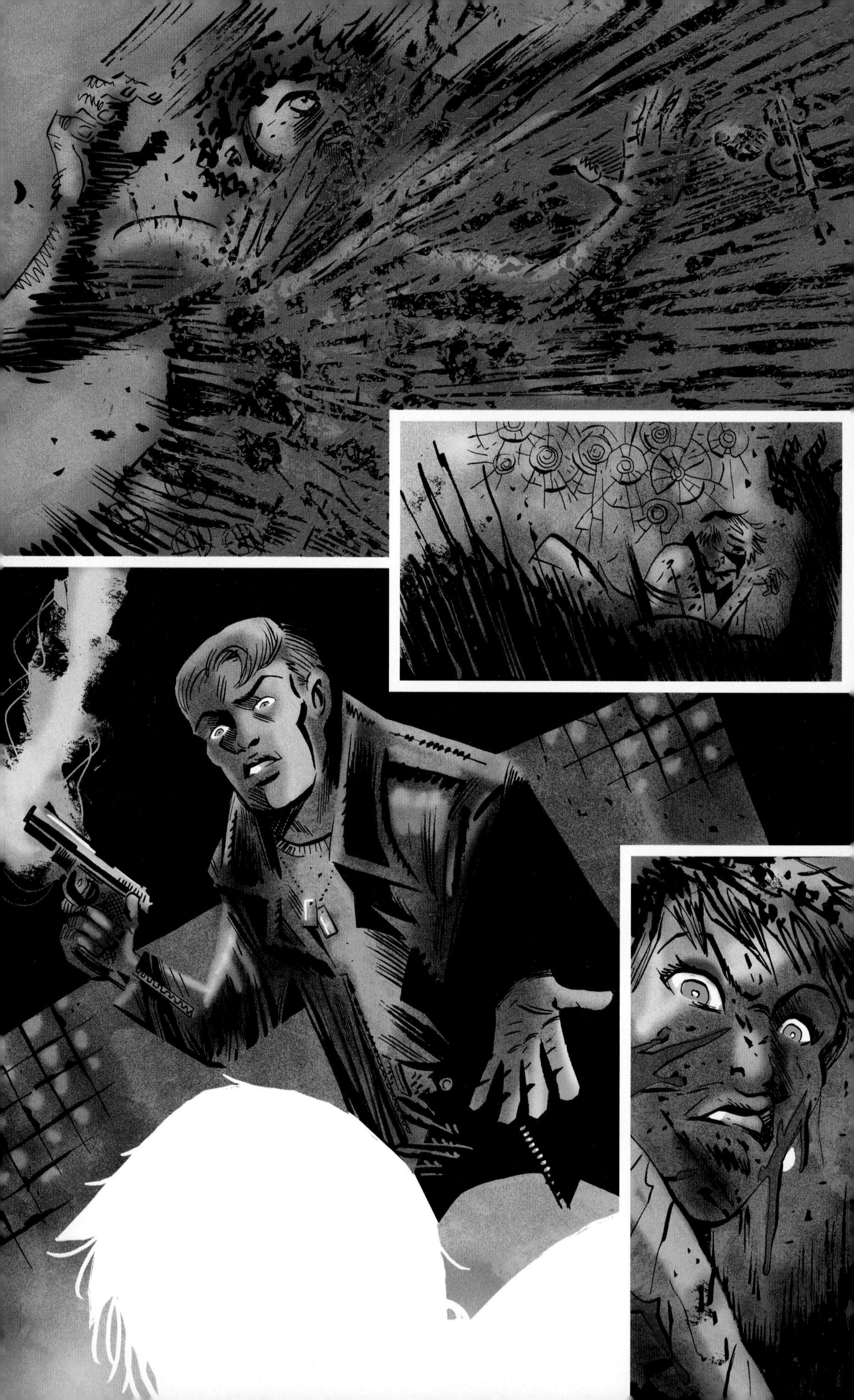

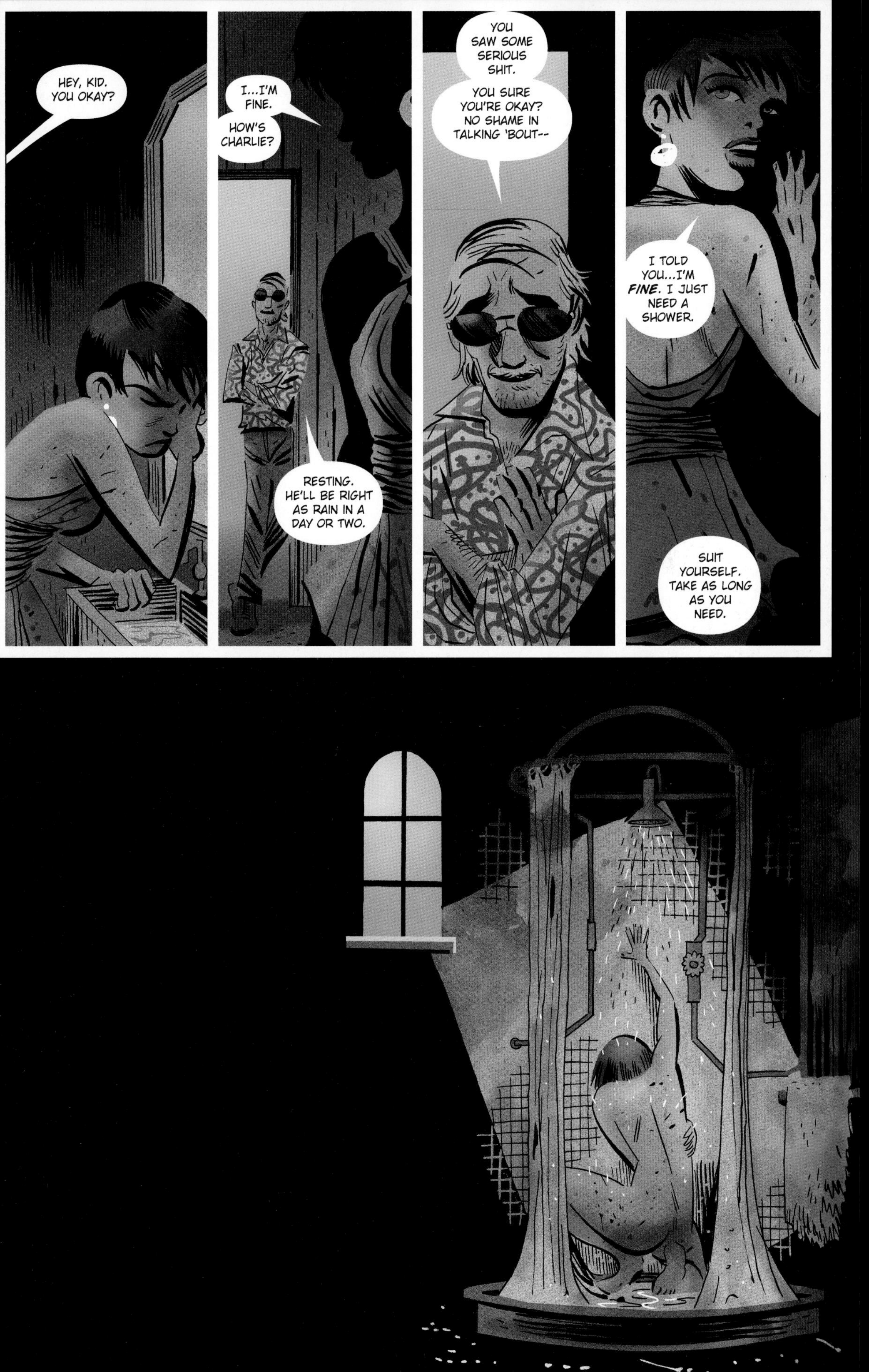
HEY, KID. YOU OKAY?
I...I'M FINE.
HOW'S CHARLIE?
RESTING. HE'LL BE RIGHT AS RAIN IN A DAY OR TWO.
YOU SAW SOME SERIOUS SHIT.
YOU SURE YOU'RE OKAY? NO SHAME IN TALKING 'BOUT--
I TOLD YOU...I'M FINE. I JUST NEED A SHOWER.
SUIT YOURSELF. TAKE AS LONG AS YOU NEED.

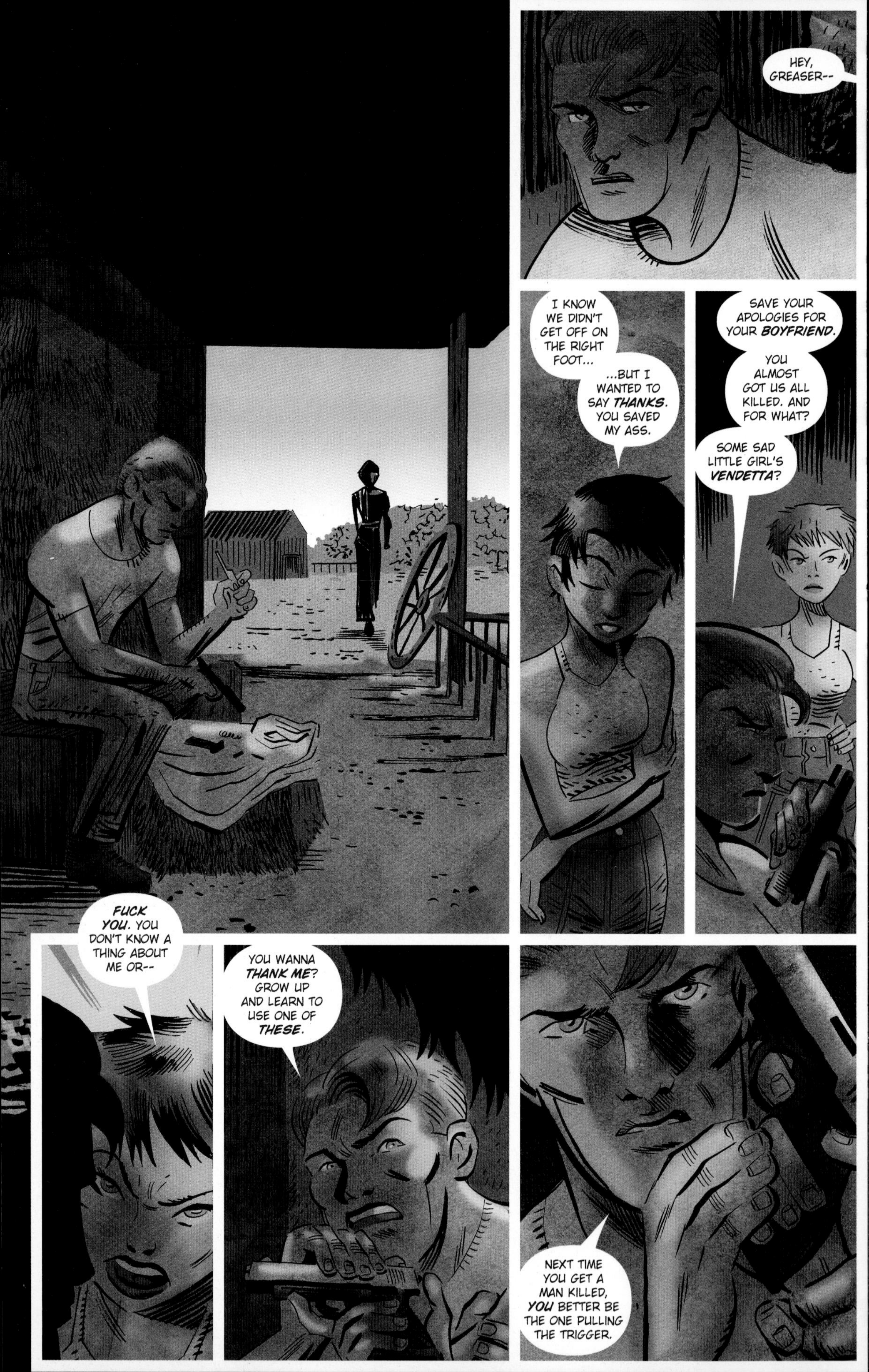
HEY, GREASER--
I KNOW WE DIDN'T GET OFF ON THE RIGHT FOOT...
...BUT I WANTED TO SAY THANKS. YOU SAVED MY ASS.
SAVE YOUR APOLOGIES FOR YOUR BOYFRIEND.
YOU ALMOST GOT US ALL KILLED. AND FOR WHAT?
SOME SAD LITTLE GIRL'S VENDETTA?
FUCK YOU. YOU DON'T KNOW A THING ABOUT ME OR--
YOU WANNA THANK ME? GROW UP AND LEARN TO USE ONE OF THESE.
NEXT TIME YOU GET A MAN KILLED, YOU BETTER BE THE ONE PULLING THE TRIGGER.

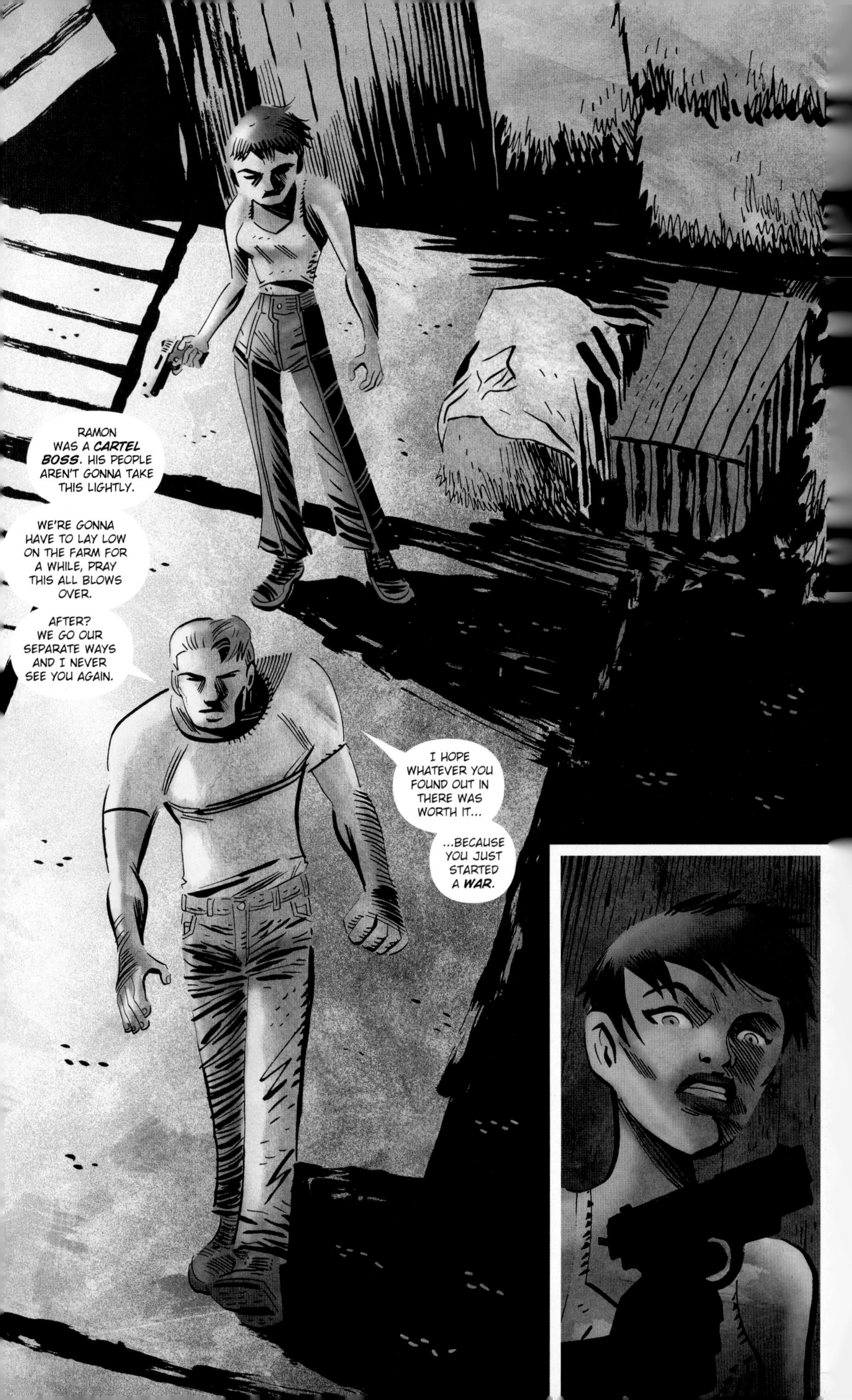
RAMON WAS A **CARTEL BOSS**. HIS PEOPLE AREN'T GONNA TAKE THIS LIGHTLY.
WE'RE GONNA HAVE TO LAY LOW ON THE FARM FOR A WHILE, PRAY THIS ALL BLOWS OVER.
AFTER? WE GO OUR SEPARATE WAYS AND I NEVER SEE YOU AGAIN.
I HOPE WHATEVER YOU FOUND OUT IN THERE WAS WORTH IT...
...BECAUSE YOU JUST STARTED A **WAR**.

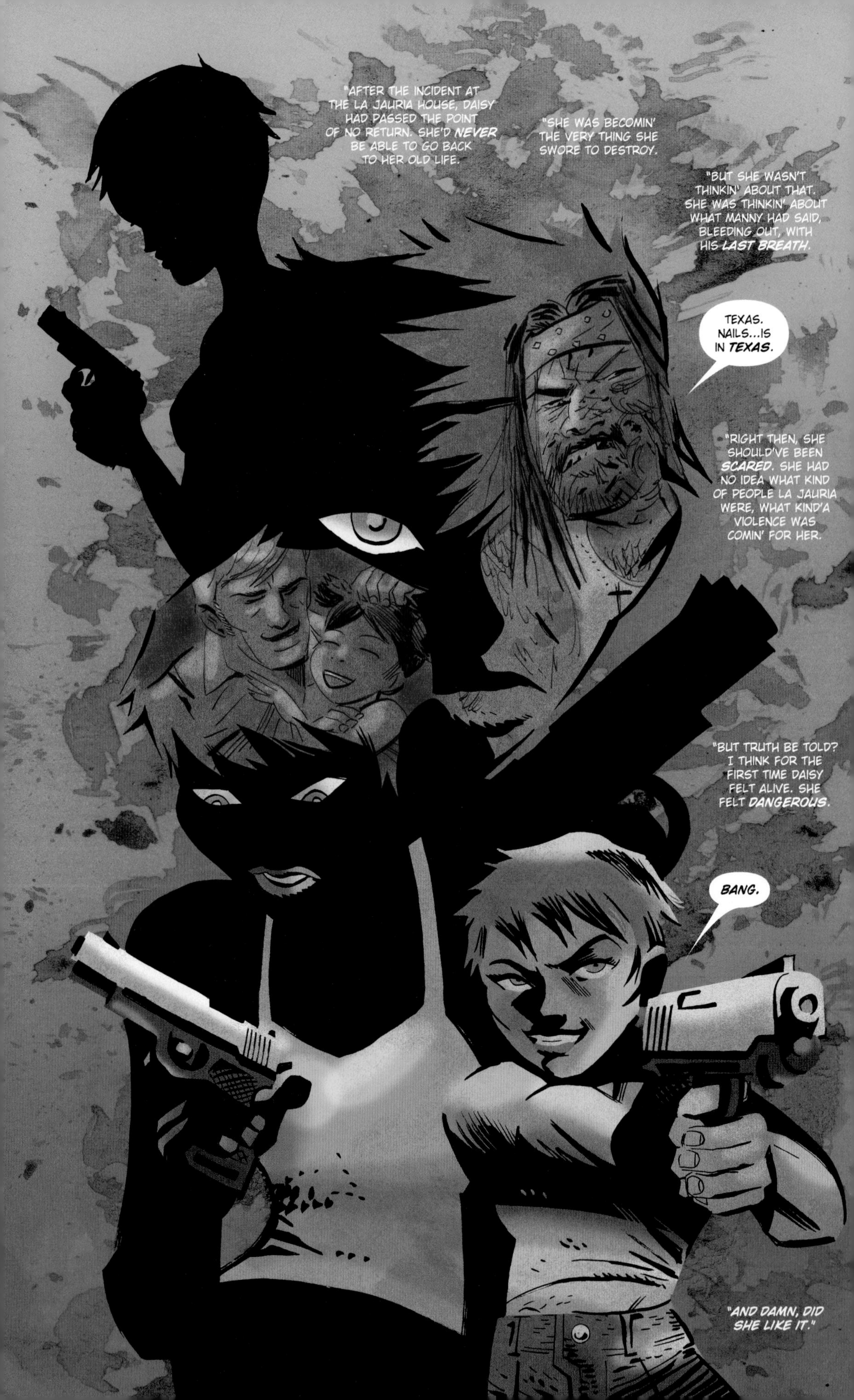
"AFTER THE INCIDENT AT THE LA JAURIA HOUSE, DAISY HAD PASSED THE POINT OF NO RETURN. SHE'D NEVER BE ABLE TO GO BACK TO HER OLD LIFE.
"SHE WAS BECOMIN' THE VERY THING SHE SWORE TO DESTROY.
"BUT SHE WASN'T THINKIN' ABOUT THAT. SHE WAS THINKIN' ABOUT WHAT MANNY HAD SAID, BLEEDING OUT, WITH HIS LAST BREATH.
TEXAS. NAILS...IS IN TEXAS.
"RIGHT THEN, SHE SHOULD'VE BEEN SCARED. SHE HAD NO IDEA WHAT KIND OF PEOPLE LA JAURIA WERE, WHAT KIND'A VIOLENCE WAS COMIN' FOR HER.
"BUT TRUTH BE TOLD? I THINK FOR THE FIRST TIME DAISY FELT ALIVE. SHE FELT DANGEROUS.
BANG.
"AND DAMN, DID SHE LIKE IT."

CHAPTER FOUR

"FINE YOUNG KNIVES"

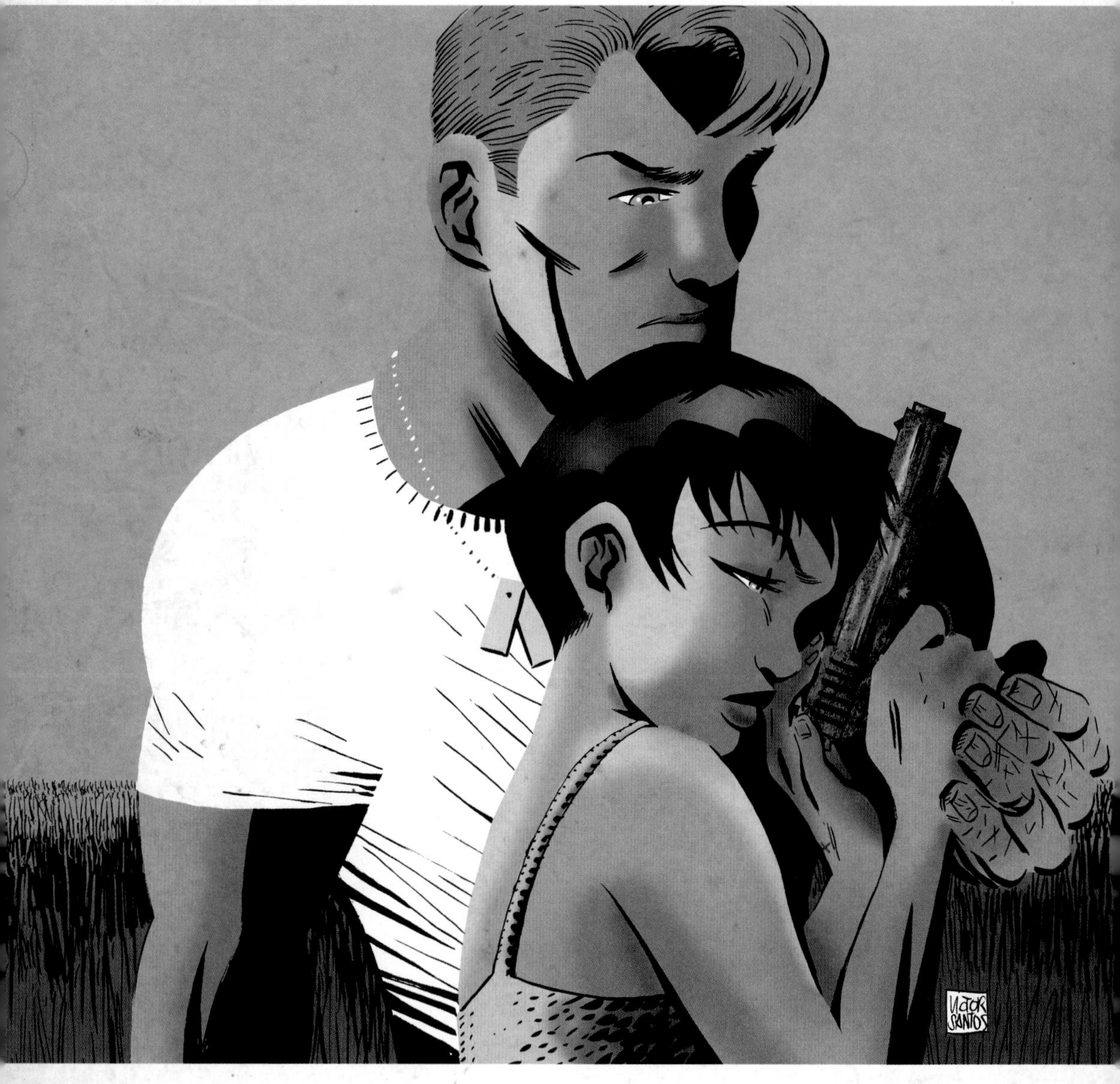

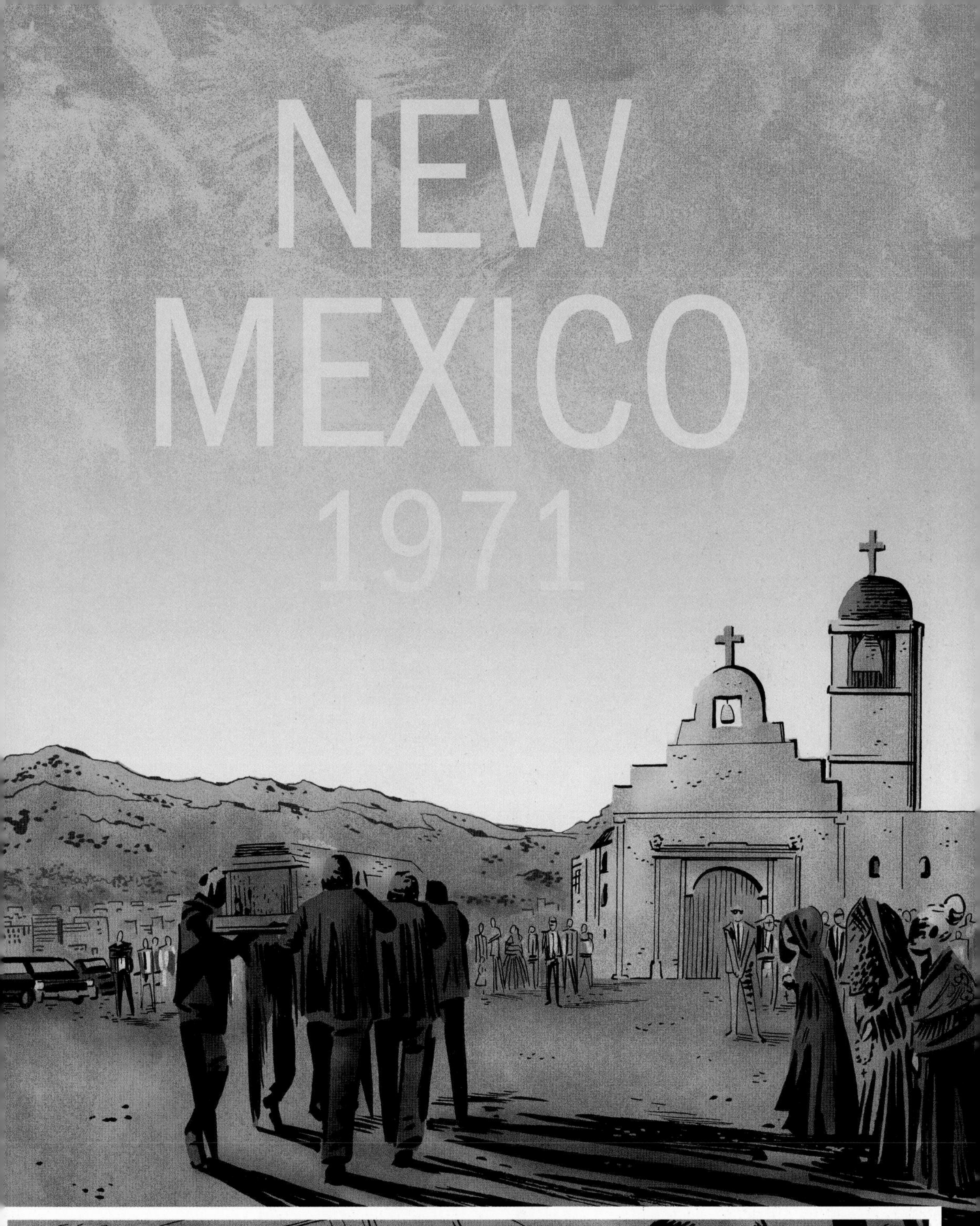
NEW
MEXICO
1971
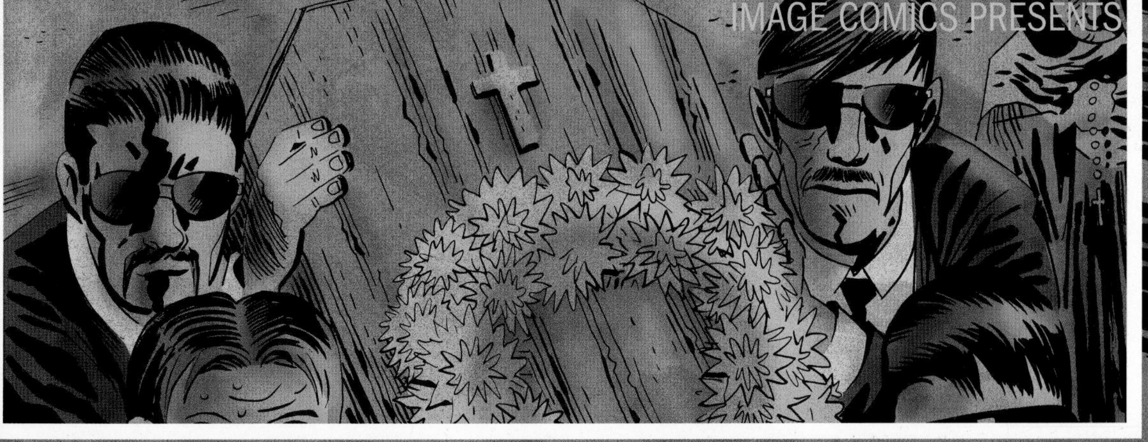
IMAGE COMICS PRESENTS

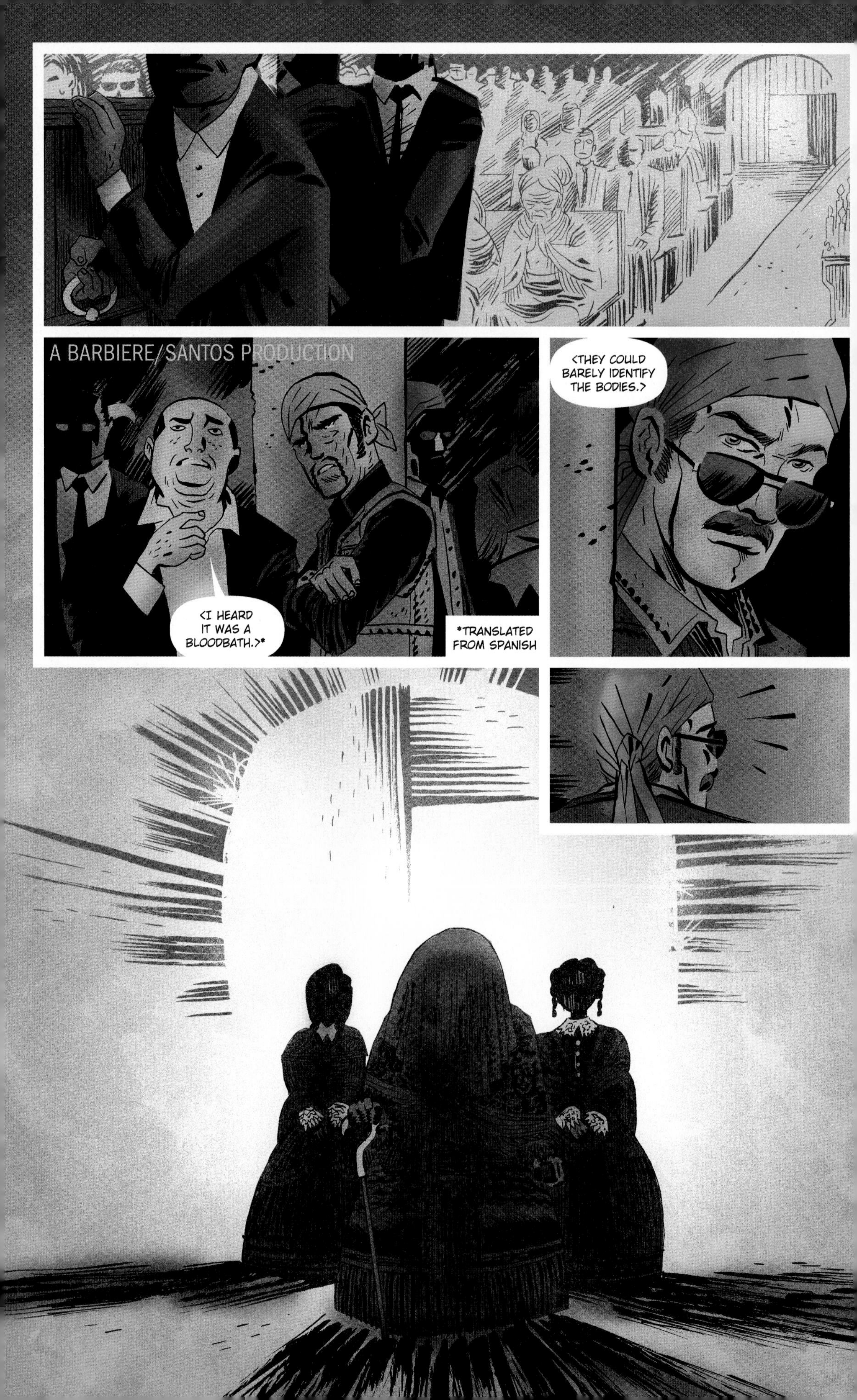
A BARBIERE/SANTOS PRODUCTION
<I HEARD IT WAS A BLOODBATH.>*
*TRANSLATED FROM SPANISH
<THEY COULD BARELY IDENTIFY THE BODIES.>

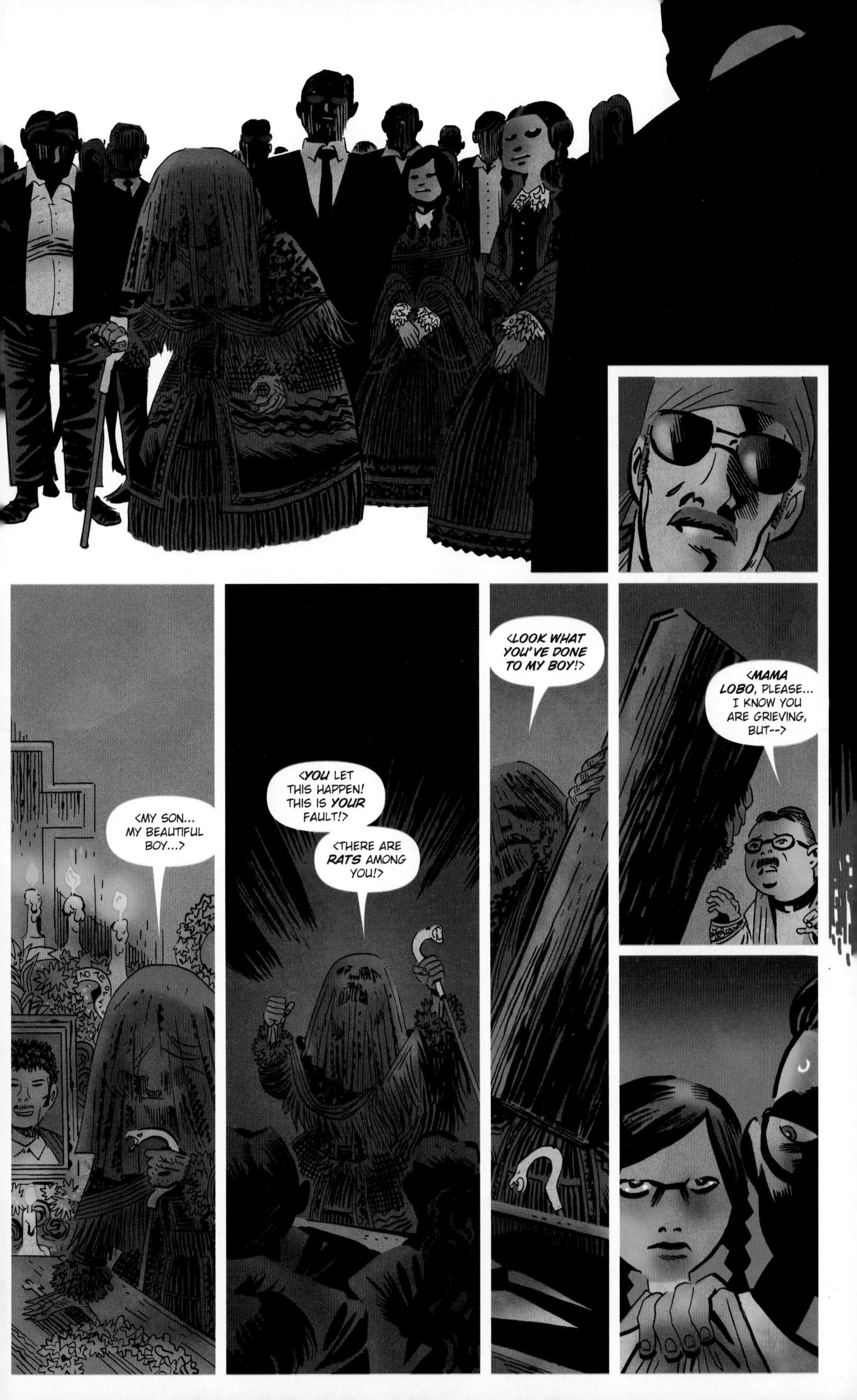
<MY SON... MY BEAUTIFUL BOY...>
<YOU LET THIS HAPPEN! THIS IS YOUR FAULT!>
<THERE ARE RATS AMONG YOU!>
<LOOK WHAT YOU'VE DONE TO MY BOY!>
<MAMA LOBO, PLEASE... I KNOW YOU ARE GRIEVING, BUT-->

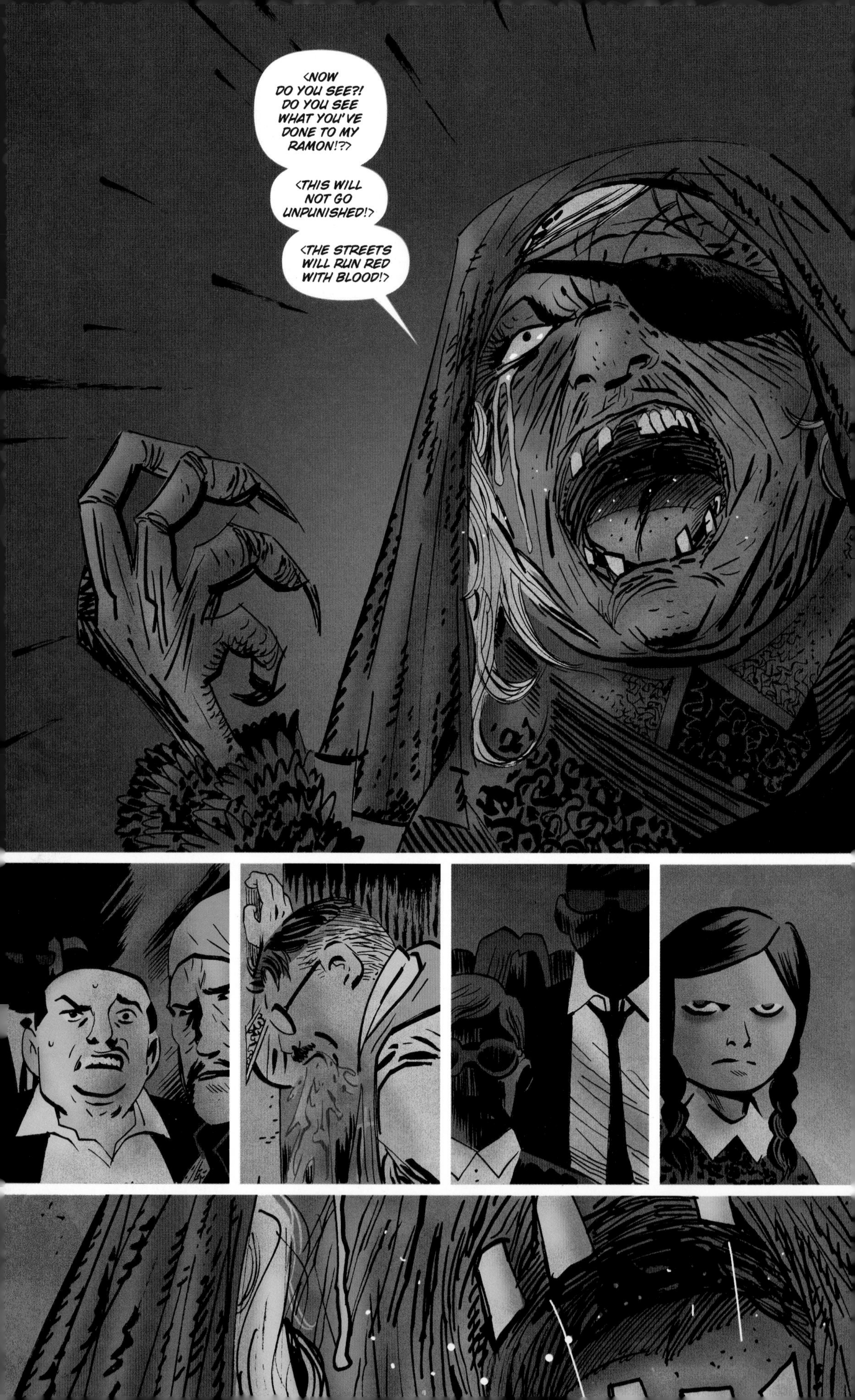
<NOW DO YOU SEE?! DO YOU SEE WHAT YOU'VE DONE TO MY RAMON!?>
<THIS WILL NOT GO UNPUNISHED!>
<THE STREETS WILL RUN RED WITH BLOOD!>

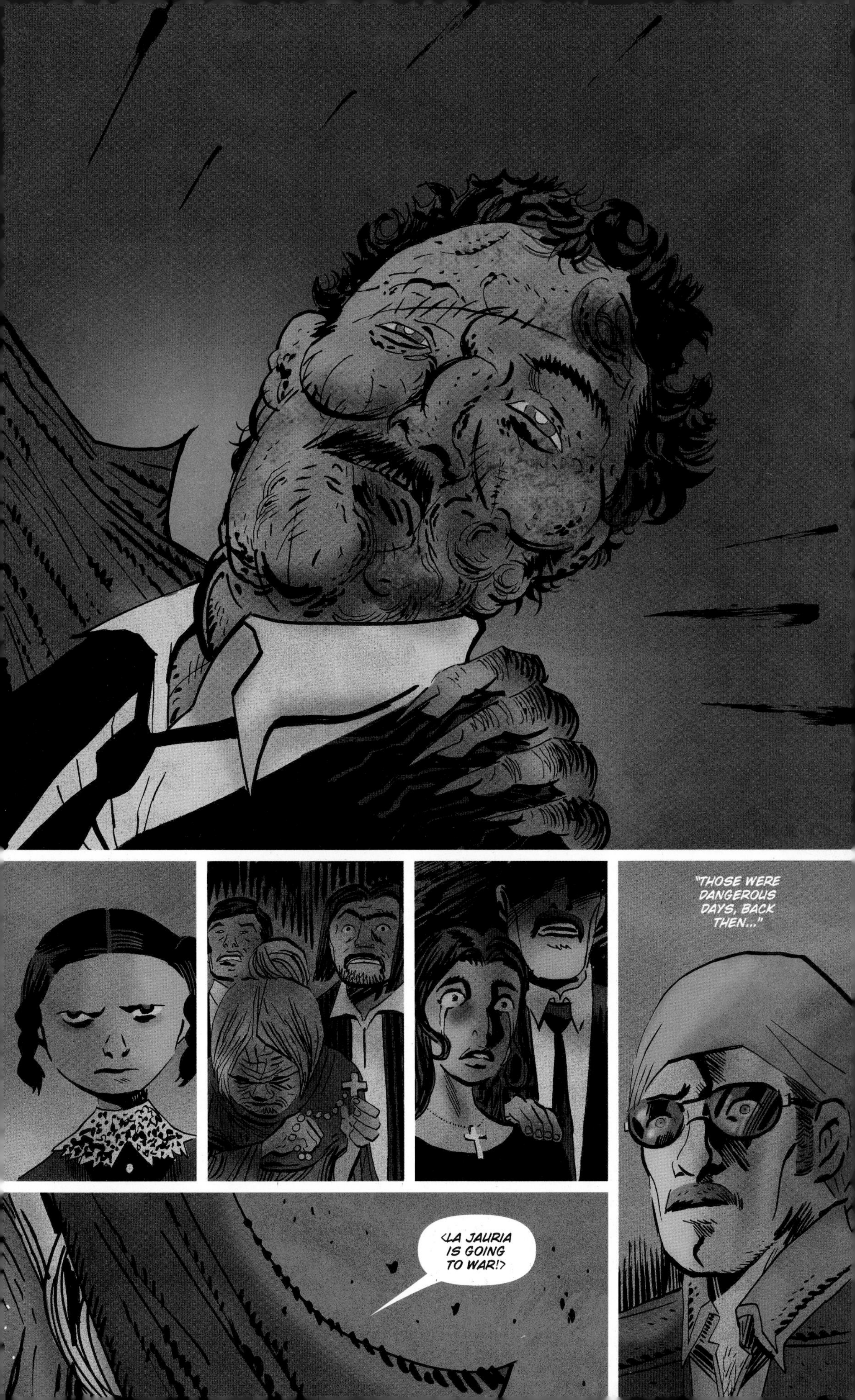
"THOSE WERE DANGEROUS DAYS, BACK THEN..."
<LA JAURIA IS GOING TO WAR!>

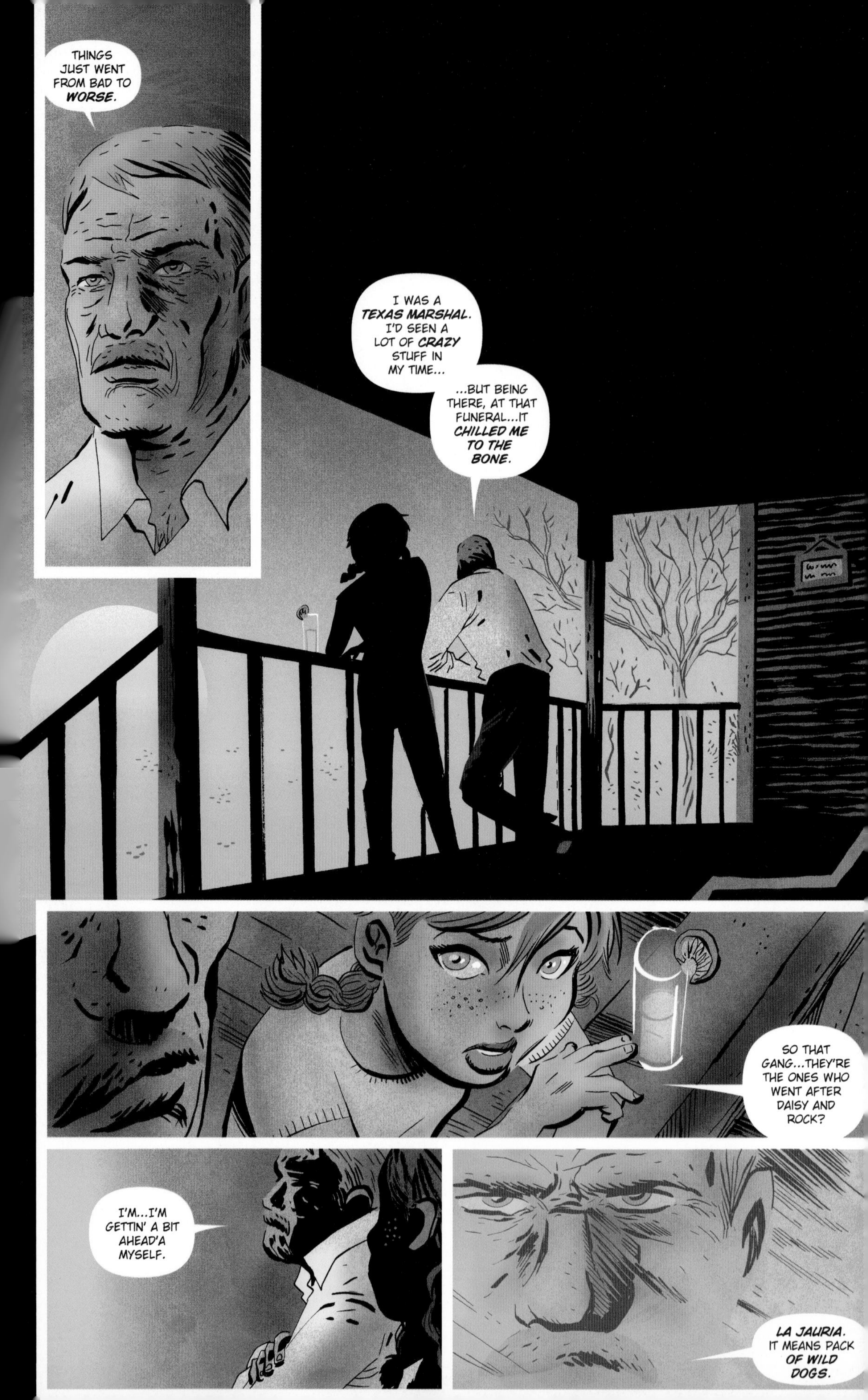
THINGS JUST WENT FROM BAD TO WORSE.
I WAS A TEXAS MARSHAL. I'D SEEN A LOT OF CRAZY STUFF IN MY TIME...
...BUT BEING THERE, AT THAT FUNERAL...IT CHILLED ME TO THE BONE.
SO THAT GANG...THEY'RE THE ONES WHO WENT AFTER DAISY AND ROCK?
I'M...I'M GETTIN' A BIT AHEAD'A MYSELF.
LA JAURIA. IT MEANS PACK OF WILD DOGS.

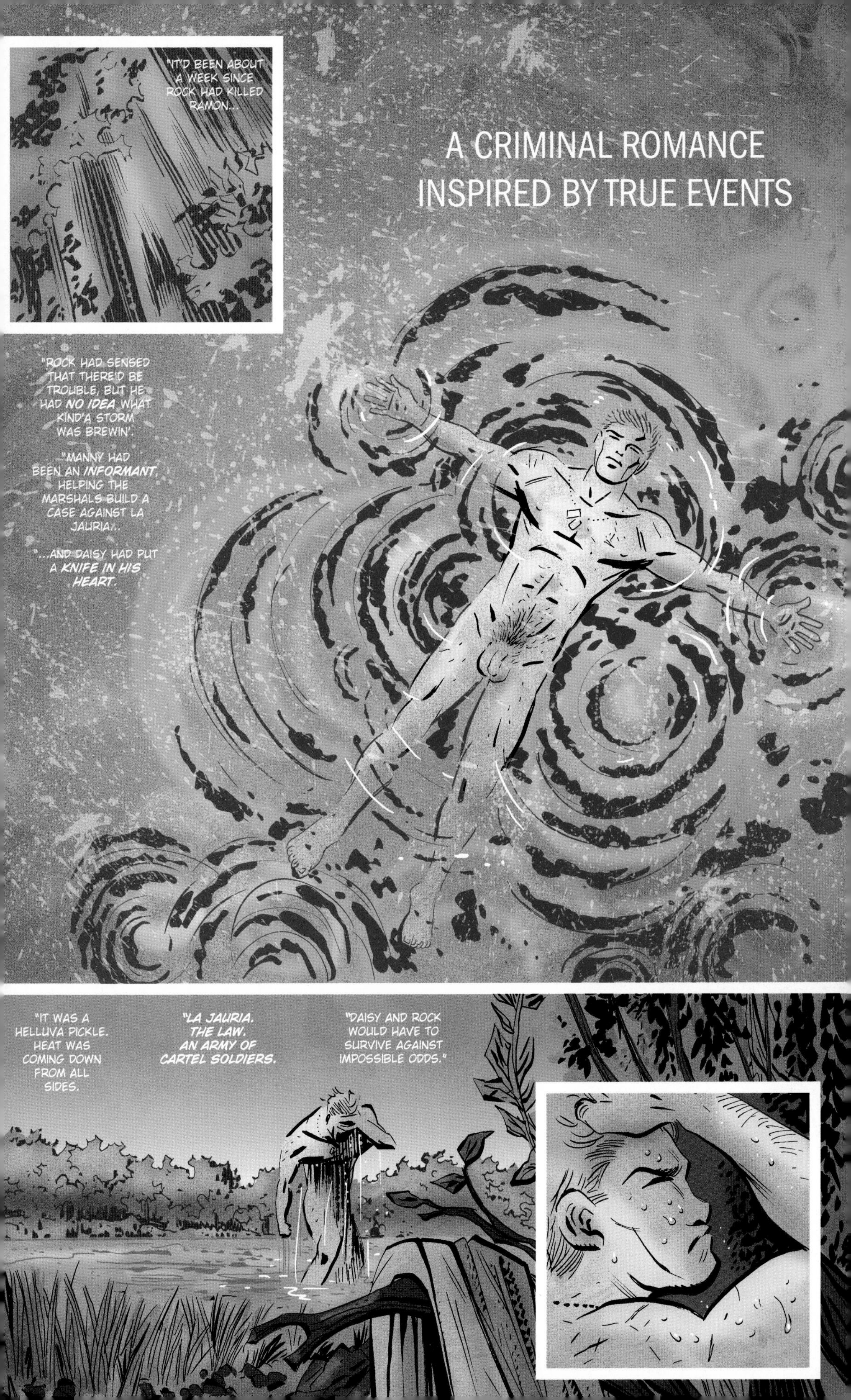
"IT'D BEEN ABOUT A WEEK SINCE ROCK HAD KILLED RAMON...
A CRIMINAL ROMANCE INSPIRED BY TRUE EVENTS
"ROCK HAD SENSED THAT THERE'D BE TROUBLE, BUT HE HAD *NO IDEA* WHAT KIND'A STORM WAS BREWIN'.
"MANNY HAD BEEN AN *INFORMANT*, HELPING THE MARSHALS BUILD A CASE AGAINST LA JAURIA...
"...AND DAISY HAD PUT A *KNIFE IN HIS HEART*.
"IT WAS A HELLUVA PICKLE. HEAT WAS COMING DOWN FROM ALL SIDES.
"LA JAURIA. THE LAW. AN ARMY OF CARTEL SOLDIERS.
"DAISY AND ROCK WOULD HAVE TO SURVIVE AGAINST IMPOSSIBLE ODDS."

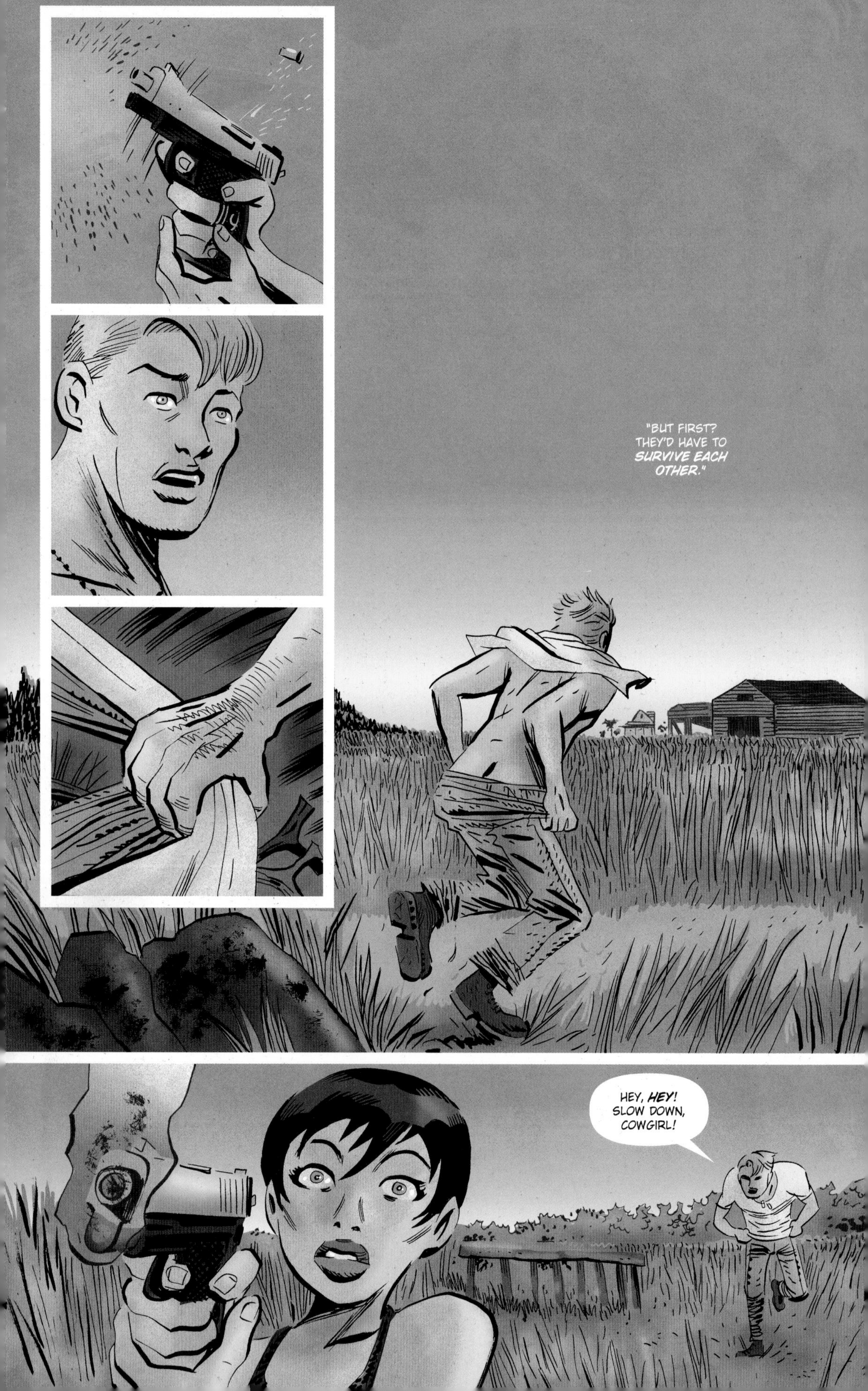
"BUT FIRST? THEY'D HAVE TO SURVIVE EACH OTHER."
HEY, HEY! SLOW DOWN, COWGIRL!

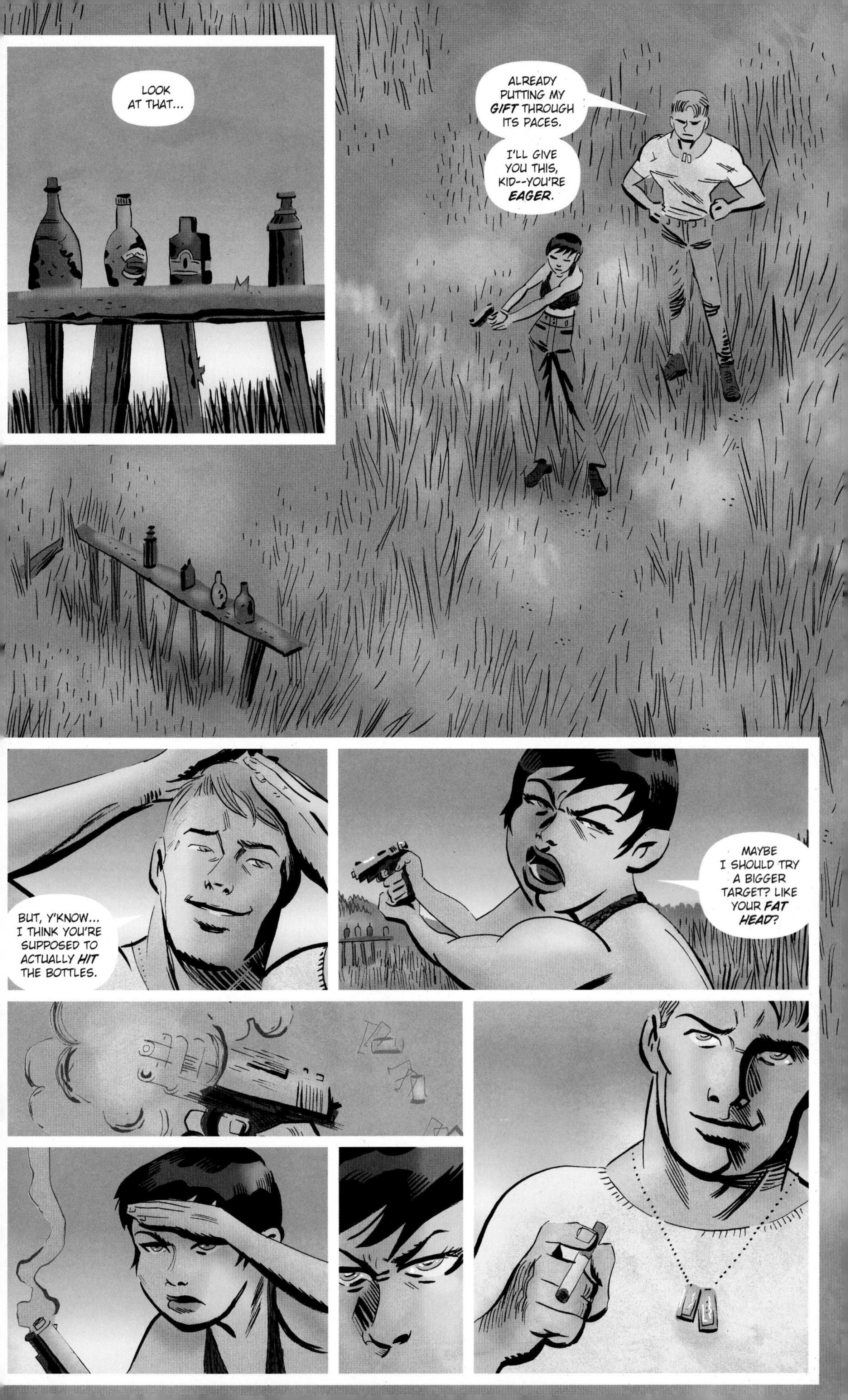
LOOK AT THAT...
ALREADY PUTTING MY GIFT THROUGH ITS PACES.
I'LL GIVE YOU THIS, KID--YOU'RE EAGER.
BUT, Y'KNOW... I THINK YOU'RE SUPPOSED TO ACTUALLY HIT THE BOTTLES.
MAYBE I SHOULD TRY A BIGGER TARGET? LIKE YOUR FAT HEAD?

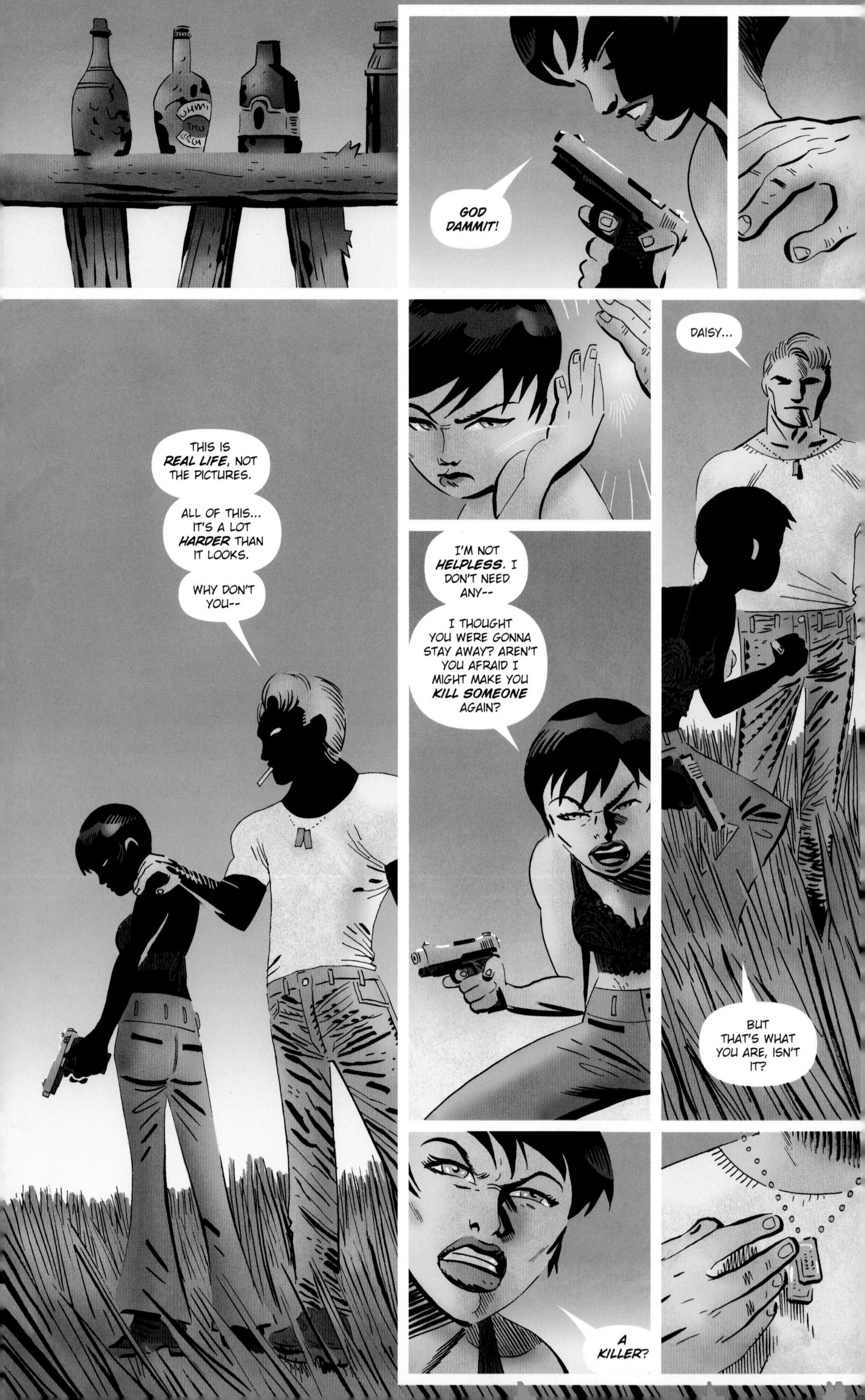
GOD DAMMIT!
THIS IS REAL LIFE, NOT THE PICTURES.
ALL OF THIS... IT'S A LOT HARDER THAN IT LOOKS.
WHY DON'T YOU--
DAISY...
I'M NOT HELPLESS. I DON'T NEED ANY--
I THOUGHT YOU WERE GONNA STAY AWAY? AREN'T YOU AFRAID I MIGHT MAKE YOU KILL SOMEONE AGAIN?
BUT THAT'S WHAT YOU ARE, ISN'T IT?
A KILLER?

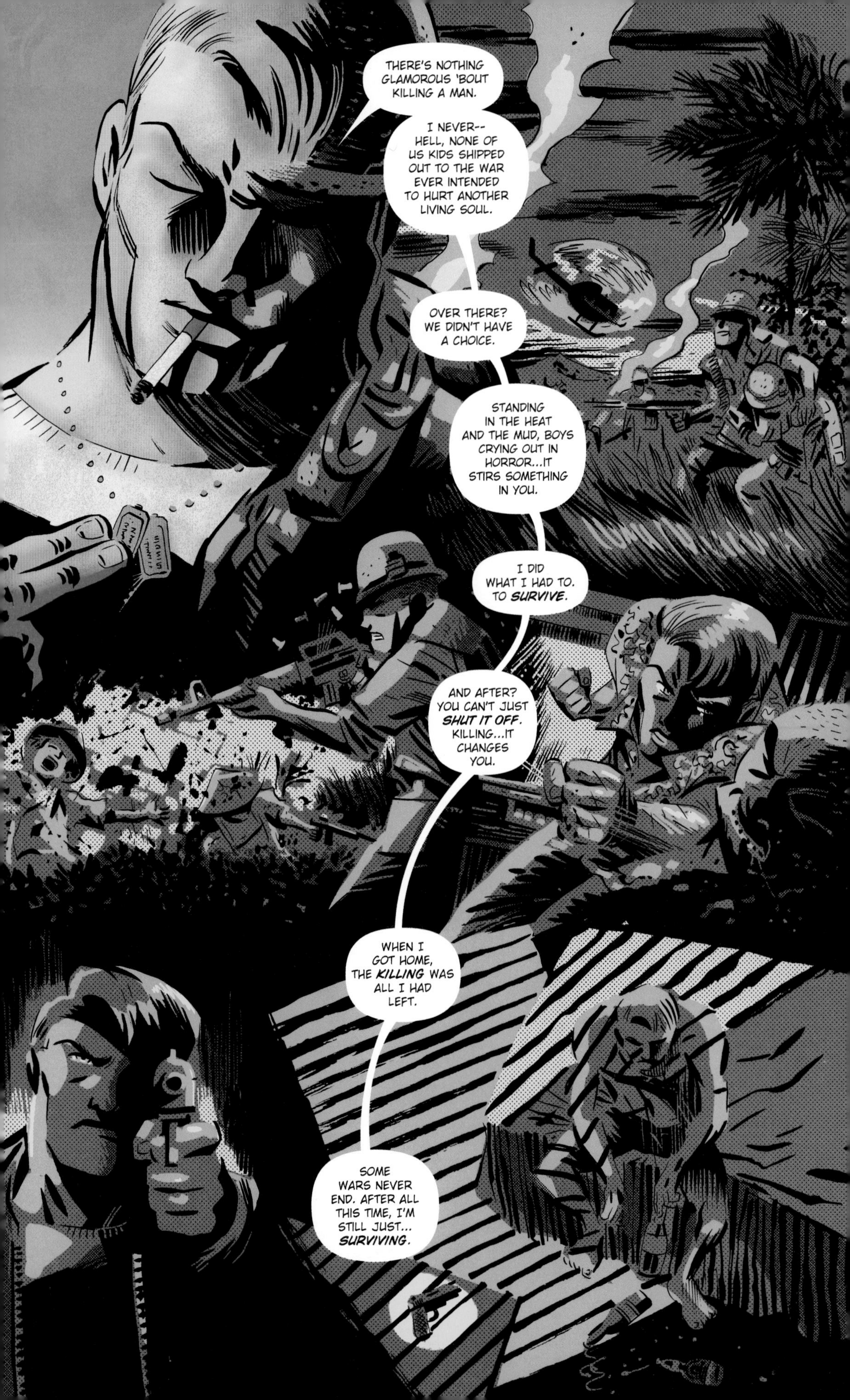

THERE'S NOTHING GLAMOROUS 'BOUT KILLING A MAN.
I NEVER-- HELL, NONE OF US KIDS SHIPPED OUT TO THE WAR EVER INTENDED TO HURT ANOTHER LIVING SOUL.
OVER THERE? WE DIDN'T HAVE A CHOICE.
STANDING IN THE HEAT AND THE MUD, BOYS CRYING OUT IN HORROR...IT STIRS SOMETHING IN YOU.
I DID WHAT I HAD TO. TO *SURVIVE*.
AND AFTER? YOU CAN'T JUST *SHUT IT OFF*. KILLING...IT CHANGES YOU.
WHEN I GOT HOME, THE *KILLING* WAS ALL I HAD LEFT.
SOME WARS NEVER END. AFTER ALL THIS TIME, I'M STILL JUST... *SURVIVING*.

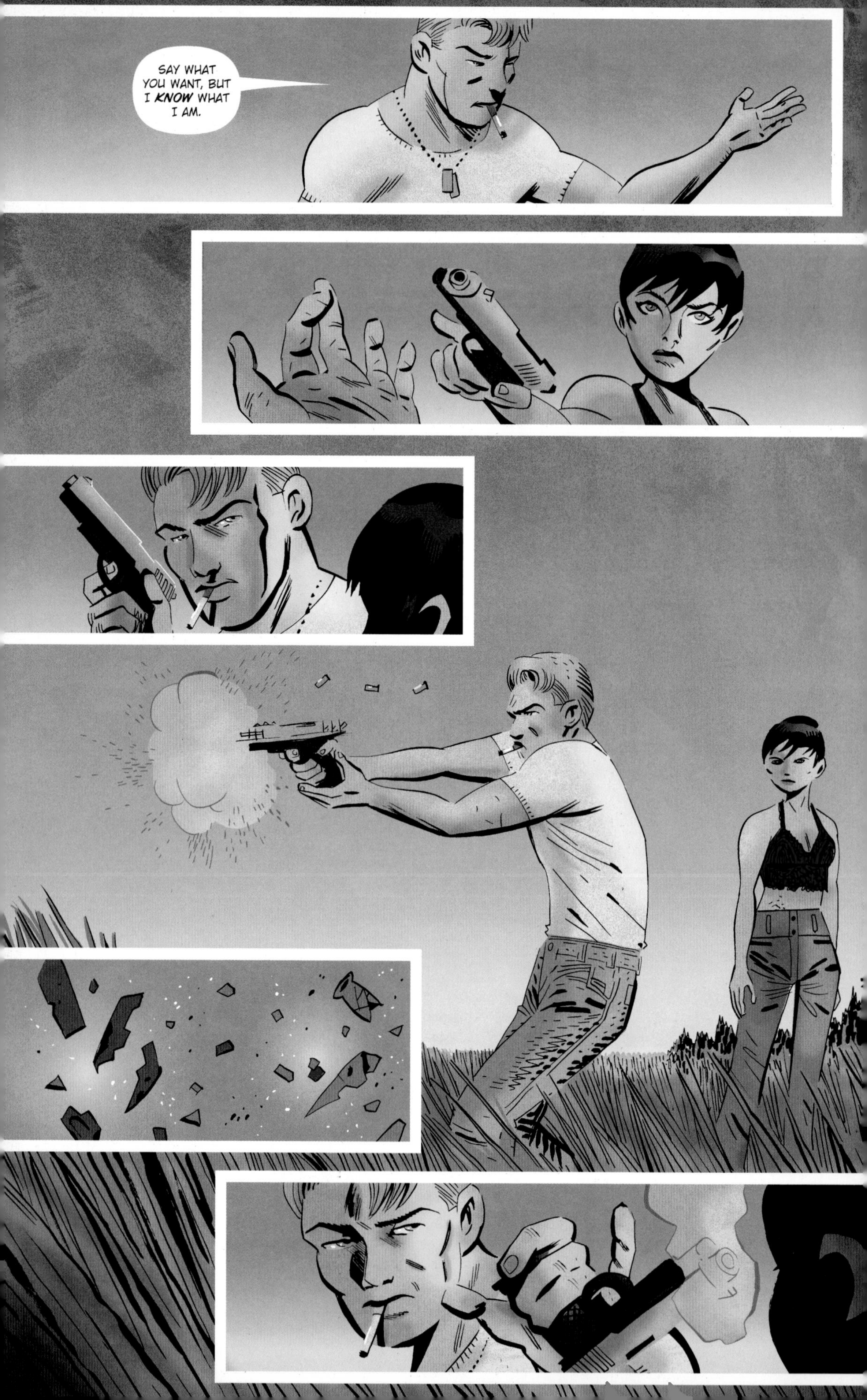
SAY WHAT YOU WANT, BUT I **KNOW** WHAT I AM.

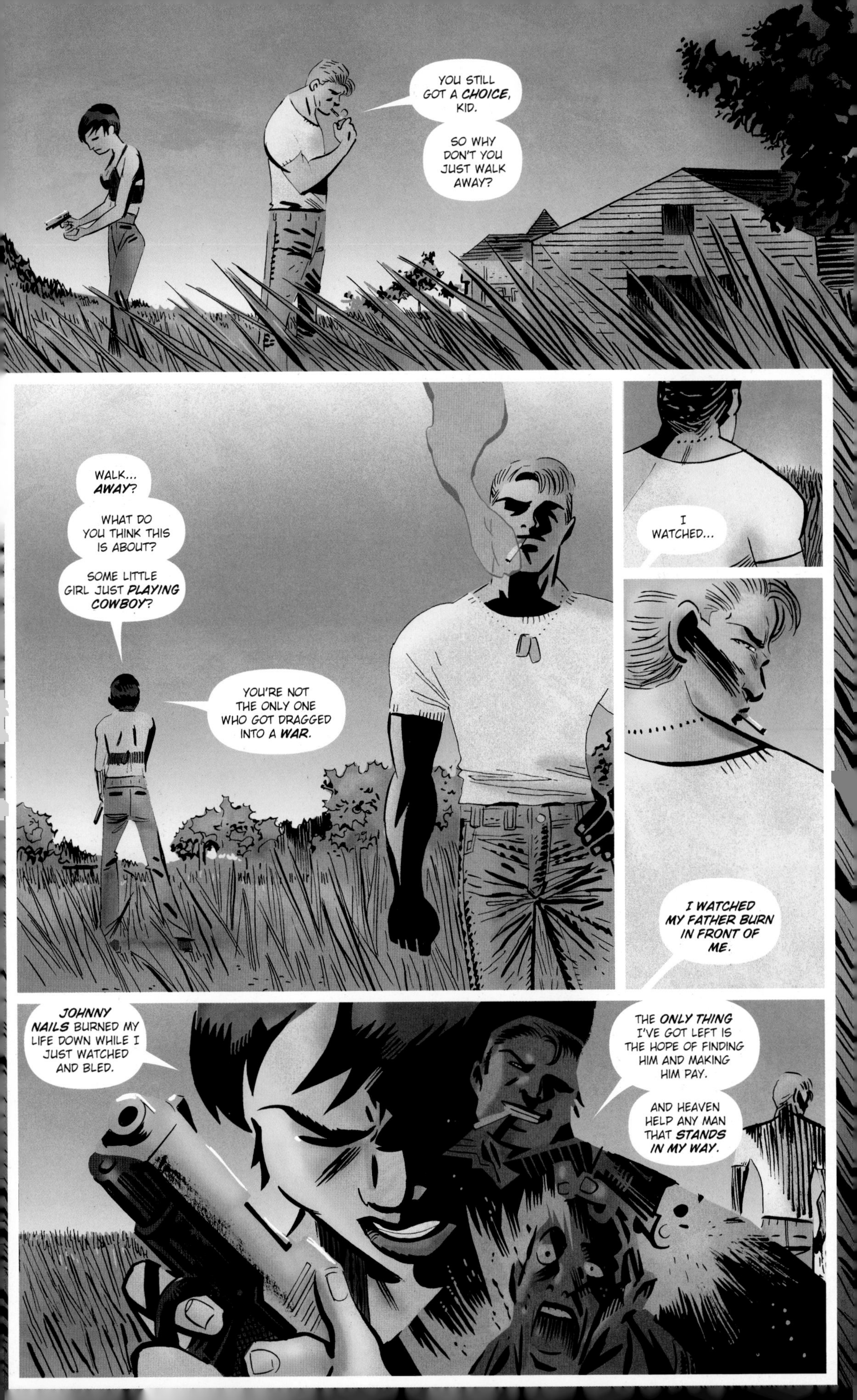
YOU STILL GOT A CHOICE, KID.
SO WHY DON'T YOU JUST WALK AWAY?
WALK... AWAY?
WHAT DO YOU THINK THIS IS ABOUT?
SOME LITTLE GIRL JUST PLAYING COWBOY?
YOU'RE NOT THE ONLY ONE WHO GOT DRAGGED INTO A WAR.
I WATCHED...
I WATCHED MY FATHER BURN IN FRONT OF ME.
JOHNNY NAILS BURNED MY LIFE DOWN WHILE I JUST WATCHED AND BLED.
THE ONLY THING I'VE GOT LEFT IS THE HOPE OF FINDING HIM AND MAKING HIM PAY.
AND HEAVEN HELP ANY MAN THAT STANDS IN MY WAY.

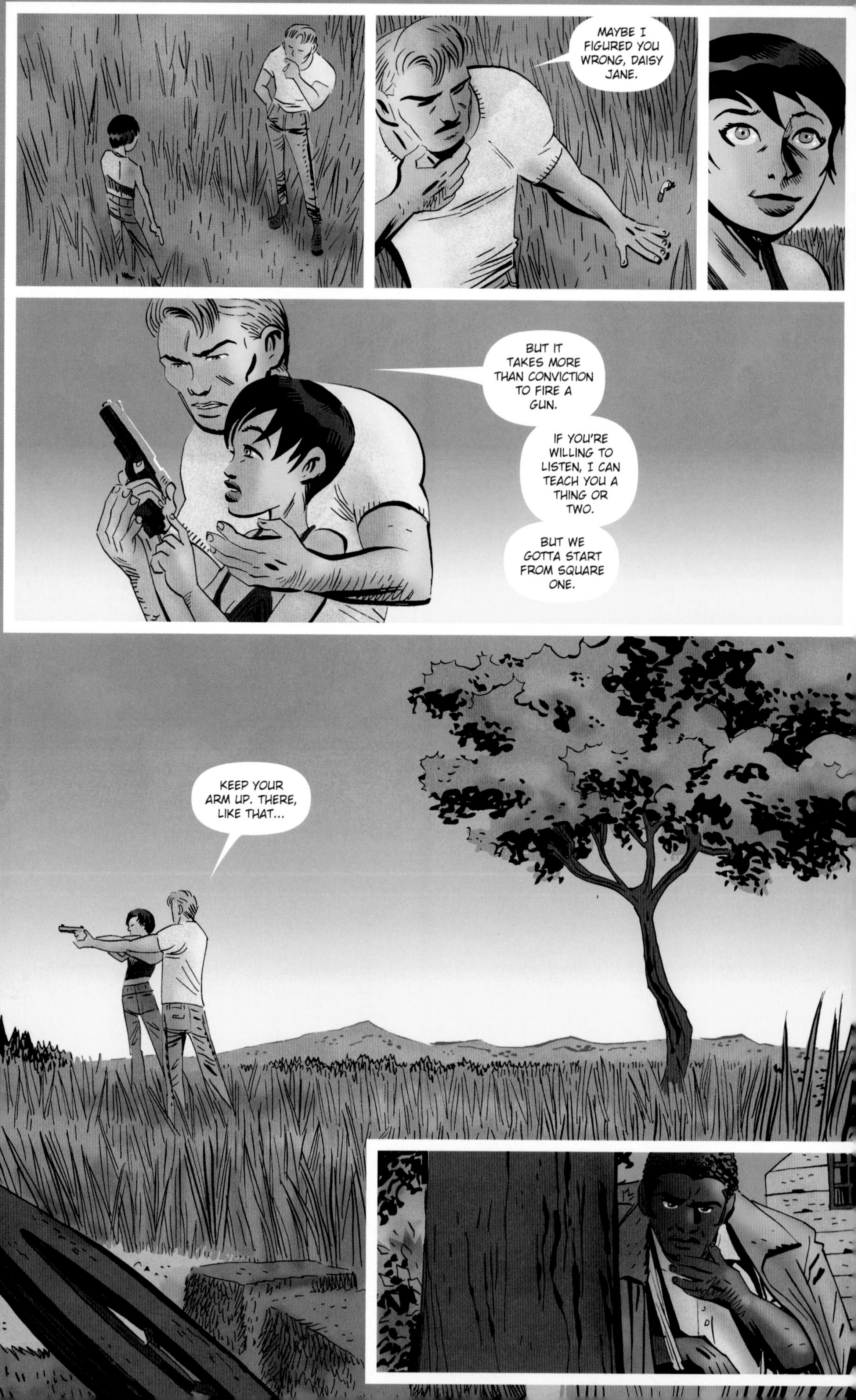
MAYBE I FIGURED YOU WRONG, DAISY JANE.
BUT IT TAKES MORE THAN CONVICTION TO FIRE A GUN.
IF YOU'RE WILLING TO LISTEN, I CAN TEACH YOU A THING OR TWO.
BUT WE GOTTA START FROM SQUARE ONE.
KEEP YOUR ARM UP. THERE, LIKE THAT...

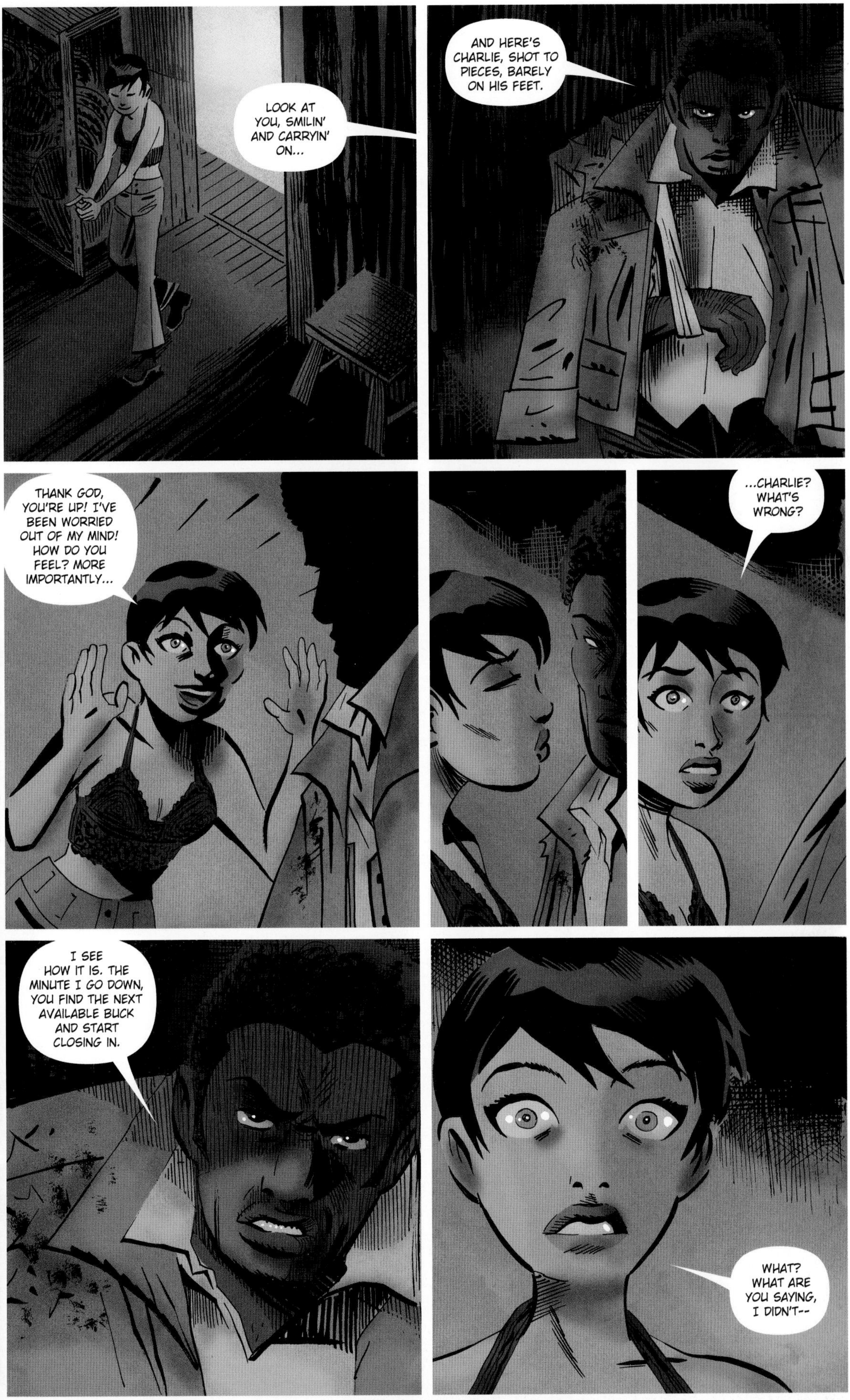
LOOK AT YOU, SMILIN' AND CARRYIN' ON...
AND HERE'S CHARLIE, SHOT TO PIECES, BARELY ON HIS FEET.
THANK GOD, YOU'RE UP! I'VE BEEN WORRIED OUT OF MY MIND! HOW DO YOU FEEL? MORE IMPORTANTLY...
...CHARLIE? WHAT'S WRONG?
I SEE HOW IT IS. THE MINUTE I GO DOWN, YOU FIND THE NEXT AVAILABLE BUCK AND START CLOSING IN.
WHAT? WHAT ARE YOU SAYING, I DIDN'T--

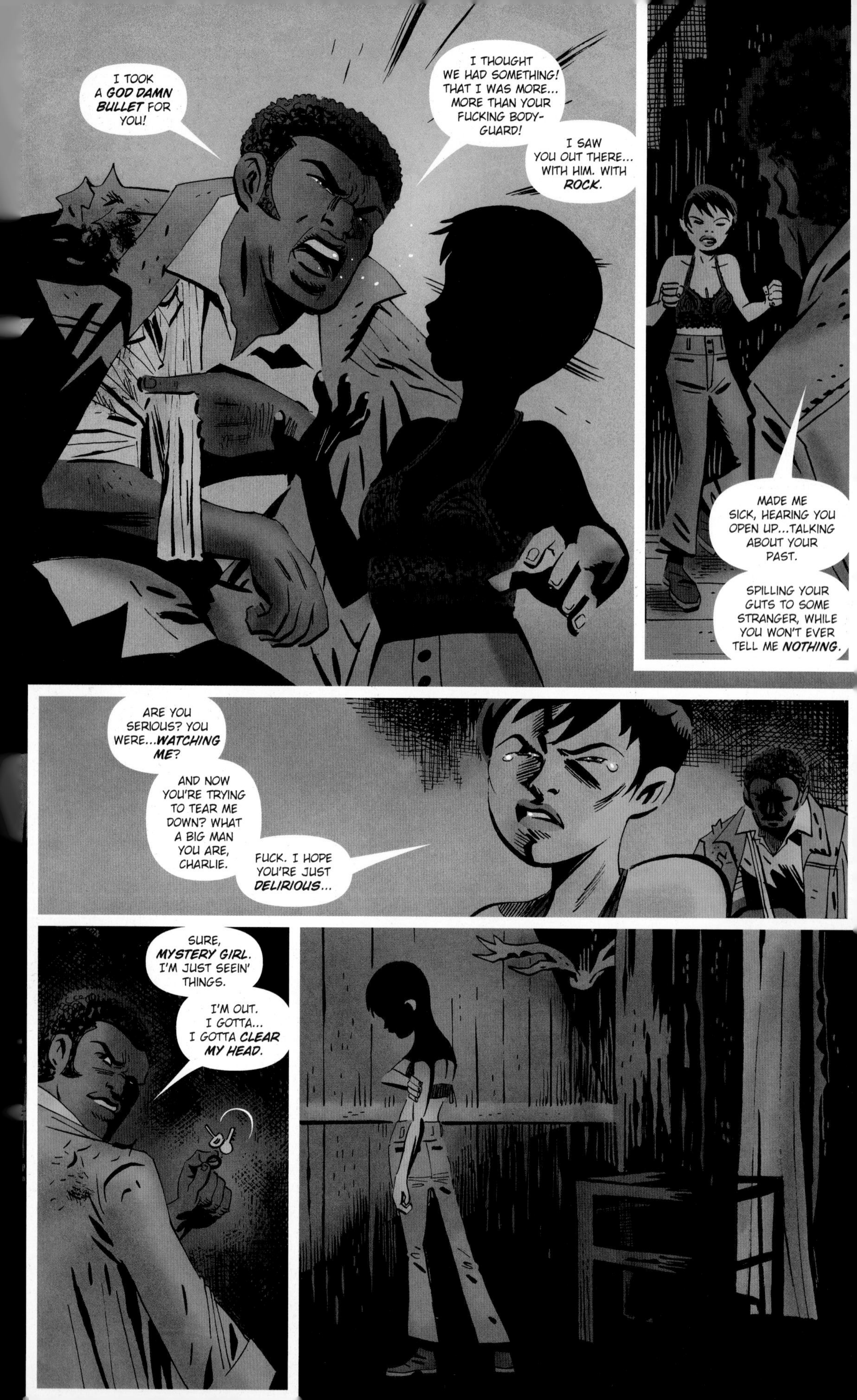
I TOOK A GOD DAMN BULLET FOR YOU!
I THOUGHT WE HAD SOMETHING! THAT I WAS MORE... MORE THAN YOUR FUCKING BODY-GUARD!
I SAW YOU OUT THERE... WITH HIM. WITH ROCK.
MADE ME SICK, HEARING YOU OPEN UP...TALKING ABOUT YOUR PAST.
SPILLING YOUR GUTS TO SOME STRANGER, WHILE YOU WON'T EVER TELL ME NOTHING.
ARE YOU SERIOUS? YOU WERE...WATCHING ME?
AND NOW YOU'RE TRYING TO TEAR ME DOWN? WHAT A BIG MAN YOU ARE, CHARLIE.
FUCK. I HOPE YOU'RE JUST DELIRIOUS...
SURE, MYSTERY GIRL. I'M JUST SEEIN' THINGS.
I'M OUT. I GOTTA... I GOTTA CLEAR MY HEAD.

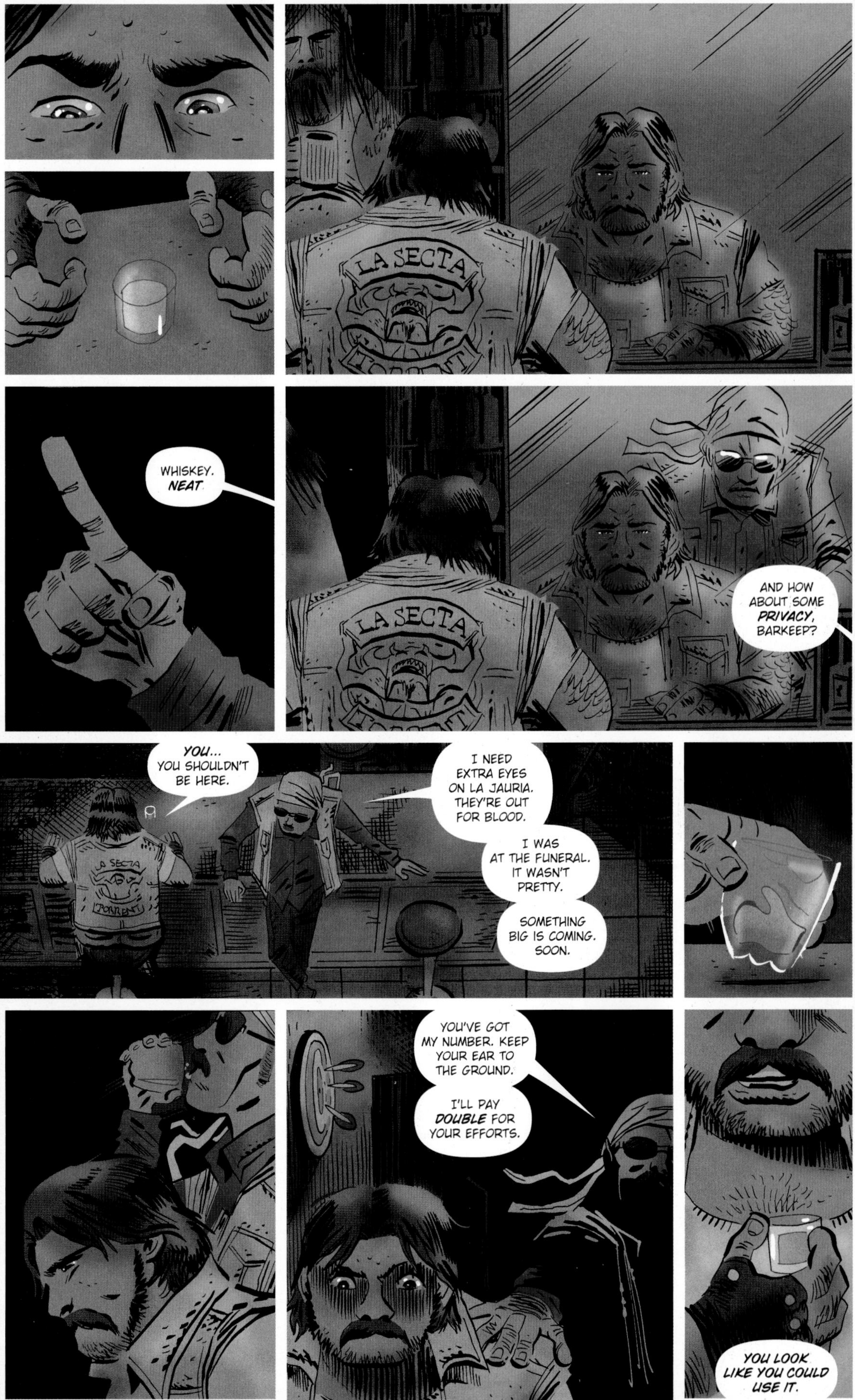
LA SECTA
TORRENT
WHISKEY. NEAT.
LA SECTA
TORRENT
AND HOW ABOUT SOME PRIVACY, BARKEEP?
YOU... YOU SHOULDN'T BE HERE.
LA SECTA
TORRENT
I NEED EXTRA EYES ON LA JAURIA. THEY'RE OUT FOR BLOOD.
I WAS AT THE FUNERAL. IT WASN'T PRETTY.
SOMETHING BIG IS COMING. SOON.
YOU'VE GOT MY NUMBER. KEEP YOUR EAR TO THE GROUND.
I'LL PAY DOUBLE FOR YOUR EFFORTS.
YOU LOOK LIKE YOU COULD USE IT.

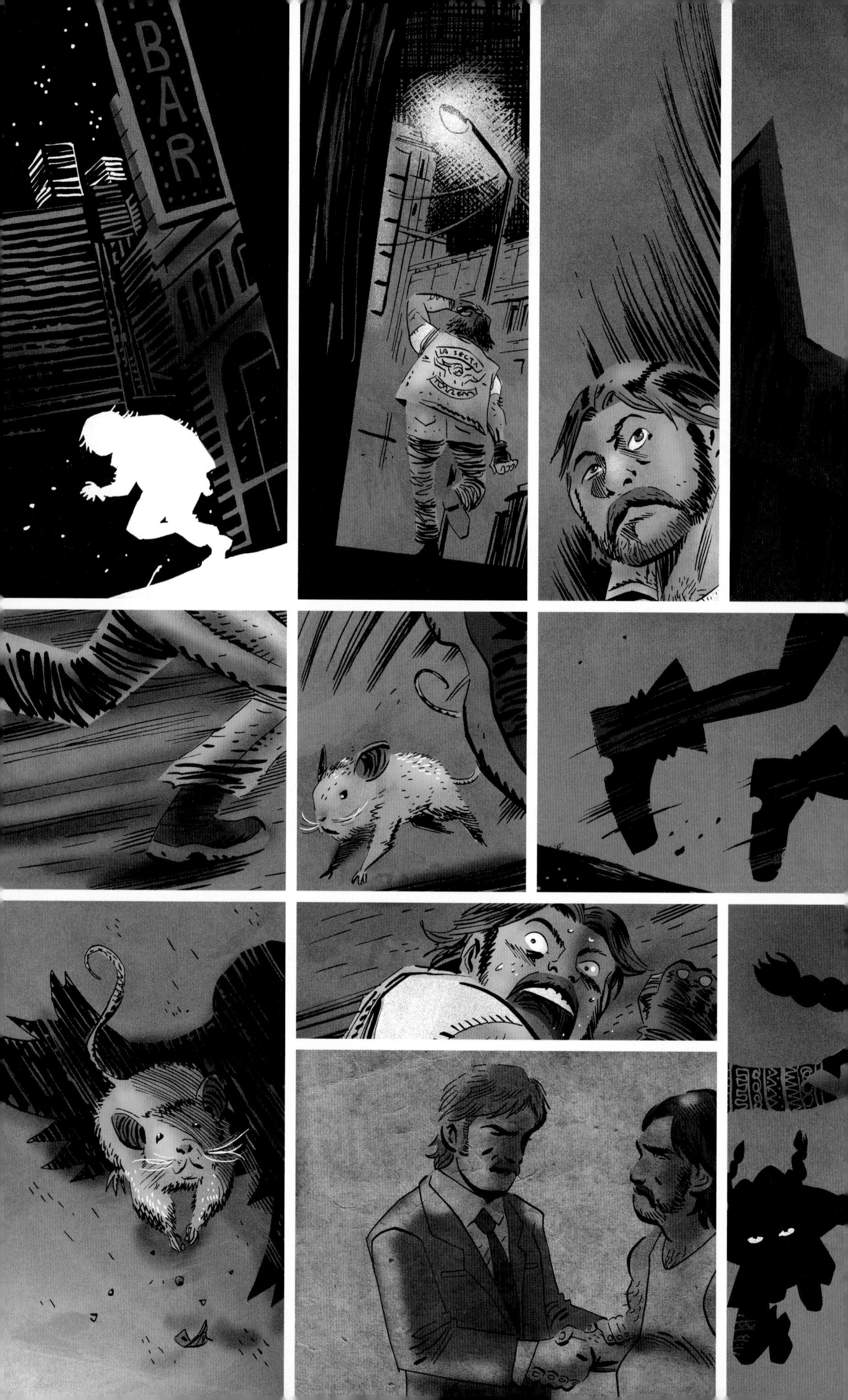

BAR
LA SECTA

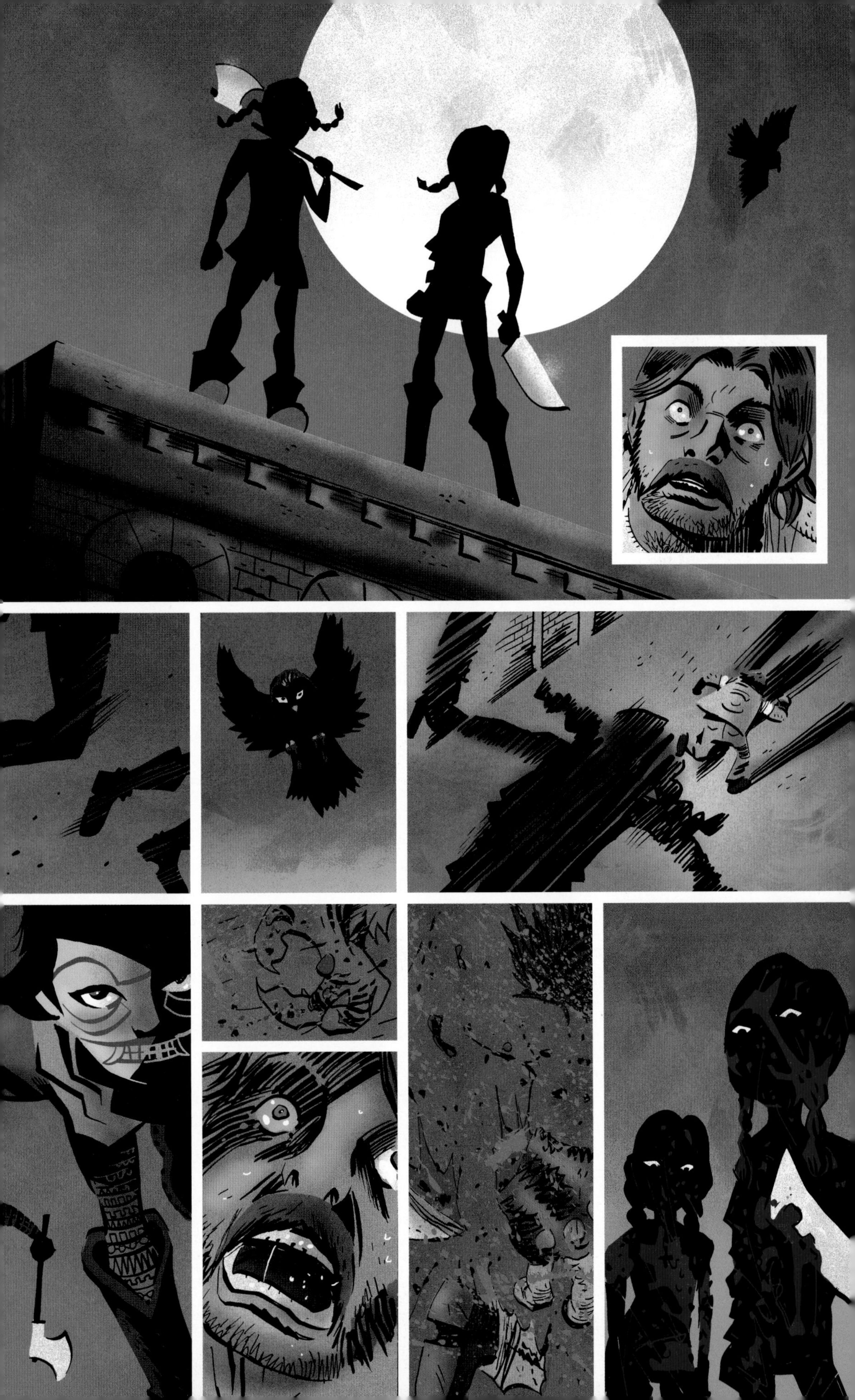

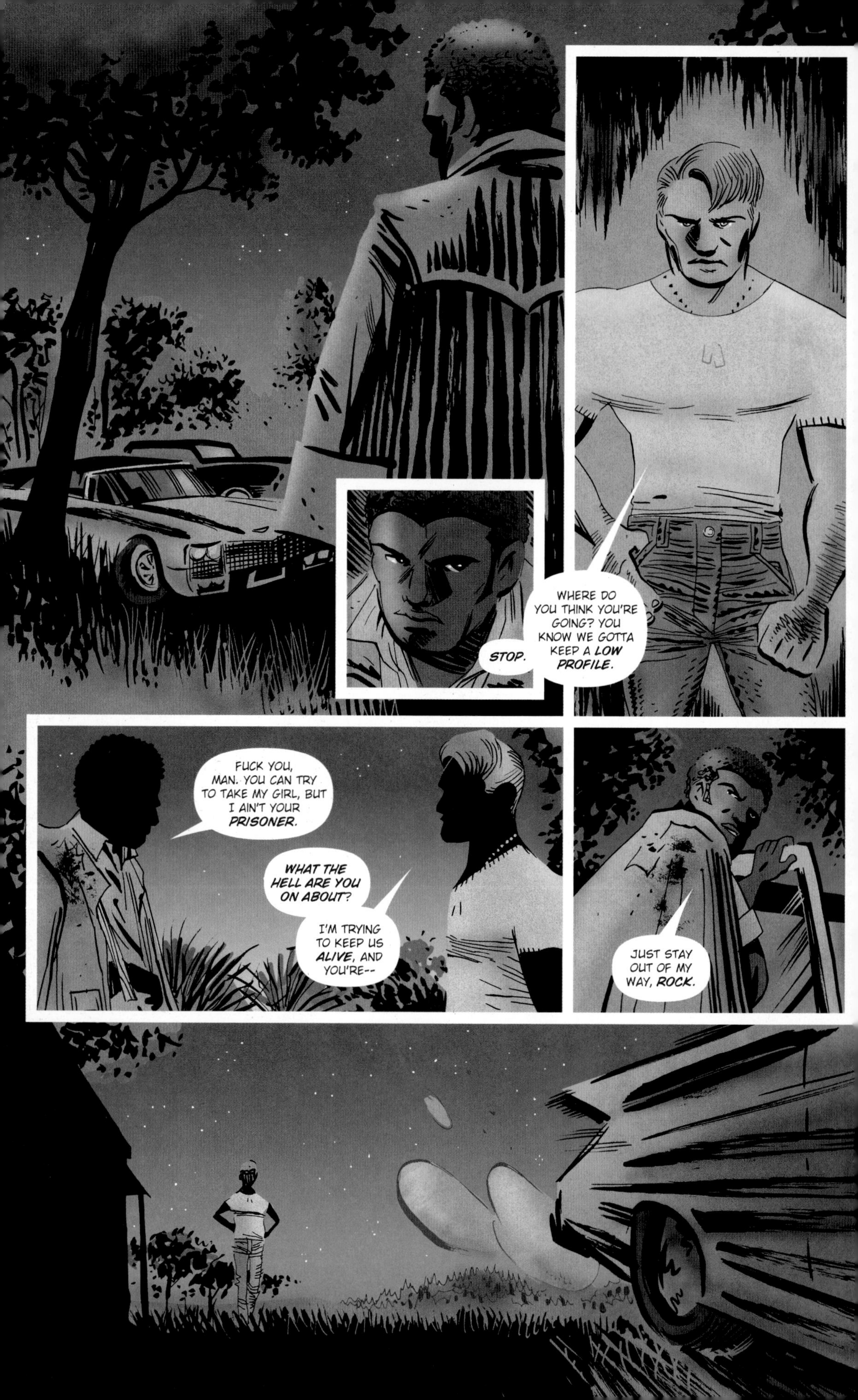
STOP.
WHERE DO YOU THINK YOU'RE GOING? YOU KNOW WE GOTTA KEEP A LOW PROFILE.
FUCK YOU, MAN. YOU CAN TRY TO TAKE MY GIRL, BUT I AIN'T YOUR PRISONER.
WHAT THE HELL ARE YOU ON ABOUT?
I'M TRYING TO KEEP US ALIVE, AND YOU'RE--
JUST STAY OUT OF MY WAY, ROCK.

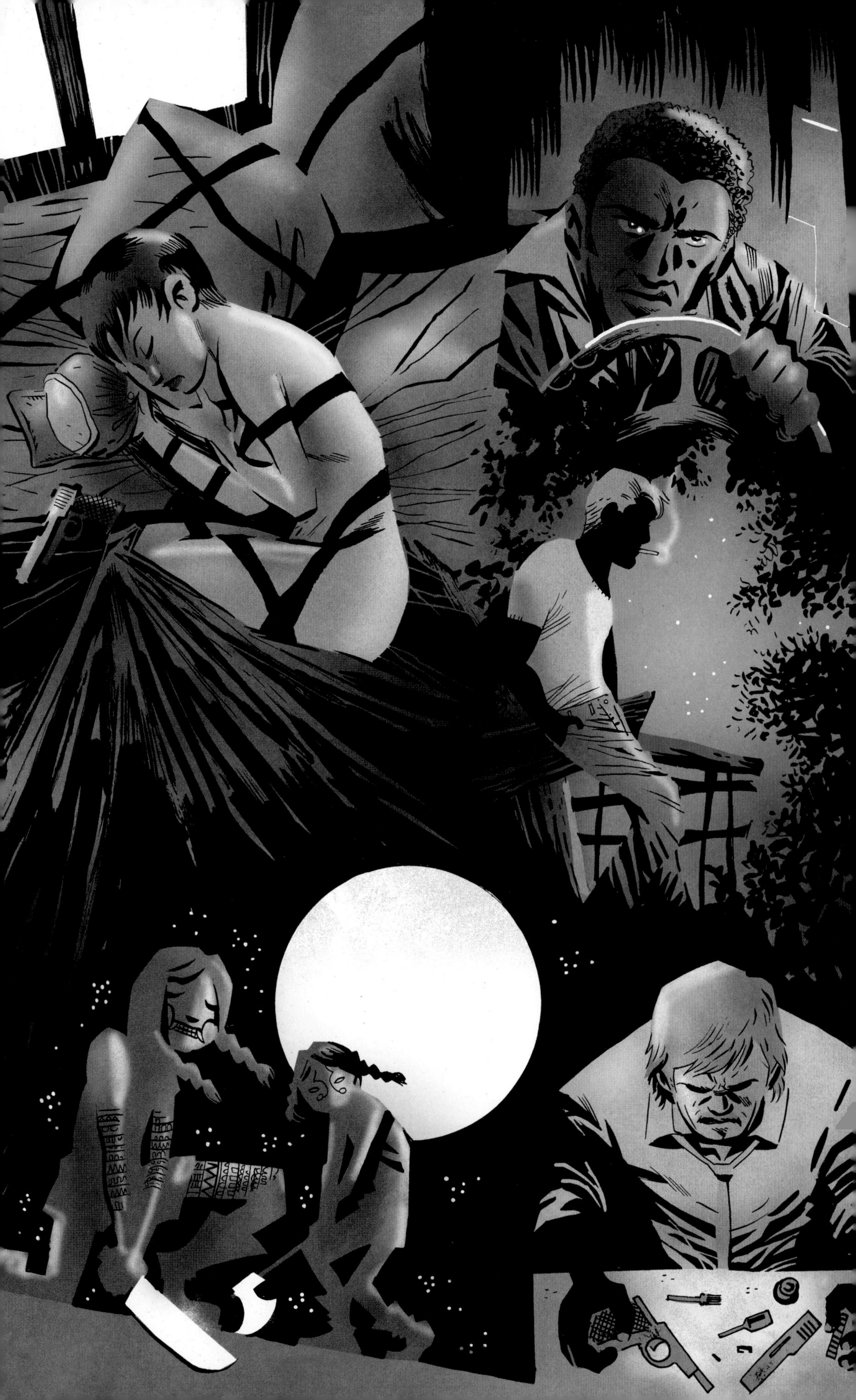

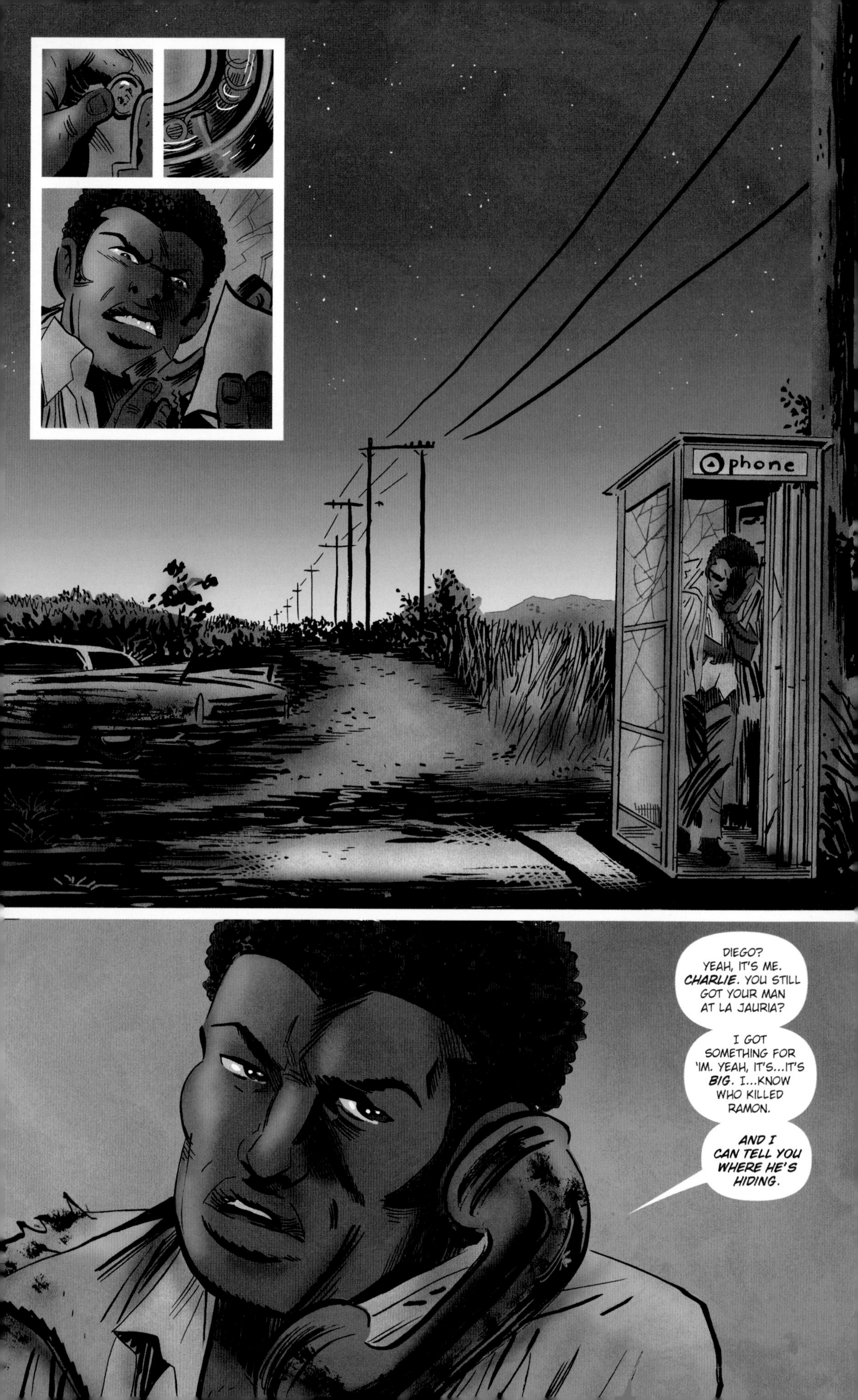
phone
DIEGO? YEAH, IT'S ME. CHARLIE. YOU STILL GOT YOUR MAN AT LA JAURIA?
I GOT SOMETHING FOR 'IM. YEAH, IT'S...IT'S BIG. I...KNOW WHO KILLED RAMON.
AND I CAN TELL YOU WHERE HE'S HIDING.

CHAPTER FIVE

"WHERE HAVE ALL THE GOOD TIMES GONE?"

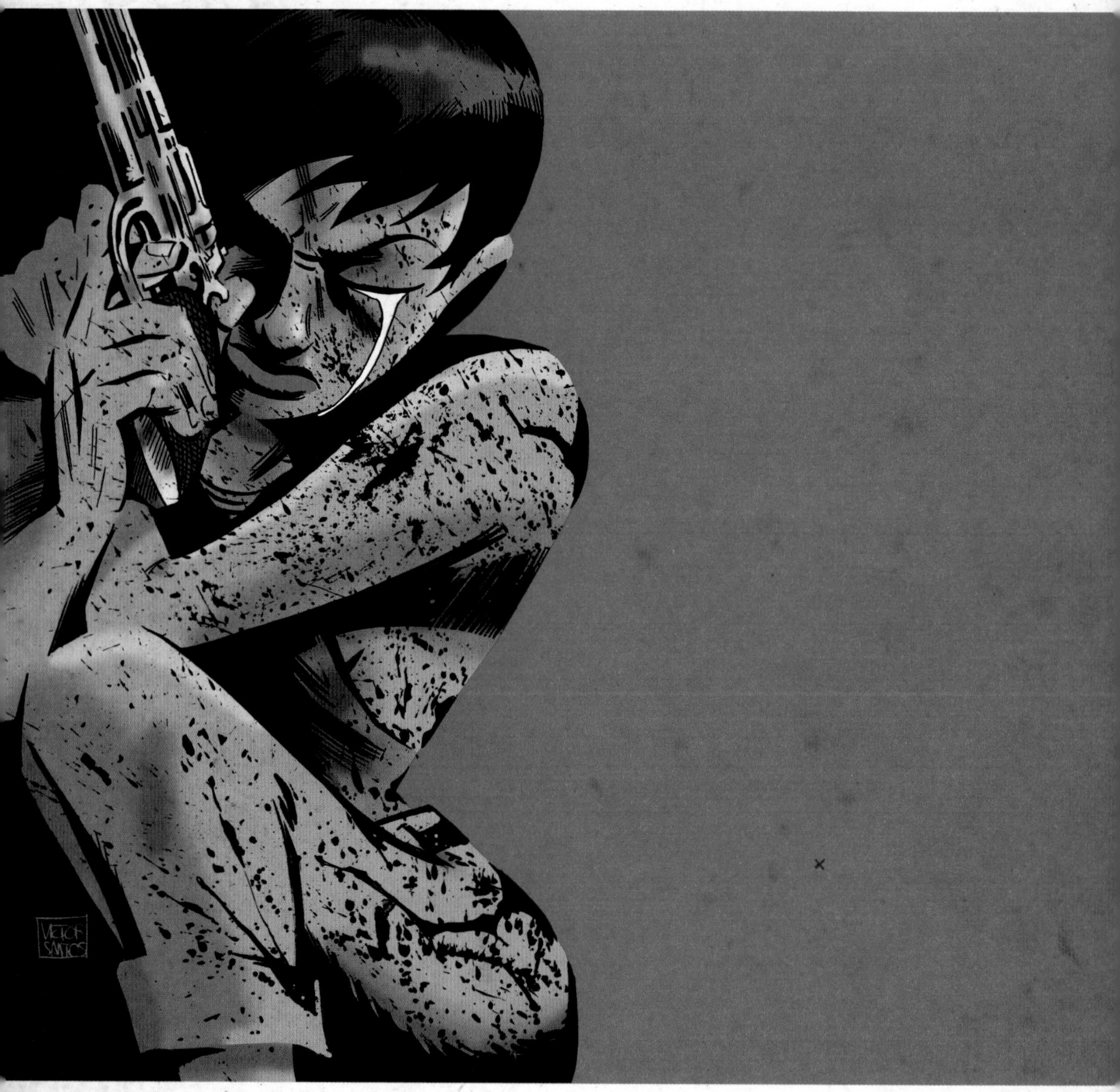

CALIFORNIA
1970

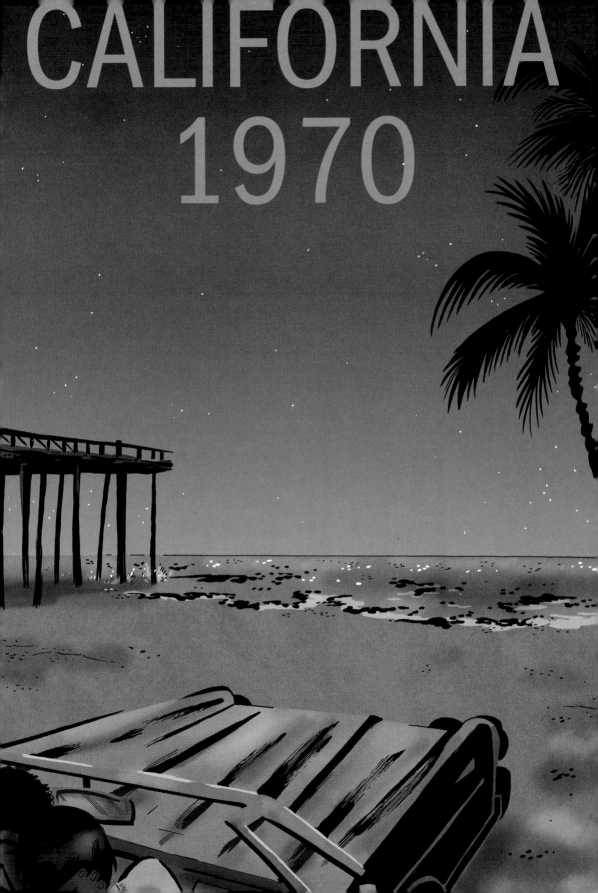

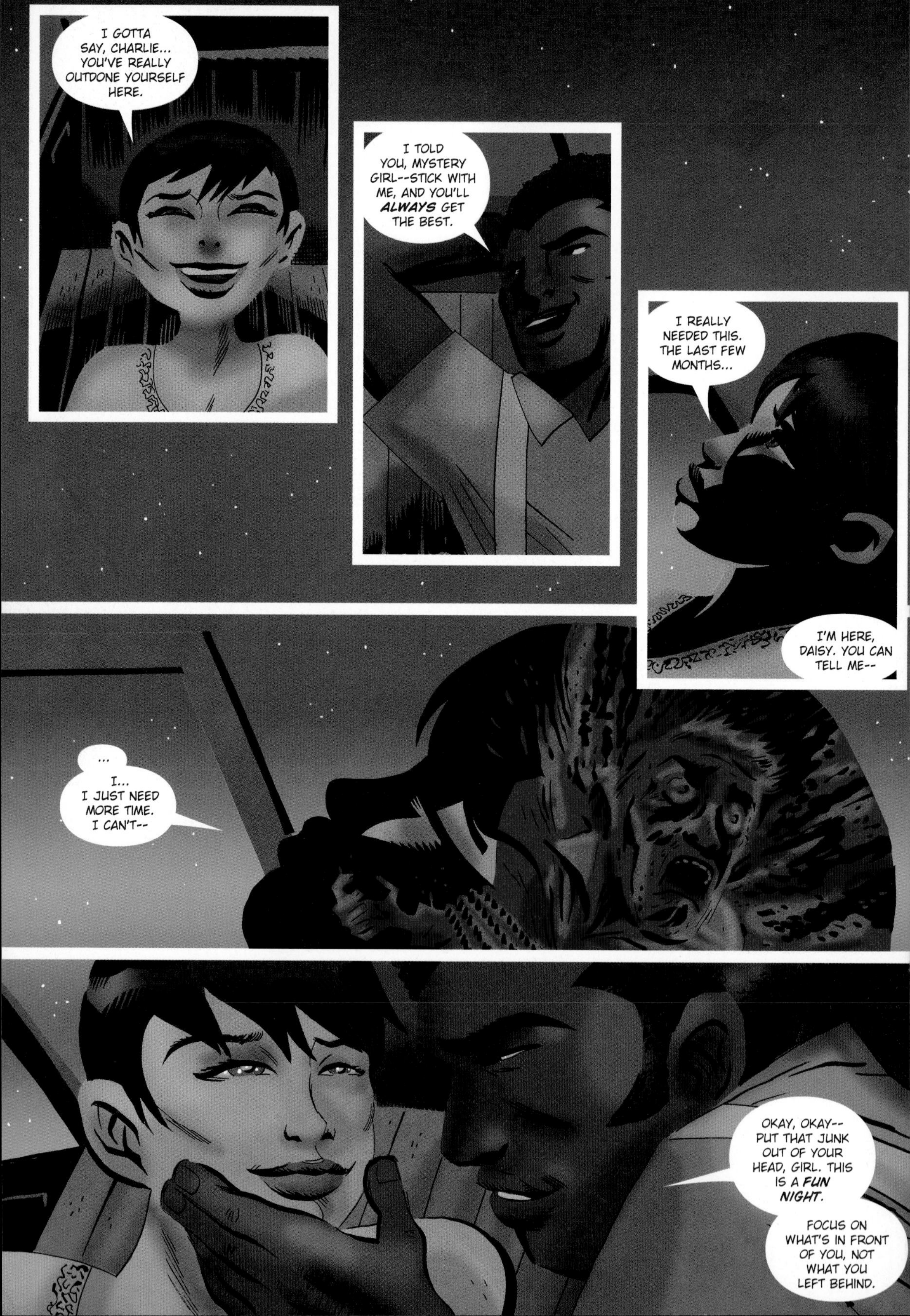
I GOTTA SAY, CHARLIE... YOU'VE REALLY OUTDONE YOURSELF HERE.
I TOLD YOU, MYSTERY GIRL--STICK WITH ME, AND YOU'LL ALWAYS GET THE BEST.
I REALLY NEEDED THIS. THE LAST FEW MONTHS...
I'M HERE, DAISY. YOU CAN TELL ME--
...
I... I JUST NEED MORE TIME. I CAN'T--
OKAY, OKAY--PUT THAT JUNK OUT OF YOUR HEAD, GIRL. THIS IS A FUN NIGHT.
FOCUS ON WHAT'S IN FRONT OF YOU, NOT WHAT YOU LEFT BEHIND.

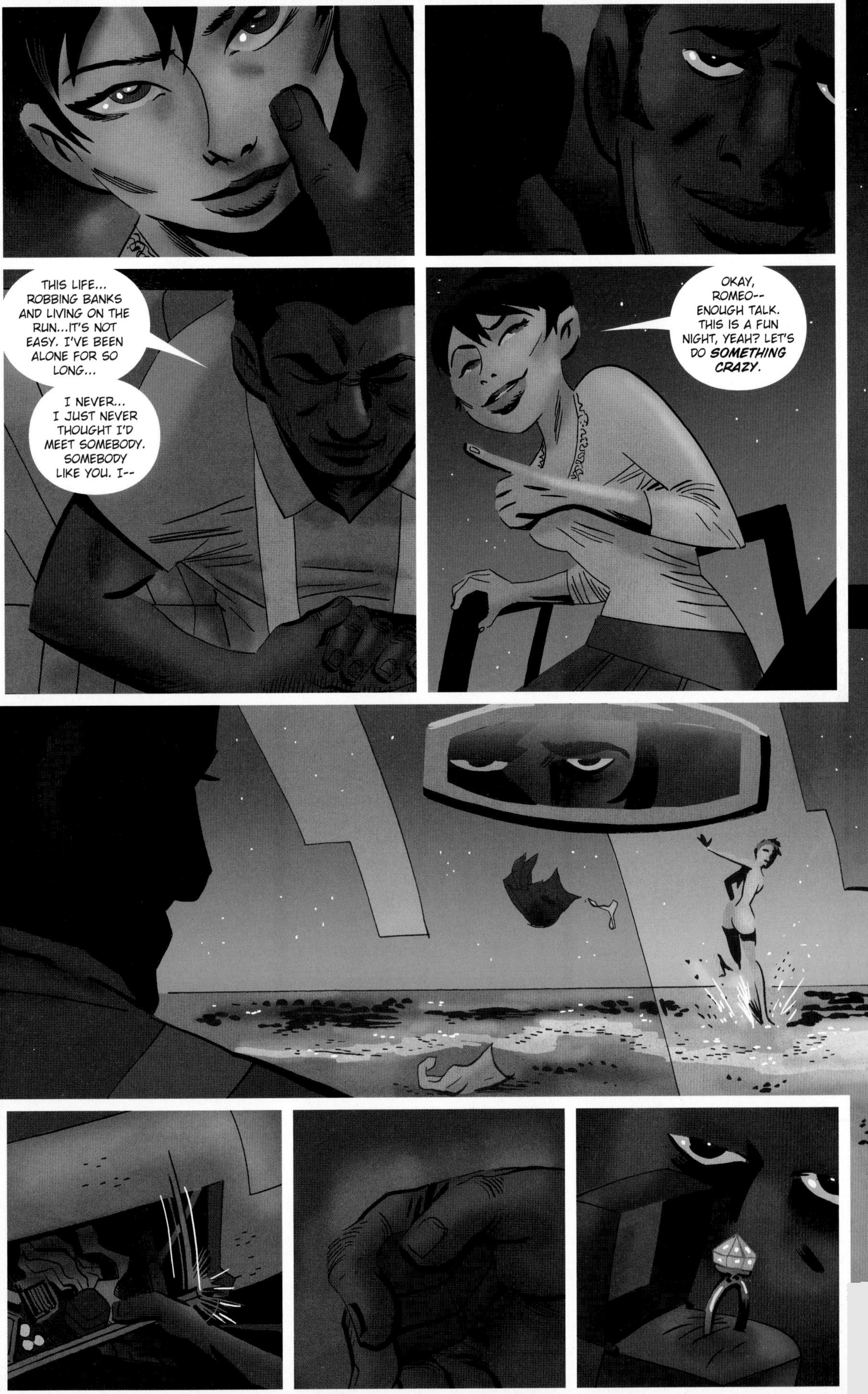
THIS LIFE... ROBBING BANKS AND LIVING ON THE RUN...IT'S NOT EASY. I'VE BEEN ALONE FOR SO LONG...
I NEVER... I JUST NEVER THOUGHT I'D MEET SOMEBODY. SOMEBODY LIKE YOU. I--
OKAY, ROMEO-- ENOUGH TALK. THIS IS A FUN NIGHT, YEAH? LET'S DO SOMETHING CRAZY.

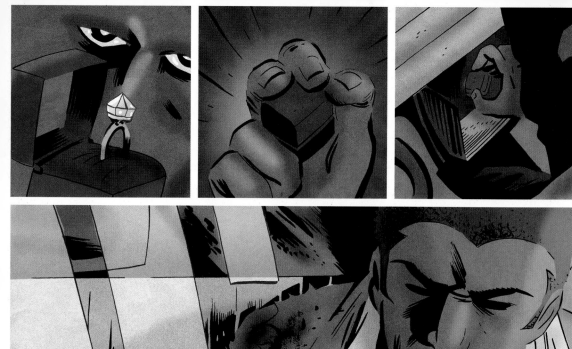

NEW MEXICO
1971

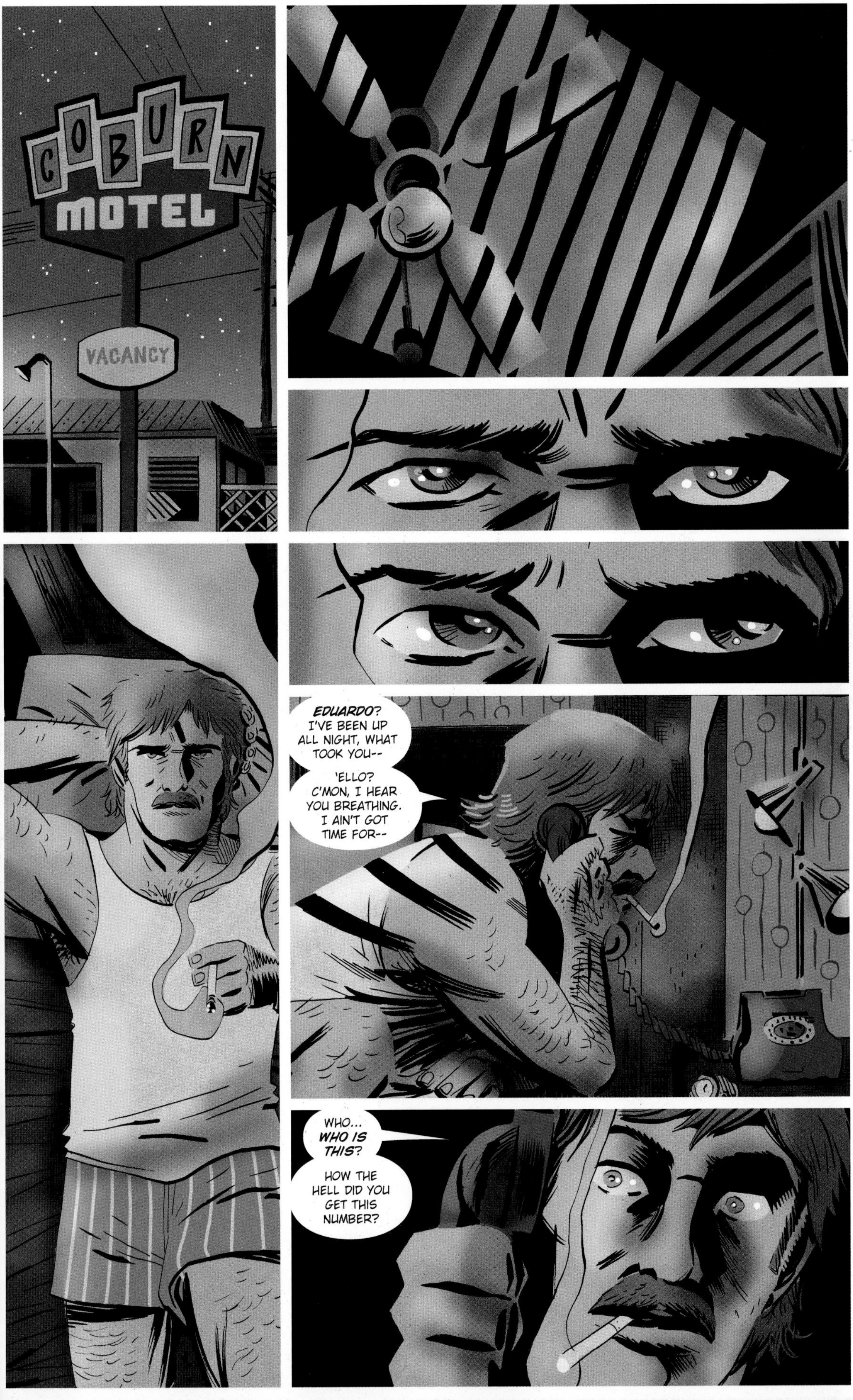
COBURN
MOTEL
VACANCY
EDUARDO? I'VE BEEN UP ALL NIGHT, WHAT TOOK YOU--
'ELLO? C'MON, I HEAR YOU BREATHING. I AIN'T GOT TIME FOR--
WHO... WHO IS THIS?
HOW THE HELL DID YOU GET THIS NUMBER?

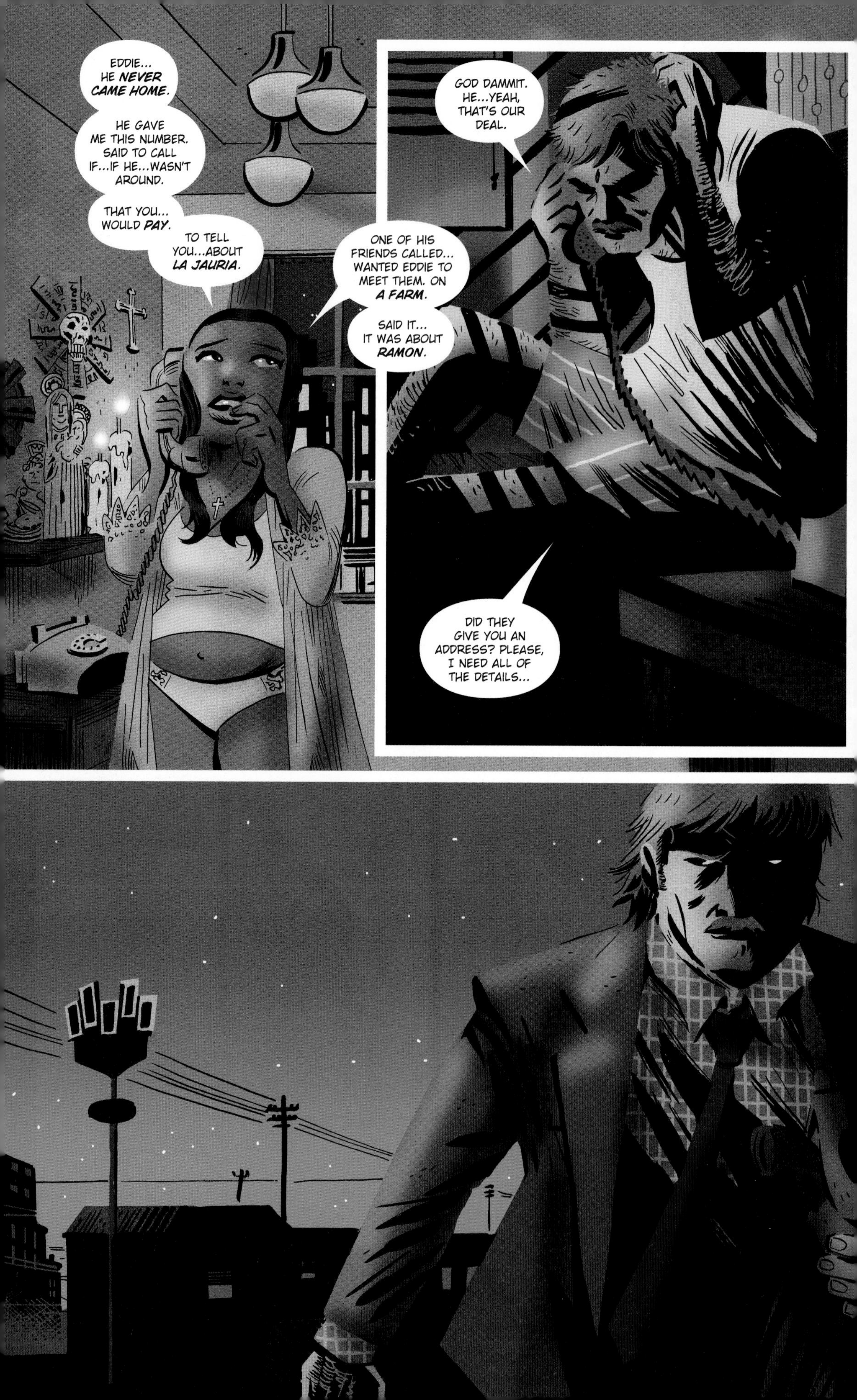
EDDIE... HE NEVER CAME HOME.
HE GAVE ME THIS NUMBER. SAID TO CALL IF...IF HE...WASN'T AROUND.
THAT YOU... WOULD PAY.
TO TELL YOU...ABOUT LA JAURIA.
GOD DAMMIT. HE...YEAH, THAT'S OUR DEAL.
ONE OF HIS FRIENDS CALLED... WANTED EDDIE TO MEET THEM. ON A FARM.
SAID IT... IT WAS ABOUT RAMON.
DID THEY GIVE YOU AN ADDRESS? PLEASE, I NEED ALL OF THE DETAILS...

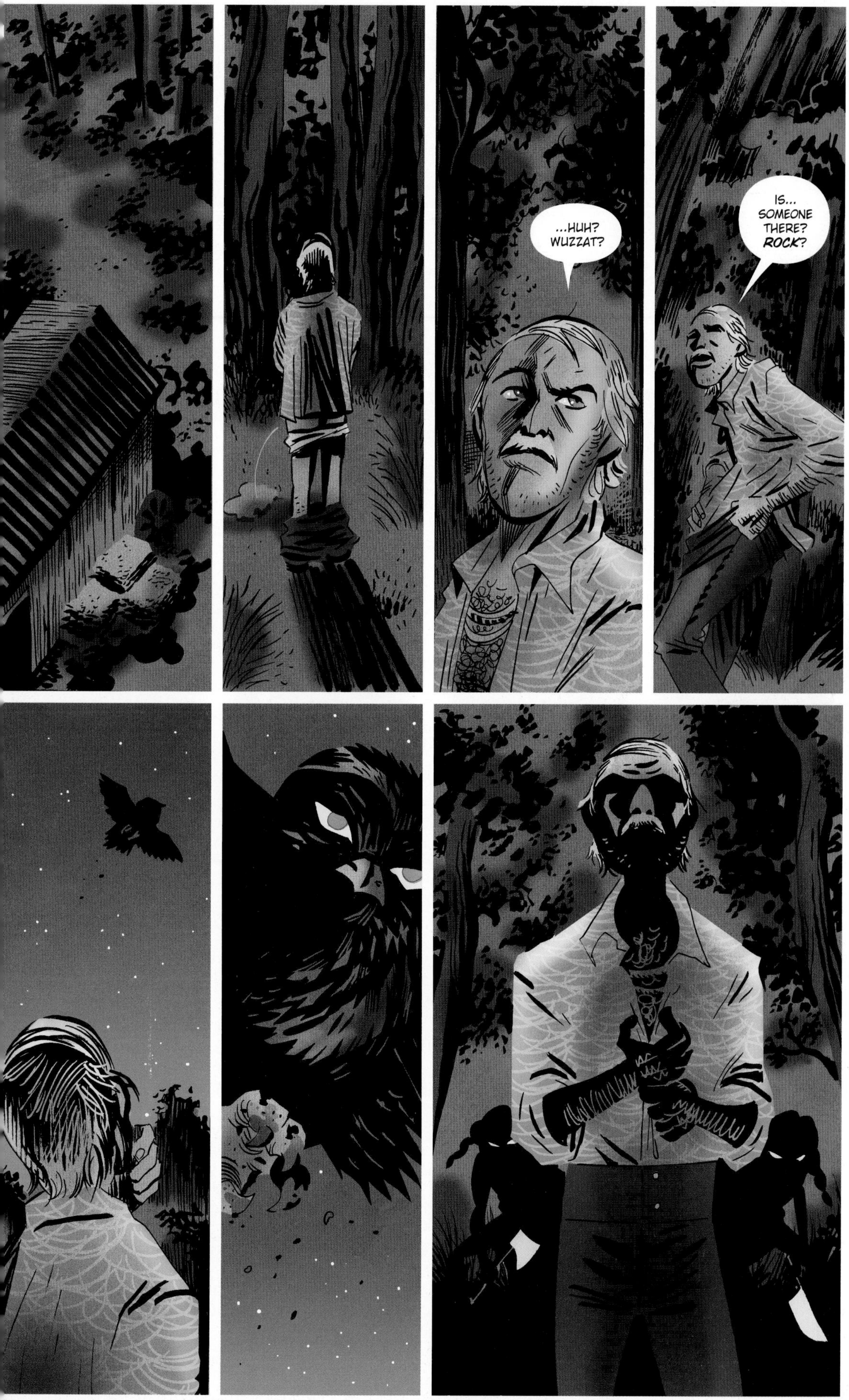
...HUH?
WUZZAT?
IS...
SOMEONE
THERE?
ROCK?

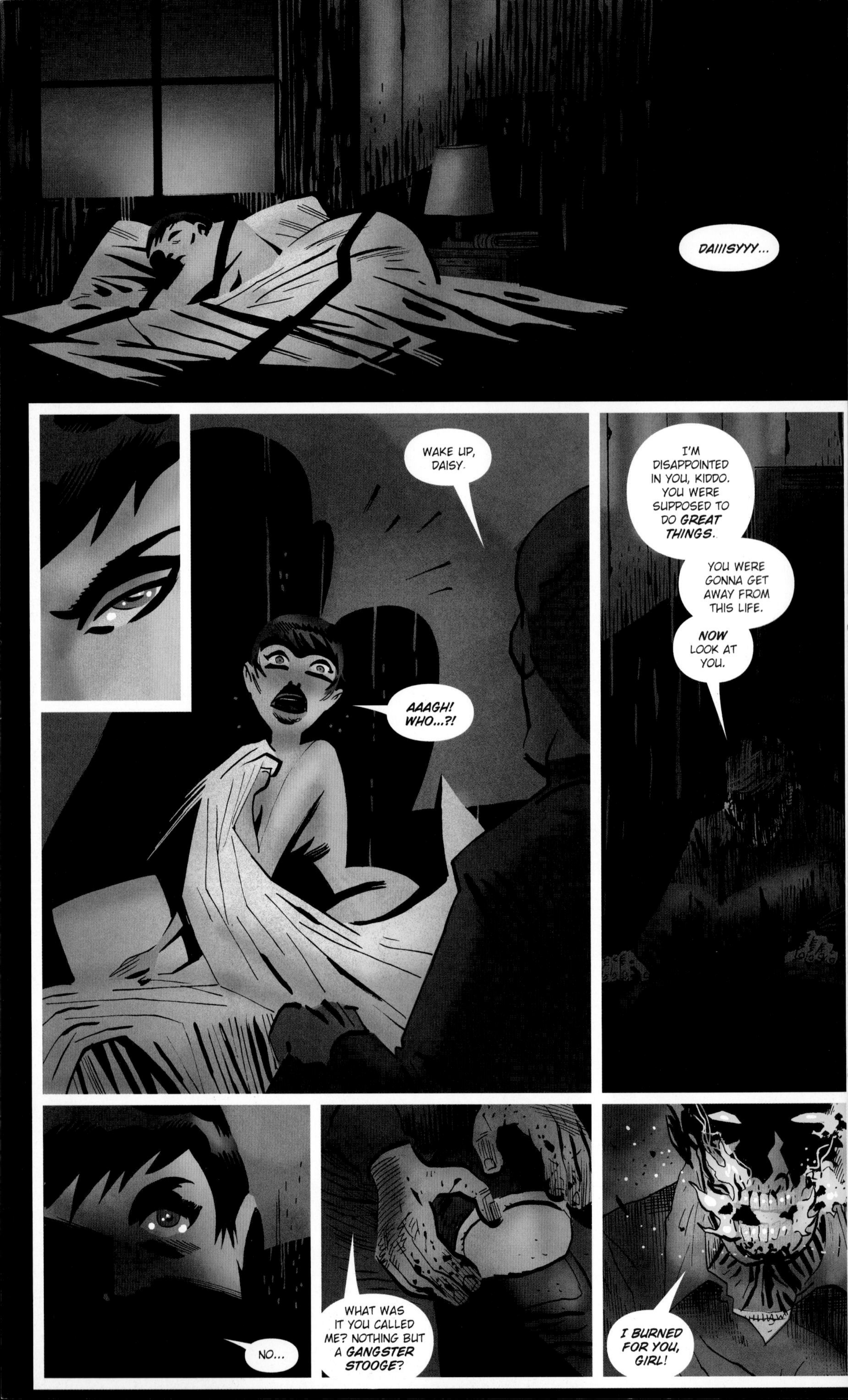
DAIIISYYY...
WAKE UP, DAISY.
AAAGH! WHO...?!
I'M DISAPPOINTED IN YOU, KIDDO. YOU WERE SUPPOSED TO DO GREAT THINGS.
YOU WERE GONNA GET AWAY FROM THIS LIFE.
NOW LOOK AT YOU.
NO...
WHAT WAS IT YOU CALLED ME? NOTHING BUT A GANGSTER STOOGE?
I BURNED FOR YOU, GIRL!

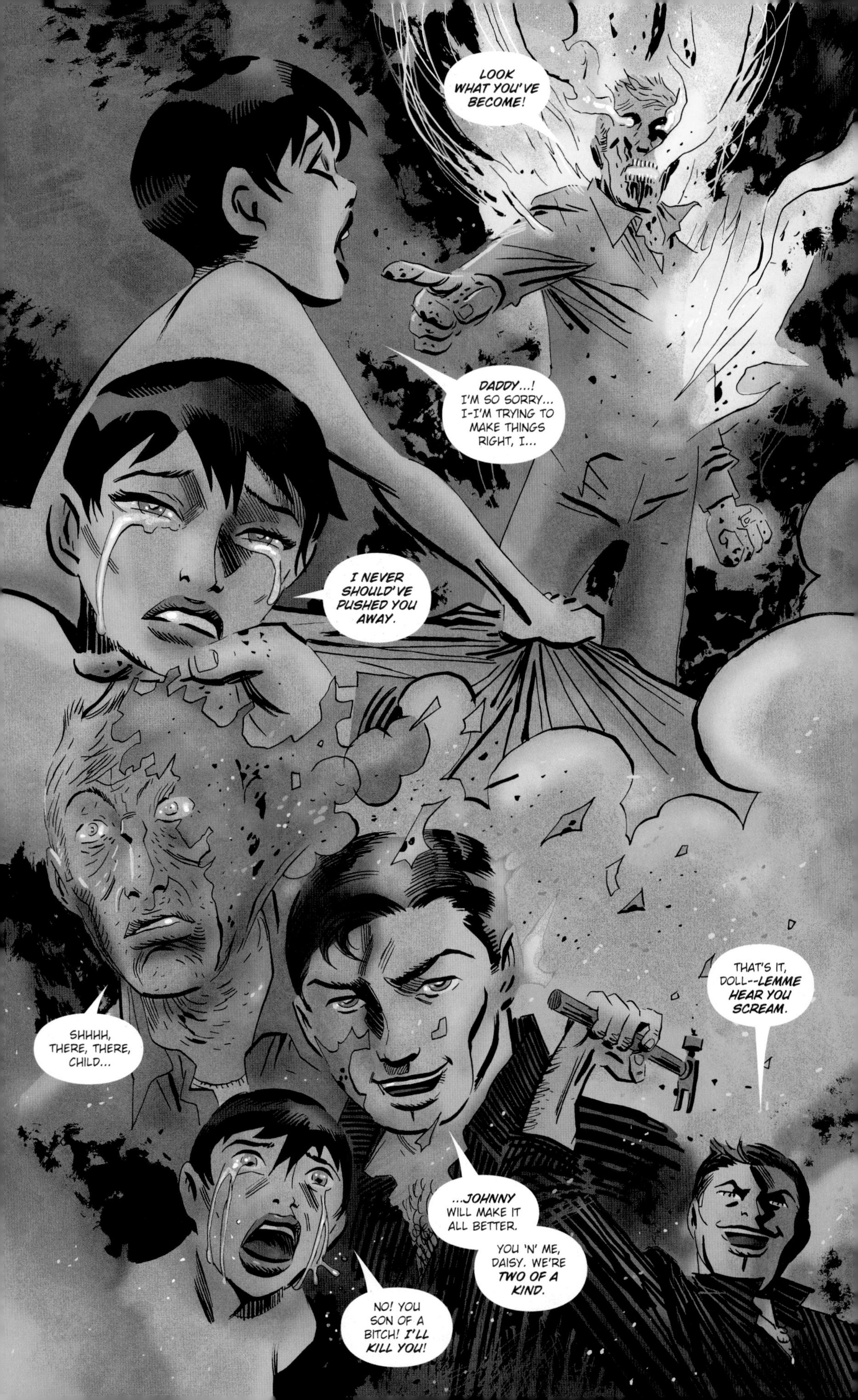
LOOK WHAT YOU'VE BECOME!
DADDY...! I'M SO SORRY... I-I'M TRYING TO MAKE THINGS RIGHT, I...
I NEVER SHOULD'VE PUSHED YOU AWAY.
SHHHH, THERE, THERE, CHILD...
...JOHNNY WILL MAKE IT ALL BETTER.
THAT'S IT, DOLL--LEMME HEAR YOU SCREAM.
YOU 'N' ME, DAISY. WE'RE TWO OF A KIND.
NO! YOU SON OF A BITCH! I'LL KILL YOU!

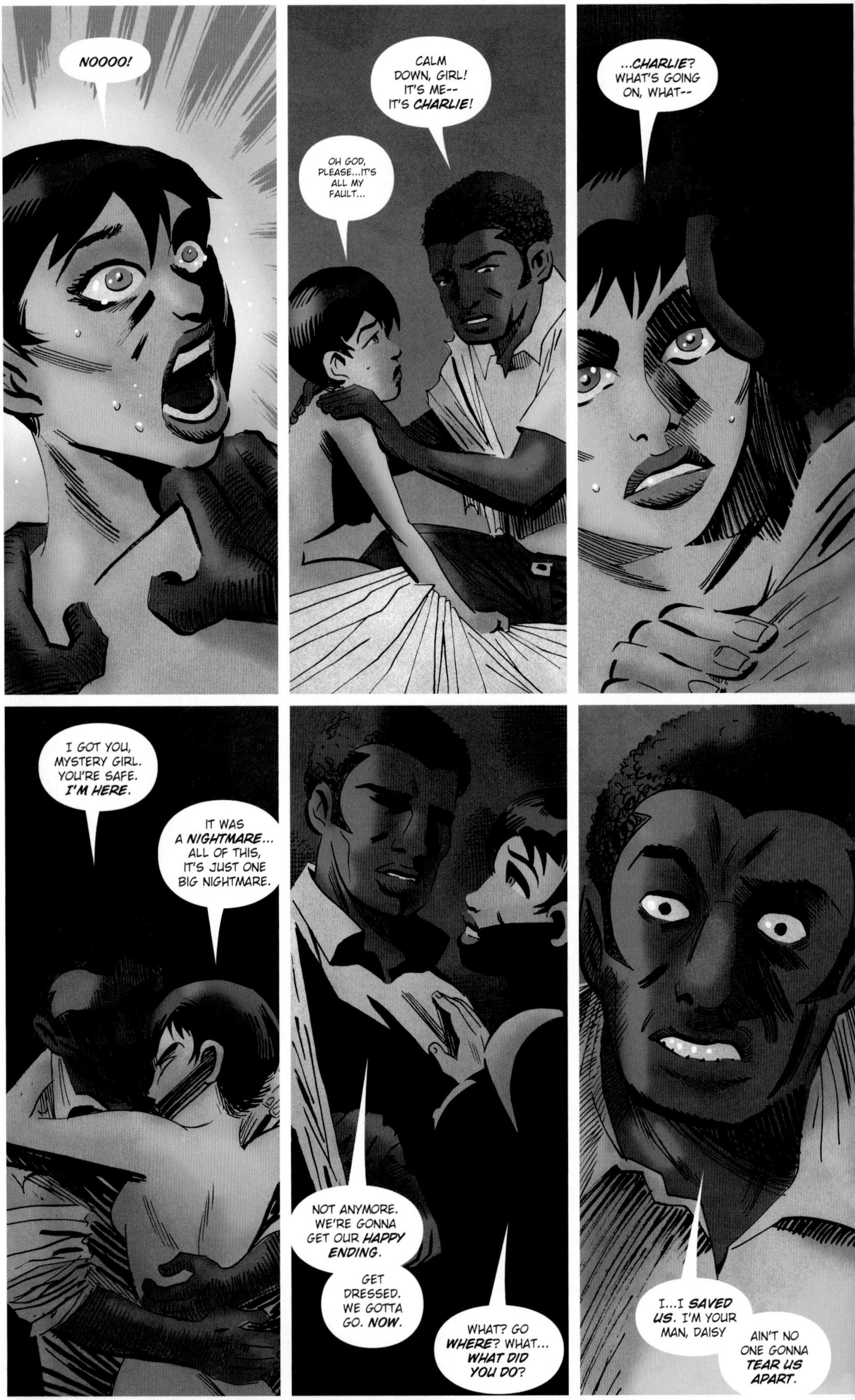
NOOOO!
CALM DOWN, GIRL! IT'S ME-- IT'S CHARLIE!
OH GOD, PLEASE...IT'S ALL MY FAULT...
...CHARLIE? WHAT'S GOING ON, WHAT--
I GOT YOU, MYSTERY GIRL. YOU'RE SAFE. I'M HERE.
IT WAS A NIGHTMARE... ALL OF THIS, IT'S JUST ONE BIG NIGHTMARE.
NOT ANYMORE. WE'RE GONNA GET OUR HAPPY ENDING.
GET DRESSED. WE GOTTA GO. NOW.
WHAT? GO WHERE? WHAT... WHAT DID YOU DO?
I...I SAVED US. I'M YOUR MAN, DAISY
AIN'T NO ONE GONNA TEAR US APART.

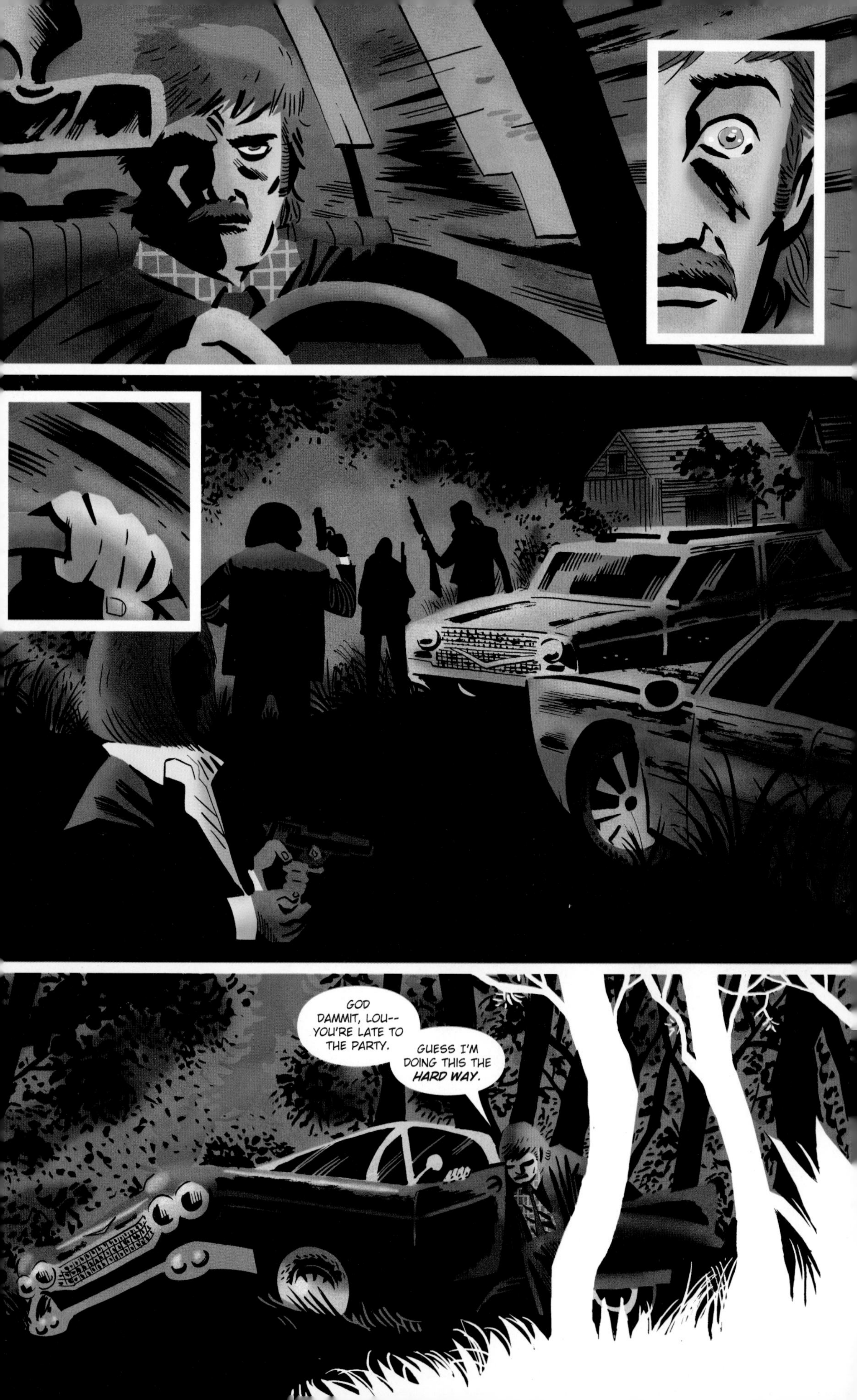
GOD DAMMIT, LOU-- YOU'RE LATE TO THE PARTY.
GUESS I'M DOING THIS THE HARD WAY.

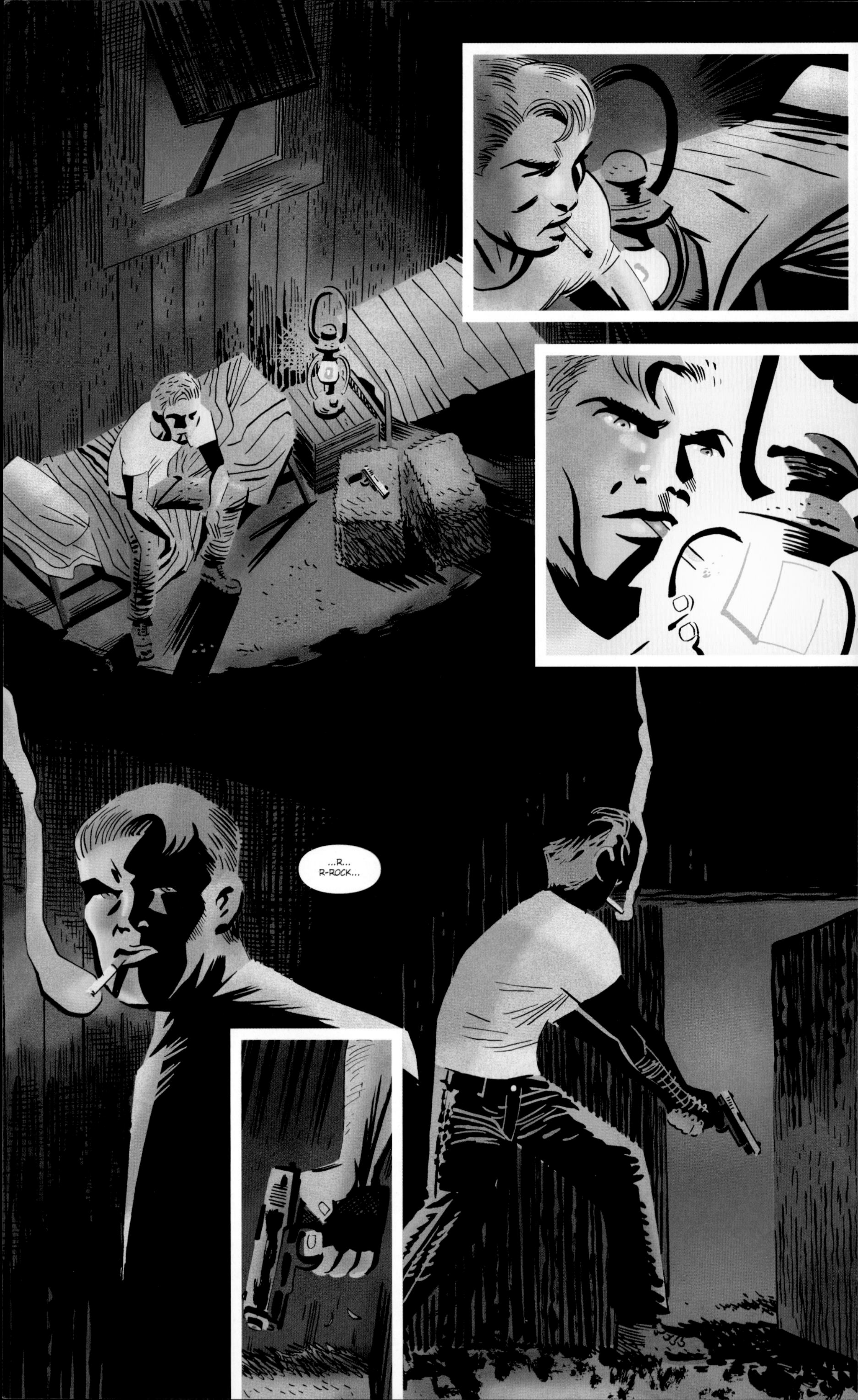
...R...
R-ROCK...

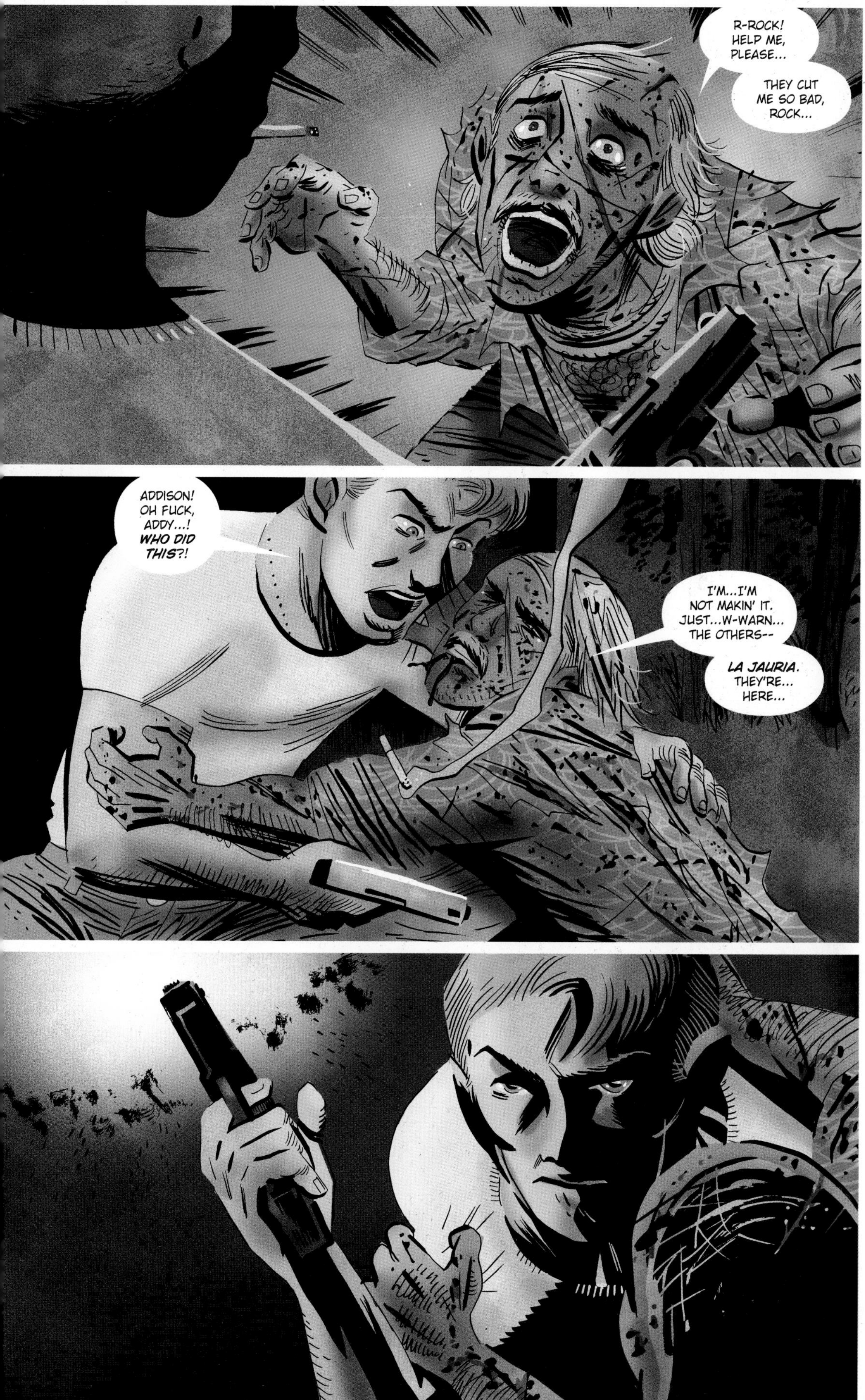
R-ROCK! HELP ME, PLEASE...
THEY CUT ME SO BAD, ROCK...
ADDISON! OH FUCK, ADDY...! **WHO DID THIS?!**
I'M...I'M NOT MAKIN' IT. JUST...W-WARN... THE OTHERS--
LA JAURIA. THEY'RE... HERE...

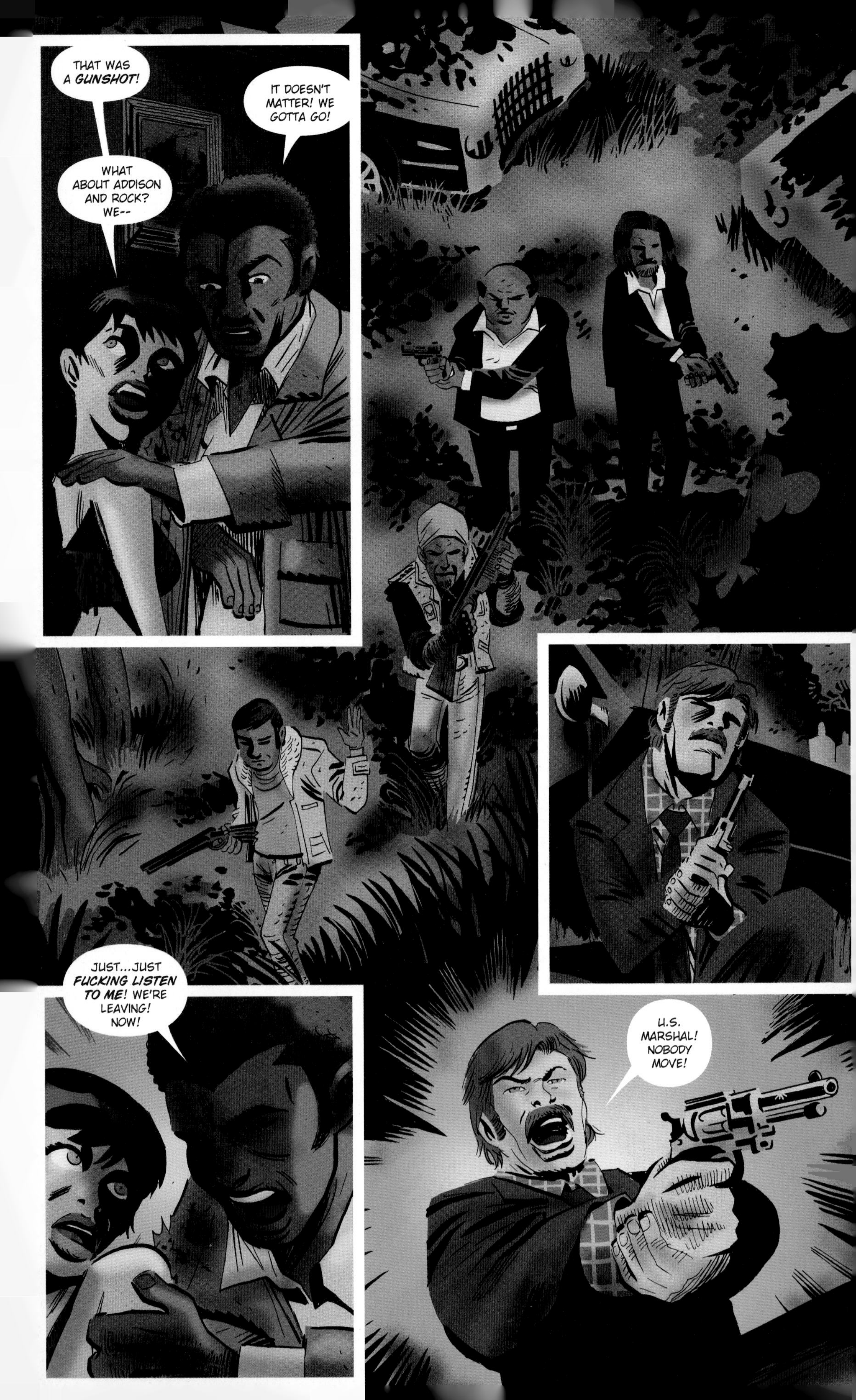
THAT WAS A GUNSHOT!
WHAT ABOUT ADDISON AND ROCK? WE--
IT DOESN'T MATTER! WE GOTTA GO!
JUST...JUST FUCKING LISTEN TO ME! WE'RE LEAVING! NOW!
U.S. MARSHAL! NOBODY MOVE!

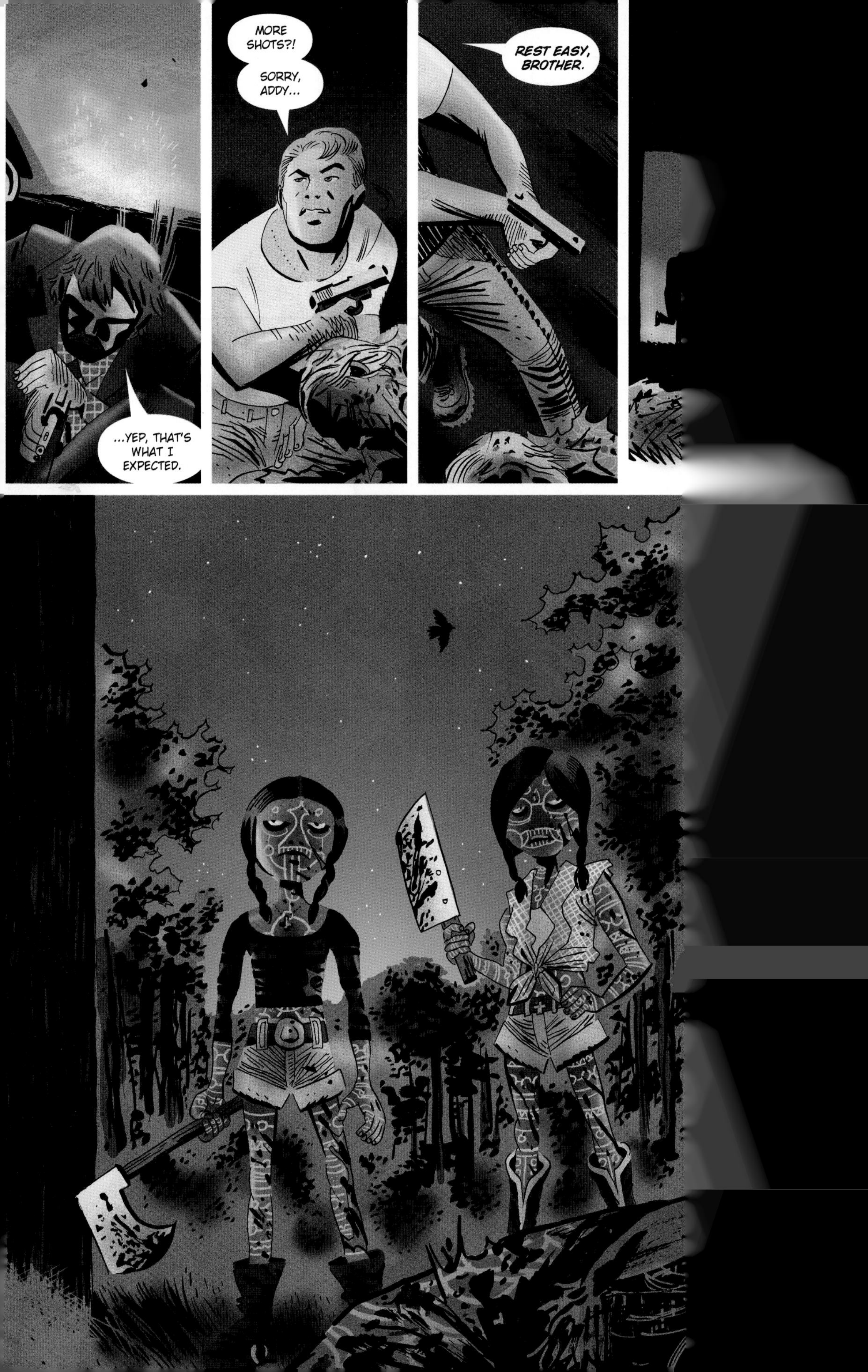

...YEP, THAT'S WHAT I EXPECTED.
MORE SHOTS?!
SORRY, ADDY...
REST EASY, BROTHER.

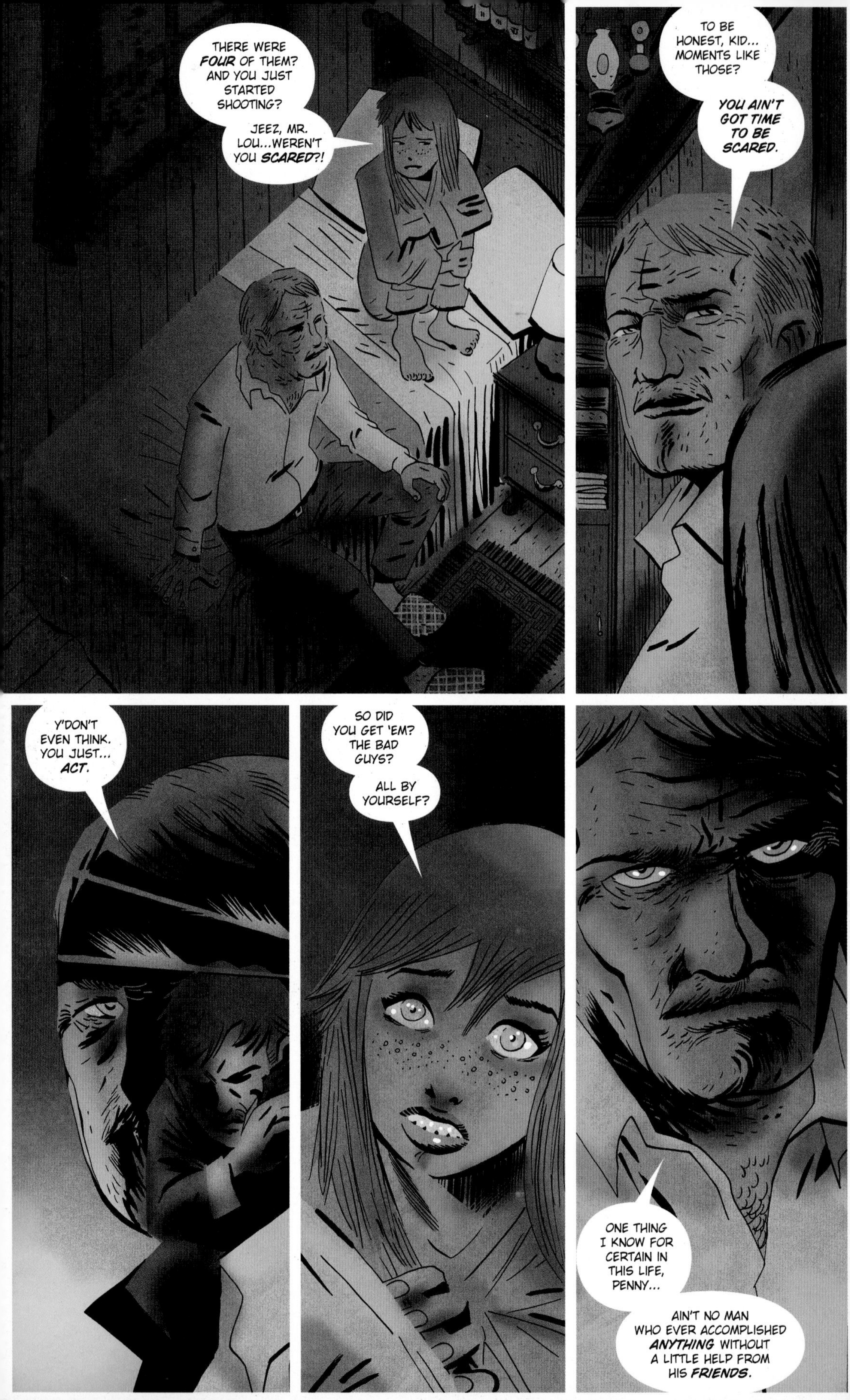
THERE WERE FOUR OF THEM? AND YOU JUST STARTED SHOOTING?
JEEZ, MR. LOU...WEREN'T YOU SCARED?!
TO BE HONEST, KID... MOMENTS LIKE THOSE?
YOU AIN'T GOT TIME TO BE SCARED.
Y'DON'T EVEN THINK. YOU JUST... ACT.
SO DID YOU GET 'EM? THE BAD GUYS?
ALL BY YOURSELF?
ONE THING I KNOW FOR CERTAIN IN THIS LIFE, PENNY...
AIN'T NO MAN WHO EVER ACCOMPLISHED ANYTHING WITHOUT A LITTLE HELP FROM HIS FRIENDS.

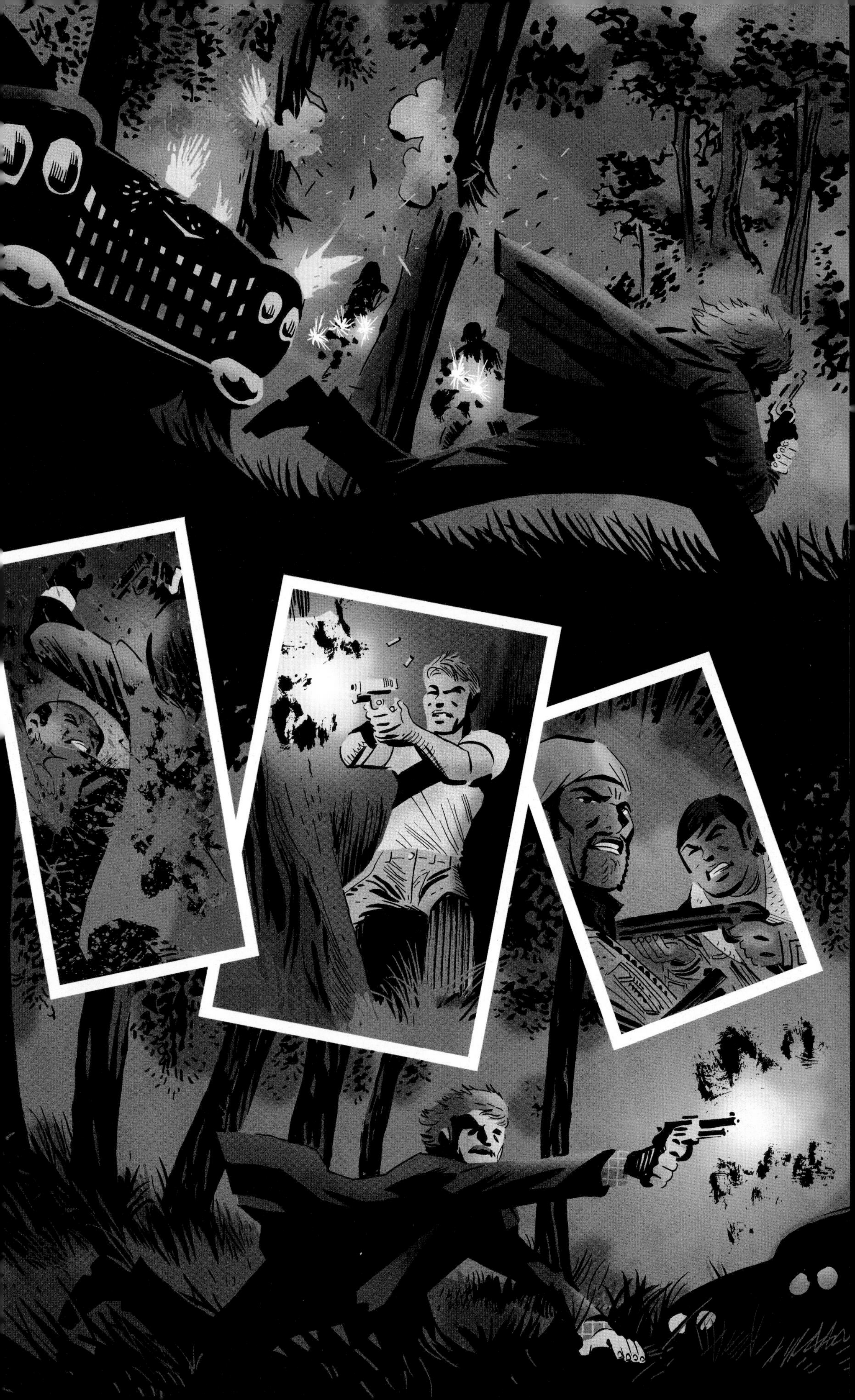

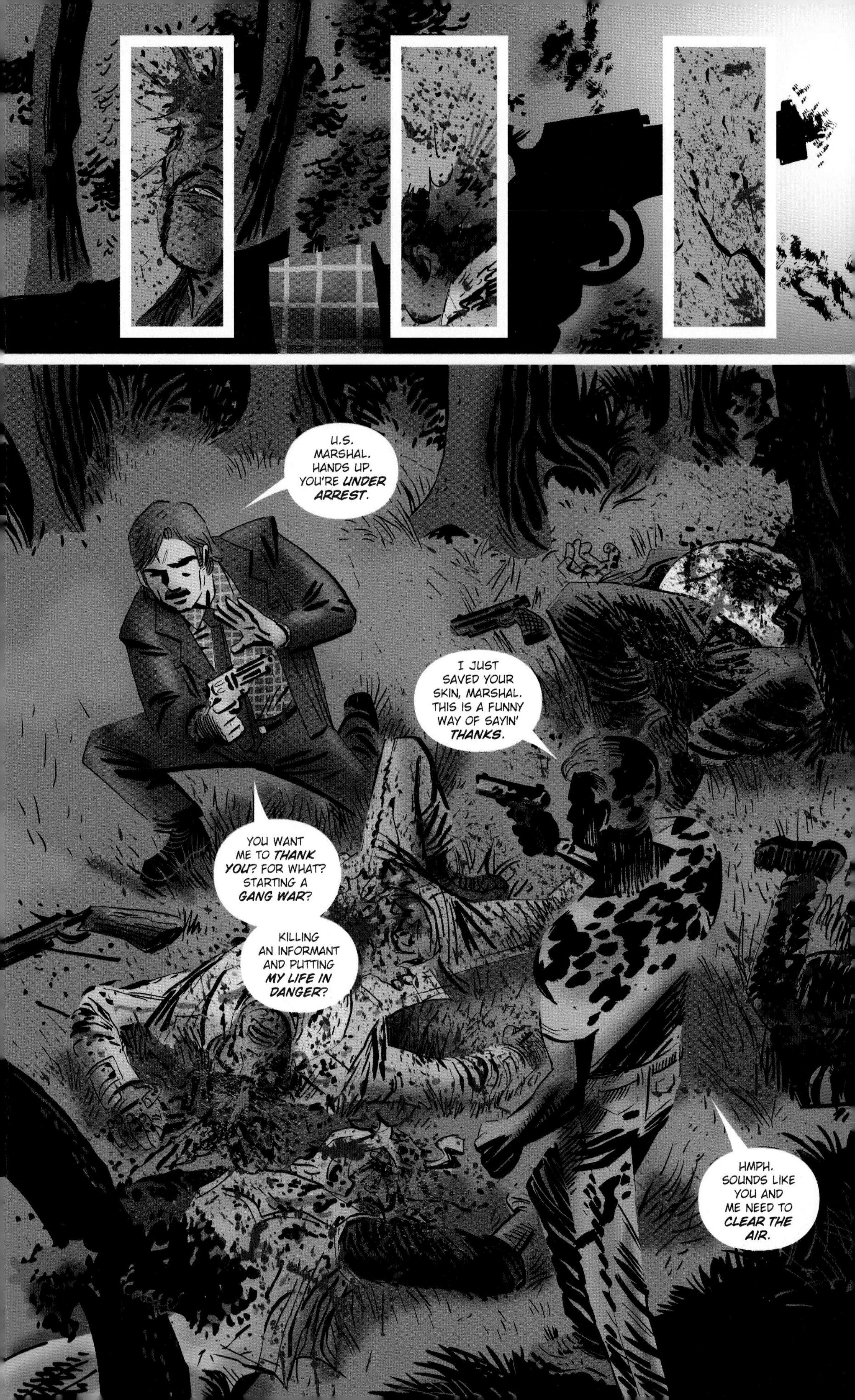
U.S. MARSHAL. HANDS UP. YOU'RE **UNDER ARREST**.
I JUST SAVED YOUR SKIN, MARSHAL. THIS IS A FUNNY WAY OF SAYIN' **THANKS**.
YOU WANT ME TO **THANK YOU**? FOR WHAT? STARTING A **GANG WAR**?
KILLING AN INFORMANT AND PUTTING **MY LIFE IN DANGER**?
HMPH. SOUNDS LIKE YOU AND ME NEED TO **CLEAR THE AIR**.

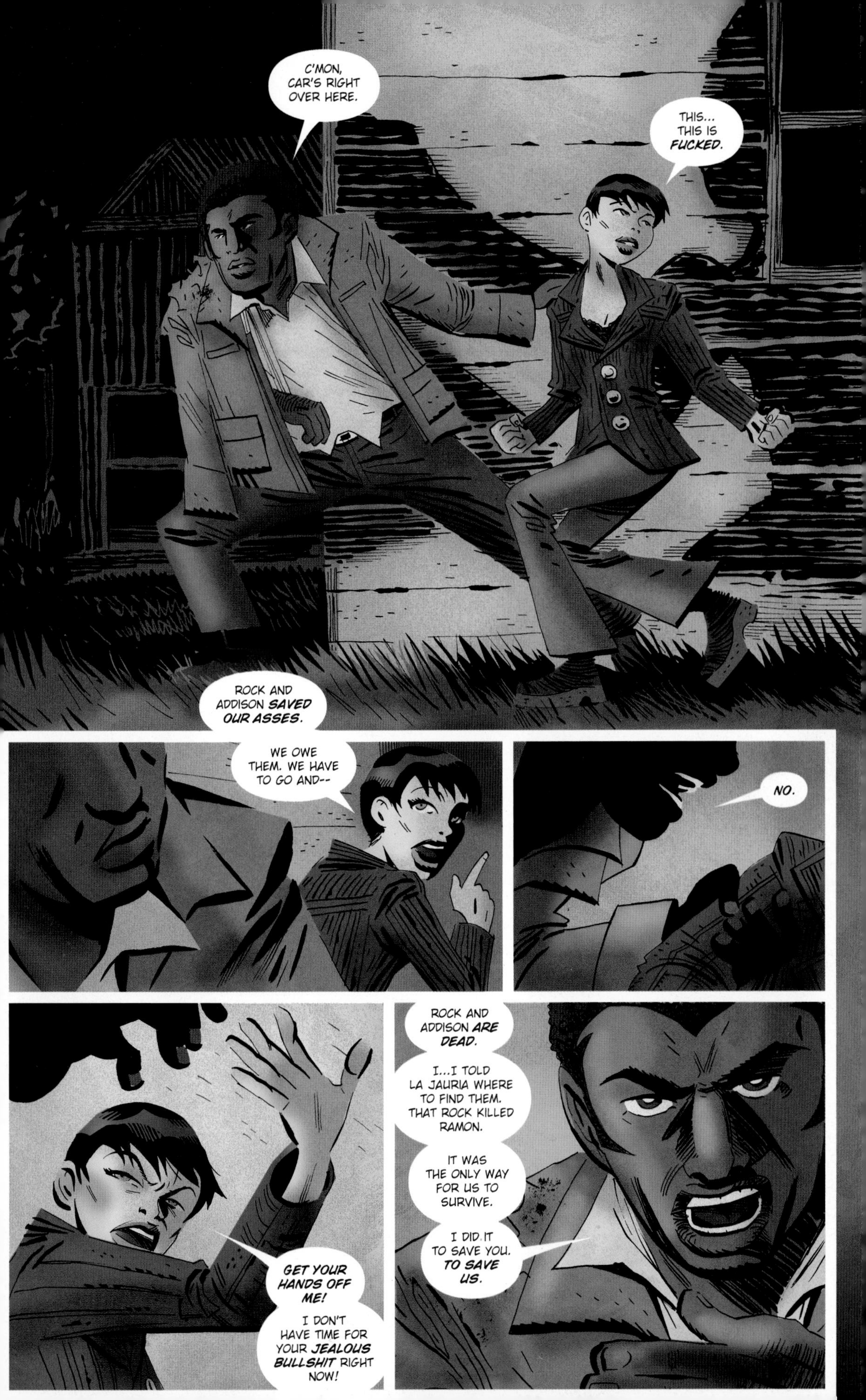
C'MON, CAR'S RIGHT OVER HERE.
THIS... THIS IS FUCKED.
ROCK AND ADDISON SAVED OUR ASSES.
WE OWE THEM. WE HAVE TO GO AND--
NO.
GET YOUR HANDS OFF ME!
I DON'T HAVE TIME FOR YOUR JEALOUS BULLSHIT RIGHT NOW!
ROCK AND ADDISON ARE DEAD.
I...I TOLD LA JAURIA WHERE TO FIND THEM. THAT ROCK KILLED RAMON.
IT WAS THE ONLY WAY FOR US TO SURVIVE.
I DID IT TO SAVE YOU. TO SAVE US.

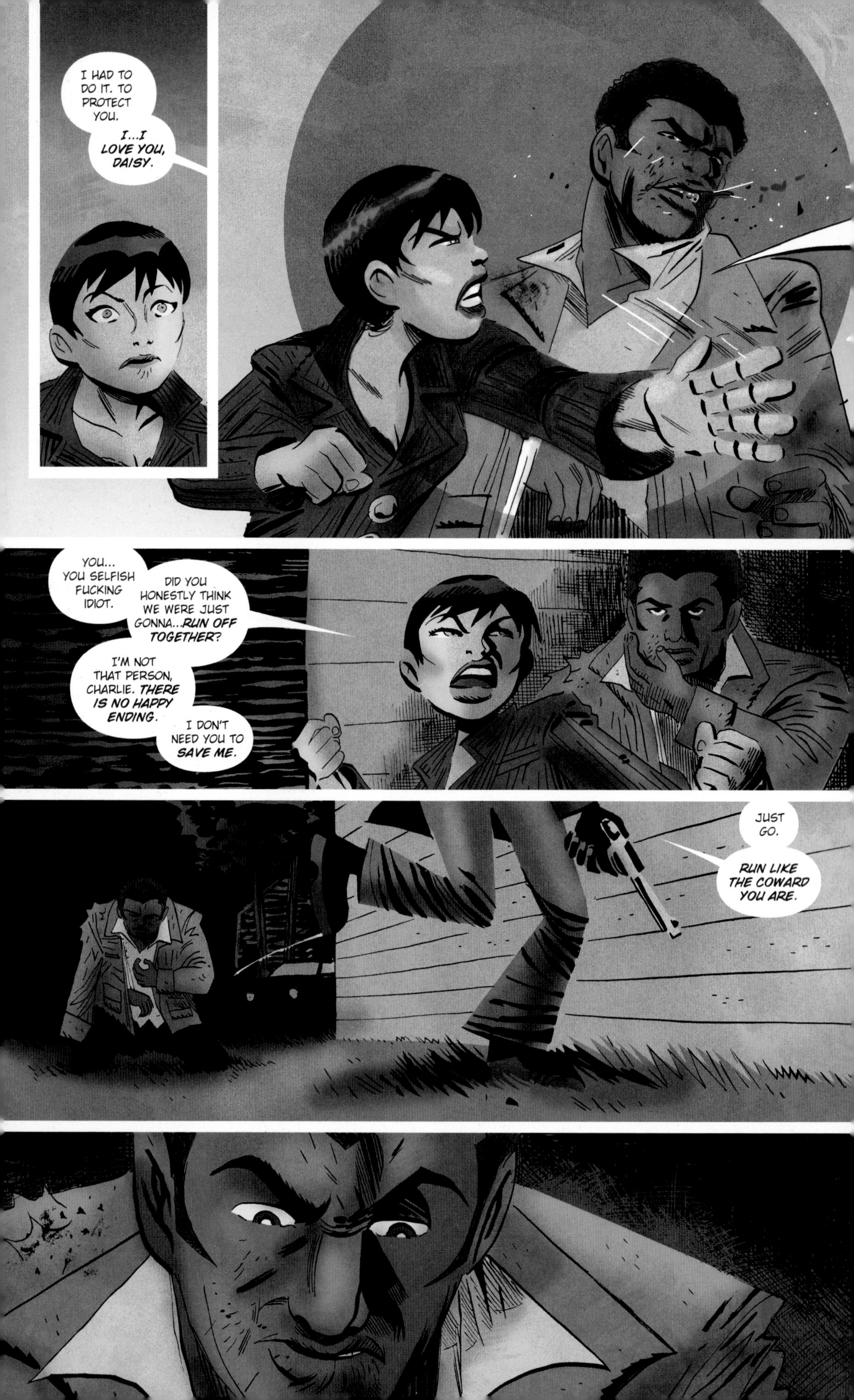
I HAD TO DO IT. TO PROTECT YOU.
I...I LOVE YOU, DAISY.
YOU... YOU SELFISH FUCKING IDIOT.
DID YOU HONESTLY THINK WE WERE JUST GONNA...RUN OFF TOGETHER?
I'M NOT THAT PERSON, CHARLIE. THERE IS NO HAPPY ENDING.
I DON'T NEED YOU TO SAVE ME.
JUST GO.
RUN LIKE THE COWARD YOU ARE.

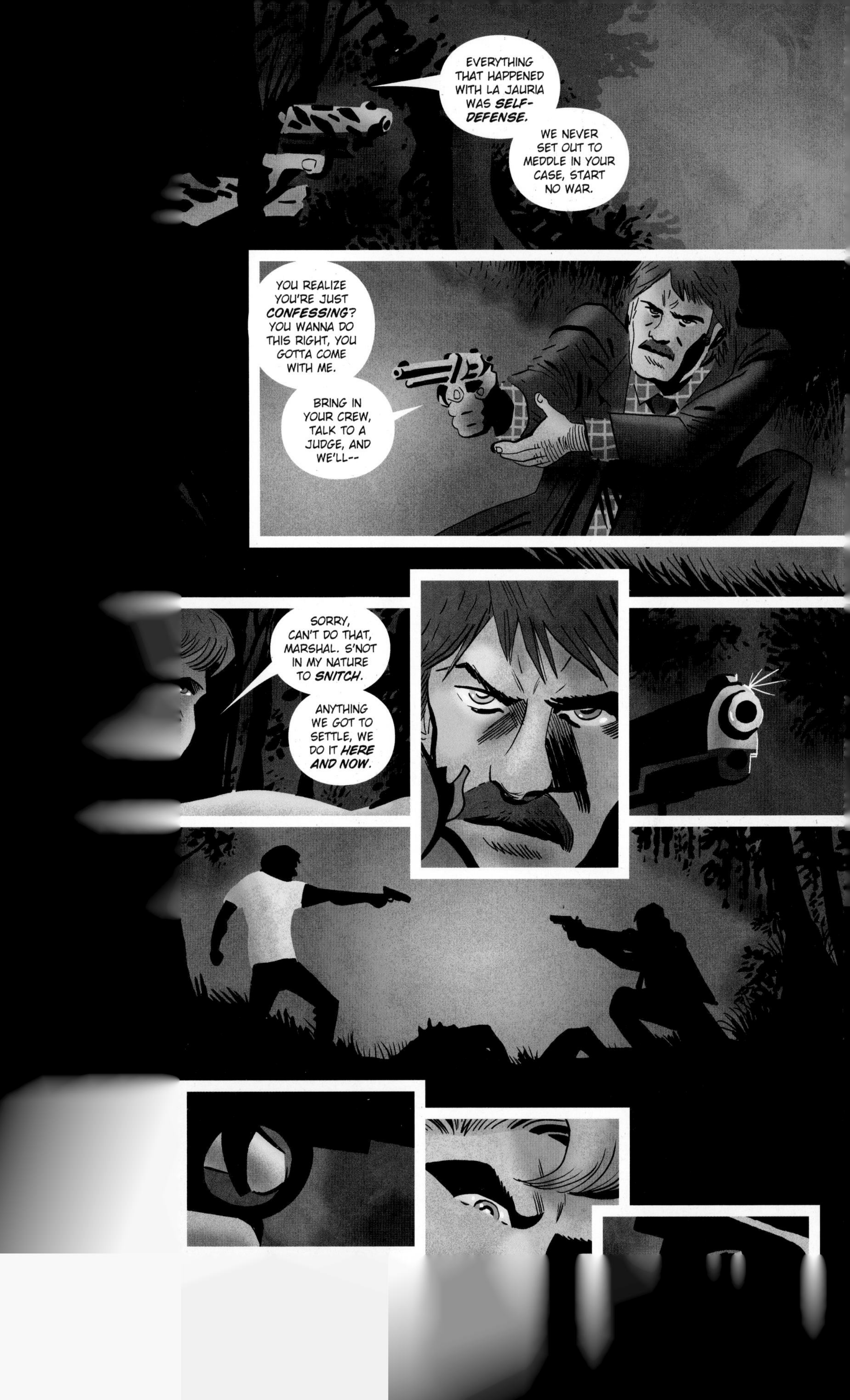
EVERYTHING THAT HAPPENED WITH LA JAURIA WAS SELF-DEFENSE.
WE NEVER SET OUT TO MEDDLE IN YOUR CASE, START NO WAR.
YOU REALIZE YOU'RE JUST CONFESSING? YOU WANNA DO THIS RIGHT, YOU GOTTA COME WITH ME.
BRING IN YOUR CREW, TALK TO A JUDGE, AND WE'LL--
SORRY, CAN'T DO THAT, MARSHAL. S'NOT IN MY NATURE TO SNITCH.
ANYTHING WE GOT TO SETTLE, WE DO IT HERE AND NOW.

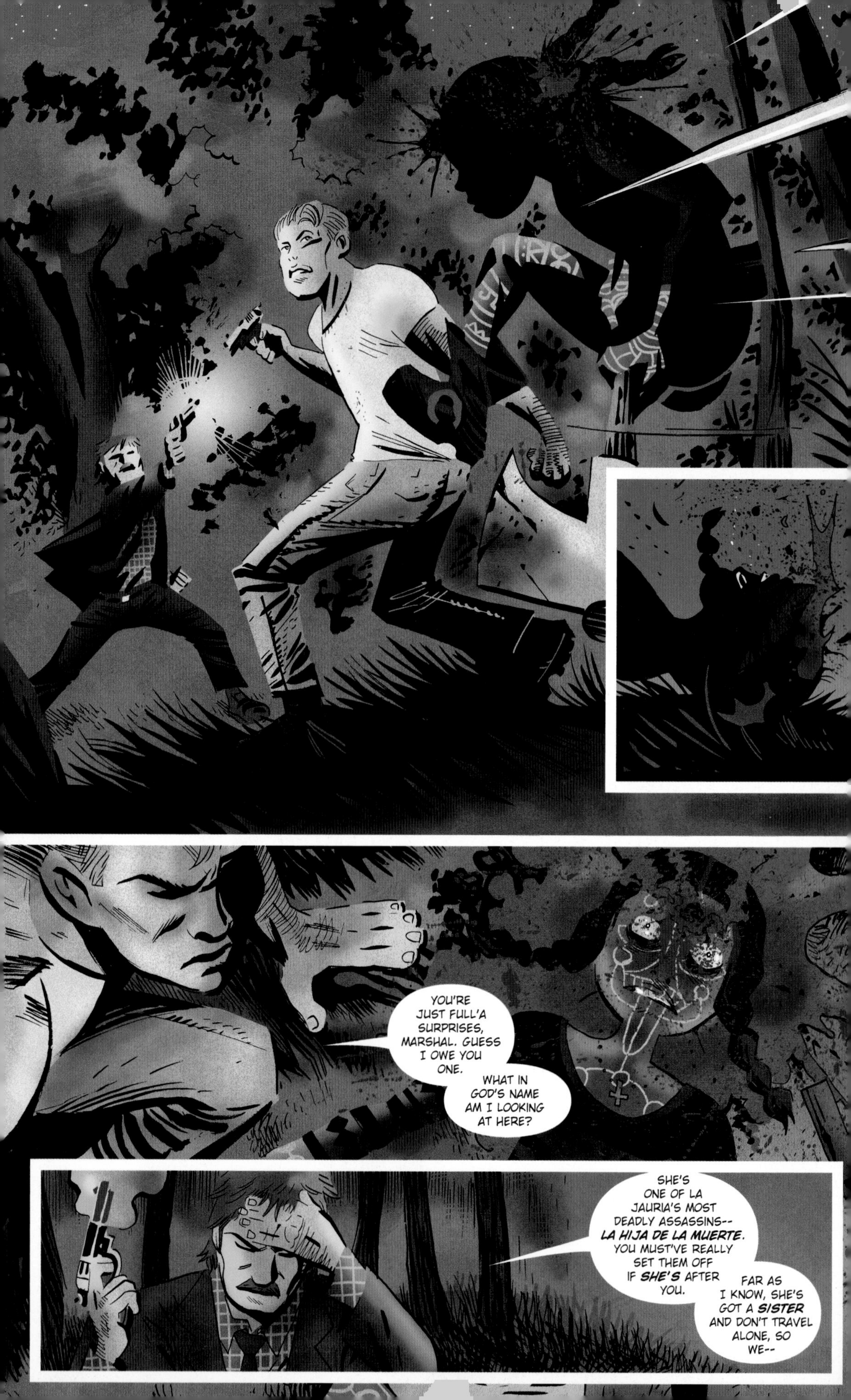
YOU'RE JUST FULL'A SURPRISES, MARSHAL. GUESS I OWE YOU ONE.
WHAT IN GOD'S NAME AM I LOOKING AT HERE?
SHE'S ONE OF LA JAURIA'S MOST DEADLY ASSASSINS-- LA HIJA DE LA MUERTE. YOU MUST'VE REALLY SET THEM OFF IF SHE'S AFTER YOU.
FAR AS I KNOW, SHE'S GOT A SISTER AND DON'T TRAVEL ALONE, SO WE--

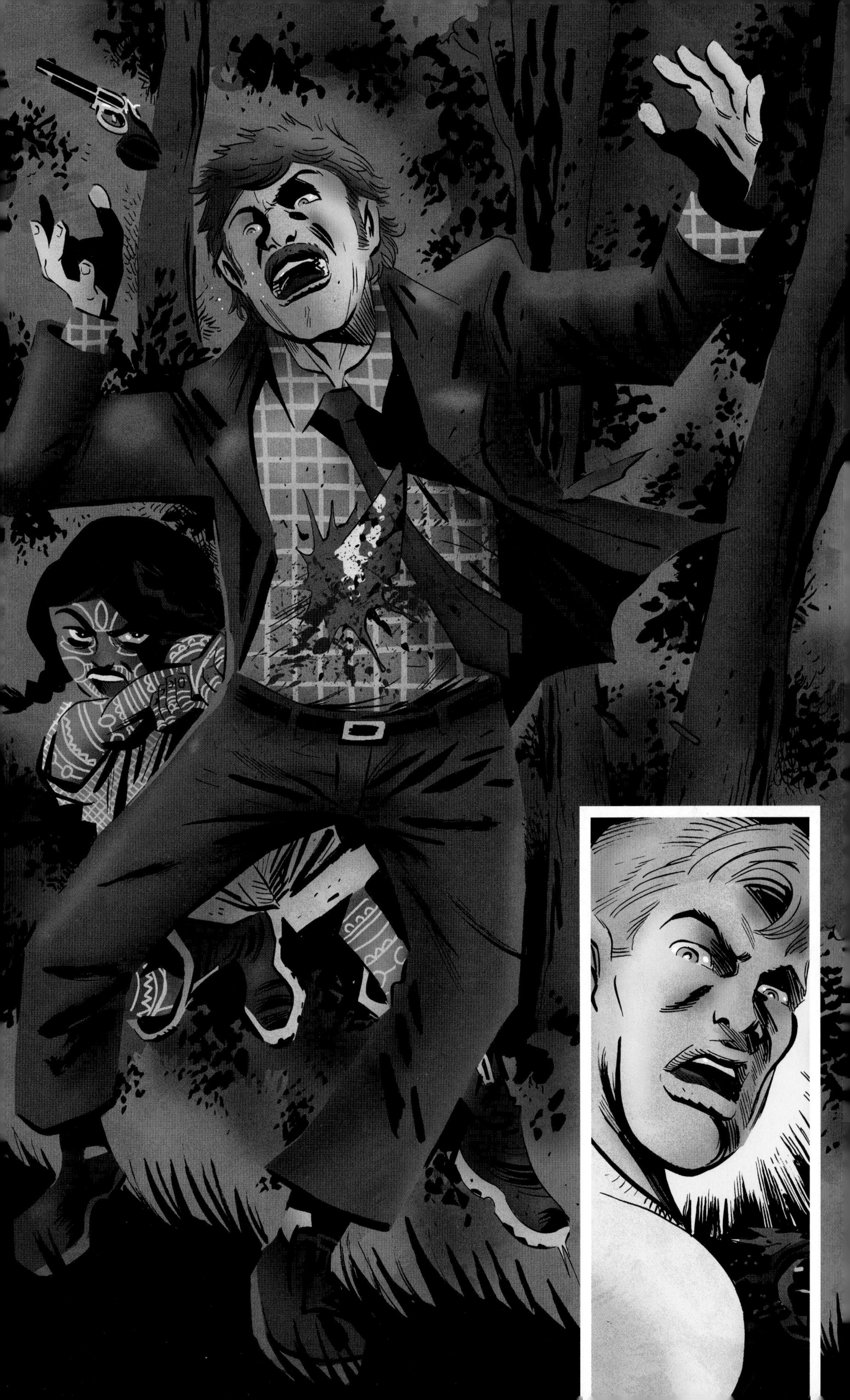

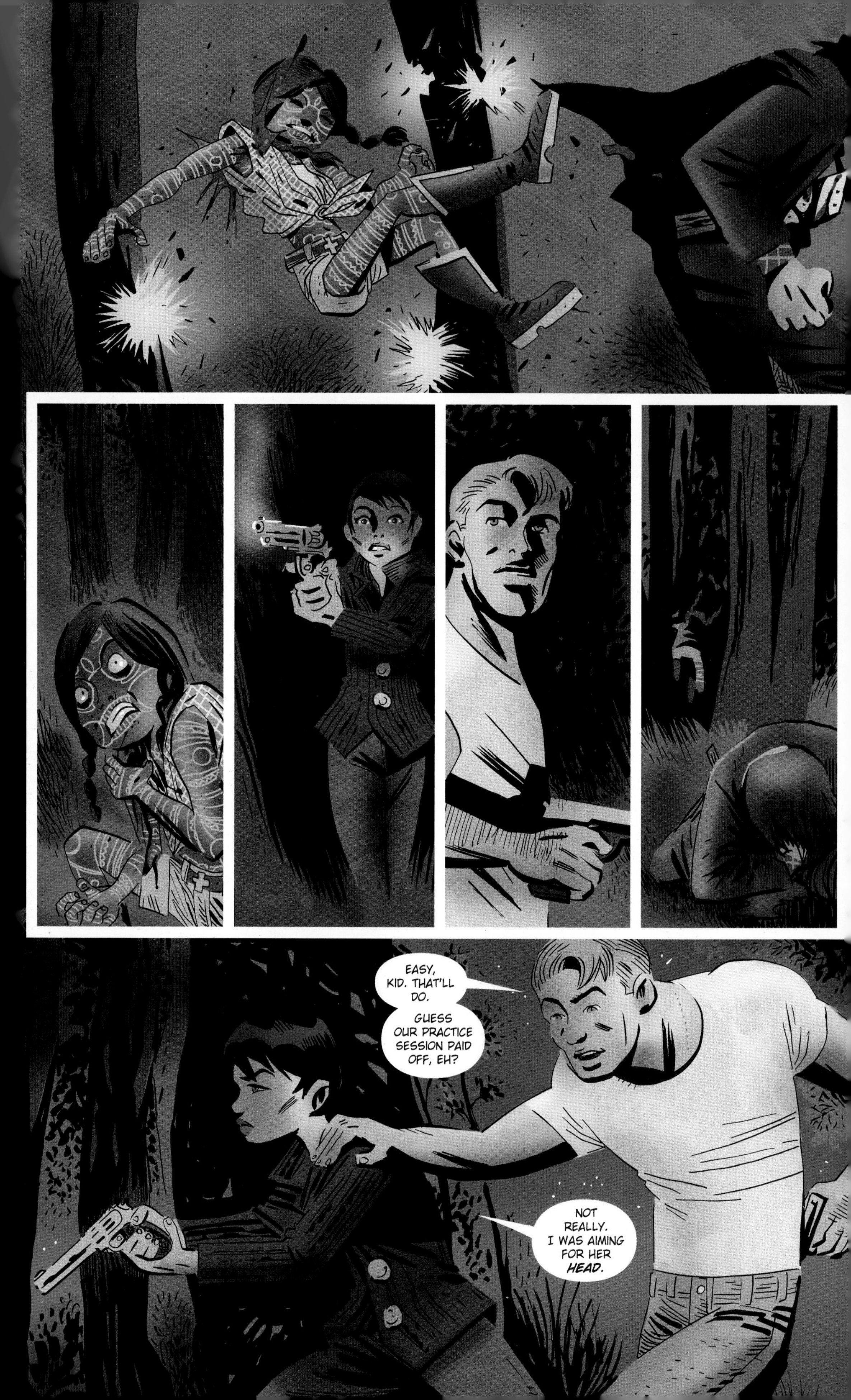
EASY, KID. THAT'LL DO.
GUESS OUR PRACTICE SESSION PAID OFF, EH?
NOT REALLY. I WAS AIMING FOR HER HEAD.

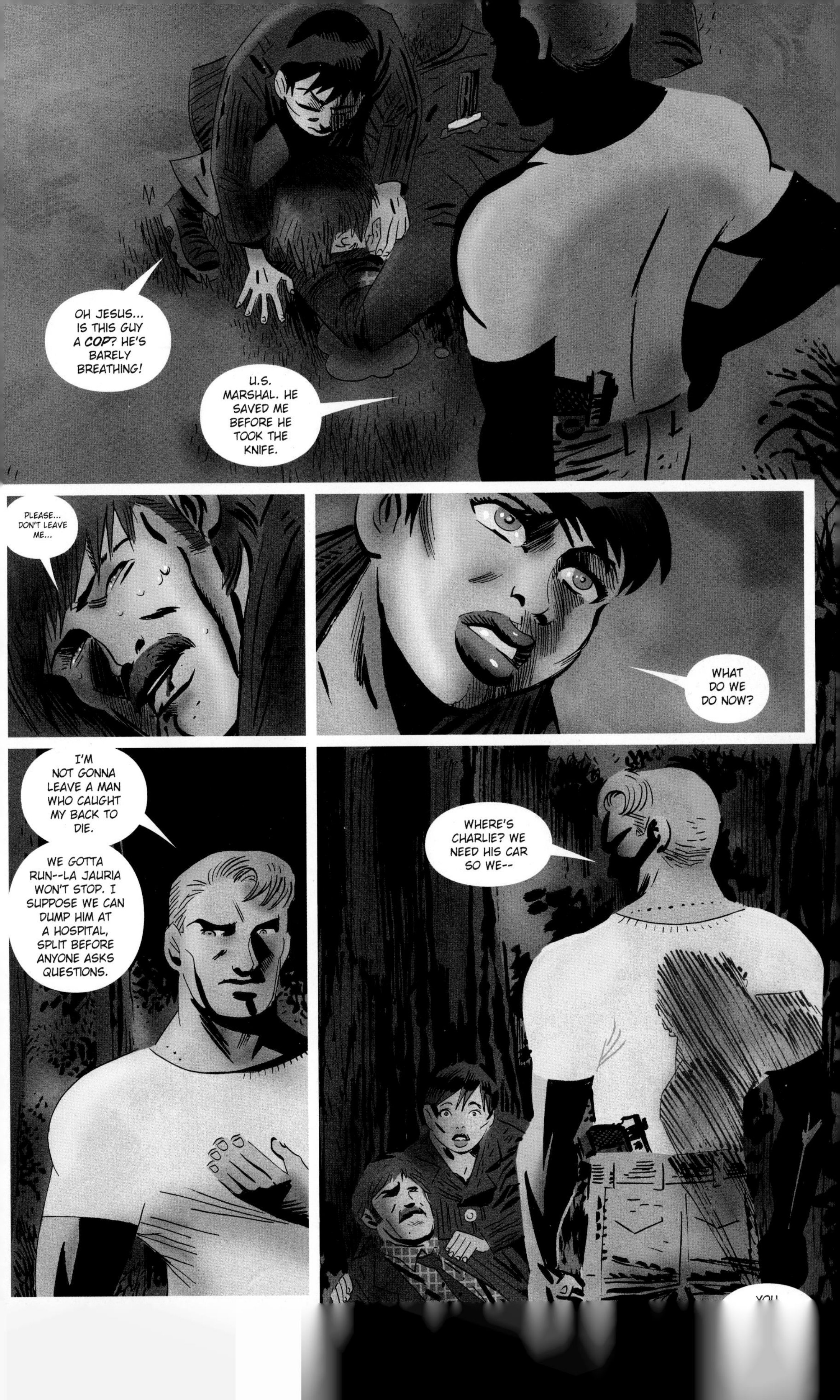
OH JESUS... IS THIS GUY A *COP*? HE'S BARELY BREATHING!
U.S. MARSHAL. HE SAVED ME BEFORE HE TOOK THE KNIFE.
PLEASE... DON'T LEAVE ME...
WHAT DO WE DO NOW?
I'M NOT GONNA LEAVE A MAN WHO CAUGHT MY BACK TO DIE.
WE GOTTA RUN--LA JAURIA WON'T STOP. I SUPPOSE WE CAN DUMP HIM AT A HOSPITAL, SPLIT BEFORE ANYONE ASKS QUESTIONS.
WHERE'S CHARLIE? WE NEED HIS CAR SO WE--
YOU

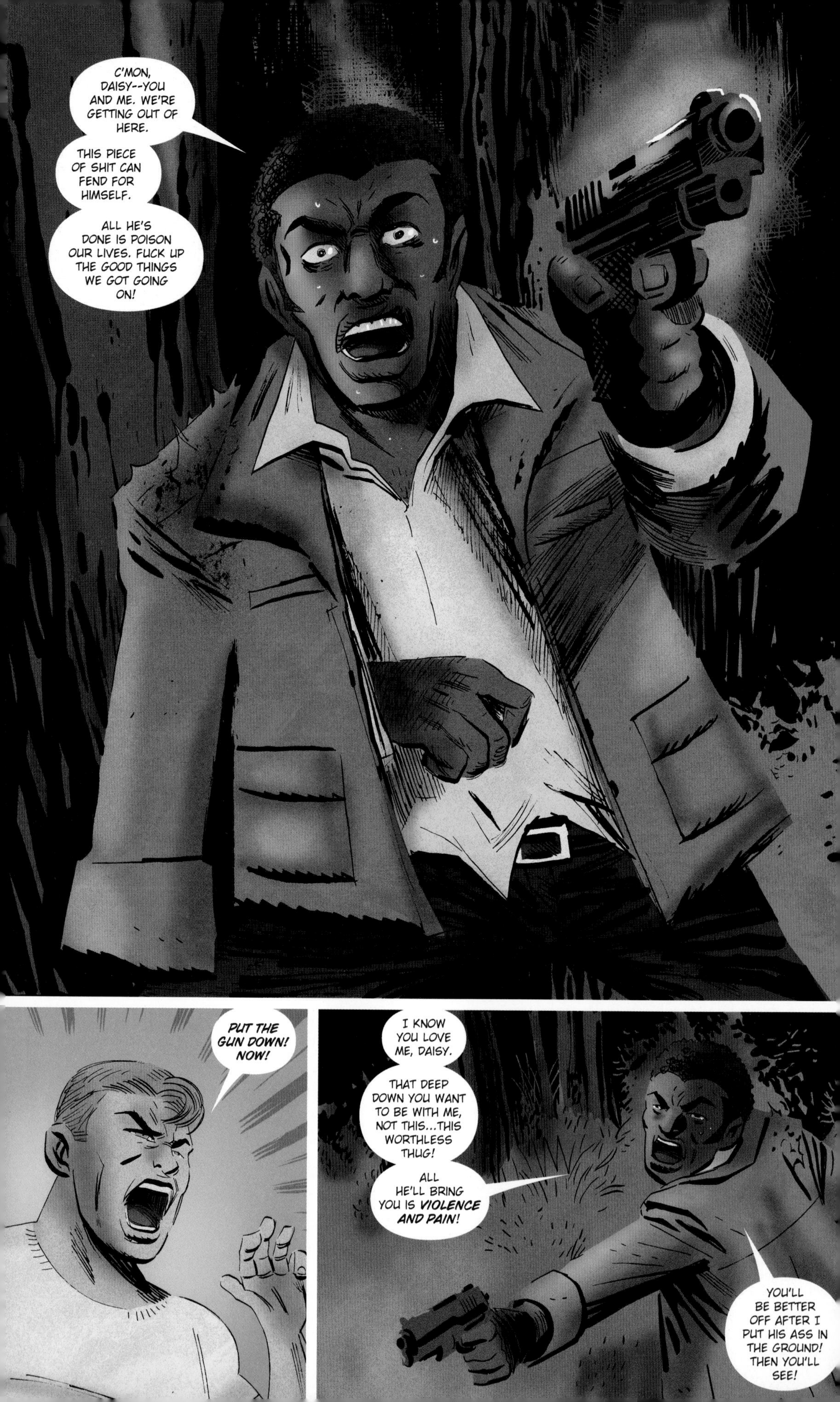
C'MON, DAISY--YOU AND ME. WE'RE GETTING OUT OF HERE.
THIS PIECE OF SHIT CAN FEND FOR HIMSELF.
ALL HE'S DONE IS POISON OUR LIVES. FUCK UP THE GOOD THINGS WE GOT GOING ON!
PUT THE GUN DOWN! NOW!
I KNOW YOU LOVE ME, DAISY.
THAT DEEP DOWN YOU WANT TO BE WITH ME, NOT THIS...THIS WORTHLESS THUG!
ALL HE'LL BRING YOU IS VIOLENCE AND PAIN!
YOU'LL BE BETTER OFF AFTER I PUT HIS ASS IN THE GROUND! THEN YOU'LL SEE!

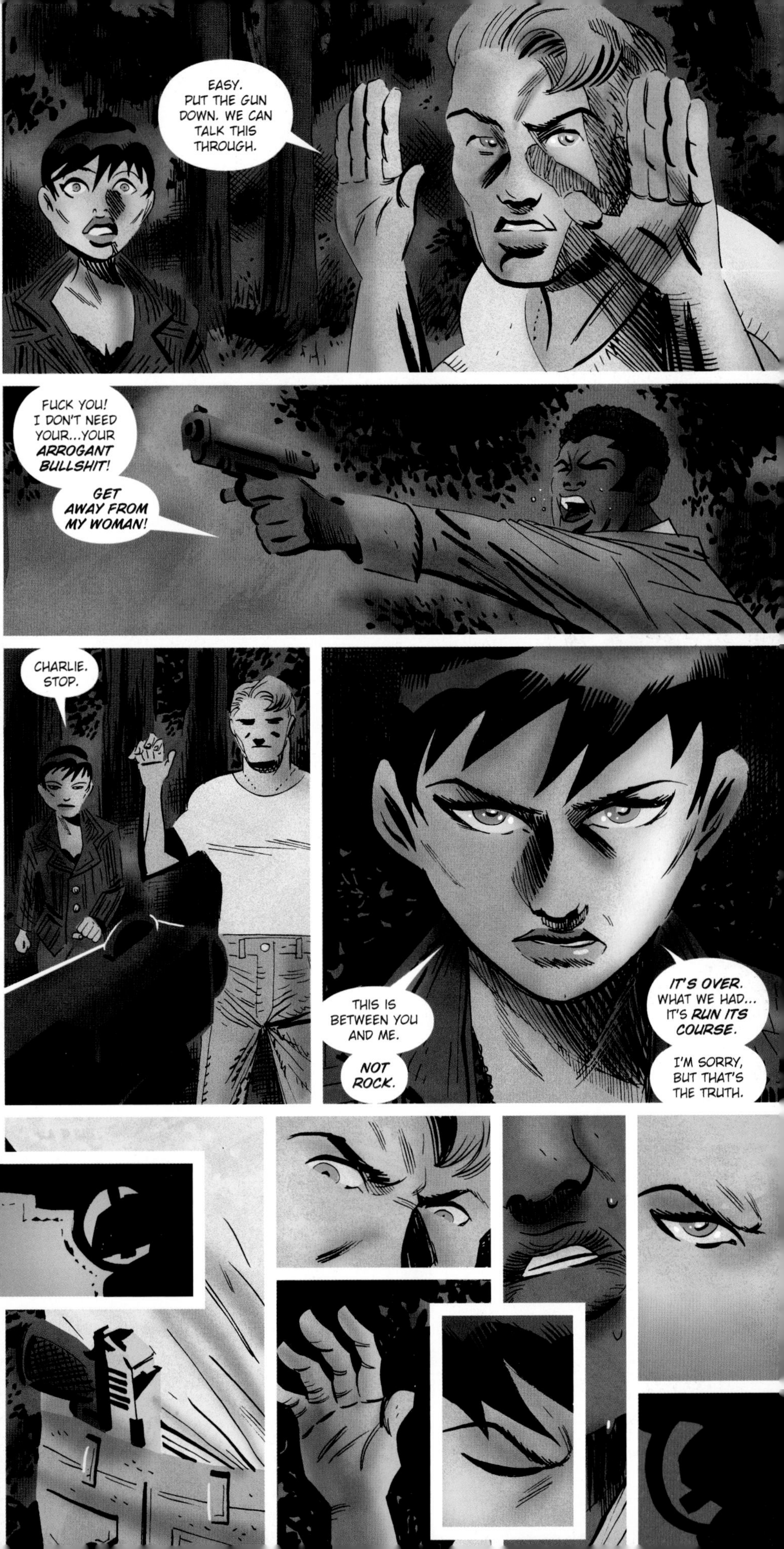
EASY. PUT THE GUN DOWN. WE CAN TALK THIS THROUGH.
FUCK YOU! I DON'T NEED YOUR...YOUR ***ARROGANT BULLSHIT!***
GET AWAY FROM MY WOMAN!
CHARLIE. STOP.
THIS IS BETWEEN YOU AND ME.
NOT ROCK.
IT'S OVER. WHAT WE HAD... IT'S ***RUN ITS COURSE.***
I'M SORRY, BUT THAT'S THE TRUTH.

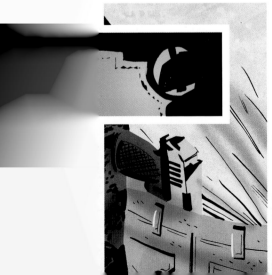

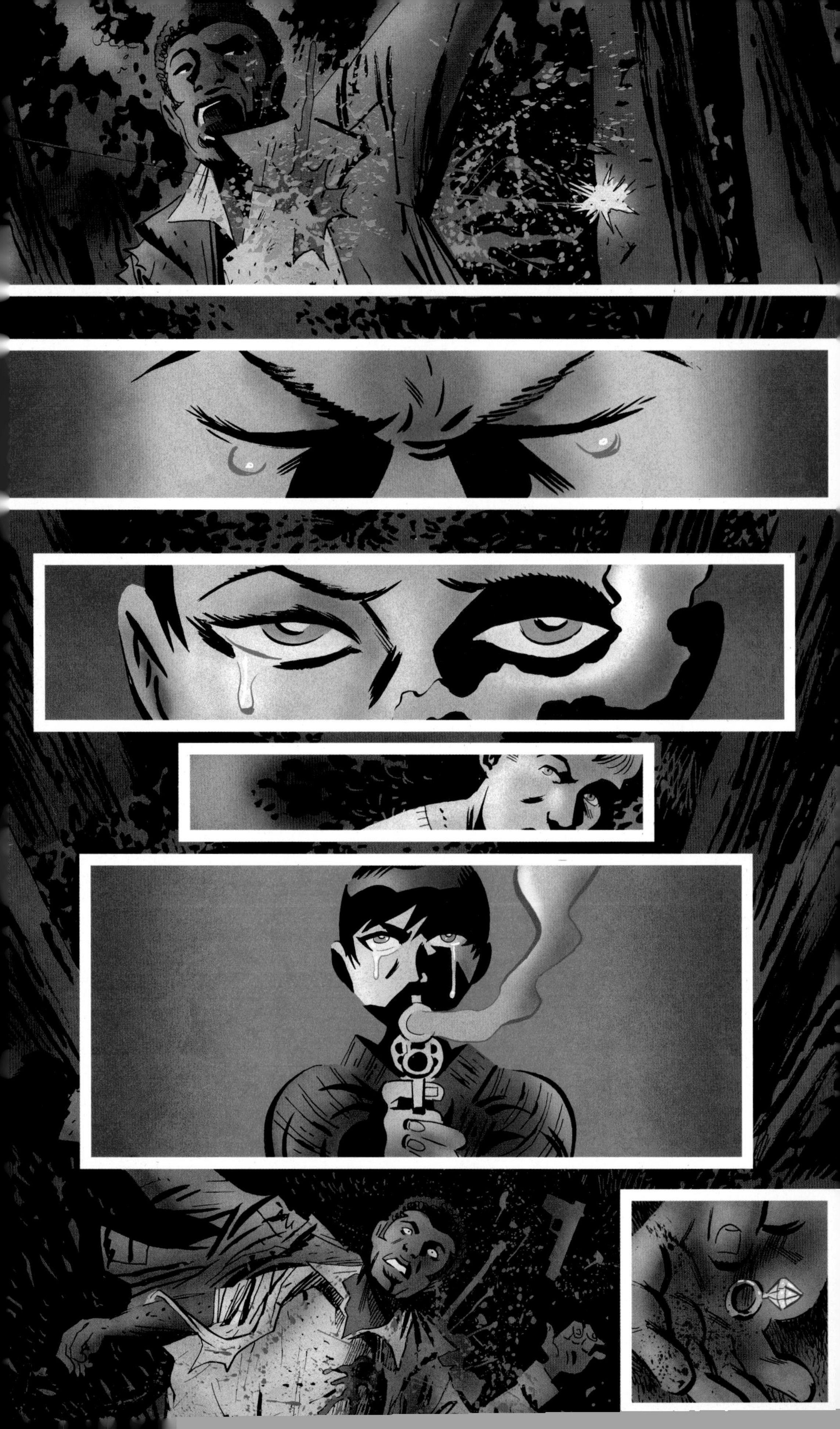

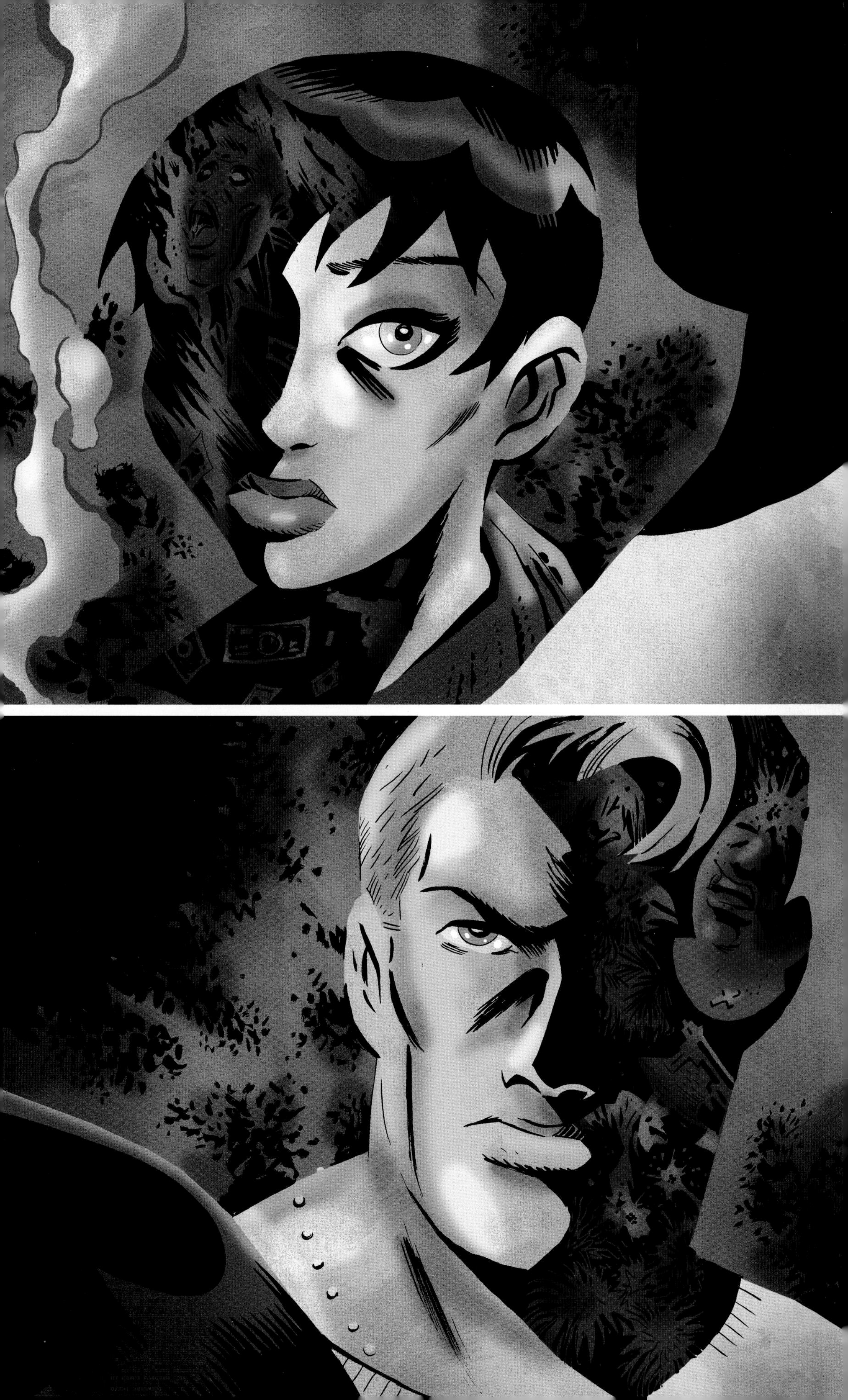

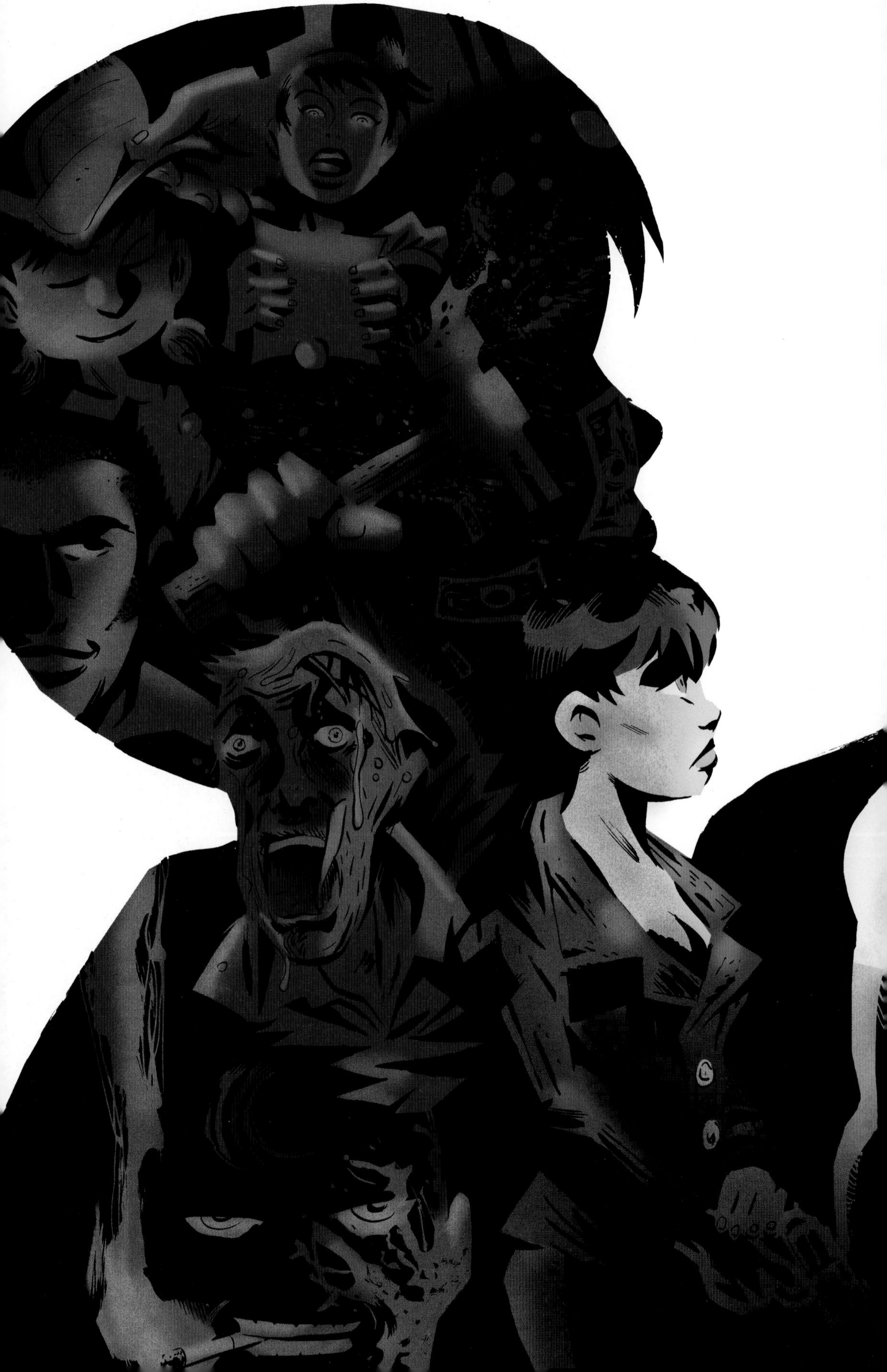

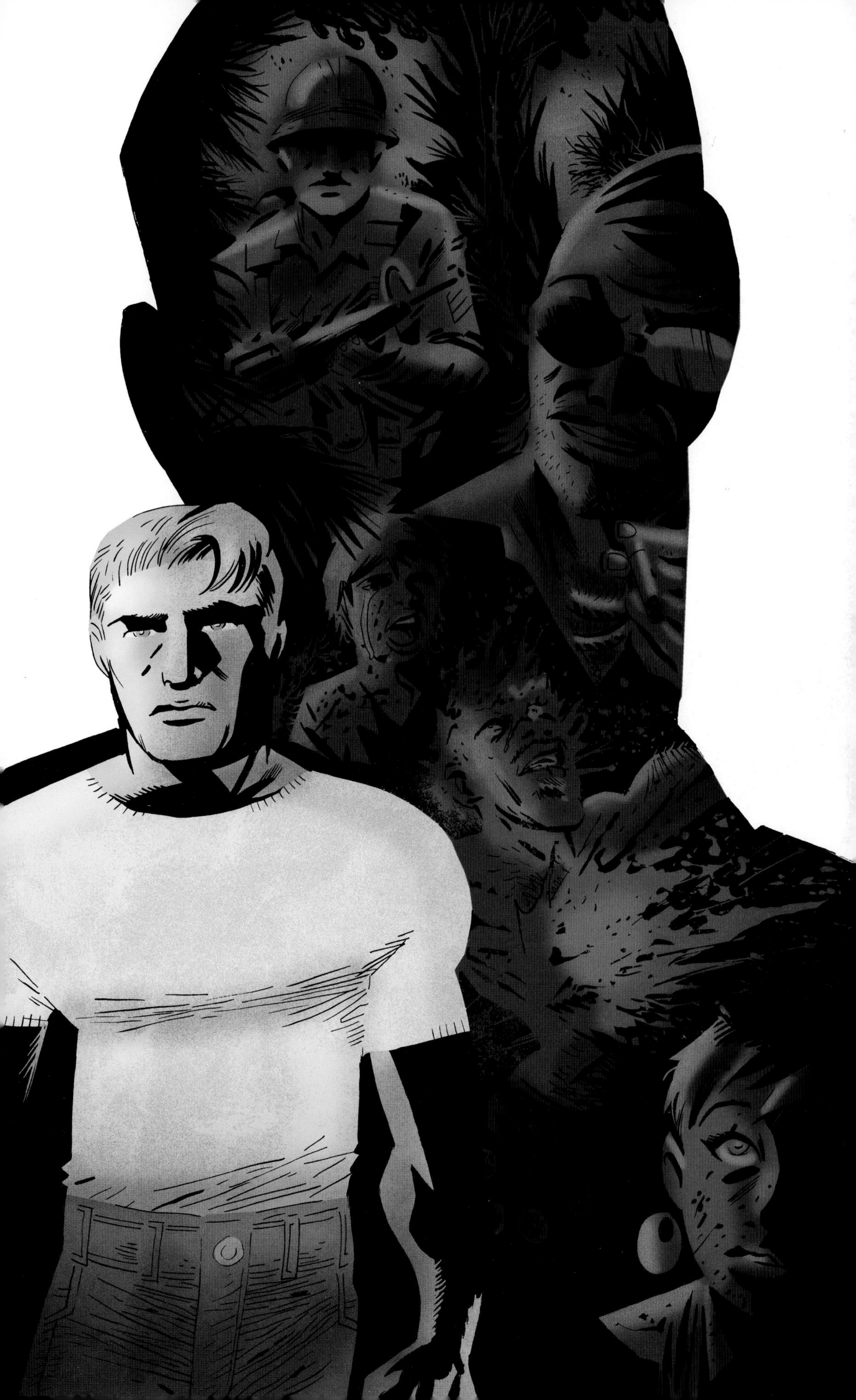

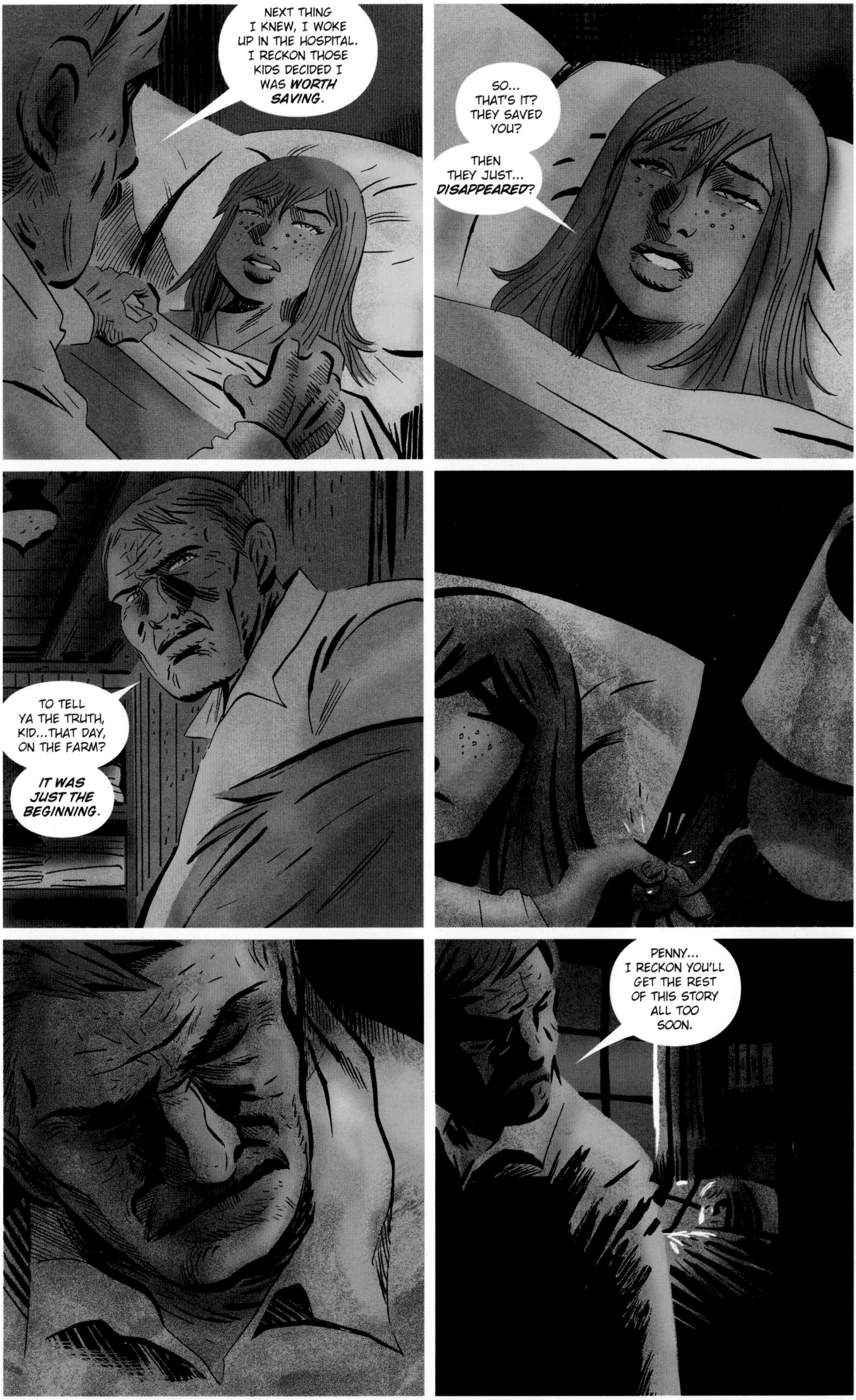
NEXT THING I KNEW, I WOKE UP IN THE HOSPITAL. I RECKON THOSE KIDS DECIDED I WAS **WORTH SAVING**.
SO... THAT'S IT? THEY SAVED YOU?
THEN THEY JUST... **DISAPPEARED**?
TO TELL YA THE TRUTH, KID...THAT DAY, ON THE FARM?
IT WAS JUST THE BEGINNING.
PENNY... I RECKON YOU'LL GET THE REST OF THIS STORY ALL TOO SOON.

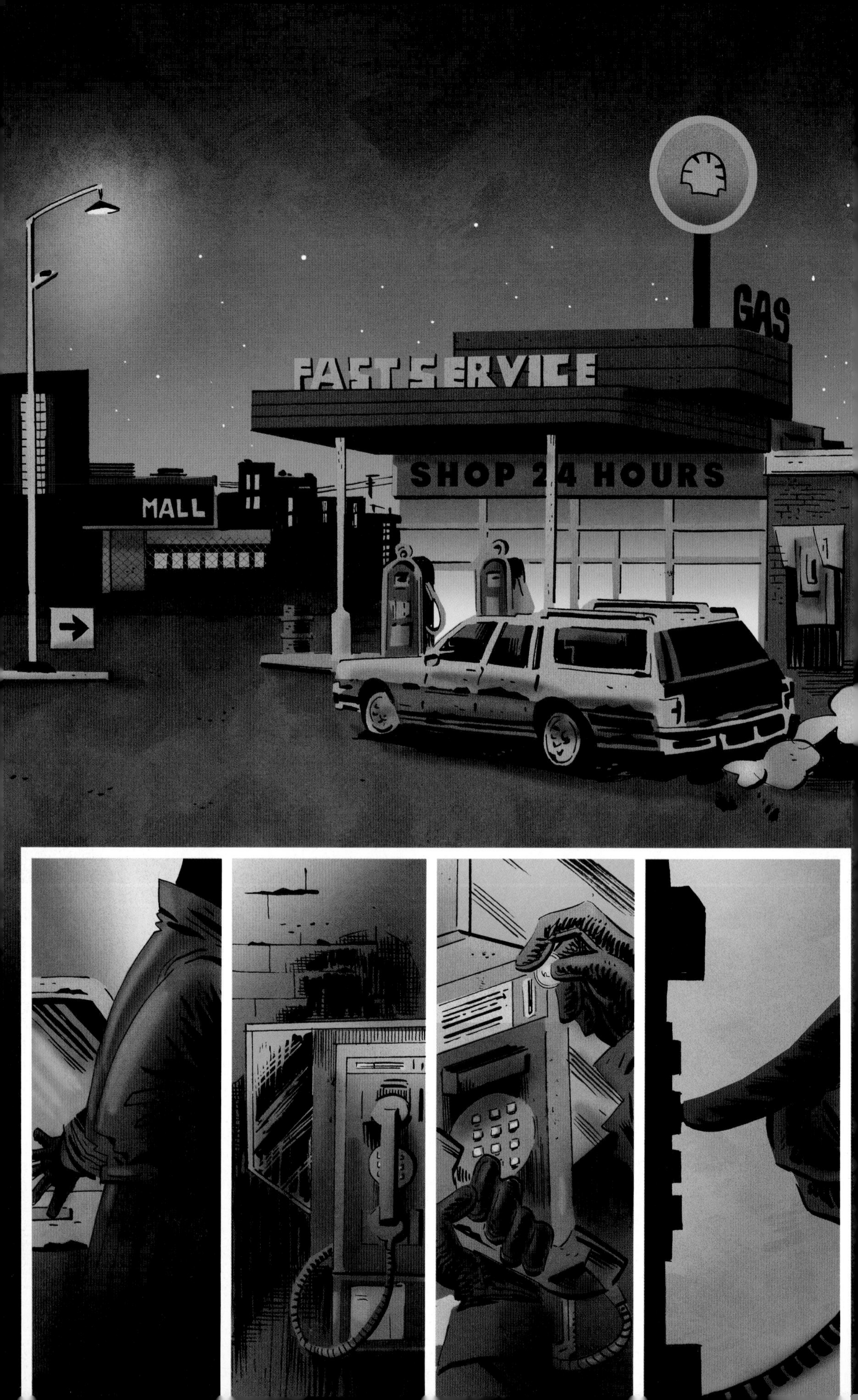
GAS
FAST SERVICE
SHOP 24 HOURS
MALL

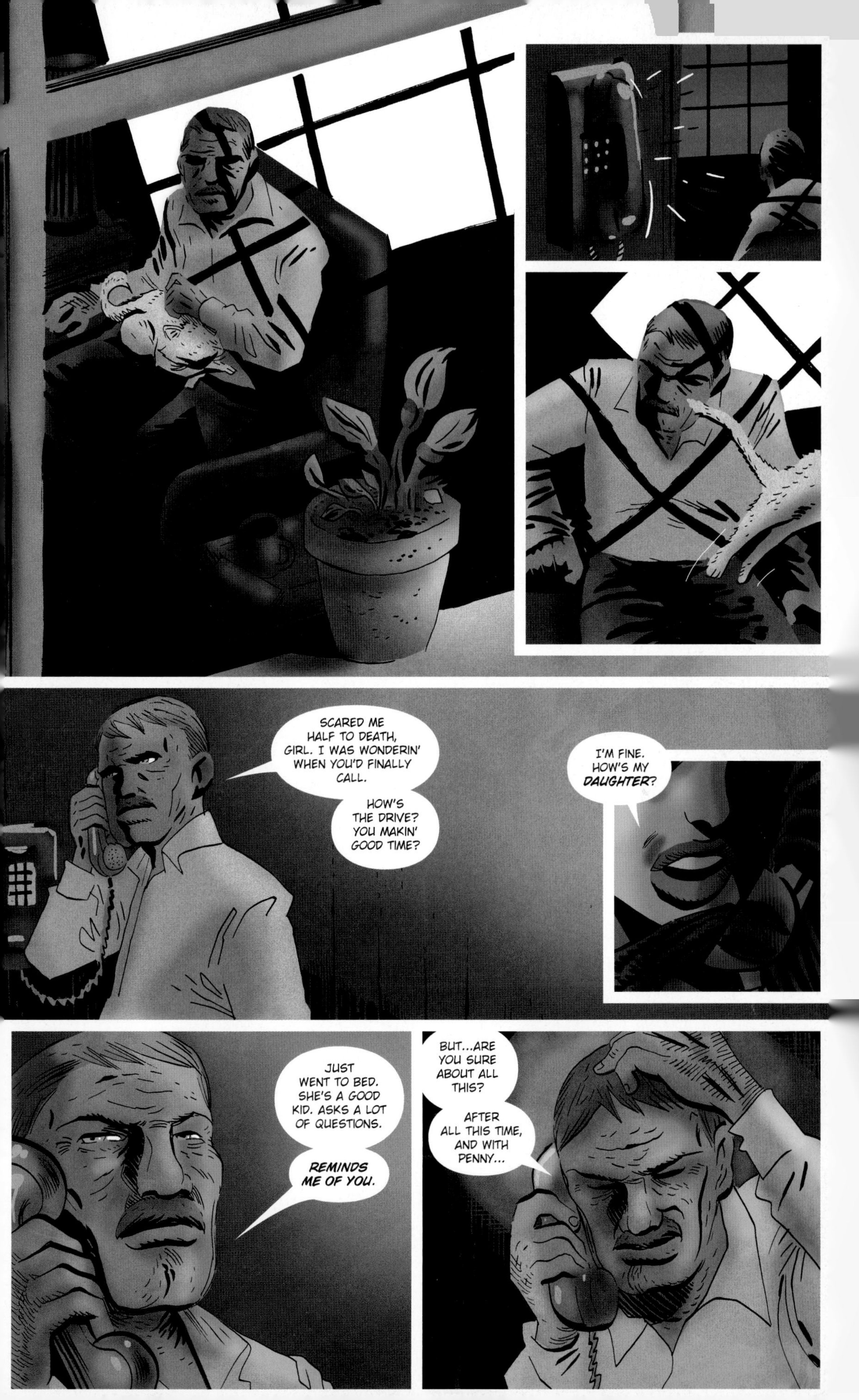
SCARED ME HALF TO DEATH, GIRL. I WAS WONDERIN' WHEN YOU'D FINALLY CALL.
HOW'S THE DRIVE? YOU MAKIN' GOOD TIME?
I'M FINE. HOW'S MY *DAUGHTER*?
JUST WENT TO BED. SHE'S A GOOD KID. ASKS A LOT OF QUESTIONS.
REMINDS ME OF YOU.
BUT...ARE YOU SURE ABOUT ALL THIS?
AFTER ALL THIS TIME, AND WITH PENNY...

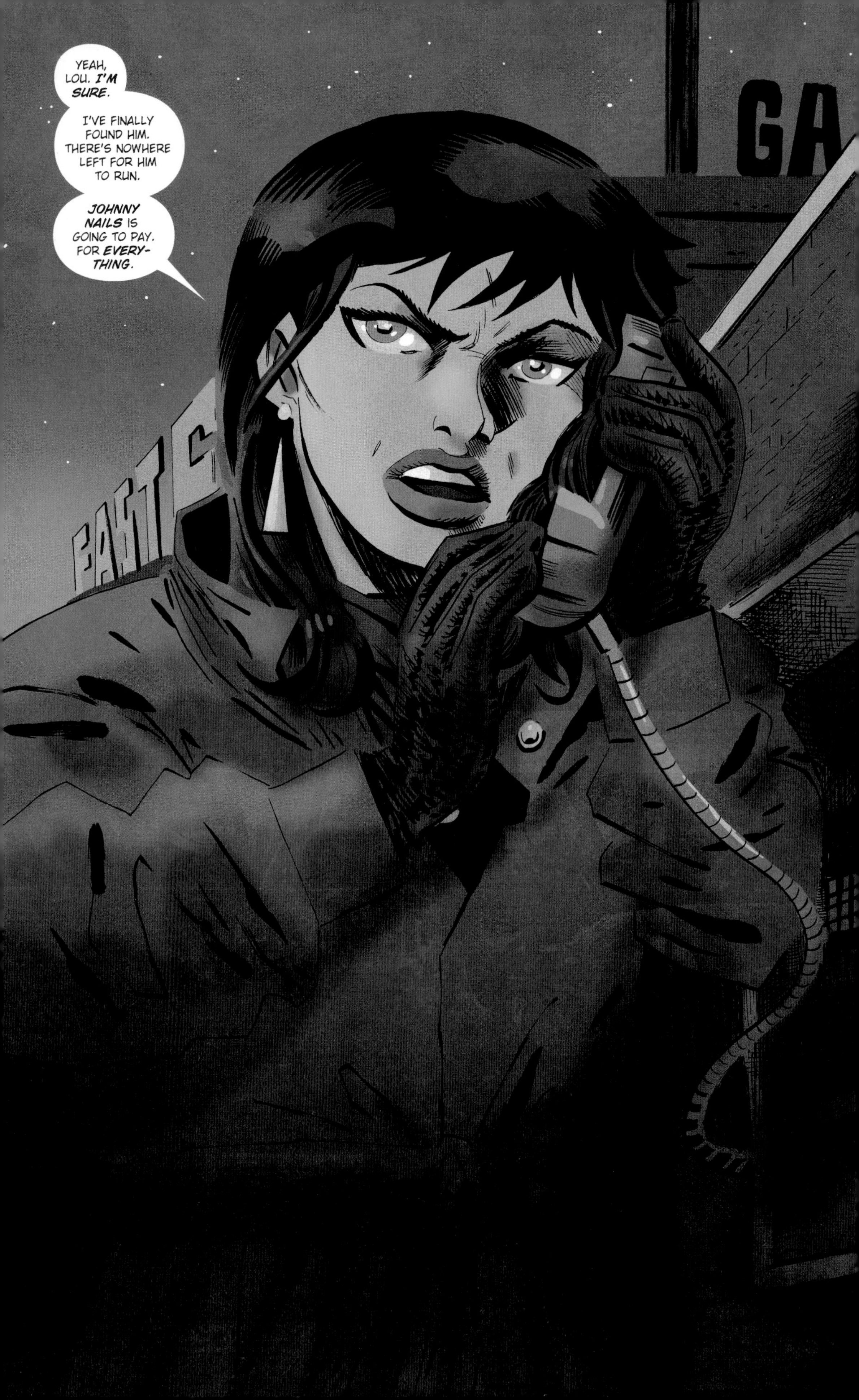
YEAH, LOU. I'M SURE.
I'VE FINALLY FOUND HIM. THERE'S NOWHERE LEFT FOR HIM TO RUN.
JOHNNY NAILS IS GOING TO PAY. FOR EVERY-THING.
GA

VARIANT COVERS

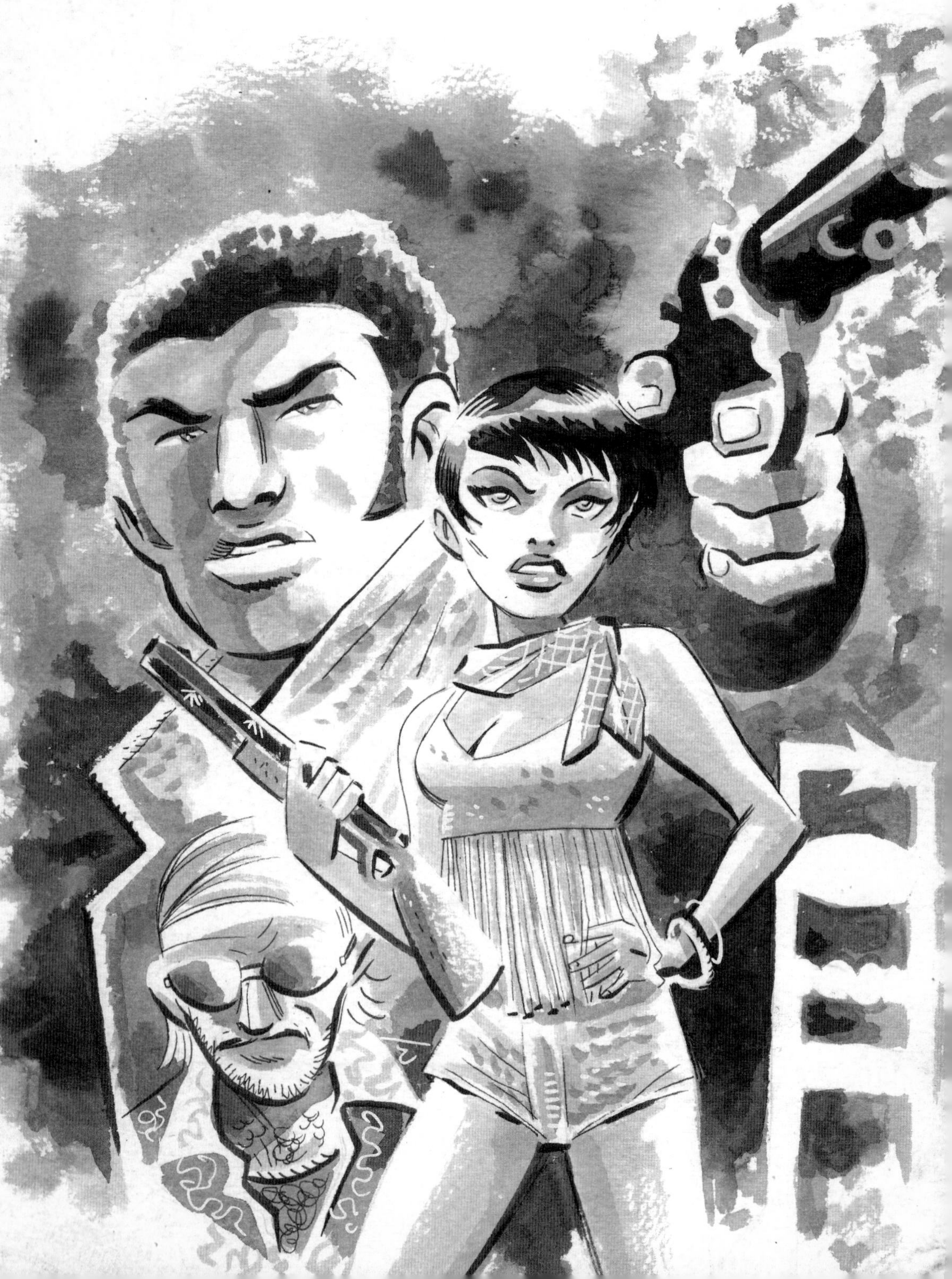

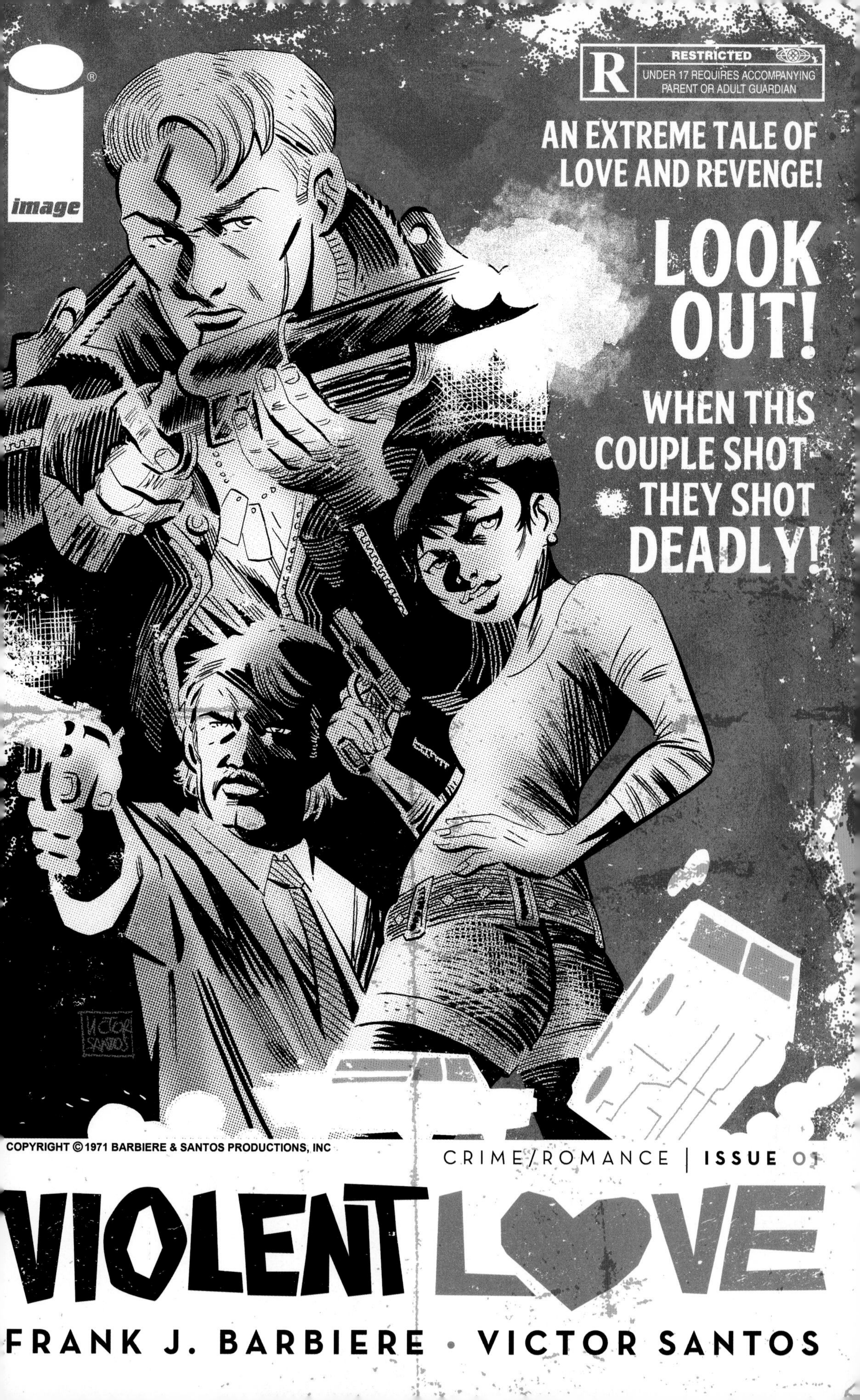

image
R RESTRICTED
UNDER 17 REQUIRES ACCOMPANYING PARENT OR ADULT GUARDIAN
AN EXTREME TALE OF LOVE AND REVENGE!
LOOK OUT!
WHEN THIS COUPLE SHOT THEY SHOT DEADLY!
VICTOR SANTOS
COPYRIGHT © 1971 BARBIERE & SANTOS PRODUCTIONS, INC
CRIME/ROMANCE | ISSUE 01
VIOLENT LOVE
FRANK J. BARBIERE • VICTOR SANTOS

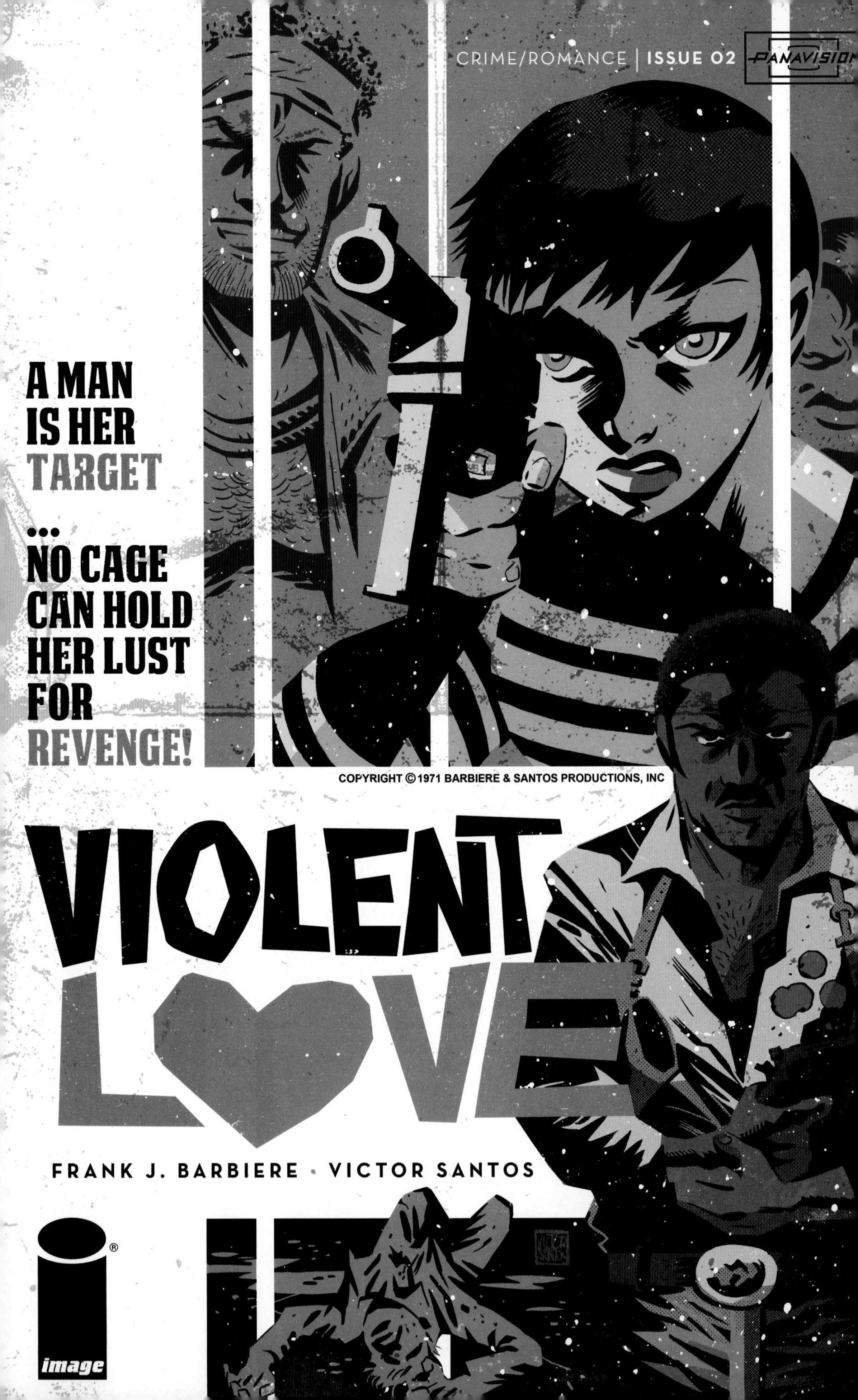
CRIME/ROMANCE | ISSUE 02
PANAVISION
A MAN IS HER TARGET
...
NO CAGE CAN HOLD HER LUST FOR REVENGE!
COPYRIGHT © 1971 BARBIERE & SANTOS PRODUCTIONS, INC
VIOLENT LOVE
FRANK J. BARBIERE · VICTOR SANTOS
image

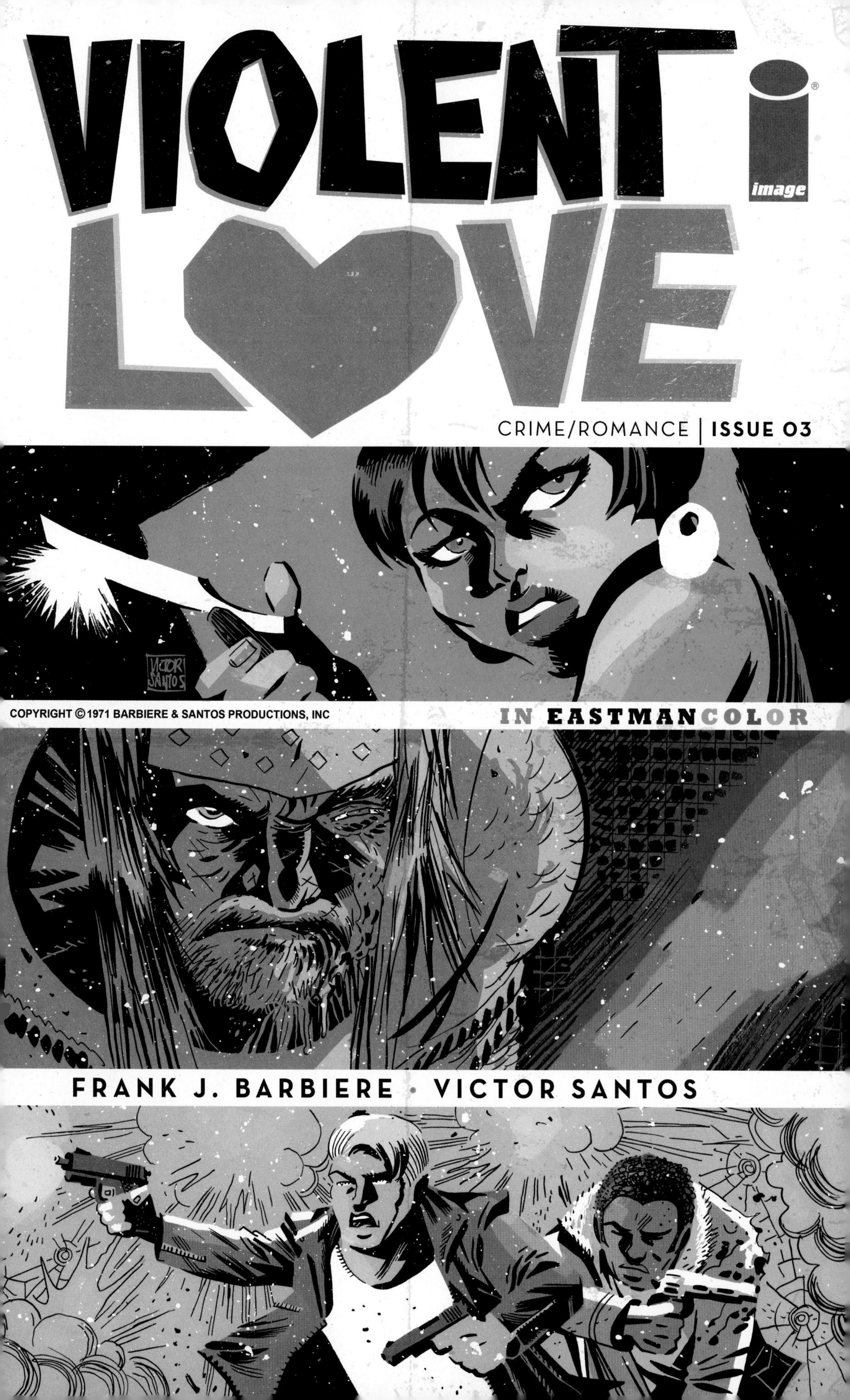
VIOLENT LOVE
image
CRIME/ROMANCE | ISSUE 03
VICTOR SANTOS
COPYRIGHT © 1971 BARBIERE & SANTOS PRODUCTIONS, INC
IN EASTMANCOLOR
FRANK J. BARBIERE · VICTOR SANTOS

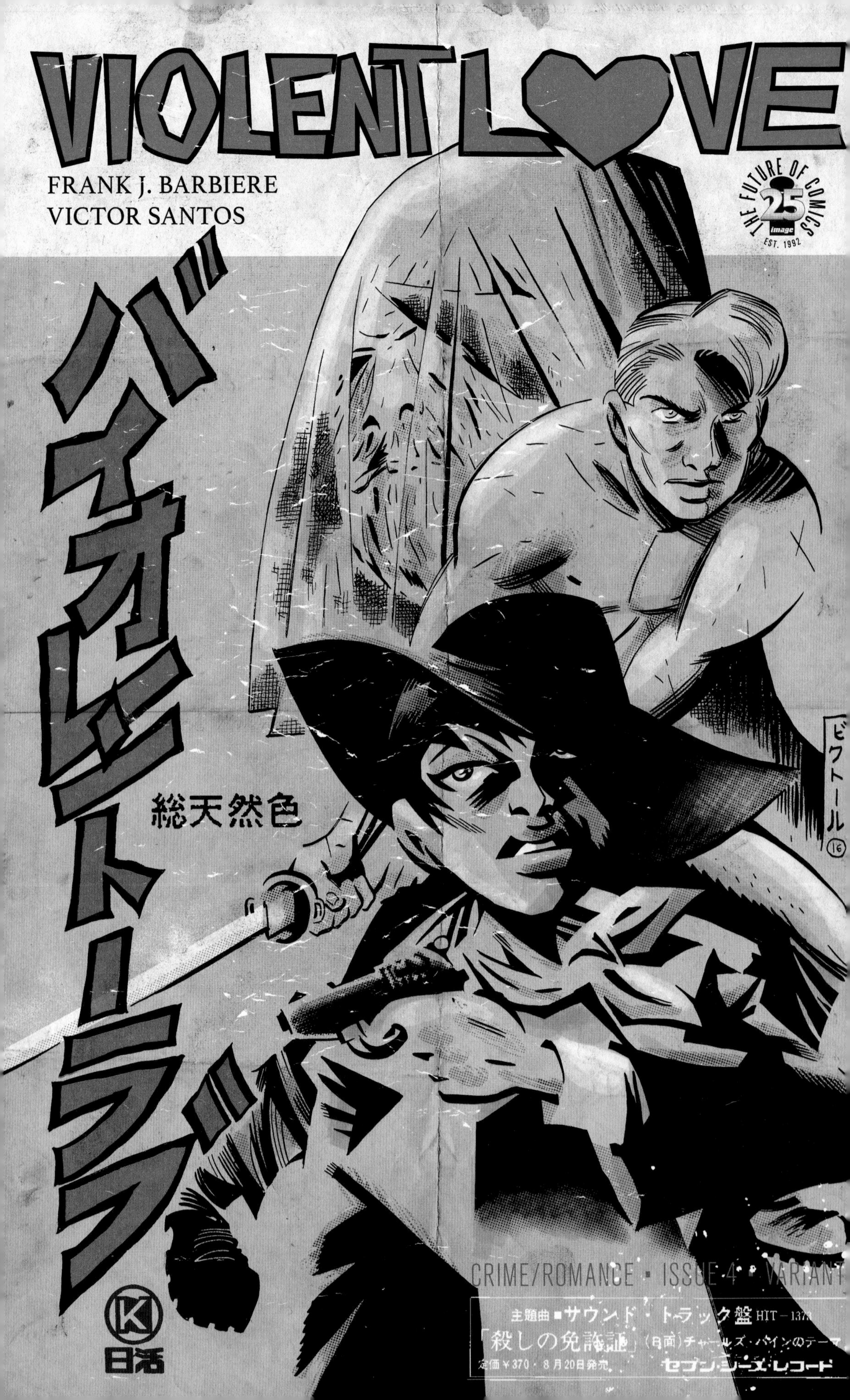

VIOLENT LOVE
FRANK J. BARBIERE
VICTOR SANTOS
THE FUTURE OF COMICS 25 image EST. 1992
バイオレントラブ
総天然色
ビクトール 16
日活
CRIME/ROMANCE ▪ ISSUE 4 ▪ VARIANT
主題曲■サウンド・トラック盤 HIT－1373
「殺しの免許証」(B面)チャールズ・パインのテーマ
定価￥370・8月20日発売
セブン・シーズ・レコード

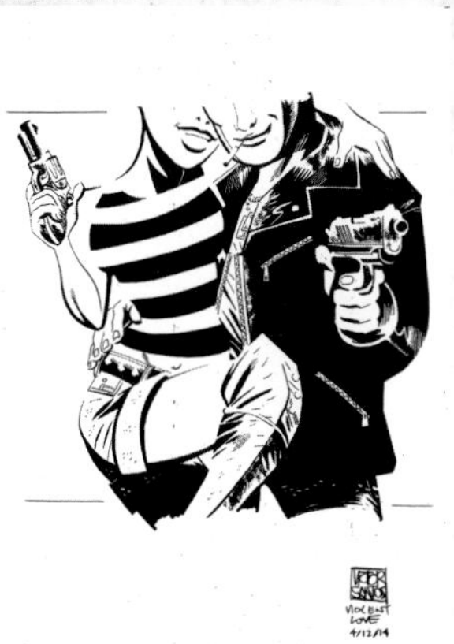

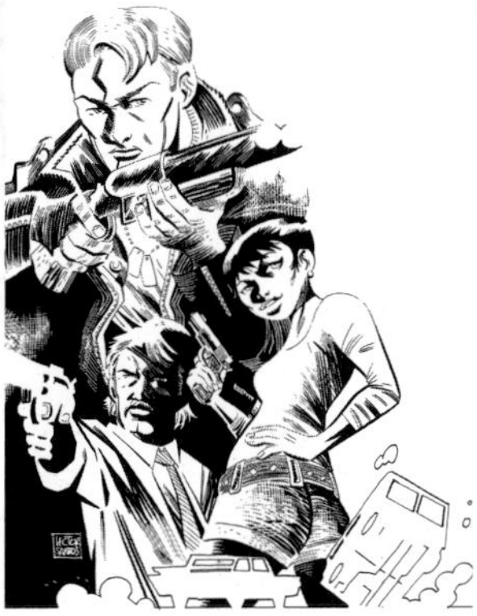

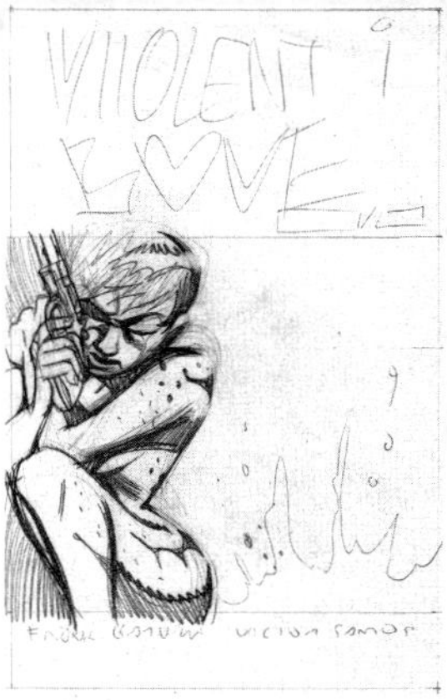
VIOLENT
LOVE

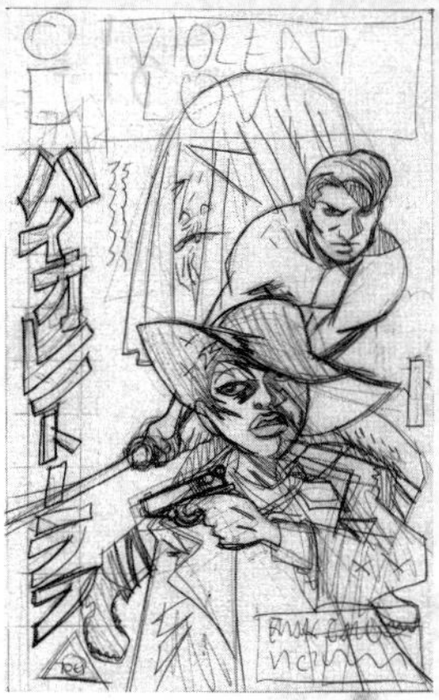
VIOLENT
LOVE

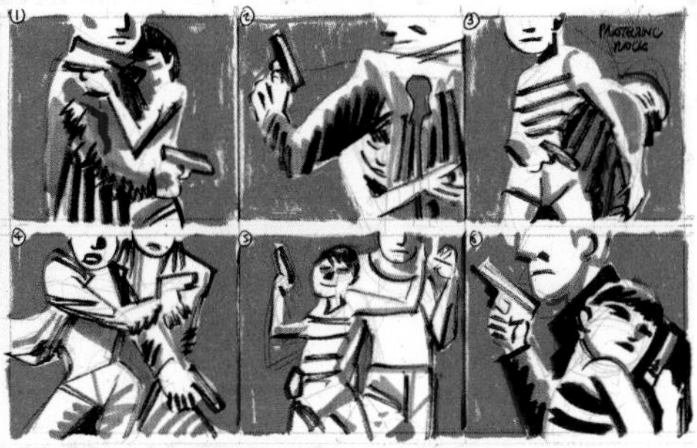

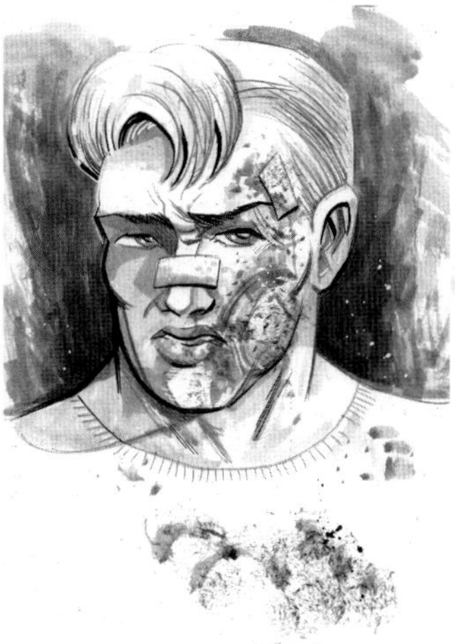

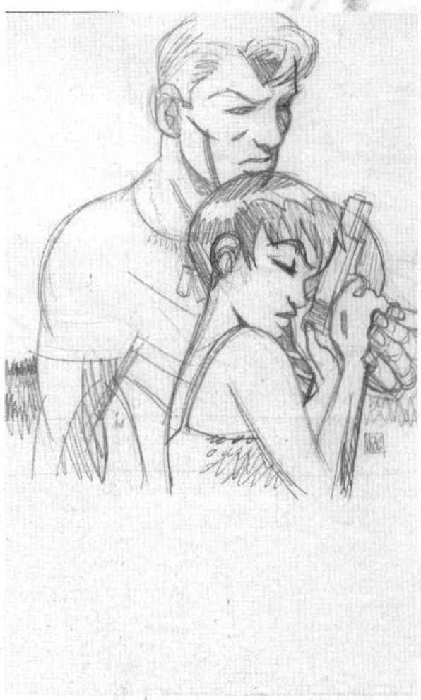

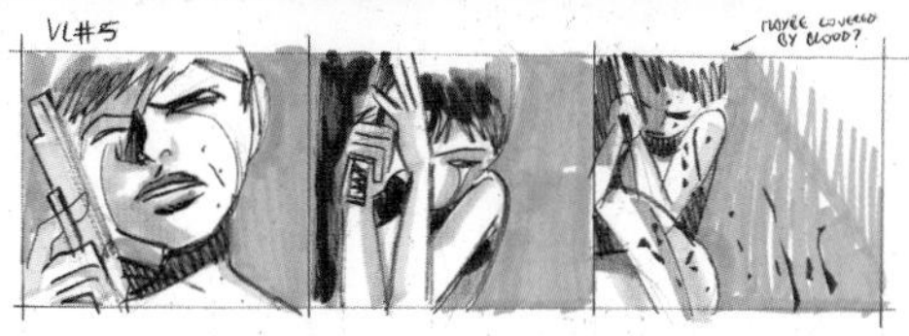
VL#5
MAYBE COVERED BY BLOOD?

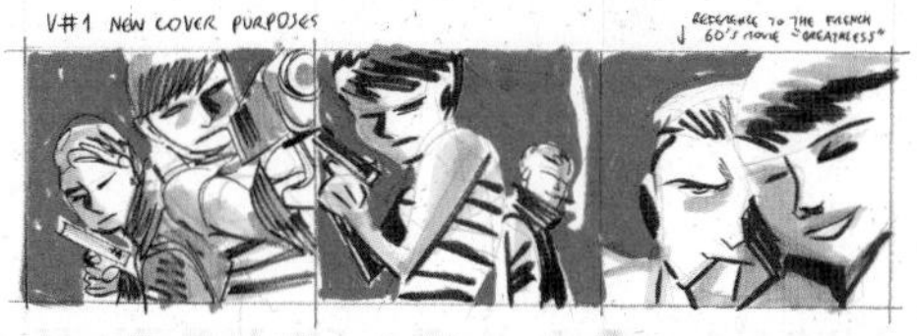
V#1 NEW COVER PURPOSES

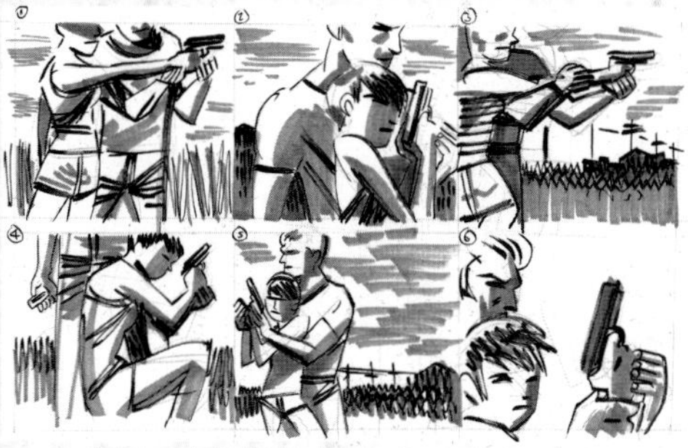

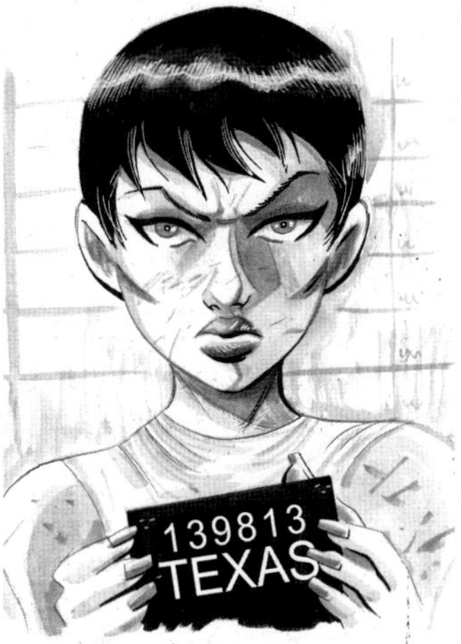
139813
TEXAS

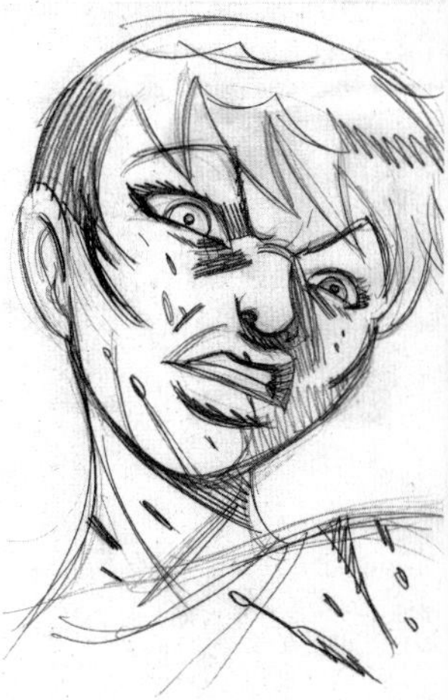

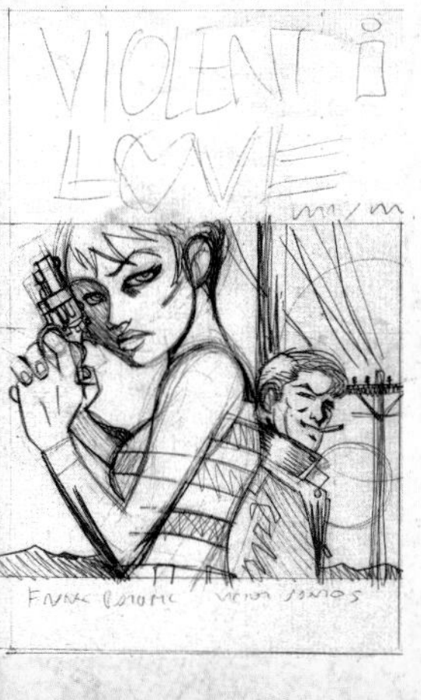
VIOLENT
LOVE

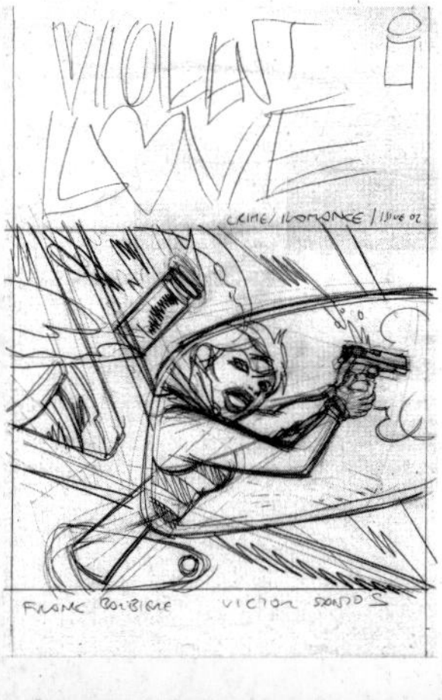
VIOLENT
LOVE

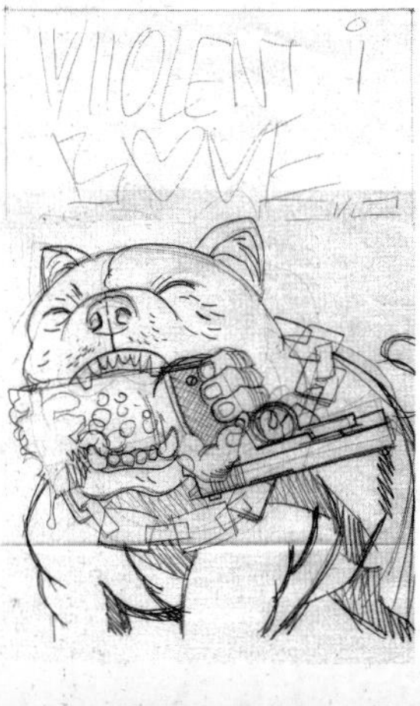
VIOLENT
LOVE

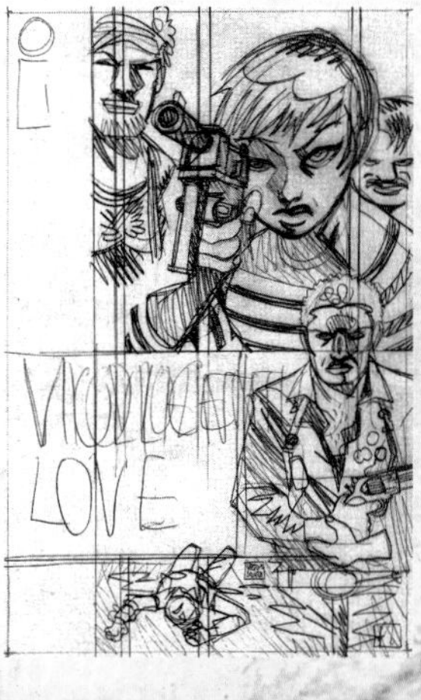
LOVE

FRANK J. BARBIERE is a writer from New Jersey. A former English teacher, Frank is a graduate of Rutgers University and the Graduate School for Education.

Frank broke into the industry with the creator-owned hit *FIVE GHOSTS* (Image Comics) and has since worked for every major publisher in the US, as well as having a global presence in France (Glenat Comics) and Italy (Cosmo Editoriale) with his creator-owned work. His body of work includes notable runs on *AVENGERS WORLD* and *HOWLING COMMANDOS OF S.H.I.E.L.D.* at Marvel Comics, as well as the creator-owned series *BLACK MARKET* & *BROKEN WORLD* (BOOM! Studios), *THE REVISIONIST* (Aftershock Comics), and *THE WHITE SUITS* (Dark Horse Comics).

www.atlasincognita.com | @atlasincognita

Born in Valencia in 1977, **VICTOR SANTOS** has written and illustrated a variety of comics in Spain and France, including *LOS REYES ELFOS*, *PULP HEROES*, *INTACHABLE* and *RASHOMON*, where he won six awards from the Barcelona international comic convention and three from the Madrid con. Since 2006, he has worked on numerous creator-owned comics in the United States including *THE MICE TEMPLAR*, written by Bryan Glass and Mike Oeming, *FILTHY RICH*, written by Brian Azzarello, *BLACK MARKET*, written by Frank J. Barbiere, and *FURIOUS*, written by Bryan Glass. He recently returned to France with the graphic novel *SUKEBAN TURBO*, written by the french writer Sylvain Runberg.

Victor has balanced these independent works with franchise series like *GODZILLA*, *SLEEPY HOLLOW*, *AXIS*, *DEAD BOY DETECTIVES* and *BIG TROUBLE IN LITTLE CHINA* for publishers like IDW, Marvel, DC and Boom! Studios.

His most personal work as a complete creator is the *POLAR* trilogy from Dark Horse Comics, optioned by Constantin Films and in development as a motion picture. He was nominated to a Harvey Award in 2014 for his work on the first volume, *POLAR: CAME FROM THE COLD*.

victorsantoscomics.tumblr.com | @polarcomic

DYLAN TODD is a writer, art director and graphic designer. When he's not reading comics, making comics, writing about comics or designing stuff for comics, he can probably be found thinking about comics. He likes Star Wars, mummies, D-Man, kaiju and 1966 Batman. He's the editor of the *2299* sci-fi comics anthology and, alongside Mathew Digges, is the co-creator of *THE CREEP CREW*, a comic about undead teen detectives.

bigredrobot.net | @bigredrobot

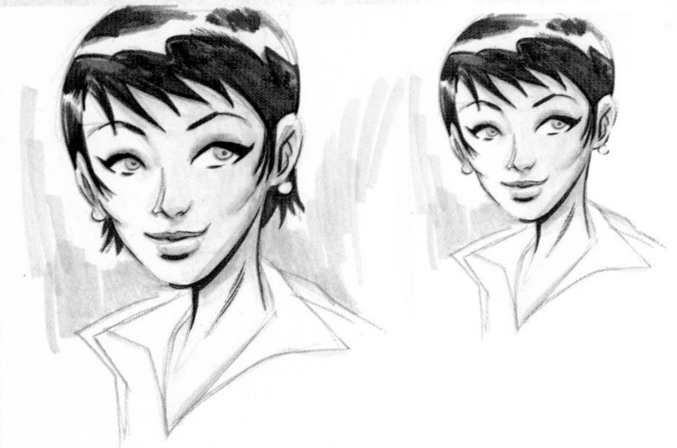
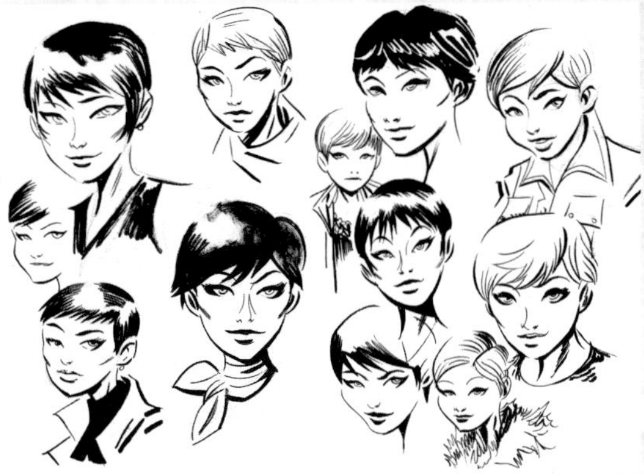
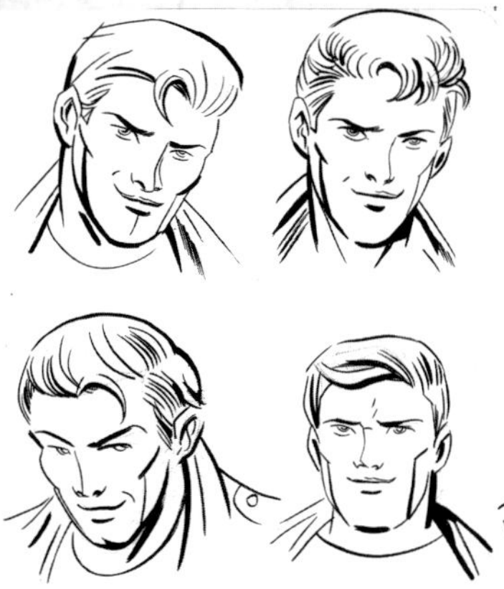
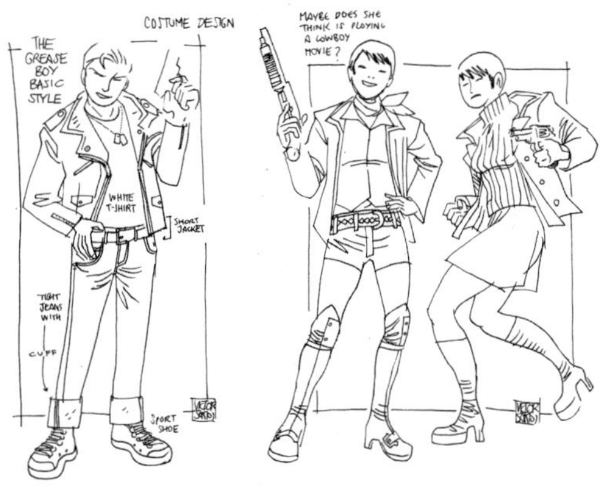
COSTUME DESIGN
THE GREASE BOY BASIC STYLE
WHITE T-SHIRT
SHORT JACKET
TIGHT JEANS WITH CUFF
SPORT SHOE
MAYBE DOES SHE THINK IS PLAYING A COWBOY MOVIE?
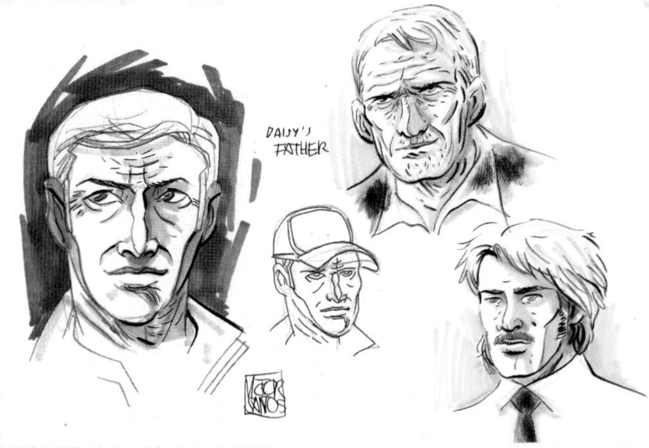
DAISY'S FATHER
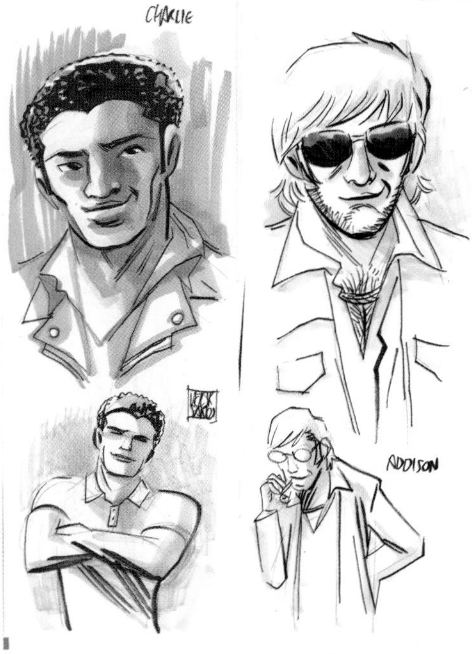
CHARLIE
ADDISON
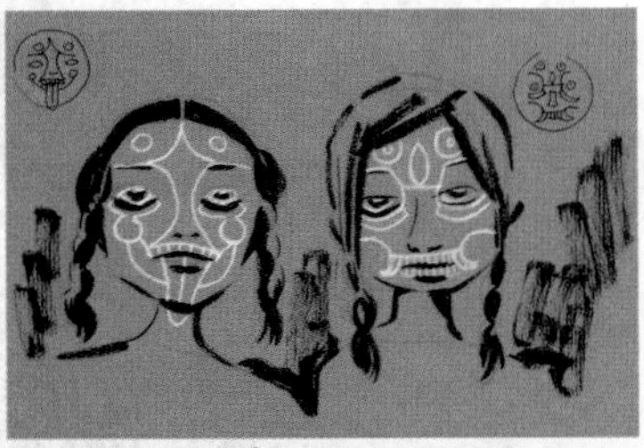
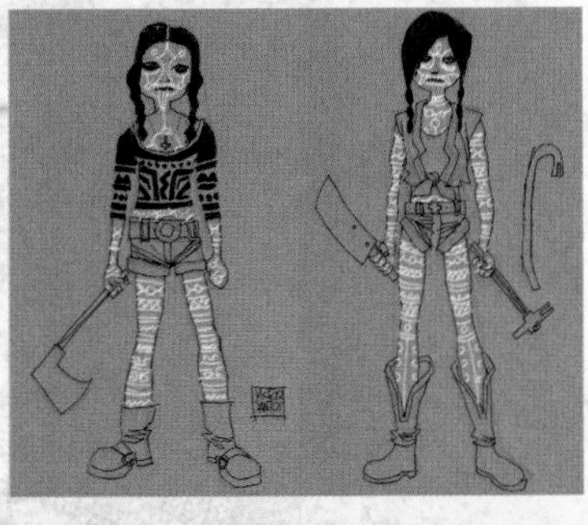
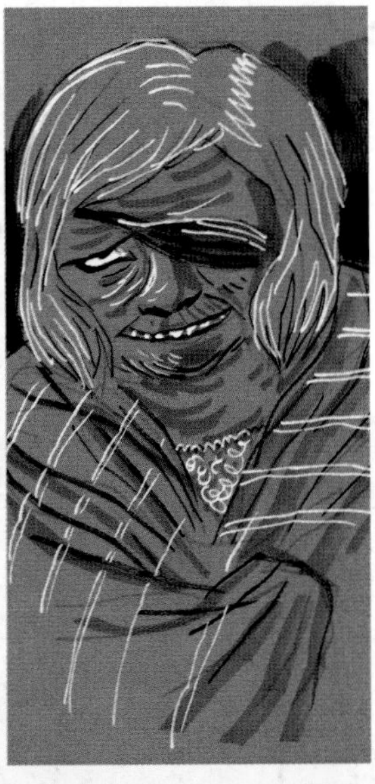
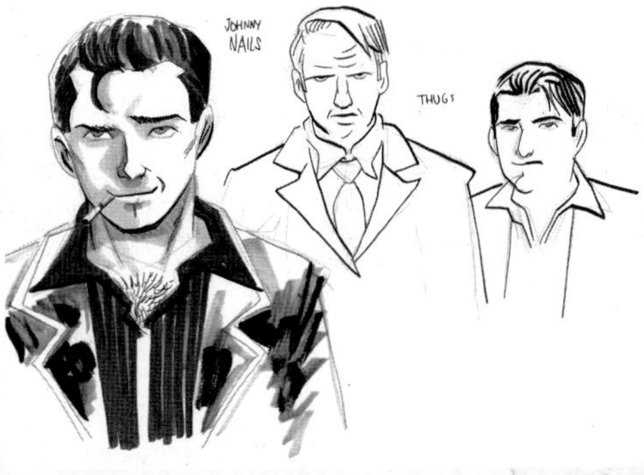
JOHNNY NAILS
THUGS

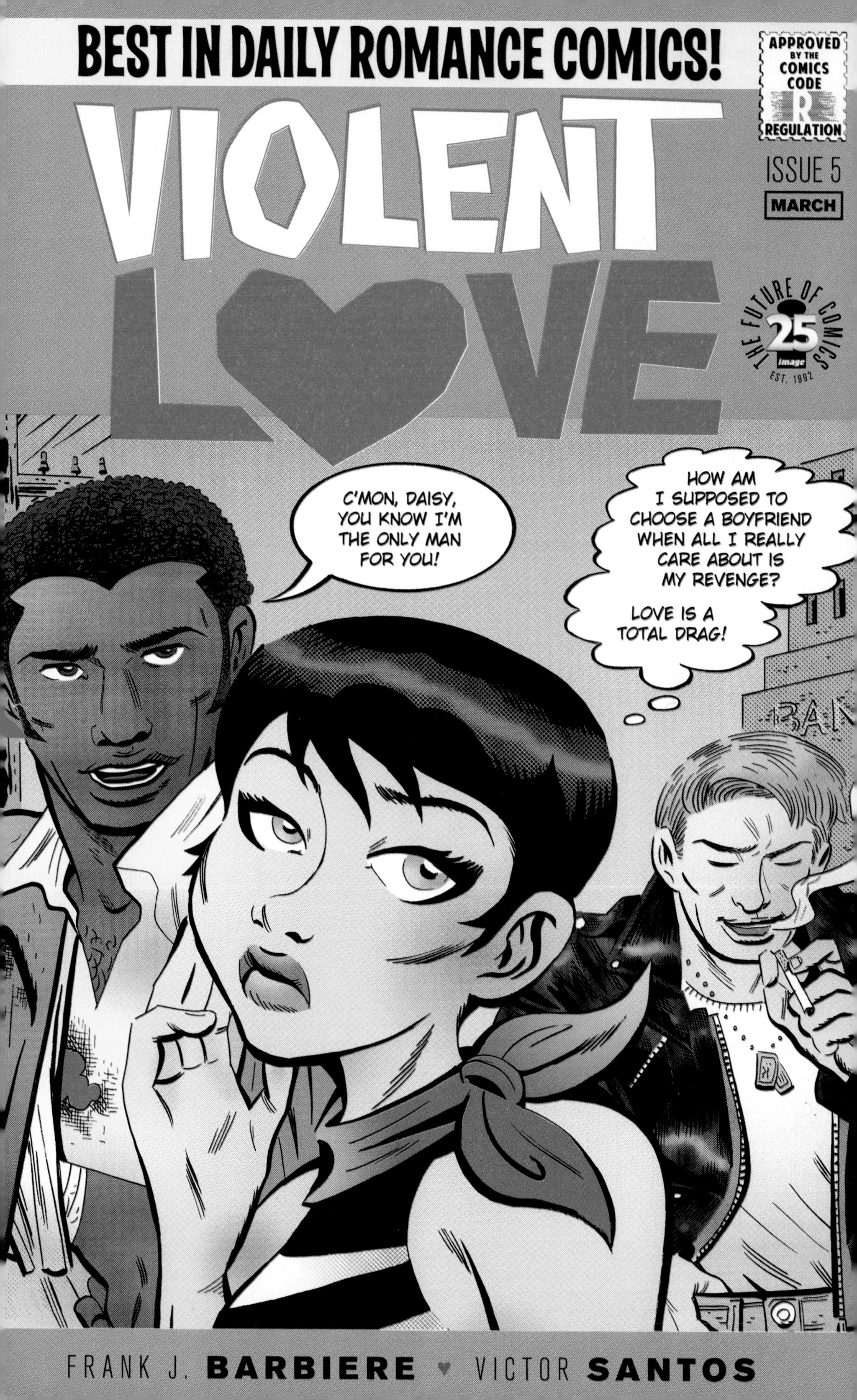
BEST IN DAILY ROMANCE COMICS!
APPROVED BY THE COMICS CODE R REGULATION
VIOLENT LOVE
ISSUE 5
MARCH
THE FUTURE OF COMICS 25 image EST. 1992
C'MON, DAISY, YOU KNOW I'M THE ONLY MAN FOR YOU!
HOW AM I SUPPOSED TO CHOOSE A BOYFRIEND WHEN ALL I REALLY CARE ABOUT IS MY REVENGE?
LOVE IS A TOTAL DRAG!
FRANK J. BARBIERE ♥ VICTOR SANTOS